"Are your fingers numb?" he asked.

"I don't know. I can't feel them."

He laughed, his chest rumbling beneath her cheek. "Let's sit down."

He led her to the sofa, where they sat with the blanket tented around their shoulders. He gently chafed her frozen hands between his large warm ones.

As his body heat seeped into hers, Claudia became aware of the man next to her, of his planes and edges, muscles and bones. She knew better than to trust this man, a stranger really, but she relaxed. Because of the cold, she'd been holding herself stiff for hours. No, for days. She'd been constantly on guard since the night she'd fled her apartment, and the tension had exhausted her. Right now it felt good to just let go, to dissolve into a puddle of warmth.

She'd worry about the danger again when her body temperature returned to normal.

Dear Reader,

I loved writing *Accidental Bodyguard*! The heroine, Claudia Romero (nee Goodwin), was a minor character in *The South Beach Search*, a 2014 Superromance, and her backstory always tugged at me. She's a courageous woman willing to testify against her murdering ex-husband even though she's been warned to keep her mouth shut. Her ex bribed someone in the US attorney's office, so she doesn't trust the federal government to protect her and refuses to go into a safe house. She doesn't dare involve her family or risk endangering them. Claudia is on her own, on the run and struggling to stay alive.

I had to know what happened to her. How did she avoid being killed by the terrorists that want to keep her quiet? She needed help, so Jackson Richards, sexy ex-cop and security expert extraordinaire, stepped up as her bodyguard.

Claudia doesn't trust anyone. Not herself and certainly not a man who turns her on every time she looks at him. Since Claudia lied her way onto the ritzy island where Jack works as security director, he's convinced she's a con artist stringing along a wealthy sugar daddy.

I hope you enjoy watching the sparks fly when these two strong-willed people fall in love.

Namaste,

Sharon

SHARON HARTLEY

Accidental Bodyguard

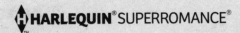 HARLEQUIN® SUPERROMANCE®

Recycling programs
for this product may
not exist in your area.

ISBN-13: 978-0-373-61008-2

Accidental Bodyguard

Copyright © 2016 by Sharon S. Hartley

Printed in U.S.A.

www.Harlequin.com

Sharon Hartley recently survived (barely) a move from Miami to St. Petersburg, Florida. She still doesn't know where most of her clothes are, but hopes they'll turn up soon. Her orchids survived the trip, and, fortunately, so did her computer, where she can be found every morning creating stories where people make mistakes, endure perilous journeys, learn about life and always find a happy ending. She misses her friends in South Florida, but the birding is fabulous on Tampa Bay and she can practice yoga anywhere. Sharon loves to hear from her readers. Please visit her website at sharonshartley.com.

Books by Sharon Hartley

HARLEQUIN SUPERROMANCE

The Florida Files
The South Beach Search

Her Cop Protector

To Trust a Cop

Other titles by this author available in ebook format.

For my sister, Sandy Clark. I miss you every day.

CHAPTER ONE

CLAUDIA GOODWIN DROVE into her assigned parking space at Brasilia Apartments, turned off her demon car and held her breath. This time the engine kept chugging for only about five seconds before it finally hiccupped to a stop. With a weary sigh, she pulled herself out of the old clunker and into the cool late-January evening.

Thank the nursing gods she was off tomorrow and could sleep late. Although first she had to check on Maude Spalding.

Claudia entered the pleasantly lit courtyard of the small complex and reminded herself she loved her job at West Miami Children's Hospital. She'd chosen the option of working three days straight and then four off. One of those seemed-like-a-good-idea-at-the-time deals. Funny how lots of things seem like a good idea at first and later prove, hey, not so much.

Pushing away useless regret, she took a deep breath and inhaled the fragrance of night-blooming jasmine. She closed her eyes to savor the scent and relaxed her shoulders. The courtyard was filled with tropical foliage—towering palms, hibiscus, terrestrial orchids and bromeliads. Even a live oak or two.

Meant to remind visitors of a mini rainforest, this garden-like refuge was why she'd moved in.

And she'd move again as soon as the trial was over. A niggle of worry about her testimony crept into her thoughts, but Claudia shrugged it away, rapping on her downstairs neighbor's door.

Though it was after midnight, Maude would be up. The feisty eighty-six-year-old seldom slept. She'd lived by herself in the Brasilia for over thirty years and refused to go into assisted living.

"Maude?" Claudia called softly.

"Come on in," Maude answered in her breathy voice.

Claudia entered and, as always, felt like she'd been transported into an over-the-top holiday extravaganza. Every available surface contained some red-and-green or gold ornament. There were Santas, Mrs. Santas, snowmen, elves, wreaths, twinkling lights and hundreds of Christmas trees, big and small. Glitter everywhere.

Claudia called Maude Our Lady of Perpetual Christmas.

December 25th was long gone, but Maude kept Christmas year-round, never putting away any of her knickknacks. They reminded her of happier times, of her family, now all dead.

Claudia approached her tiny, gray-headed neighbor in the large recliner where she spent most of her time watching television, noting she was using her oxygen.

"You been upstairs yet?" Maude demanded, with an odd, excited expression. Her eyes appeared huge behind her thick glasses.

"No," Claudia answered, feeling for her neighbor's pulse. "Any palpitations tonight?"

"Was some kind of ruckus in your unit," Maude blurted.

Claudia dropped Maude's wrist. "Ruckus?"

Maude nodded. "Sounded like furniture being moved, dishes being thrown every whichaway. I almost called the police, but I didn't want to get you in no trouble."

Claudia stepped back, her stomach cramping hard. Had Carlos finally decided to take action against her? "Why would you think—"

"I been around a long time, Miss Claudia. I can tell when someone's got something in their past they're not proud of."

Claudia looked up. Her unit was directly over Maude's. "I promise I'm not wanted by the police. My problem is I agreed to help them."

"You may not be hiding from the law, but you're keeping your head down trying to avoid trouble."

Hoping my ex forgets about me. Claudia swallowed, suddenly worried about Moochie, the black stray cat who'd adopted her when she moved in to the Brasilia.

"Did you see anyone?"

"Two men ran down the stairs after the commotion. I didn't notice them going up." Maude sighed.

"With my eyesight, I couldn't tell you nothing about the way they looked."

"I'd better go see what's going on," she said.

"You still got that stun gun?"

Claudia nodded and patted her purse.

"Have it at the ready."

Claudia hurried up to her apartment. Had Carlos decided she was a liability? Maybe it was time to go in to hiding.

Her front door stood open. Not closed and locked as she'd left it. She took a deep breath. Now the jasmine seemed sickeningly sweet, making her faintly nauseous.

Most people would call the police before entering, but she couldn't do that. Not because she was hiding from them as Maude thought, but because she didn't trust them to protect her. Cops could easily be bought. Her ex, the infamous Carlos Romero, had taught her that. So she'd made her preparations months ago. The day she realized she was being followed.

She was on her own.

Everything she needed, courtesy of a grateful patient's father, waited for her in a safe-deposit box.

Claudia pushed the door wide and gasped. She waited at the threshold, absorbing the chaos before her. Maude's description had nailed the condition of her home. Furniture had been tossed and ripped. Drawers opened and thrown. Dishes and appliances smashed on the kitchen floor.

No doubt they were looking for her journal.

"Moochie?" She stepped into the living room, her heart beating so hard and fast her blood pressure had to be off the charts. "Moochie," she called again. "Where are you?"

She entered the bedroom and discovered more destruction. They'd ripped her nursing scrubs into shreds. Fearing the worst, she kept searching.

In the bathroom she found Moochie, drowned in the toilet.

She clamped a hand over her mouth, her shoulders shaking. *Oh, Moochie. You poor sweet thing. I'm so sorry.*

She raised her eyes to the mirror and stared at words scrawled in red lipstick: KEEP YOUR MOUTH SHUT.

JACKSON RICHARDS ACCEPTED the coffee he'd ordered from the dark-haired barista, thanked her and took a hesitant sip. Strong and hot. Just as he remembered. No one brewed a better cup than the Collins Island Café.

Jackson exited the café into a cool, salt-laden breeze off the Atlantic Ocean and walked the short distance to the security office. He had a golf cart at his disposal, but he preferred to walk.

Colorful tropical landscaping and the soothing sound of waterfalls surrounded him. He was on the job, but this assignment was more like a forced vacation. His boss insisted he needed a break after his last two missions, which, yeah, had both been bitches. He took another sip of the excellent coffee.

Maybe Lola was right, but he'd resisted taking this cushy gig as Security Director on Collins Island, a private island off Miami Beach accessible only by boat where his employer, the Protection Alliance, provided security. PA operatives rotated in and out as the live-in chief, usually delighted for the opportunity.

Most of the residents were seasonal, and this was the height of the season. Crime was nonexistent on this island paradise. All he had to do for the next month was keep his staff on schedule, act friendly to the wealthy residents and enjoy the resort-like atmosphere.

But it was always boring as hell. And he hated sucking up to trust fund slackers.

A blast of hot air greeted him when he pushed open the door to the security office. He groaned at the decor as he moved to shut down the heat. Pink-and-gray Art Deco was definitely not his style. And what idiot had decided heat was needed just because a weak cold front had swept through south Florida last night? Not him. He was a north Florida man. Jackson opened a window.

He shrugged off his jacket and hung it in the closet. Another thing he didn't like about this gig was the requirement to wear a blue blazer. Damn thing made him feel like a polo player. His khakis and the knit shirt featuring the Collins Island logo over the pocket were enough of a uniform.

He sat at the desk to review the security force schedule. The most critical duty was clearing arrivals for the ferry on the Miami side. The ferry ran every fifteen minutes, and no one was allowed to place a toe on Collins Island without clearance from an owner. Even daily maids were checked and their bags searched. Two guards handled that assignment on three eight-hour shifts, with two more guards on the island side to supervise debarkation. Another two circulated the island on golf carts, constantly alert for any sort of trouble. Of which there was, fortunately, seldom any.

He noted all six positions on all three shifts were staffed with regular PA personnel for the next week. Excellent. That made the transition easier, but he'd make a late-night visit to the docks to ensure no one was catching a nap, looking to take advantage of the new guy in the director's chair. Not likely, though. Guards loved this job because it came with a lot of perks like big tips and expensive gifts—especially during the winter season.

Still, you never knew what could happen. He wanted no screw-ups during his stint as chief.

Looking for any anomalies, he reviewed the security logs for the last week and reached for the phone when it rang.

"Security."

"Hey, Action Jackson. Are you bored yet?"

Lola, the office manager from Protection Alliance's main office. He pictured her pink hair, always worn in short spikes. She looked crazed but possessed a laser-sharp mind and never forgot a thing. Jackson relaxed back in his chair, making the leather squeak.

"I've only been on the job forty-five minutes, Lola."

"That's usually all it takes."

"Maybe I'm looking forward to a month of not having to duck bullets."

"Yeah, right. I'll remind you of that in a week."

"Hey, this was your idea, boss. I'm ready to go back in the field anytime."

"You are in the field."

Jack snorted. "Field of dreams."

"Did you get settled in the apartment? Everything to your liking?"

"Ocean view. Great coffee. I can walk to work through a tropical paradise. What's not to like?"

"Don't be sarcastic, Jack."

"I'm going with the flow."

Lola laughed, a throaty sound. "By the way, we received a very nice thank-you bonus from that rapper Jazzy Bones Boy yesterday. He's grateful for your services."

He ought to be. The jerk almost got me killed. "How grateful?"

"I think your cut will make you happy," Lola said.

"Is that why you called? Couldn't have already been a complaint about me."

"I wanted you to know there's a tenant arriving sometime today." Jackson listened as Lola shuffled through paper. "A Mr. Rodolfo Santaluce has rented the pool house of his villa. He wants us to assist with the arrival, make sure security doesn't hassle his new tenant."

"Isn't renting a bit unusual? I can't imagine the owners here needing extra income."

"It put up a red flag for me, too, so I questioned his assistant, who informed me that Mr. Santaluce got where he is today by being frugal. The assistant's tone suggested it wasn't any of my business what his boss did." Lola hesitated, then added, "I'm thinking it's a mistress."

"Who's Santaluce?"

"Big deal Italian businessman. Married, two kids. The family is in Hong Kong for the winter."

"What business?"

"Questionable."

"Got it," Jack said. "Give me his address. I'll meet the mistress and expedite her transition into the love shack."

"Thanks, Jack. Her name is Louise Clark."

After disconnecting, Jack donned his jacket and exited the office for a trip to the docks to give clearance for one Louise Clark, a lucky lady with a mega-rich sugar daddy. He could do that by phone, but wanted to introduce himself to his staff and make certain they alerted him when Ms. Clark boarded the ferry on the Miami side.

He climbed into the golf cart with *Security Director* stenciled on the rear and turned a key conveniently in the lock, shaking his head. Weren't many places in south Florida where you could leave a key in the ignition without worry of theft. The quiet electric motor ignited immediately, and he headed toward the dock. Not a speck of trash anywhere on the streets or the neatly mowed grass. Palms, oaks and other landscaping were trimmed to perfection. Gently cascading fountains sounded all around him, clear of any leaf debris because they were cleaned twice a day.

Jack couldn't imagine—but could easily find out—what the monthly maintenance fee was on Collins Island. Had to be astronomical because per square foot there weren't that many residences. Only ten large villas on the eastern shore of the island—where Ms. Clark would soon take up residence—and forty town homes on the west housed in four three-story buildings.

The graceful structures were constructed in a coordinated Mediterranean style with coral-color barrel-tile roofs, featuring arches and supporting decorative columns. Colorful ceramic tile mosaics detailed many of the architectural elements, including the addresses.

Nobody out on this fine Monday morning, except a maid actually dressed in a starched gray uniform walking two French bulldogs. Jack nodded at her, and she responded with a shy smile.

The 10:00 a.m. ferry, laden with only six vehicles, approached the dock when Jack arrived. He parked his cart by the guard shack—constructed in the same architectural style—and watched the dock personnel do their job. Tanned men and women in blue shorts and crisp white shirts efficiently tied the boat to the landing, secured the sturdy metal ramp and motioned for the cars to drive off in a particular order. Three walk-aboards also exited.

The guard on duty, a uniformed twentyish black male, watched the process with alert attention. All clearance was completed on the Miami side, so all he had to do was make a head count, answer questions and direct approved visitors to their destination.

When debarkation was complete, Jack approached the guard and shook his hand. "Jackson Richards."

"Ike Gamble. We were expecting you today, sir. Welcome to Collins Island."

"Thanks, Ike." Jack crossed his arms to observe the ferry staff prepare for the next trip. "Everything go okay this morning?"

Ike shrugged. "We seldom have any glitches, sir."

Jack winced at constantly being called *sir*. He was maybe five or six years older than this guy, but understood it was a matter of respect. "You can call me Jack."

"Yes, sir."

So much for informality. "I need to talk to the guards on the other side," he told Ike.

"Of course, sir."

Ike removed a walkie-talkie from his belt, contacted the Miami guards, who responded in seconds, and handed the device to Jack. Viewing the distant guardhouse across the channel, a shipping lane also used by enormous cruise ships, Jack explained about the new tenant and approved her to board the ferry.

"Make sure you call the office when Ms. Clark shows. Leave word for the next shift if you go off duty before she arrives."

Confident his instructions would be followed, Jack returned to his cart. He sat for a moment, watching the ferry depart, wondering what the mistress looked like and when Mr. Santaluce would arrive. A clandestine love affair on an island this small would be hard to hide. A lot of people could be hurt. Jack's thoughts drifted to his momma—which trashed his relaxed good mood.

His divorced momma didn't believe in the sanctity of marriage vows either, but her lover, a north Florida sheriff and his old boss, was nowhere near Collins Island rich. Did that make her indiscretions worse or better? He could hear Momma's voice as she explained her lies, *I'm in love, Jack. You don't understand. You've never been in love.*

Considering what a fool Momma had made of herself over Chuck Wheeler, he seriously hoped he never fell in love. Who needed that shit?

CLAUDIA DRUMMED HER fingers on her steering wheel as the Collins Island ferry chugged across the narrow channel. Her windows were down, and a stiff ocean breeze flowed into the car, cooling her flushed face. She wished she could stand at the railing, but didn't dare. Too exposed.

She focused on the dock, watching it get closer and closer. *Almost there. I've made it this far. I should be okay.*

Similar self-pep talks had helped her through each step of the journey. She'd checked in and out of a fleabag motel without getting blown to bits. She'd made it to the bank vault to retrieve her fake IDs and the Glock, and emerged still breathing. She'd even managed to purchase new clothes in a mall she never frequented. That was the most nerve-racking but couldn't be helped because she'd left everything behind in her trashed apartment in case they'd put a tracking device somewhere. Better to be safe.

And she'd made it out of the grocery store without a hitch. Could Carlos's people hack into her credit card records? Probably, but she didn't have to touch her maxed-out cards again. Once she got to this island with its legendary security, there was no way anyone could get to her.

She'd crammed her car with enough groceries to last until Carlos's trial. She would have loved to obtain a new vehicle, but lack of time and funds made that impossible.

She'd be fine as long as she kept out of sight and remembered her new name. It'd been three days, and so far she'd stayed beneath their radar.

The last and most difficult step was boarding this ferry. It was a wonder she hadn't stroked out while the security guard checked for her name on his list. He'd frowned at her rusted twenty-year-old vehicle, scrutinized her fake driver's license, then looked at her face for so long she thought he was trying to memorize her features. His gaze had shifted back to the license, then the car again to check out all the bags in the backseat.

Finally, his jaw clenched in obvious disapproval, he scanned the license with a small device, made a note on his clipboard and motioned her aboard.

She closed her eyes, remembering her near panic. God, what would she have done? Accept the US Attorney's offer of a safe house? No way. Carlos had bragged that he'd bribed an employee, so that was a sure death sentence.

Her ex had taught her to trust no one. The attorney she'd been working with on her testimony would worry when he couldn't contact her, but she wanted her trail ice-cold. She'd reach out to him later.

She felt a gentle bump and opened her eyes. Relief swamped her. They'd reached the other side. She was safe.

The car in front of hers, a bright red sporty Mercedes, started its motor. Claudia turned her key to do the same and heard nothing but an empty click.

Please, not now. Not when I'm almost there.

She tried the key again, but still nothing. Of course

her devil car had chosen this exact moment to quit working.

The Mercedes proceeded down the ramp, and a ponytailed, brown-haired female ferry attendant motioned for Claudia to follow. With a sigh, she popped her hood and exited the car.

"What's wrong, ma'am?" the attendant asked politely.

"My battery is dead," Claudia replied.

The attendant, whose name tag read *Julie*, frowned. "Okay. Let me get the rest of the vehicles off and we'll see what we can do."

Speaking into a walkie-talkie in one hand, with the other Julie motioned for the next line of vehicles to exit the ferry.

Uneasy in the open, Claudia searched the Collins Island dock and beyond where attendants sprayed water over arriving vehicles to wash off salt residue.

No one should have her in their sights from that direction. Was she too far from the mainland for a clean shot? She glanced back across the channel. Maybe not.

As vehicles circumvented her and drove away, she moved to the front of her car, seeking the protection of the open hood.

Julie, accompanied by two male attendants, hustled toward her. Claudia flinched when one of the males slammed the hood with a loud bang.

"We're going to push you," Julie said. "Put the transmission in Neutral and steer off the ramp."

When her vehicle's wheels rolled off the ferry and onto Collins Island, Claudia offered a silent prayer and tried her ignition again. *Please, please.* Still just a sad click. She pounded on the dash.

Wishing she could make herself invisible—hey, if she could arrange for superpowers, why not just fly to Mr. Santaluce's villa—Claudia climbed out of her car just as a tall, ruggedly handsome man in a blue blazer arrived.

She looked up into piercing green eyes, noticed sun-streaked light brown hair and for a moment forgot where she was.

She tried to speak, to say hello and explain, ask for help, but had to swallow to moisten her throat.

She'd had this instant, gut-churning reaction to a male once before in her life, but those eyes had been an unfathomable, brooding brown, not a lively green. She'd been foolish enough to marry that man, and he'd nearly destroyed her.

And he might still.

CHAPTER TWO

JACK EVALUATED THE stranded woman with the rusted heap of a car and arranged his expression into a mask of professional concern. This fresh-faced young woman without a speck of makeup around sky-blue eyes was a rich man's mistress? Pretty, yes, no question, but more wholesome than seductive.

She'd pulled back her long dark hair in a casual ponytail. Hardly glamorous. She wore loose-fitting shorts and a short-sleeve blouse that revealed no cleavage from her generous breasts. No flashy jewelry; just tiny gold ear hoops.

Louise Clark was not what he'd expected.

"Ms. Clark?" he asked.

Frowning, the woman stared at him, as if confused. Didn't she know her own name? Was she a druggie? She didn't look like one. In fact, Ms. Clark appeared to be exactly the type of woman he was normally all over.

He extended his arm to shake her hand. "I'm Jackson Richards, Security Director. Aren't you Louise Clark?"

Her expression cleared, and Ms. Clark clasped his

hand with both of hers as if she was drowning and he was her lifeline. "Yes, yes. I'm Louise Clark."

She offered a killer smile which transformed her face from pretty into stunning, which explained Mr. Santaluce's interest. Jack felt an unexpected stab of envy.

"Please forgive me, Mr. Richards," Ms. Clark continued. "I'm embarrassed by the trouble, but my demon car chose this awkward moment to quit working."

"No trouble at all, ma'am. Mr. Santaluce requested we make certain you get settled in your new home."

"Oh, that was kind of him," Ms. Clark said.

Kind of him? Jack reevaluated the scenario before him. His gaze swept over the rattletrap vehicle, noting a backseat heaped with plastic bags from a local grocery. Apparently Ms. Clark wasn't planning on expensive dinners out with her lover. Hell, maybe she was a gourmet cook and that was what had attracted the man. A looker and a cooker? If so, a far better reason for jealousy.

"Will a jump start help?" Jack asked. "I've called our maintenance department for an assist."

She shrugged. "I don't know. This is the first time it hasn't started. Usually it won't stop running."

"Maybe it's time for a new car."

"Wouldn't that be nice. Maybe when I win the lottery."

Jack forced a smile. "Yes, ma'am." Damn, but Santaluce was one cheap sugar daddy. You'd think he'd want her driving a flashier vehicle onto his ritzy winter home.

The huge maintenance pickup truck approached, and Ms. Clark slid behind the wheel of her car. Jack retrieved jumper cables from the truck and hooked its battery to the clunker's.

"Give it a try," he yelled over the truck's powerful engine.

The old car shook and rumbled to life. Jack let its battery run off the truck's for a minute or two to allow a better charge, then disconnected the cables, handed them to the maintenance man and returned to speak to Ms. Clark.

"Thank you," she said meaningfully. "Thank you so much."

"No problem, ma'am. I recommend you get that battery checked out. It's possible you need a new one."

"But now that I'm here, I won't need my car," she said.

"I suppose not." Jack nodded, but her words made no sense. Was the woman planning to never leave Collins Island? Considering the amount of food in her backseat—and no telling how much more in her trunk—maybe so.

Maybe Santaluce planned to keep her in the bedroom. Or maybe he'd had lured her here with promises of a shiny silver Porsche.

"Follow me," Jack said, "I'll lead you to your new home."

On the short drive to the east end of the island, Jack considered Louise Clark, her rattletrap vehicle—which fortunately kept chugging along behind him—her mounds of groceries and the questionable business of one Rodolfo Santaluce.

The more Jack thought about Ms. Clark, the more his bullshit alarm sounded loud and clear. Something didn't add up. Maybe Lola had assessed the relationship between Santaluce and Ms. Clark all wrong. Maybe the pretty young woman was indeed a paying tenant.

Jack stopped in front of Santaluce's tall, arched, wrought-iron gate topped with the name, Villa Alma, in block letters, and Ms. Clark pulled next to him. Why would she drive that battered jalopy if she could afford the rent this spectacular villa would command? She wouldn't. Yeah, she was moving in to the pool house, but he'd seen the so-called cabanas in these villas. A small family would have room to spare.

Clutching a slip of paper, Ms. Clark exited her car, punched a code into the alarm pad and the gate swung open. She turned and offered him another one of her brilliant smiles.

"Thanks so much for your help, Mr. Richards."

"Let me help you carry in those groceries," he offered.

Her smile faded, replaced by wariness. In fact, she looked afraid of him. Why was that?

"No, thanks," she said. "I can manage."

"Are you sure? I don't mind."

"Absolutely. I've been enough trouble already." She waved a graceful hand, the one holding the code, which had been scribbled on some sort of preprinted memo pad with a letterhead. He could make out the word *Hospital* in large letters, but nothing more.

"I'm certain you have more important duties," she continued.

Jack shrugged, disappointed. *Important duties? This place practically runs itself.*

His main function was to assess all possible security threats. Was Ms. Clark a threat to the security of Collins Island? Maybe. Something was off about her.

He definitely needed to learn more.

She looked at him with raised eyebrows, obviously expecting—no, wanting—him to drive away.

He didn't want to go, but waved and motored west into the sinking sun, back toward the security office.

Lola had been right on about one thing. His day had been boring as plain white toast before Ms. Clark's arrival, but now things were getting interesting. He had a project.

Of course, he should keep a watchful eye on Collins Island's newest resident—which shouldn't be too hard since Ms. Clark was easy on the eyes.

And it was, after all, his job.

CLAUDIA UNLOADED HER car and hid it in a garage at the rear of Mr. Santaluce's estate. She quickly filled the refrigerator—empty but for three lonely

Coronas—with perishable fruits, vegetables and dairy items. She'd run out of fresh produce before the trial date in four weeks, but that couldn't be helped. She'd divide her meat into single portions and stuff the freezer later—after she'd locked herself in. At least she wouldn't starve.

She left the Glock on the counter within easy reach while she worked. She'd keep her weapon close at hand, always loaded and ready to fire. She'd taken a course and knew how to shoot. She could usually hit the target, if nowhere near the bull's-eye.

Closing the refrigerator for the last time, she took a deep breath.

Dear Mr. Santaluce had provided detailed instructions on the alarm system, but first she needed to confirm all openings were locked or otherwise secure.

She grabbed the gun and exited the cabana through the front door into twilight. A shiver caused her to hug her arms. Claudia inhaled deeply to calm herself, noting the cool, salty ocean breeze. Because of the wall, she didn't have a view of the tantalizingly close Atlantic Ocean.

But no one had a view of her, either.

Maybe she could go out occasionally—late at night—and take a peek at the waves. Maybe not.

Claudia walked the villa's grounds looking for any weakness, a location where someone could breach the eight-foot concrete wall. The activity helped settle her, reminded her of patrolling the pediatric unit on the night shift when her patients, poor sick kids, were all sleeping. She missed her job. How long would it be before she could go back to work?

She discovered there was only one gate, the one she'd driven through, and that it had an electronic lock and an alarm. Carlos's henchmen would have to ram a truck through, making a ton of noise, definitely attracting the attention of that eagle-eyed security director. She doubted he missed anything.

She shivered again, wondering at her reaction to Jackson Richards, who in no way resembled her dark-headed, dark-eyed ex. Still, she'd had the same visceral reaction to him she'd had to Carlos: the urge to rip off his clothes. Unfortunately, she'd acted on that impulse with Carlos. To the horror of her family, two weeks after that explosive first meeting she'd married the jerk.

Within three months of the vows, she'd realized her deadly mistake.

Deciding all was secure, Claudia moved back to the pool area and eyed the impressive three-story main house. She had a key, but had no intention of entering Mr. Santaluce's winter home. Her benefactor didn't plan a Miami visit until mid-March, and she'd be gone by then. She didn't want her presence to put his family in danger.

She pictured the angelic face of Rosa Santaluce, a sweet child who had suffered through way too many painful nights in the pediatric ICU. Her father had been there for most of them, suffering right along with his daughter.

For the thousandth time, Claudia felt a rush of gratitude toward the man she believed had saved her life by offering this refuge. The irony was he was thanking her for saving his daughter's life.

Claudia paused by the well-lit pool, which reminded her of promotional brochures for an expensive resort with its landscaping, fountains and gurgling cascades. But that pool, right outside her front door, was also her biggest concern, since the island contractor came once a week to test the water and add the necessary chemicals. Santaluce had given her the schedule, so she could hunker down inside and make nary a peep so no one would know of her presence. Ditto with the lawn maintenance people.

But otherwise she'd be left alone. She could sit out here to study and use the pool to exercise. She just couldn't show her face beyond the wall.

Inside the cabana, she repeated her patrol, checking each window, door and every possible entrance into the structure. When done, she armed the security system and stared at the blinking red light. If someone breached or she pushed the nearby bright yellow panic button, who would respond? The island security director? She hoped not. She was a woman who learned from her mistakes, and history had taught her she needed to avoid Jackson Richards as much as she avoided contact with Carlos or infectious bacteria.

What was similar about two such different-looking men that caused her to become tongue-tied with desire? Had to be some trait hidden underneath their physical appearance, something she sensed intuitively and her treacherous body reacted to. Carlos was much smaller than Richards, but slick and sneaky as a fox. Richards was built more like a gladiator with his powerful shoulders and arms. While he worked with her car, she'd had the odd sensation he controlled a capacity for extreme violence.

Just like Carlos.

So she liked aggressive males? Dear God, what was wrong with her? She couldn't be trusted around men. For some sicko reason, she was attracted to dangerous types, the ones your mother warns you to stay away from.

Her stomach cramped at the thought of her mom. It'd been three days since she'd contacted any member of her family, and she knew they were sick wondering where she'd vanished to. She'd sent a text to her dad that first night—with hands shaking so badly she couldn't control the tiny keyboard—telling him she was okay but had to disappear until Carlos's trial. Then she'd smashed that phone under the tires of her demon car and purchased a prepaid throwaway the next day.

A noise from the kitchen made her whirl and raise the Glock—but she relaxed her stance, realizing it was just the motor of the huge Thermidor refrigerator switching on in the eerie silence. She'd hadn't yet learned the rhythms and sounds of her new home. She'd probably lie awake all night listening, wondering if anyone lurked outside her protective wall.

Claudia wandered into the living room and collapsed on the plush sofa, placing the gun on a table beside her.

No one could know where she was. She loved her family, but they were all a bunch of gossips—especially her two sisters—and she might as well put an ad announcing her location in the *Miami Herald*. For sure there'd be a flurry of traceable emails and texts, and hints of Collins Island would probably even leak to Facebook. Everyone dreamed of living on this ritzy isle. Julie, her eldest sister, would insist on a visit.

Of course that could never happen. Carlos's very own domestic terrorist group—at least that was what the US Attorney called them—the Warriors for Self Rule, might even be watching her family in hopes they'd lead them to her. She prayed that wasn't true, but she wouldn't put it past Carlos. His terrorist friends had killed Moochie to warn her. She wouldn't underestimate them again.

The next month would be the most difficult in her life, but it was her own fault for allowing lust to overcome common sense and the advice of the people who loved her. No, she had to go through this alone. She'd find a way to make contact eventually, but the less her family knew, the safer it was for everyone.

And she couldn't get sick. She didn't dare go to a doctor, hospital or even a clinic and use her insurance.

Carlos's Warriors had expert hackers among the faithful.

THREE DAYS LATER, Jack still wondered about the enigmatic Louise Clark who'd disappeared behind the walls of Villa Alma and hadn't emerged once. He knew that for a fact because he'd reviewed the surveillance camera on the front gate. Not even a solitary walk on the beach.

What was she doing in there? Writing a book?

He didn't have access to the feed from any security cameras inside the compound. If they were even turned on.

He'd expected Santaluce to arrive on the island by now. So far that hadn't occurred, although Santaluce's assistant phoned to confirm Ms. Clark had moved in. When Jack had inquired about the arrival of the villa's owner, he'd been informed that information was on a need-to-know basis, as if Santaluce was part of some covert op.

No question something funky was going on, and as the security director he needed to know what.

So where had Ms. Clark lived before arriving on Collins Island?

Jack booted up the computer. Every visitor had to provide proof of identity to board the ferry, and the guard always scanned that ID into a database.

Curious about what he'd find, he clicked the file for the date of her arrival. When her driver's license appeared on the screen, he zoomed in.

The address was in the southwest part of Miami-Dade County, a settled, middle-class area, full of homes that held their value even through the recession. So why the junker car?

He placed the address into a search engine, and discovered it didn't exist. He confirmed the digits to be sure he hadn't made a mistake. He ran the address through Miami-Dade County's database and got the same results.

The address on her driver's license was fake.

Was the license itself?

Jack studied the image. If it was a phony, it was a damn good one. Made by people who knew what they were doing. He needed the license itself to confirm its authenticity.

Well, well, well. Jack leaned back in his chair, considering. His instincts had been right on, as usual. Ms. Clark wasn't what she seemed. Did her appearance on Collins Island have something to do with Mr. Santaluce's "questionable" business?

Was she cooking meth behind the walls of Villa Alma? Or doing something else equally dangerous?

He entered her name into a search engine and hundreds of results materialized. But Clark was as common as Smith. He narrowed the options to Florida, waded through them, but didn't find the Louise Clark living in Santaluce's cabana. So that likely wasn't her real name, which explained the woman's confusion when he'd first addressed her.

He called Lola in the Alliance office.

"Yeah, Jack?" she answered in her throaty voice.

"I'm going to email you a driver's license. Run the image through our facial-recognition program and see if you get a hit."

"Something going on?"

"Maybe. I don't know yet." He hit the send button.

"I know you're bored, Jack, but don't go looking under rocks for trouble."

"Noted."

After a pause, Lola said, "I've got it. Louise Clark. Isn't this the new tenant?"

"Right, but she doesn't exist. Neither does the address."

"So Santaluce has her under wraps. What's she done?"

"Nothing, but my radar is lit up."

"Ouch. Never a good sign," Lola said, her tone now serious. "I'll let you know what I find."

Jack scrolled through the security feed until he got to the camera on the front of Villa Alma and froze the image. No sign of the new tenant. What was going on behind that imposing gate? He decided to pay a little visit and see what response he got from the lovely Louise.

When he arrived at Villa Alma, he exited the golf cart and rang the delivery bell, staring up into the security camera. After a few moments he heard a breathy "Yes?" on the intercom.

"Ms. Clark?" he inquired.

"Yes."

"It's Jackson Richards, Security Director."

"Yes, Mr. Richards?" she responded, politely impatient.

"Just a courtesy call to see if everything is all right."

"Everything is fine, Mr. Richards. Is there some problem?"

"None of my staff has seen you since your arrival, and we wanted to make certain you were okay in there."

After a pause she said, "Thank you for checking, Mr. Richards, but please don't concern yourself with me. You probably won't see me around much."

Thinking it awkward to have a conversation with a camera, Jack said, "I wanted to let you know there's a weekly happy hour on Friday night in the clubhouse for all residents."

"Thank you, but I'm here for some rest."

"Happy hours can be restful."

"Yes. Well, if there's nothing else, I need to go."

Go where? Do what? Jack's phone sounded the alarm for an emergency text. He found a message from Ike Gamble: CODE 99.

An unknown boat was attempting to land on the island's private beach.

Jack saluted to Villa Alma's camera and remounted

his golf cart. He needed to handle this situation but wasn't overly alarmed. A beach landing wasn't exactly a common problem, but every so often someone—usually a local cruising around Biscayne Bay under the influence of too many beers—decided to check out Collins Island on a whim. People were curious about the good life, and since there was no bridge from the mainland, a boat was the only method to arrive. The interlopers usually zoomed away with huge rooster tails when waved off.

And if they didn't, they'd soon regret it. The developers had positioned huge rocks a hundred feet offshore to prevent any unsanctioned vessels from approaching. The rocks were submerged but clearly marked and on all nautical charts as a hazard.

But when Jack approached the beach he saw a thirty-foot Mako had been driven hard onto the sand, leaving an ugly trench in its wake. The white hull rested on its side and huge gashes from the rocks marred the fiberglass.

What? Damn fools. Unlikely that boat would ever float again.

Ike Gamble, assigned today as a roving guard, was involved in a heated confrontation on the beach with two thirtysomething bearded men wearing backpacks. Jack alerted the Miami Beach police, then jumped from his cart and hurried to assist Ike.

"I'm sorry, gentlemen," Ike said forcefully. "As I've explained, this is a private island. You'll have to remain with your vessel."

"The hell with that," the larger of the men said, and brushed past Ike. "Come on, Smitty."

"Hold it." Jack extended both arms, displaying the shoulder holster beneath his jacket.

The man cursed and stopped moving.

"Ike, use your phone to record this," Jack called out. "Just in case the surveillance cameras don't have a good view."

"Got it, boss." Ike raised his phone.

"What's your name, sir?" Jack asked pleasantly, lowering his arms.

"Jeff Baldwin." Baldwin met Jack's gaze with a hostile stare.

"Didn't you see the hazard warnings, Mr. Baldwin?"

"Didn't see any warnings," he spat out in a manner that made Jack's alarm bells loudly sound off. This man had deliberately steered his boat over those rocks and onto the island. Why? Did he hope to pull some sort of scam on the wealthy residents with an expensive lawsuit? Others had tried it, and failed. Maritime law was clear on the subject.

"That's hard to believe, sir," Jack said. "There are at least ten markers on the other side of the rocks. Maybe you've been drinking? The Miami Beach Police are on their way."

Baldwin shot a glance to the buddy he'd called Smitty, who waited beside Ike. Smitty appeared nervous. What did these guys have planned?

"I need to find a phone," Baldwin said. "I'll need help to move the boat."

"Don't you have a cell phone?"

Baldwin raised his chin. "What if I don't?"

"Then I'll let you borrow mine," Jack said. "You're not leaving this beach until the police arrive."

"But you can't arrest me, can you, hotshot?" the man sneered. Baldwin again glanced to Smitty, who gave a quick nod.

Jack tensed.

"You can't keep me here," Baldwin stated, clenching and unclenching his fists at his sides.

"Sir, I am requesting that you remain where you are," Jack said. "You've been informed this is private property and that you are trespassing. We will render whatever assistance is needed, but if you attempt to leave this area, I will have no choice but to restrain you."

"You and who else?"

"I don't need anyone else."

"Right. You're going to shoot me?"

"Not unless you shoot first."

Baldwin narrowed his eyes, obviously calculating. After another harsh curse, he rushed into Jack with his shoulder.

When he made contact, Jack grabbed Baldwin's wrist with his left hand, twisted hard and flipped the trespasser onto the sand. He pressed a knee into his kidney.

"Hey," Smitty yelled, stepping forward.

In one smooth movement, Jack withdrew his Sig Sauer and leveled it in the center of Smitty's body mass. "Stay there," Jack instructed.

Smitty halted. Ike's eyes widened.

"Is your Taser ready, Ike?" Jack barked.

Smitty shot his arms into the air and stepped away from Ike. "Don't tase me, man. I'll wait on the boat."

Jack nodded. Smitty had obviously been tased before.

"How about you?" Jack asked, looking down at Baldwin who was still eating sand.

"Yeah, sure," Baldwin muttered. He raised his head and spit. "Just let go before you break my arm."

An hour later, the trespassers stood on the deck of the Miami Beach PD's patrol boat on their way back to the mainland. Jack sighed as he watched the boat's wake grow smaller. So much for his peaceful month on Collins Island. The wrecked Mako remained on the beach, an eyesore that he'd definitely hear about from the home owners' association.

Baldwin and Smitty had refused to make arrangements for the boat. They'd been given a week for removal, or a salvage crew would disassemble the vessel for scrap. For some bizarre reason, they didn't seem to care about the boat, which made Jack wonder about their motive.

What the hell were they up to? And what had been in those backpacks?

FRIDAY AFTERNOON, WISHING the pool guy would get here already, Claudia tossed her textbook aside and padded in socks to what she now thought of as security central. She studied the static image of the front gate, but no one was visible. What time would the serviceman show? She'd closed all the window coverings so he couldn't see in while he worked. She'd been antsy all morning and wouldn't be able to relax until the pool maintenance was completed.

Not that she'd been doing much relaxing for the last four days. Her grand intention, her goal during her solitary confinement, was to study for certification as a physician's assistant, a job she considered the wave of the future in health care and one that paid far better than working the floors of a hospital. She had all the material she needed in old-fashioned hardbound books. No way was she venturing on the internet to leave a footprint for Carlos's bogeymen to trace, even though an excellent free course existed online to help her cram.

But every morning, after two hours of reading and taking notes, she'd grow restless and unable to focus. A walk around the estate released tension, as did a swim in that gorgeous heated pool. But going outside was off-limits today until the pool had been checked and proper chemicals added.

She glared at the television, which also provided an escape. She suspected by the end of her confinement she'd hate TV. Either that or she'd be one of those weird addicted viewers who couldn't miss an episode of *Hoarders*. But she didn't dare turn up the sound this morning.

Where was the pool guy? Alert for the slightest noise, she soundlessly returned to the sofa and grabbed her book. Not even a week, and already she longed to venture beyond the walls of Villa Alma. She'd seen photos of a gorgeous beach. The golf course—all of the holes with a view of the Atlantic—looked prettier than the one on Pebble Beach.

Claudia forced her attention back to techniques for taking a good patient history. She found the subject interesting. She really did. She wanted to learn how to— Her head jerked up at a noise outside. The gate opening?

She crept to the monitor. Yes, the gate stood wide open. A red-haired young man, maybe an older teenager, walked into the image carrying a yellow bucket in each hand. He wore shorts and a T-shirt, but soon disappeared off the monitor.

Claudia tiptoed back to the couch and slowly, oh so carefully, set her butt down. No one—especially not young maintenance men who might be susceptible to bribes—could know she was here. She considered Jackson Richards and his team a weak link, but had to assume the security of übersafe Collins Island was trustworthy.

But maybe not. Carlos had taught her you couldn't trust anyone. Ever.

She wrapped her arms around her knees and waited, forehead down, barely breathing. She couldn't see the screen from here, but testing a pool's water couldn't take long. She closed her eyes, her stomach churning. When the kid left, she'd planned to put on sunscreen, recline on a lounge chair and stare at a clear blue sky. She already had on her bathing suit beneath her cutoffs, so maybe a quick dip, too. That would be the—

The door to the living room swung open. The pool guy sauntered inside pocketing a key, focused on the kitchen.

Heart pounding, Claudia reached for her Glock. She rose and backed toward security central, raising the weapon with both hands. How had Carlos found her so quickly?

The pretend pool guy hadn't yet noticed her.

Never taking her gaze off the intruder, she pushed the panic button.

Nothing happened. A chill traced her spine. Had the lines been cut?

Whistling as if he hadn't a care in the world, Carlos's hit man moved into the kitchen and opened the refrigerator door.

"What the—" He jumped back as if stung. He swung his head.

That's when he saw her. And screamed—just like a little girl.

Claudia stiffened her elbows. The gun was becoming heavy. "Hands up," she said, amazed her voice sounded calm.

He shot his arms in the air, his face bright red. "Oh, God. Please. Please don't shoot me."

"Did Carlos send you?" she demanded.

"Who? No." He swallowed hard, his Adam's apple bobbing.

"Who are you?"

"I work for AquaClear. I service the pool. No one is supposed to be here. I keep beer in the fridge and—oh, God. I'm going to be—"

He vomited all over the spotless kitchen floor.

CHAPTER THREE

WHEN THE ALARM from Villa Alma sounded, Jack bolted from the security office and onto his golf cart. He punched the accelerator, but the slow-ass worthless piece of junk wouldn't go over ten miles an hour. Hell of a thing in an emergency. He could jog faster than this.

He needed to find out what was going on inside Villa Alma.

As he approached Santaluce's estate, he noted AquaClear's service truck outside a wide-open gate.

Jack unsnapped the holster beneath his shoulder. Moving cautiously through the opening, he glanced up to the camera mounted high on the gate. Was Ms. Clark watching?

Ignoring the main house, he jogged toward the smaller cabana. He couldn't see inside. Every window was covered.

The two on-duty guards arrived on their carts. He held up his hand to signal them to hold.

This wasn't a police op, so he needed to follow the emergency protocol established by the home owners' association.

At the front door, he placed his ear against the wood and listened. All quiet.

He motioned for his backup to approach. He positioned them at each end of the structure—although they were all but useless since their only weapon was a Taser.

Jack removed his Sig Sauer, pointed the barrel skyward and rapped hard on the door.

"Ms. Clark, Island Security. Please respond."

Protocol dictated to wait five minutes and then breach. Five minutes was too long if someone was inside bleeding.

The door opened. Ms. Clark appeared. No blood visible.

Jack relaxed slightly.

"Took you long enough," she said.

"What's the emergency?" Jack demanded.

"Intruder alert." With a Glock awkwardly clutched in her right hand, she motioned him inside.

"Watch where you point that thing," Jack said. By the way she held the weapon, he doubted she knew how to use it. He signaled for his backup to stand down and stepped inside the cabana.

A foul smell was his first sensory impression. Next was how the place was closed up tight as a tomb.

P.J., the kid who serviced the pools, lay on a sofa with a washcloth over his eyes. He looked sick.

"This is your intruder?" Jack asked.

"Yep." Ms. Clark moved to the kitchen, placed

the gun on a counter, pulled on plastic gloves and squatted to clean up puke on the floor. That explained the smell.

Jack glanced back to the sofa. "What happened?"

P.J. groaned and sat up. He worked the washcloth between nervous fingers. "I keep Coronas in the fridge. This is my last stop of the day, so I pop a cold one and take a dip in the pool."

"What?" A slow burn of anger ignited in Jack's gut. "How do you get inside?"

"Santaluce gave AquaClear a key for some plumbing job last year." Looking miserable, P.J. sighed. "I made a copy." He met Jack's gaze with pleading eyes. "No one is ever here. I never hurt anything, don't look in any drawers."

As the scenario unfolded in his head, Jack nodded. P.J. must have walked in unannounced, and Ms. Clark pulled her gun on him. Stupid kid. "You could have been killed."

P.J. closed his eyes. "I thought I was dead."

And so he puked out of fear. At the stringent smell of bleach, Jack glanced toward the kitchen where Louise Clark continued to work. "You ought to make him clean up the mess."

"I'm used to it," she said. "And he'd just throw up again."

"I'm sorry," P.J. said. "I'm really, really sorry."

Louise stood. "That's about the hundredth time you've apologized."

"Please don't tell my boss," P.J. begged. "I know I'm not supposed to ever—"

"You should have thought about that before you trespassed," Jack said.

"Trespass?" The kid's eyes widened.

"Ms. Clark could file charges."

"Charges? Oh, God. I'll never do it again. I swear."

"No, you won't, because you'll never set foot on this island again."

P.J. rose. "I'm fired?"

At his expression, Jack worried the kid might hurl again. "Or your employer loses the most lucrative pool contract in Miami. Yeah, I think you're fired."

"Please, don't do that," Louise said in a small voice.

Jack turned. She stood in the kitchen holding an aerosol can of Lysol. "What?"

Stripping off gloves, she moved into the living room. "How old are you, P.J.?"

"Nineteen."

"In school, right?"

"FIU." He swallowed. "I'm studying hospitality management."

A smile flitted cross her lips as she met Jack's gaze. She was probably thinking, as he was, that P.J.'s behavior hadn't been exactly hospitable.

"I won't press charges," she said.

"The home owners' association has strict rules," Jack said. "There's no option here."

"But you don't have to tell." She looked at P.J. "You'll never do this again, right?"

Hope blossomed on the kid's face. "Never," he said. "Never. I swear."

"Can't you cut him a break?" she asked.

Jack stared at her. Nice lady. "I have to document the incident."

"Blame it on me. Say I made a stupid mistake, new tenant and all. I pushed the button wondering what it did. He's just a kid, really. I'm certain he's learned his lesson."

"I'll think about it," Jack told her. He turned back to P.J. "Give me the key."

P.J. removed a key from his shorts and handed it over.

"Have you completed your work?" Jack asked.

"Yes, sir. I always do that first."

"Then take off. You'll be hearing from me."

With a grateful look at Ms. Clark, P.J. scurried out.

"Are you sure about this?" Jack asked Louise.

She nodded. "He scared me when he burst in here, but no harm done."

"Everything else all right? I still haven't seen you around the island."

"Everything is fine." She looked away. "Thank you for coming."

"You're welcome. By the way, I arrived exactly four minutes after the alarm sounded."

She glanced up. "You timed it?"

"I did."

She shrugged, and looked down again. "Seemed a lot longer."

"Yeah, it did to me, too, actually." Jack evaluated Louise Clark as she nibbled on her bottom lip, noting long, firm legs beneath the frayed edge of denim cutoffs. She wore a pale yellow bathing suit top, firm breasts as full as he'd imagined straining against the thin fabric.

Down, boy. She's off-limits for a whole lot of reasons.

Ms. Clark was one fine-looking woman, but she couldn't hold his gaze. Did she have something to hide? Maybe she didn't want to file charges because she didn't want any involvement with law enforcement. He'd been shocked when she opened the door holding an automatic. Why did this woman own a gun? Or maybe it was Santaluce's weapon.

"Will I see you tonight at the clubhouse?" he asked.

She made eye contact, looking interested. "What's going on at the clubhouse?"

"Happy hour every Friday night during season. Remember I told you about it?" He couldn't participate in the festivities, but his job required him to observe.

"Oh," she murmured. "No, I can't make it."

"Other plans?"

"Right," she said, again looking away. "I have other plans."

Doubting she'd even leave the villa, Jack moved

toward the door. He had no excuse to linger and learn more about Louise Clark, much as he might want to.

"Please don't report P.J.," she said. Her words held him at the threshold.

"Are you always so forgiving?" he asked, looking down at her serious expression.

"Forgiving?" she asked, sounding amused, blue eyes widening in obvious surprise. Her gorgeous mouth curled into a smile, illuminating her face with that beauty he'd noticed on their first meeting, and he suddenly needed to know what she was thinking.

CLAUDIA STARED AT Jackson Richards. *This man thinks I'm forgiving? Man, does he have it wrong.* She would never forgive her ex for the things he'd done. Her testimony would ensure the murdering bastard remained behind bars the rest of his life.

"Some people would disagree with you about that," she said.

"What people are those?" Richards asked.

She shook her head. "Never mind."

Memories of her ex curtailed fleeting amusement. Really, there was nothing funny about her situation.

And the reason she wanted Richards to cut P.J. a break was so the kid wouldn't hold a grudge. Carlos taught her that people who held grudges were dangerous. What if Carlos's friends found P.J. and asked questions, offered money for information? The teenager would jump at the chance to turn on the woman who'd cost him his job.

She couldn't take that chance. Better to make P.J. an ally. And now that she thought about it, same thing with Jackson Richards. She needed him on her side, to be her friend. She nibbled her bottom lip, the phrase *friends with benefits* springing into her head. What she wanted from this hunk of a gladiator was definitely not friendship.

What would it be like to peel off this guy's clothing, see what that magnificent body looked like au naturel? She crossed her arms in front of her chest so she'd keep her hands to herself. *What is wrong with me?*

She needed to get this man out of her sight before she reached out to test the strength of his impressive biceps with a quick squeeze. From the looks of those shoulders, she'd bet he could lift her with one arm. And once she touched him, she wouldn't be able to stop.

"Enjoy the happy hour tonight," she said, in a voice meant to encourage him to leave, yet not sound too rude. She needed this ally. "And thanks again for coming to my rescue."

"You're sure you can't come?" he asked.

He was halfway out the door. He needed to go. *Please go.*

"I've got to study," she said.

"What are you studying?"

She sighed. *Me and my big mouth.* "For the physician's assistant exam." She gripped the doorknob, signaling she meant to shut it, shut him out, that she wanted him to leave.

"You'll need to take a break at some point."

"But I shouldn't drink booze on that break. Thanks again, Mr. Richards, but I need to get back to it."

Still he hesitated, glancing back inside the cabana. "Are you proficient with that Glock?" he asked.

The quick change in subject caught her off guard, making her blurt out the truth. "I can pull the trigger, but don't usually hit where I want."

His gaze refocused on her. His eyes were insanely intense. Did this man know how he affected her? Probably. Likely all women reacted to him the same way. How could any heterosexual female help herself? She took a deep breath, feeling her resolve slip away.

"Practice makes perfect," he murmured.

Remembering his gun when he'd arrived at the door, she wanted to ask if he was an expert shot. Of course he was. He was the security chief. Could he teach her how to hit her targets? Yeah, and what else could he show her?

She felt a delicious pull low in her belly, and opened her mouth to ask him to stay and begin a few lessons, but swallowed the words. *Get a grip, Claudia. Remember—you can't trust anyone.*

"See you around," Richards said and finally, thankfully moved outside.

Claudia closed the door and leaned against it. She

closed her eyes, disgusted with herself. She was practically panting.

She waited until Richards had closed the gate and driven away on his cart, pulled off her shorts and dived into the pool. The blast of water was better than a cold shower.

BACK IN THE security office, Jack replayed his encounter with Louise Clark in his head. He'd been blown away by the fact that she didn't want P.J. fired, figuring she'd want the kid's balls nailed to the wall. Yet he was madder about the security breach than she was. He was considering cutting the kid a break, but could never trust him again. He'd feel compelled to check the security feed and the timing each time P.J. serviced the pools.

So Louise owned a gun and, from what she said, had obviously done some target practice. Was shooting a hobby or did she need to be proficient because of some threat? And who were these mysterious people who didn't think she was forgiving? Why was she used to cleaning up puke? She was studying to be a PA, so maybe she was a nurse.

Damned perplexing. But he loved to solve a good riddle. Besides, what else did he have to do?

Ike Gamble, one of the guards on roving duty today, motored to a stop out front on his electric cart. The other, Rafael Garcia, arrived a minute later on his. They'd completed a circuit and were taking their afternoon break. The two entered the office animatedly discussing the excitement at Villa Alma.

"Good job today, guys," Jack told them. "I appreciate how fast you responded."

"Man, what a rush," Rafael said in his slight accent. He was a new hire, a Hispanic man in his thirties carrying a few extra pounds. "That's the first time I ever responded to an alarm."

"And hopefully the last," Jack said.

"Everything all right inside Villa Alma?" Ike asked.

"Yeah, false alarm. The new tenant pushed the panic button by mistake."

Ike nodded. "That happens every so often."

"Sure broke up the day," Rafael said. "I wish it happened *more* often."

"You wouldn't say that if someone had been inside bleeding or dead," Jack said. Yet he'd once felt the way Rafael did. As a deputy sheriff in Marion County, he'd craved action like a junkie craves smack. But Rafael had no military or police experience. All he knew was the boredom of Collins Island. He didn't understand how in a heartbeat a thrill could turn tragic.

The phone rang, and Jack reached to answer. "Break is over," he told the guards.

"Okay, boss," Rafael said, hiking up his belt, his hand moving protectively over the Taser as if he was on his way to the OK Corral.

Jack grinned. "Be careful out there."

Ike rolled his eyes as he left the office.

"Security," Jack barked into the phone.

"This is Lola," she said needlessly in her distinctive voice. "I'm calling to remind you about the all-hands meeting tomorrow morning."

"I forgot about that."

"Conveniently, as usual. Thus the call. You know how I look out for you, Jack."

"Can I skip it this time? Those meetings are nothing but a time suck."

"Yet required for all available operatives. You're expected at 9:00 a.m."

"Yeah, yeah. I'll be there," Jack grumbled. He'd have to take the 8:00 a.m. ferry to make the meeting on time.

"I also wanted to let you know the facial recognition program didn't get a hit on Louise Clark."

"Too bad." Jack suppressed a stab of disappointment. Damn. Was he craving action now, too? "Well, at least she's not a known criminal."

"She's not in any law enforcement database we have access to," Lola said, "so she's never been arrested."

"Good to know. Thanks, Lola."

"So what are you going to do about her?"

"I'm not sure."

"Liar."

"I'm wounded," he said, deliberately making his voice aggrieved.

"No. You're curious and you won't let it alone until you figure out what bothers you."

"I have work to do," he said, and disconnected.

Which *wasn't* a lie. He wanted to complete the paperwork documenting the alarm this afternoon. Even as a deputy sheriff, Jack's work habit was to get the paperwork out of the way immediately. Putting off drudgery only made a boring task loom larger and harder to initiate.

He pulled up the form on the flat-screen monitor, renamed a file for today's incident and stared at the blanks he needed to complete. Lola had labeled him a liar, a dig that bothered him. She knew how much he valued the truth. What she didn't know was he was about to file a false report, something he'd never done in his career.

And why was he doing it? What P.J. had done was not only against every Collins Island rule, but criminal. Although, yeah, no harm done except to Louise Clark's mental health. Would it be better to fire the kid to teach him a hard lesson about following the rules? That lesson could alter his life. He might need the money for tuition and have to drop out of school. Jobs were still hard to come by for kids. An angry teenager could turn sullen and bitter.

Jack closed the file without entering a single word. He wanted to think about what he'd put in his report a little longer. Maybe he'd watch P.J. for a few weeks, see what happened. The report wasn't due until the end of his stint as director.

Jack's gaze drifted to the surveillance feed switching from camera to camera around the island. Everything remained calm. *As usual*, he thought, mimicking Lola's comment.

When the stream landed on Villa Alma's impressive front gate, he froze the image on a secondary monitor and leaned back in his chair. Was he considering cutting P.J. a break because Louise Clark had asked him to? He thought about his time inside the walls of Santaluce's estate, searching for anything unusual, out of place. He hadn't seen the junker car Ms. Clark had driven to her new home. Likely she'd secreted it in Santaluce's garage. She'd indicated she didn't plan to drive anywhere.

Surveillance cameras took a snapshot of every car loading the ferry. It'd take some digging, but why not get the car's license plate and run her down from there? She could have switched plates, but maybe not. At least he'd have more information.

He pulled up the database from the date of her arrival, accessed the log and found the name Louise Clark on the 5:00 p.m. ferry. The camera time stamped every photograph, and the shot would have been taken around that time. In case the clock was off—a common occurrence with surveillance cameras—Jack began his search with photographs after 4:00 p.m. He scrolled through photo after photo, and finally found what Louise Clark called her devil car. Her twenty-year-old clunker was easy to spot among the Bentleys, Porsches and Teslas.

He enlarged the screen and wrote down the name of the tag, double-checking the digits. He sure didn't need to start this little treasure hunt with bad intel.

Remembering the happy hour in the clubhouse, he glanced at the time. He was already late. The phone would ring any minute and Dr. Diane Kirkman, the home owners' association president, would demand his presence.

Entering Ms. Clark's tag number into the Florida Department of Motor Vehicles database would have to wait.

Jack slipped into his blazer and walked to his cart deep in thought. He wanted to skip this cocktail party, another giant waste of time. He was expected to mingle with the socialite island residents, be available to answer any questions about security protocols, listen to them outbrag each other about their latest investments.

He'd much rather continue his investigation into Ms. Clark, but the answers would have to wait.

Lola was right. He couldn't let it alone until he unraveled the mysteries of the new tenant.

Who was she? What was she doing on Collins Island? His gut told him something was going on with Louise Clark, something he needed to know about.

At 2:00 A.M. Claudia dressed in black jeans and a black sweatshirt with a hoodie and tucked the Glock in her waistband. She moved to Villa Alma's front gate.

A brisk northeast wind, the leading edge of a strong cold front sweeping into south Florida, whipped palm fronds. It would start raining in an hour, maybe less. Clutching the cool wrought iron, she scanned the street in front of the estate and saw no one. She looked up at a clear night sky with thousands of stars and heaved a huge breath.

The Weather Channel claimed this front would drop the temperature close to freezing, a rare event in Miami. There might even be frost by dawn. Hopefully that meant nobody would be out.

Good. Because she couldn't stand it any longer. She felt like a bird in a gilded cage and needed to break out of her prison for a short time. She'd be back inside before the rain started.

She entered the security code and cautiously stepped outside with her back flat against the wall. The catch relocked with an automatic click when she closed the gate. Staying close to the wall, wary of anyone else out at this ungodly hour, she jogged toward the ocean.

As she neared, she could hear waves crashing on Collins Island's private beach. The wind had also stirred up the surf.

She slowed her pace, breathing hard. God, but it felt good to get her blood pumping. She scanned the beach nervously, but quickly determined the area was deserted except for the hull of an empty beached boat. No one sat at the many lounge chairs and tables.

That's what she had hoped. The moon was only the thinnest silver crescent, so it didn't provide much light.

She'd be too obvious if she relaxed in a lounger. A line of coconut palms dotted the sand, and she collapsed in front of the thickest one hoping no one would see her from the street. She wouldn't stay long. A few minutes.

She lowered the hoodie and stared at the water. The endless ocean stretched out before her, white-caps bouncing on the waves.

She'd been miserable and lonely ever since Jackson Richards left late this afternoon. After her plunge in the pool, she'd stood by the gate for a long time, listening to the faint sounds from the happy hour in the clubhouse. People were laughing, talking, enjoying themselves. She'd longed to join the party, but of course couldn't.

This was bad, very bad. She'd been in exile less than a week and was already going crazy. What would she be like at the end of a month? This is what Carlos had done to her. She'd become a pitiful recluse hiding on a deserted beach in the middle of the night. She used to love people. Now she didn't trust anyone.

Not even the US Attorney who'd convinced her to testify.

She brushed away a tear. *Yeah, great, Claudia. Just what you need, a pity party.*

Her hatred for Carlos Romero threatened to swamp all that remained of the old carefree, fun-loving

Claudia, the woman who wanted to help the hurting people of the world. That was why she'd become a nurse. Was there anything left of that person?

Sometimes she thought her quest for justice was all she had to live for, her belief that someone had to ensure Carlos was punished for his irrational violent rampage. Yes, she'd been stupid to marry him, but he'd lied to her. He'd pretended to be something he wasn't.

Or had she been too much in lust to see it? No, she'd watched him change. And he changed her with him, drumming his paranoid philosophy into her head night and day. Claudia swiped a tear from her face, her anger churning again. What kind of a life would she have after the trial? Would she ever return to the woman she used to be?

"Are you all right?"

CHAPTER FOUR

CLAUDIA LEAPED TO her feet and whirled. Her heart pounded. She felt for the weapon at her waist, but hesitated before yanking it out.

Before her stood an elegant, gorgeous woman of about forty smiling at her with what looked like sympathy. She held a wineglass in her long graceful fingers, one displaying a giant pear-shaped diamond. Luxuriant red hair framed her face, falling to her shoulders.

"You are weeping," she said in softly accented words. Not Spanish. Maybe French.

"I—I—" Breathing hard, Claudia shook her head. She'd been feeling so sorry for herself that this sophisticated woman, obviously one of the wealthy residents out for a late-night walk, had snuck up on her. Her chic white slacks, which fit as if designed for her perfect body, likely cost thousands of dollars. She wore a loose, gauzy blouse, which looked pale yellow in the moonlight, tucked into the waist.

"I startled you, didn't I? I am so sorry, *cherie*."

"Yes," Claudia finally managed to say. "I thought I was alone."

"A woman should never come to the beach in the middle of the night to cry alone."

Claudia swallowed, knowing she should turn and run, but said, "No?"

"Never to cry." The woman held up her glass and took a sip of red wine. "Drink, yes. Of course that is always appropriate and far more effective in drowning one's sorrows."

Claudia felt a laugh threaten to bubble up. Maybe she was close to hysteria.

"My name is Marsali," the woman said.

"I'm—Louise."

"Would you like to join me for a glass of wine, Louise?"

"I really need to get back."

Marsali swirled the liquid in her glass. "This particular bottle of Bordeaux cost my husband over ten thousand dollars, and it really is quite good. You must give it a try."

"Ten thousand dollars?" Claudia choked out.

"Yes. But of course it is very old. Like my husband." Marsali raised her eyebrows. "A woman as young as you, as lovely, who is weeping alone beneath the moon deserves to taste this spectacular grape. Please join me."

Claudia hesitated, tempted. Lordy. When would she ever get another opportunity to taste such expensive wine?

She took a step away. No. What was she doing? This was too dangerous. "I really can't."

"Ah, *cherie*. Believe me, he is not worth your tears."

"You think I'm crying over a man?"

"Are you not?"

"Yeah." Claudia sighed. "I guess I am."

Marsali smiled sadly. "I know the symptoms only too well." She motioned toward a table a few feet away where Claudia spotted a bottle and another graceful wineglass. She was certain the table had been empty when she'd arrived at the beach.

"Please join me," Marsali said again.

Almost convinced she'd already be dead if this woman were working for Carlos, Claudia walked with her new friend toward the table. "Are you expecting someone else?" Claudia asked, nodding at the second glass.

Marsali dribbled dark liquid into the second glass, ending the pour with a practiced twist. "I always bring two stems when I come to the beach with wine. A woman never knows when she might meet someone interesting."

Still suspicious, Claudia reached for her wine, marveling at how light the glass felt in her hands, and knew it had to be real crystal. "To the next man in your life," Marsali said, touching her crystal against Claudia's with a musical clink.

"I'm done with men," Claudia said, taking a careful sip, not wanting to waste a drop of the wine. She'd do the math later and try to approximate how much each swallow cost. The liquid flowed smoothly across her tongue. Wow. Delicious, but of course she was no expert.

"Done with men? Have you perhaps become a lesbian?" Marsali wondered in her charming accent.

Claudia almost choked. "No, no. It's not that."

"Then you must never think of being done with men, *cherie*, even in the blackest hour of the darkest night. Men make life interesting." Her eyes swept Claudia's face approvingly. "You have many males ahead of you to tame."

"To tame?"

Marsali shrugged. "Men are wild animals that must be subdued. Some are slinky, sexy lions, some energetic bears. Unfortunately, some—like my current husband—are more like water buffalo. Definitely a challenge to domesticate. But all types have their uses and advantages."

Claudia stared at Marsali and wondered about her age. Maybe she was older than she appeared. No question a stunningly beautiful woman, but on closer look older than forty. And perhaps she'd undergone some top-notch plastic surgery around the eyes.

"How many husbands have you had?"

"Lloyd is my fourth legal husband."

"Oh," Claudia murmured, confused by her emphasis on *legal*.

"And you, Louise? Are you married?"

"Divorced." Claudia grimaced at how bitter she sounded, and took another swallow of the wine, which really was extraordinary.

"Ah. Divorce is a nasty business," Marsali said. "Could that be the reason for your tears?"

Claudia shrugged. "Not really. I was well rid of the bum, but can't imagine going through that humiliating experience three times."

"Agreed," Marsali said. "Divorce is far too expensive."

"But aren't you—"

"I'm three times a widow," Marsali stated with a dramatic sigh. "The tragic result of falling passionately in love with the money of older men."

Claudia opened her mouth to offer sympathy, but closed it when the words registered.

Marsali grinned. "I wish you could see your face, *cherie*."

"Sorry." Claudia gulped more wine.

"There have been many generous men in my life. Believe me, I loved every single one, but of course I couldn't marry them all." Marsali shook her head, her hair swinging. "An intelligent woman must be careful before committing. It is fortuitous that we met tonight, no?"

"I'm sorry?" Claudia asked, confused again. Either that or the wine was going to her head.

"I suspect you are in need of some guidance."

"You're probably right about that."

Marsali sipped her wine before speaking. "You are young yet. You see a handsome young man—a stud I think you Americans call them—and the hormones take over, no?"

Claudia laughed, thinking of Jackson Richards. Could this woman read her mind?

"And it is perfectly okay to enjoy yourself on occasion," Marsali said. "But youth and beauty are your most precious assets. You must learn to spend them wisely."

Spend them wisely? Claudia stared at Marsali, trying to process a philosophy alien to anything she'd ever considered. She'd never met a woman like this. Maybe she'd seen a few in movies, but thought they were mostly fictional.

"What did you gain from your marriage?" Marsali asked.

"Not a damn thing." Claudia finished the wine and placed her glass on the table, her mood vastly improved even though they were discussing her disastrous marriage to Carlos. Was it the wine or the company? She grinned. "I wanted out so badly I gave him everything."

"Oh, dear," Marsali said with a disapproving frown. "Definitely a blunder. I wonder if it is too late to—"

A drop of cold rain fell on Claudia's arm. Several more quickly followed. Claudia looked up. She'd been so engrossed in this illuminating conversation, she hadn't noticed the wind had died down.

"Run for home, *cherie*," Marsali squealed, gathering the wine and glasses. *"Au revoir."*

Until we meet again. Wishing she *could* see the wonderful Marsali again, Claudia dashed for Villa

Alma. But that couldn't happen. She'd let her guard down and put herself in danger. Marsali had seen her face.

Too bad, though. It'd been nice having someone to talk to.

JACK WAS UP before daylight Saturday morning, stoked when he exited his apartment into a frigid morning. It had rained hard last night, and the plunge in temperature from the cold front resulted in a smattering of frost, a fricking miracle in Miami, something he hadn't seen since leaving Ocala.

But now the sky was clear and bright blue. Wearing sweats for the first time in years, he jogged two glorious miles along the beach and completed an upper body workout in the island's state-of-the-art gym, another perk of his stint as the security director. The downside was how much time it took to get anywhere off island because of the ferry. To be safe, he'd have to be in line at 7:45 to catch the 8:00 a.m. departure. Lola would provide bagels at the meeting, so breakfast could wait.

After a quick shower, he grabbed coffee at the Island Café and walked to the security office to run down Louise Clark's tag number. He had maybe thirty minutes. He didn't quite understand why he was in such a hurry. Learning about Ms. Clark wasn't an emergency—or he hoped not, anyway. Yet his gut told him he needed to know the truth ASAP.

He brought up the Department of Motor Vehicles website and entered the tag number.

After a few prompts, the name Claudia Jean Goodwin materialized.

Well, well, well.

Was this Louise's real name, or had she stolen the vehicle? The tag matched the vehicle description so she hadn't switched plates. He jotted down the address, which was in the southwest section of Miami near Louise Clark's bogus addy.

So the woman in Villa Alma wasn't who she said she was. He'd known something was off about her. She was either a thief or used a fake ID. Although another possibility was the Goodwin woman recently sold the car to Clark and the sale hadn't yet corrected the website. Jack rejected that explanation. Clark claimed she'd owned her rusted car a long time.

Was she on the run from the police? Did Santaluce know she wasn't what she seemed? Would he find warrants under the name Claudia Goodwin?

Needing a photo to confirm her identity, Jack entered Claudia Goodwin into a search engine and got hundreds of hits. He scrolled, found one for a nursing registry and clicked on the link, recalling the word *hospital* on the paper with the alarm code for Villa Alma.

Sure enough, a photograph of a smiling Claudia Goodwin stared back at him. Louise Clark was a registered nurse, and her name was Claudia Goodwin.

He itched to continue the hunt, but he had a meeting to attend. No time to sift through the links now to learn more about the woman residing in Villa Alma. How was he supposed to do his job with so many useless events crowding his schedule? And when had running down a license tag ever given him such a jolt of excitement?

He looked forward to discussing all this with the lovely Ms. Clark. And why was that? He knew she was a fraud, but her very presence in Villa Alma tugged at him with an insistence that he didn't understand. He constantly searched for logical excuses to show up at that impressive front gate. He resisted the urge to invent a security concern so he could talk to her again.

She wasn't a danger to Collins Island. He'd seen no evidence of criminal activity. Definitely no meth lab. Any threat was purely to Santaluce's bank account. Jack shook his head. Yeah, and her being a gold digger didn't hold together, either. Not with that hunk-of-junk car.

He needed to go back into the field and dodge bullets. The mystery of Louise Clark was making him bonkers.

Jack decided to leave Ike Gamble in charge while off island, so he finalized his instructions and returned to his apartment to retrieve his SUV. Driving the huge vehicle felt weird after motoring around in the tiny golf cart. Like a return to reality after spending a week in Disney World.

After an uneventful trip across the channel, Jake

noted an agitated, red-faced man arguing with a Miami-side guard. The fool had no clearance from a resident, so he was denied permission to board the next ferry. Clueless people, especially tourists, thought they could take a free joyride over to Collins Island and party on the exclusive beach. Happened all the time, although this guy seemed especially pissed.

Jack waited for the outcome of the encounter to provide backup if his guard needed assistance. But the angry man finally gave up. He drove past Jack with a phone pressed against his ear.

Out of habit, Jack jotted down the tag number.

TWO HOURS LATER, Jack sat at a polished conference table in the Protection Alliance's office with Lola and the four other operatives working in the south Florida area. Agents grumbled about the all-hands meetings, but Lola insisted on a monthly gathering to keep everybody grounded, especially the men and women working undercover or in other dangerous circumstances.

Jack suspected that Lola wasn't just the office manager, but also the owner. Her position and source of authority remained murky, but no one argued with the fact that she was in charge.

He'd almost completed his report on Collins Island, detailing how the security department ran smoothly.

"What? No cougars this month?" asked Greta, a

blonde German operative fluent in five languages, with a black belt in karate. "Too bad, Jack." Everyone in the room laughed.

"Don't get too used to the good life," said Brad, an investigator who usually worked as a celebrity bodyguard. "It's my turn to run paradise next month."

"There's one thing, though," Jack said.

"Louise Clark?" Lola inquired.

Jack met her dark stare and nodded. Her pink spikes appeared especially pointy today.

Lola worked her keyboard and put Louise's driver's license up on the screen as Jack chronicled what he'd learned about her, the most damaging item being her fake name and ID. As he laid out the details, he wondered what set off his alarms.

"Not unusual for a beautiful woman to carry a firearm," Greta offered.

"But why isn't Santaluce with her?" asked Tony, another operative. He grabbed a grape from the fruit platter in the center of the table, eyebrows raised. "And why doesn't she ever come out? Sounds like she'd hiding."

"Maybe she's working on a top secret cookbook and that explains all the groceries," Brad said.

"Or maybe Santaluce is really a rich uncle providing her with a quiet location to study for that exam," Greta suggested. "Are you sure you're not just impressed by her ta-tas, Jack? You've always been a breast man."

Jack leveled a glance at Greta. The razzing would only get worse if he reacted.

"Any chance she could be a twin?" This suggestion came from Tony.

"The different names could be because of marriage," Greta said.

"Watch her, Jack," Lola said, putting an end to the discussion. "If she does anything that could interfere with the serenity of Collins Island, you know what to do."

"Understood," Jack said.

An hour later, the meeting completed, Jack slid behind the wheel of his vehicle. He stared at the facade of the run-down strip mall that housed the Protection Alliance's headquarters. The signage on PA's door read Security in small, peeling black decals. No one would ever guess the amount of high-tech bells and whistles that lurked behind a tiny reception area with one ordinary desk and file cabinet.

Just like no one knew what was behind the beautiful face of Louise Clark.

Deception. It could be and often was a dangerous game. What kind of a game was Louise Clark, also known as Claudia Goodwin, playing? Most likely a con game on an unsuspecting wealthy man. Maybe bilking sugar daddies was her primary source of income. He considered the idea that had germinated while listening to a report from a fellow operative.

He ignited his vehicle's powerful engine. Why not visit the address that the Department of Motor

Vehicles listed for Claudia Goodwin? Maybe Louise did have a twin.

The odds were that he'd find nothing. He'd already determined the DMV address did exist, an apartment complex called Brasilia. The addy could also be a ruse, but what the hell. Brasilia was only a ten-minute drive away. He was off island. Why not take the opportunity to check it out?

He parked his SUV in a visitor space and walked into a lush courtyard, alert for anything unusual. But it was early afternoon, so quiet. Goodwin's apartment number indicated the second floor, so Jack jogged up the stairs, and knocked on her door. No one answered.

He knocked again and yelled, "Ms. Goodwin?"

No response.

Jack tried the knob. It turned easily in his hand. Interesting.

He loosened the snap on the holster under his jacket, kept his hand near the weapon and pushed the door open, ready for anything.

He stared inside, evaluating the status of a thoroughly wrecked room. Was this vandalism or had someone been looking for something? Definitely not ordinary theft. The perpetrator of this violence either wanted something specific, something small since cushions had been sliced, or wanted to leave an impression on the owner of the possessions.

Was Claudia Goodwin, also known as Louise Clark, that owner?

How long ago had the apartment been ransacked? He stepped inside and used his elbow to flip a switch, noting that the electricity hadn't yet been turned off. He moved to the refrigerator. Using a paper towel, he opened the door and checked for expiration dates. Skim milk was only a day gone.

Whoever abandoned this place had only been gone a week to ten days. Rent wouldn't be due until next week, the first of the month. Management likely didn't yet know about the condition of this apartment.

His gaze fell to a magazine on the floor with a smiling woman wearing nursing scrubs on the cover. He squatted and read the label. Claudia Goodwin, this address.

Jack moved into the bedroom and found slashed nursing uniforms on the floor.

In the bathroom, he found toothbrush, toothpaste and over-the-counter meds. Something had been written in lipstick on the mirror but smeared so it couldn't be read. His gaze swept the small tiled room and zeroed in on traces of blood inside the toilet bowl.

Not a good sign. Had Louise killed someone, deserted her home and run to hide on Collins Island?

He used the paper towel to swipe the blood. He might need to get DNA from the sample.

Thoughts churning, Jack departed, using another paper towel to close the door behind him.

When he got to the bottom of the stairs, he heard a frail voice call out, "Young man."

Jack turned toward the sound and found an elderly woman standing at the doorway of an apartment leaning on a walker. Her thin hair, weathered face and shrunken body told him she was pushing ninety.

"Yes, ma'am?" he asked.

"You went inside Claudia's apartment, didn't you?" she asked with a suspicious tone.

"Yes, ma'am," Jack replied. "I'm looking for her."

"Are you a friend of hers?"

"Yes, ma'am." He stepped forward, hoping for some intel. "I'm Jack, and worried about Claudia. What's your name, ma'am?"

"Maude Spalding."

"Do you know where Claudia is, Ms. Spalding?"

"No." The old woman struggled to take a breath. "I haven't seen her for over a week, and she always used to check on me."

"Claudia is a nurse," Jack stated, hoping for confirmation.

"And a damn good one." Maude narrowed her eyes. "Had someone messed up her rooms?"

"Why do you ask?"

Maude sucked in a deep breath. "Wait. I need my oxygen."

Jack followed Maude into her apartment and came to a shocked halt. He didn't think anything could surprise him anymore, but the explosion of Christmas decorations that assaulted his vision made him blink. A staggering number of twinkling lights, Santa Claus figures and snowmen overflowed every surface of the room. Maude collapsed in a recliner and inserted an oxygen tube in her nostrils. After inhaling deeply several times she said, "That's better."

"I guess you like the holidays," Jack said, still dazed.

"Tell me about Claudia's place," Maude demanded, definitely more feisty now that she could breathe. "Was her cat locked up inside? I've been worried about Moochie since she disappeared."

"No cat," Jack said. "And the door wasn't locked."

Maude's eyes widened. "Not locked?"

"No. And she didn't take her belongings."

"I didn't think so. Didn't hear her move out."

"Why did you ask if her rooms were messed up?"

"I heard someone up there." Looking upward, Maude dropped her voice, as if worried that someone would overhear. "Sounded like they trashed the place. I warned her that night before she went upstairs. Then I never saw her again."

"Why didn't you call the police?"

Maude drew herself up. "Not my business to call down the police on a sweet thing like Claudia."

Jack interpreted that to mean Maude knew Claudia had something to hide from the authorities. "Anything else you can tell me?"

"Just I figure whoever is after her is still watching her apartment, looking to see if she comes back so's they can snatch her."

"What makes you say that?"

Maude shifted her gaze toward her window, which had a good view of the stairs and the courtyard beyond. But the old lady wore glasses an inch thick. "Seen some strange folks around lately."

"Strange folks?" Jack prompted. "Can you explain?"

"Mean talking men. I'm home all day. Got nothing else to do but watch folks come and go, and I don't like the looks of some of these 'uns."

"Have you seen them today?"

"No. And I didn't see 'em the night Claudia left, but I'm thinking it was them that drove her off."

"Thank you, Ms. Spalding. I appreciate your help."

"You look like a right capable young man," Maude said, meeting Jack's gaze imploringly. "Nothing like those other fellows. Please find Ms. Claudia and help her. She always helped me."

Jack drove back to the ferry with more questions than answers rippling through his thoughts. He needed a conversation with Claudia Goodwin.

If that was her real name.

CHAPTER FIVE

IN AN EFFORT to preserve body heat, Claudia wrapped her arms around her knees and made herself as small as possible.

She was living in a gazillion-dollar villa and the heat didn't work. How ridiculous was that?

She'd dressed in two layers of clothing, including the black hoodie, and still couldn't get warm. It didn't help that she had to constantly pee because of all the hot green tea she sipped. Although wrapping her palms around the warmth of the cup definitely felt good. If only her knuckles weren't numb.

She tucked her hands under her armpits. She'd lived in Miami her whole life and never owned a pair of gloves. Even if she did, why would anyone bring mittens for exile on a tropical island? How could she possibly know that last night's temperature would set a record in south Florida?

While the sun remained high overhead, sitting outside helped, especially huddled beneath a blanket. But as the afternoon wore on, the sun disappeared and the wind kicked up again, so she'd been forced back inside.

She'd tried to reach Mr. Santaluce, but he hadn't

returned her messages. And who knew what the time was in Hong Kong. Her brain was too frozen to compute the time difference.

Huddled on the couch, she knew what she had to do. She'd resisted the idea all day, but she had no choice but to call island maintenance to come fix the heater. That meant another person would have eyes on her, remember what she looked like and possibly report her presence to Carlos's hit men.

But the Weather Channel had forecast tonight to be even colder. She believed them. The second night of a cold snap was always worse.

Claudia glared at the television. Where was global warming when you needed it?

A buzz from the security system startled her and sent her heart racing. She grabbed the Glock, but her fingers were so cold she wondered if she could pull the trigger. With the blanket draped around her shoulders, she hurried to the monitor and saw Jackson Richards standing at the front gate peering into the estate's grounds.

She activated the intercom. "Yes?"

"I need to speak with you, Ms. Clark," he said.

"Do you know how to turn on the heat?"

He squinted into the camera. "What?"

"Come on in," she said and released the gate to admit him.

She opened the front door so she could watch him approach. Wearing a blue blazer and tan slacks, Jackson moved easily, powerfully, but somehow gracefully, a man in complete control of his body. This guy was gorgeous. What she needed to do was climb inside that jacket and absorb the heat from his well-defined muscles.

He ignored the pool area as he strode forward, his gaze intent on her. He definitely looked like he had something to say, and she wondered what about. Maybe she needed to sign a statement about yesterday's false alarm.

She hoped he knew how to fix the heat.

"Good evening, Ms. Clark," he said with a polite nod.

Claudia motioned him inside and shut the door against the biting wind. With teeth threatening to chatter, she took a deep, chilly inhalation. When she exhaled, her breath mushroomed in the air before her.

Jack noticed, because his eyes widened.

"Why is it so cold in here?" he demanded.

Feeling like an idiot, Claudia wrapped the blanket more snugly around her shoulders. "I can't get the heat to come on."

He frowned. "Why didn't you contact maintenance? They're on call 24/7."

She stared at Richards, and he stared right back. What could she tell him that wouldn't sound foolish? She was too miserable to think of a logical reason for allowing herself to freeze to death. She'd thought she could tough through it. Cold weather never lasted long in Miami.

"I'm so cold," she said, which of course didn't answer his question. Oh, God. Confusion was one of the first signs of hypothermia.

"Hold on," he said. "I think I know what's wrong."

She opened her eyes. "Really?"

"Give me a minute."

He went back outside and returned five long minutes later. She followed him to the thermostat.

"The system needs to be reset manually when you switch from AC to heat," he said. "It's a safety precaution for residents that are only here seasonally."

"I hadn't even turned on the AC," she said. "The weather has been so good I didn't need to."

He pressed a button. "That explains it."

"Mr. Santaluce forgot to tell me about that," she said.

"He probably doesn't know," Jack said as he adjusted the temperature. "Maintenance normally prepares the homes for winter residents when they visit. It's part of the service."

"Nothing is happening," she complained, glaring at the thermostat.

"Give it a minute." He turned from the control and met her gaze. "You look miserable," he said.

"That's because I am."

Jack stepped close and wrapped his arms around her.

She stiffened in surprise, wanting to push him away, but he was warm. And smelled delicious.

"Body heat is the quickest thing," he said, adjusting the blanket so it draped over both of them.

Of course she knew that. She was a nurse.

"Better?" he asked after a few moments.

"Yes," she murmured. "Thank you."

She heard a whooshing sound overhead and realized the heat had just clicked on. *Oh, thank God.*

She closed her eyes, allowing Jack's delicious heat to warm her. She'd like to remain wrapped in his arms until she was old enough to have her first hot flash, but this was dangerous. *Just another moment or two until I thaw out.*

"Are your fingers numb?" he asked.

"I don't know. I can't feel them."

He laughed, his chest rumbling beneath her cheek. "Let's sit down."

He led her to the sofa where they sat with their thighs touching and the blanket tented around their shoulders. He gently chafed her frozen hands between his large warm ones.

As his body heat seeped into hers, Claudia became aware of the man next to her, of his planes and edges, muscles and bones. Because of the cold, she'd been holding herself stiff for hours. No, for days. She'd been constantly on guard since the night she'd fled her apartment and the tension had exhausted her. Right now it felt good to just let go, to dissolve into a puddle of warmth.

She knew better than to trust this man, a stranger,

really. She'd worry about the danger again when her body temperature returned to normal.

Jackson quit rubbing her hands, intertwined his fingers with hers and met her gaze, their faces inches apart. She remembered those intense green eyes, but she didn't remember them being so kind. She hadn't noticed that small white scar over his left eye, either. Her gaze dropped to his mouth, so temptingly close.

"Socks work," he said.

"Socks?"

"For keeping your hands warm when you don't have gloves."

"Good idea," she murmured, noticing the strong lines of his jaw, the beginnings of a beard on his chin. Afternoon shadow. How would that stubble feel rubbing against her skin? She shivered.

"Are you still chilled?" Jack held her gaze.

"No. Thanks." She looked away. "So you've had experience with cold weather?"

"Some. I'm guessing you haven't."

"Not really."

"From this area?"

She nodded. "Born and raised."

"So who are you hiding from, Claudia?"

She stiffened. *Hiding? He knows I'm—*

She leaped to her feet. He'd called her Claudia. Jackson Richards knew her name.

She backed away from him. Where was her gun?

"Calm down." He didn't move. His gaze remained glued on her face.

He was watching her like a hawk eyeing a tasty piece of prey. Did he work for Carlos? No, that was impossible. Or was it?

"Take a breath," Jack said in an even tone.

She sucked air deep into her lungs. "How do you know my name?" she demanded.

"It wasn't that hard to find out."

"My ID was good," she insisted. "Why did you doubt it?"

"It wasn't the ID."

"Then what?"

"A combination of a lot of clues. Not recognizing your own name, for one. I'm a trained investigator. It's what I do."

"But why would you investigate me?"

"It's my job." His smile told her there was more motivation than his employment. What else? What was it?

She nodded, chilled again, and hugged herself for warmth. What now? Where could she go? There was no one she could trust.

"What are you going to do?" she whispered. Her heart beat so fast and so hard its frantic pumping had to be visible through all her layers of clothing.

"That depends on this conversation," he said.

"I don't have any money."

"That much is obvious."

She narrowed her eyes. "Obvious?"

"Your car?" he said, raising his eyebrows.

"Oh." The demon car strikes again.

"I need you to tell me what happened inside your apartment at the Brasilia."

The impact of that statement, the extent of his knowledge of her, sucked away the last of her strength. She collapsed into a plush chair beside the sofa. "You went to my apartment?"

He nodded. "This morning."

"Oh, my God. Why?"

"To learn more about you."

She closed her eyes. This couldn't be happening. All of her plans had been so carefully laid out. Why did she ever think she could outsmart Carlos?

"Because it's your job," she said. "Yeah, right."

"Right. Tell me about the blood in the toilet."

JACK WATCHED EMOTION play out across Louise's face—no, Claudia's face—looking for any tells of deception, any signs of a practiced liar. Con artists perfected the skill of twisting the truth and making it sound real.

His mention of blood caused her eyes to well up with tears. Her mouth trembled as she fought against crying. Could be a ploy to win his sympathy, but this reaction appeared honest.

"Moochie," she said, her voice breaking. "Poor sweet little Moochie."

"Moochie?"

"My cat," she said on a sob. "The bastards killed my cat."

Jack knew he was getting somewhere. He just had to be patient. Fortunately, he had nothing else to do tonight but unravel the mysteries of Claudia Goodwin. Holding her close had felt good, too good. She'd clung to him, soft and sweet, like honey melting into his flesh. He'd like nothing better than to hold her in his arms for a few more hours and generate some truly meaningful body heat.

But what bastards? And what did a cat have to do with anything?

"Why would anyone kill your cat?" he asked.

"To shut me up."

Shut her up? What the—

At his waist, Jack's phone sounded the alert for an emergency text. He checked the message. Stowaway on the six o'clock. You're needed on the dock NOW.

He stood. "I've got to go."

"What? You're leaving?"

"I'm needed at the ferry landing. But we're not done here."

"Wait. Please. Does anyone else know who I am?"

Already moving toward the door, wondering how anyone had snuck aboard a ferry, Jack turned back. Claudia was on her feet. "Just my colleagues."

She looked like she'd be sick. "The Collins Island guards?"

"No, associates at the company I work for."

"Oh, God. It's too late then."

"What's too late?"

"Please," she said, her voice ragged. "Please don't tell anyone else my real name."

Jack stared at her pale face, her expression desperate, pleading. Claudia was hiding from some serious shit. But what? He wanted to remain right here and find out what was going on, but couldn't. Protecting this island *was* his job, and right now a stowaway was the larger threat.

"Don't go anywhere," he instructed. "I'll be back as soon as I'm done at the dock."

"Don't worry." She looked down at her hands. "I don't have anywhere to go."

Jack dismissed Claudia Goodwin from his thoughts, believing she'd wait for him at Villa Alma. She couldn't get off the island without him knowing. Yeah, she was a huge question mark, but he'd learned to compartmentalize. He wouldn't prejudge the ferry attendants, either, until he received a report on the stowaway.

As he approached the landing, he noted the six-thirty ferry chugging its way to Miami, a puff of smoke visible in the cool air. Good. Normal operations hadn't been disrupted.

He exited his cart and hurried inside the security shack where Ike Gamble and Rafael Garcia loomed over a shaggy-haired dude of maybe thirty sitting behind the guards' desk. Weathered skin around his eyes and forehead told Jack this man had lived outside most of his life. His cheeks and chin were pale, though, indicating he'd recently shaved a long-time beard. The stowaway wore faded jeans and a plaid shirt, and looked seriously irritated. He continuously shifted his gaze to a dark backpack resting on a file cabinet out of his reach. Another backpack. Well, well.

"If you attempt to leave again, I'll tase you," Rafael said in a hard voice.

The man cursed, narrowing his eyes at Rafael.

"What's going on?" Jack asked, wondering about the pack. Had Ike been through it? There was obviously something important to this guy inside.

"This is Jackson Richards, our security director," Ike said in a relieved tone.

"I don't fricking care who you are," the man said, meeting Jack's gaze. "You got no right to hold me."

Jack returned the stowaway's hostile stare. So that's the way it was going to be.

"He attempted to board the five o'clock, but didn't have clearance," Ike said. "Somehow he slipped on the six o'clock with walk-ons. I don't know what happened, except there were quite a few extras, domestics and servers hired by caterers to work tonight's parties."

Jack nodded. Made sense. Saturday night in season, and the winter residents hosted glittering catered affairs. The ferry would run full all night with guests. But this man was no guest, nor a domestic.

"No excuse," Jack said.

"Agreed," Ike agreed. "But the count was off, and we detained him on this side."

"What's your name?" Jack asked, knowing he'd have to make some changes, kick some butt.

"I don't have to tell you that," the stowaway said.

"We can pull up his ID from the log of the five o'clock," Ike offered.

"Do it," Jack ordered, and Ike moved to the computer.

"Shit," the stowaway muttered, glancing at the pack again.

"Why did you sneak aboard the ferry?" Jack asked.

The man narrowed his eyes. "I had business on the island."

"Business? With who?"

"I don't have to tell you that, either, and it won't be on your damn log."

"We've already been through this," Rafael told Jack.

"This is a private island," Jack said. "No one is permitted without clearance from a resident. Can you give me the name of a resident you're visiting?"

"Yeah," the man said. "I'm here to see Claudia Goodwin."

Claudia Goodwin? Jack's pulse tripped up a notch, but he kept his face impassive. He needed to know what was inside that backpack.

"And we already told you there's no resident here by that name," Rafael said.

"So maybe I made a mistake," the stowaway said.

"A big one," Jack agreed. "You got his name, Ike?"

"I'm looking at the scanned driver's license of a James Robert Picard," Ike said, his face reflecting the glow of the monitor. "See if you think this is him."

Jack moved to check the image. Fuzzy, but definitely the stowaway. "That's him. Is he on our list of known troublemakers?"

Ike checked a clipboard. "No."

"You're going back to Miami," Jack said, and remembered an old funky old pop song. Unwanted, the tune filtered through his brain.

"Oh, you're funny," Picard said. "Hilarious."

"Glad to give you a laugh. The Miami Beach Police Department will meet you on the other side. You'll be charged with trespass. Make the call, Ike."

Ike grabbed the phone. Picard cursed, and again glanced toward his pack.

Jack knew Picard was considering a lunge for his property, which most likely contained a weapon. Jack tensed, half hoping the little jerk would try. He would have let him go with a warning since this was his first attempt to breach security, but he had to act the big, bad macho fool.

Jack opened his jacket and unsnapped his shoulder holster. Picard's eyes widened, and he settled back in the chair.

Legally, Collins Island had no right to go through the man's personal possessions. Jack wasn't a sworn officer anymore, and wasn't going to break any laws today. At least not until he finished interrogating Claudia Goodwin. What did she have to do with Picard?

Jack picked up the man's pack. It was heavy enough

to contain some sort of explosive device. What kind of disaster had they just averted?

"That's mine," Picard said in a deadly tone.

"And you'll get it back when you're on the other side," Jack said, wishing he could cuff Picard. "Ike, you're in charge while Rafael and I accompany Mr. Picard on the next ferry. We'll hand him and his possessions over to the City of Miami Beach PD."

"We're providing them with a lot of business lately," Ike said.

Jack silently agreed. A lot of strange happenings since Claudia Goodwin had moved onto the island.

CLAUDIA EXPECTED JACK to return within thirty minutes, but time dragged on and he didn't buzz at the front gate. She waited for him on the couch, too worried to even turn on the television for distraction. Where was he? Alerting Carlos to her presence on Collins Island?

What the hell was she going to do now? Jackson Richards knew her real name.

The sun set, and the room grew dark. She didn't move to turn on a light.

Should I run? Where would I go? Will the car even start?

All she could think about was Jackson Richards and whether he worked for Carlos. As she grew warmer, her brain started working again and she realized the odds of the security director of this island working for Carlos were just too astronomical.

Jack couldn't be on Carlos's payroll. She remembered how he'd cocooned her hands between his. She'd sensed the strength of his powerful muscles as he'd rubbed her hands to bring back feeling. Would a man that considerate turn her over to a monster?

Sitting close to him was enough to warm any woman, even without central heat rushing in through the vents. And those piercing green eyes. When he looked at her, it was as if he could see right through her. No. As if he knew what she looked like naked. And, man, would she ever like to see *him* naked.

She stood and yanked off her sweatshirt and long pants. Now that the heat worked, shorts and T-shirt were more than enough clothing. Or her thoughts had made her hot.

But, oh, God, he knew her name. And he'd told other people that worked for his company. That disaster pressed on her chest like a million-pound weight. How had that happened when she'd been so careful? She'd only ventured out one time. She thought carefully about her encounter on the beach with Marsali, and knew she hadn't revealed her real name.

Maybe she could stay. She needed to finish her conversation with Jack, impress on him the importance of keeping her identity secret. Should she tell him the truth? She shrunk back from that thought. No. Too dangerous. He wouldn't understand her life was truly at risk. No one knew Carlos the way she did, how focused he and his friends were on what they perceived as their mission in the world.

Jack would think she was overreacting and could easily tell the wrong person. How could she trust him? She'd have to make up some story, something believable.

So why not just say she was trying to get away from an abusive boyfriend? That wouldn't seem unreasonable. She read a version of that sad story in the *Herald* almost every day.

Claudia jumped to her feet, going through the scenario in her head. Flipping on a light, she decided to stick to the truth as much as possible. She'd tell Jack her lover constantly tracked her down and she thought she could avoid him with the tight security on Collins Island. She'd be honest about Mr. Santaluce, how he was the father of a critically ill patient grateful for her nursing skills. She'd be convincing. She could do it.

She wished Jack would hurry. What was he doing at the dock? Obviously something with the ferry. Maybe one of the residents dinged their Mercedes. Or a fingernail. Yeah, that was it. One of Marsali's rich trophy-wife friends had broken a three-hundred-dollar fingernail. What a tragedy. But she could always drown her sorrows in a ten-thousand-dollar bottle of wine.

Ashamed of her spiteful thoughts, Claudia collapsed back onto the sofa. She grabbed a pillow and hugged it to her chest, her thoughts drifting to her oldest sister and her perfectly manicured fingernails.

Missing her sister, she pressed her face into the pillow. She knew her family was worried about her, ditto the US Attorney she worked with. She needed to let him know she was okay, but they'd rehearsed her testimony and she'd given him her journal for safekeeping until the trial.

No doubt the journal was what Carlos's people had been looking for in her apartment.

KEEP YOUR MOUTH SHUT.

Claudia groaned as she pictured the hateful words on her bathroom mirror, the bedraggled, limp body of sweet Moochie in the toilet.

Damn you, Carlos Romero. I'll make you pay if it's the last thing I do.

A buzz roused Claudia from her cascade of ever-worsening memories. She checked the security monitor and exhaled. Jack had returned. Finally. She released the gate, watched him push through and hurried to meet him at the front door.

His jaw set in a hard line, Jack stepped inside holding a sheet of paper. He opened his mouth to speak, but hesitated. "Are you warm yet?"

"Yes," she said. "Thanks for your help. Much appreciated. Really."

"You're welcome. But we need to have a discussion, Claudia."

"Please don't call me that. I need to be Louise."

"And why is that, Louise? Why did you come to Collins Island under a false name?"

She took a deep breath, reminding herself to stick to the truth whenever possible. "I'm hiding from my ex-boyfriend. Collins Island is famous for its security, and I didn't think he could get to me here."

By Jack's hesitation, Claudia could tell she'd surprised him.

"He's abusive?"

"You have no idea," she said.

"What's his name?" he demanded.

She shook her head. Carlos's name was all over television and print media because of his crimes. What if Jack was sympathetic to his crazy cause? More people were than she ever imagined. "What does it matter?"

"Is his name James Robert Picard?"

"No," she said, startled. "I don't know that name."

Jack thrust the paper toward her. "Do you know this man?"

Claudia looked down at a fuzzy image of a driver's license. She didn't recognize the photograph. "Who is this?"

"This man is not your boyfriend?"

"No."

"You're sure?"

She glanced up to Jack's face. He didn't believe her. "You don't think I'd recognize the man I'm on the run from?"

"How do you know Rodolfo Santaluce?" Jack demanded.

"I'm a critical care nurse at a pediatric hospital. His daughter was one of my patients for an extended time, and I told him about my problems. He believed I saved his daughter's life and offered his winter home as a refuge out of gratitude."

"For how long?"

She blinked. "What?"

"You haven't been to work in a week. You haven't even left the confines of this villa and you brought enough food to last the entire season."

She should have known Jack would see through her story. She hadn't had enough time to think through every detail. No choice but to bluff her way through.

Straightening her shoulders, she said, "So?"

"So I don't believe you."

She handed him back the copy of the driver's license. "I'm telling you the truth."

"Maybe," he said. "But not the whole truth."

"I was told the availability of groceries on the island was limited," she said, knowing that sounded weak.

Jack held up the paper. "This man snuck aboard a ferry. He knew your name."

The earth shifted beneath her feet and suddenly she couldn't breathe. "He knew what name? Louise?" How could he?

"He said he'd come to do business with Claudia Goodwin."

"Oh, no." She swallowed, hoping to calm the nausea churning in her stomach. "They've found me."

"That's the second time you've mentioned some mysterious 'they,'" Jack said. "Your ex can't be more than one person."

Light-headed, Claudia collapsed on the sofa and placed her head between her knees. She couldn't faint. She had to think, strategize an escape plan. But was she now trapped on this island? And where could she go that would be safer than here?

"Talk to me, Claudia," Jack said.

She stared at the white tile and took deep breaths until she felt better. "What did you tell the stowaway?"

"That no one by that name lived on Collins Island."

She raised her head and leaned against the cushions. "Thank you," she whispered.

"I ran a search on your name this morning," Jack said. "I got hundreds of hits."

"Of course you did," she said wearily. So far the US Attorney had managed to keep the fact that she was Carlos's ex out of the press, but someone would dig that out eventually. Probably when they got closer to trial. What journalist could resist the story of a wife testifying to convict her terrorist ex of murder?

"I didn't have time to chase down every link," Jack said.

"I guess you're a busy guy."

What should she tell him? The truth?

Her stomach tightened. What a nightmare. She had no choice but to tell him everything. Jackson Richards was a smart guy, a trained investigator. If he kept digging on the internet, he'd discover her marriage to Romero and be angry that she'd lied again. She'd already decided she needed him as an ally, not an enemy. Lying was no way to keep a friend.

Maybe if she was honest with him, laid her entire ugly situation out for him, he'd help her. Or at least keep her secret. So far he'd been a pretty nice guy.

But could she really trust him?

CHAPTER SIX

"I ALREADY KNOW you don't have a police record." Jack sat beside Claudia on the sofa, holding her gaze. For a moment he thought she'd be sick, but she looked better now.

"I wish I'd been able to run a search on you," she said. "It'd help to know something about a man I'm about to trust with my life."

"Your life?"

"Yes."

"So why *didn't* you do a search on my name?" Not that she'd find anything he didn't want the world to know.

She sighed. "I don't dare go online. I don't know enough about security and firewalls, but I think I can assume I'd leave an easy trail to follow." She looked away, nibbling on her bottom lip. "I guess somehow I did, anyway."

"Are you really a nurse?"

"Yes. And I *am* hiding. That's the truth."

"Obviously. But there's more to it than that. Who are you hiding from?"

She met his gaze again, and Jack knew she was trying to decide what to tell him. Was she deciding on a lie? Finally, she released a defeated breath and nodded to herself.

"I'm hiding from Carlos Romero."

"Carlos Romero? The jerk who blew up the post office in Lauderdale?"

"Yes. He's trying to kill me to keep me quiet."

"What? Romero is in jail awaiting trial. It's scheduled to start in a few weeks."

She nodded. "Three weeks and counting. I'm the witness who is going to keep him locked away for life."

Jack stared at her. This woman had more guts than he gave her credit for. Carlos Romero was reputed to be a stone-cold killer.

"You're going to testify against Carlos Romero?"

She hesitated. "If I'm still alive."

"What evidence do you have against him?"

"A lot. I can even put him at the post office."

"You're an eyewitness?"

Claudia looked away, which meant she was considering whether or not to make up a story. What did she have to lie about now? She clutched her fingers so hard the knuckles showed white through her skin.

After a deep inhalation, she met his gaze again and raised her chin. "I'm Romero's ex-wife."

"You were married to Carlos Romero?"

"Briefly," she said, her voice breaking. "It was the biggest mistake of my life."

"Why isn't your name Romero?"

"After the divorce, I took back my maiden name."

Jack stood and began to pace. Wow. This whole-some, sweet-faced woman had been married to a terrorist? Or was she still lying?

He whirled on her. "If he's in custody, how is he going to silence you?"

"He's the leader of a group called the Warriors for Self Rule."

Jack nodded. Everyone knew of the group. The media referred to them as the Warriors. They were a homegrown terrorist group that claimed to believe in self-determination and the rights of the individual. Nothing wrong with that philosophy, but when the government cracked down on them for refusal to pay taxes, the group turned violent and innocent people died.

"Were you a member of the Warriors? Is that how you met him?"

"Never. I hate them." She swallowed. "When I realized something was off about the bastard, I started to keep a detailed journal of his activities. I gave it to the US Attorney I'm working with for safekeeping."

"Go on."

"Carlos gave the order to eliminate me when my name appeared on the witness list," Claudia continued. "The US Attorney says without my testimony, he could go free. I'm the linchpin of his case."

"Then why don't the prosecutors have you under wraps in a safe house?"

She shook her head. "No way. I don't trust them."

"You don't trust the federal government?"

"I don't trust anybody."

"But the feds want to put Romero away."

"Don't you read the paper?" Claudia asked, sounding exasperated. She leaped to her feet and began to pace. "The left hand doesn't know what the right is doing."

"Come on, Claudia."

She whirled on him. "Carlos told me he has someone on the inside, that he found the right person to bribe. In a safe house, I'd be vulnerable with no way to protect myself."

Paranoia strikes deep. Claudia was off the charts suspicious, and maybe with good reason considering the condition of her apartment. "So the Warriors trashed your home?"

"Yes, to scare me into silence, I think."

"Or looking for your journal."

She shrugged. "Management hasn't cleaned it up yet?"

"The place was a disaster. Did you ever meet any of these Warriors, see them with your husband?" he asked.

She shrugged. "A few. They terrified me." She looked into the distance, as if remembering. "They all wore these big, shaggy beards."

Jack handed her the copy of Picard's driver's license. "Look at that again. Picture that guy with a beard."

Claudia did as he asked. She narrowed her eyes, and he watched her face change.

"His license was recently issued, only six weeks ago," Jack said. "It's possible he deliberately altered his appearance."

Claudia collapsed on the sofa. "Pick Heart."

"What?"

She looked up. "Carlos called this guy Pick Heart, which always made me think of a sharp point being driven into someone's chest. He was one of Carlos's most loyal followers."

Jack nodded. And his name was Picard. That definitely worked as far as gruesome nicknames went.

Claudia waved the photocopy of the license in the air. "How did they find me? I'm certain no one followed me to the ferry landing. I've only used cash since I fled my apartment."

"Have you spoken to anyone on the island besides P.J.?"

Claudia hugged her arms. "I've only left this villa one time."

"And?"

"Last night I went to the beach in the middle of the night and met a lady named Marsali."

"Marsali Winthrop?"

"I don't know her last name. She's a gorgeous redhead."

"French accent?"

"Yes."

"That's her," Jack said. "Did you tell Marsali your name?"

"Of course not."

"Maybe she snapped a photo of you with her phone?"

"She didn't have a phone that I saw. Only a bottle of wine."

"That's definitely Marsali." Jack sighed. "Of all the people for you to meet."

"What's wrong with Marsali? I liked her."

"Yeah, I like her, too." Jack shook his head, trying to dispel the face of the outrageous Marsali Winthrop. A practiced con artist, Marsali flirted with every man she met, usually captivating the object of her attention with her intelligence, wit and charm.

"I doubt Marsali knows your husband. They don't travel in the same circles, but I'd like to make sure. Can I ask her to come over?"

"Come here?" Claudia's eyes widened. "Why? No. I don't want anyone to see me."

"Marsali has already seen you."

"But she doesn't know where I live."

"Would you rather go over to her villa? She's close."

Claudia shook her head. "No. Someone else might spot me."

"We need to find out if Marsali told anyone about you."

"So call her."

"Won't work," Jack insisted. "I need to see her face to judge her reactions. She's quite the practiced liar."

Claudia nibbled on her bottom lip and looked away from him. "I don't know what to do."

"Then it's a good thing I do."

She narrowed her eyes. "They've found me. What does it matter *how*?"

"It matters to me," Jack said. "I've got a dangerous security situation that I need to get a handle on. These terrorists may attempt to bring a bomb onto Collins Island."

"A bomb?"

"That's their MO," Jack said. "I don't want them exploding this villa or harming anyone on this island."

Claudia placed a trembling hand over her mouth. "I've put other people in danger by coming here. I have to leave."

"Maybe," Jack said. But he didn't like the idea of Claudia—of any woman—facing the Warriors on her own. He'd force her to contact the US Attorney's Office for protection, if it came to that. He'd already tightened security for the ferry, but if the Warriors were involved, he needed to do more. Much more.

"Before you relocate, we need to finish gathering information."

"I would never have come here if I thought anyone else could be hurt," Claudia whispered. "I swear."

Jack took her hand. "I believe you. And you're not going to be harmed, either. You're a guest of a resident, and as such you are under my protection."

"I am?"

"Damn right."

"Thank you," she said. But she looked away, chewing on her bottom lip again. She was terrified. And obviously didn't trust him. Or anyone.

"So can I call Marsali?" he asked. "I need to get ahold of her before she goes out for the evening."

She raised her chin. "Do it. But please, please don't mention Carlos Romero."

MARSALI WINTHROP SWEPT in wrapped in a luxurious knee-length fur coat that Claudia knew the animal rights activists would want to trash with buckets of paint. Marsali shrugged off the fur into Jack's waiting hands.

"Thank you, Jackson darling," she purred in her musical accent when he'd placed the coat over a chair.

Claudia gaped at Marsali's dress, a black silk sheath that hugged every curve of her slender body, revealing only a hint of cleavage. Glittering diamonds dangled from her ears and around her neck. She looked like royalty. All she needed was a tiara.

"Louise." Marsali kissed both of Claudia's cheeks, leaving behind a fragrance that likely cost as much as the wine had last night. "I hope you're feeling better tonight, *cherie.*"

"Not really," Claudia said.

Marsali turned to Jack. "I trust you intend to elevate her mood, Jackson."

"Are you going off island tonight?" Jack asked.

"The Kirkmans are entertaining," Marsali said.

"I understand they have a guest from Dubai." She shrugged gracefully. "So perhaps later an adventure to our private club on South Beach?"

"Ah. Will Lloyd accompany you to the Kirkmans'?"

"But of course. Unfortunately, as you know, he quickly grows weary and must retire early. Is that why you asked me to come over to Villa Alma, Jack? To inquire about my plans for the evening?"

"Can you sit, Marsali? I'd like to talk to you about something."

"Certainly." With a curious glance to Claudia, Marsali perched on the edge of the sofa. "Is there any wine?" she inquired.

"I'm sorry," Claudia said. "I don't have anything except a beer left by the pool guy. You're welcome to that."

"Beer?" Marsali appeared interested. "From Belgium?"

"Mexico, I think."

"No, thank you, *cherie*." She looked back to Jack. "Now, what is this about, Jackson?"

"After you met Louise last night, did you tell anyone about her?" he inquired politely.

Claudia was no judge of liars like Jack claimed to be, but Marsali definitely appeared perplexed by the question. She looked at Claudia. "Is there a problem, *cherie*?"

"Remember I told you about my ex?" Claudia said. Marsali nodded. "But of course."

"I came to Collins Island to hide from him, and now somehow he's found me."

"And you think I may have given you away?" Marsali sounded offended.

"Not intentionally," Claudia said quickly. "But maybe if you told someone about the crazy woman you met in the middle of the night—"

"Ah, *cherie*," Marsali said. "You are not crazy. Just a betrayed woman. And, no, I did not mention our chance meeting to anyone, not even to my husband. Why would I?"

"You're sure," Jack asked, staring hard at Marsali.

"Yes," Marsali said. "Did your ex beat you, *cherie*? Is that why you're hiding?"

Claudia looked away.

"Ah." Marsali rose and approached Claudia, speaking in rapid, musical words she didn't understand, most likely French. Gathering Claudia into a fierce hug, Marsali spit out, "The bastard."

Claudia hugged Marsali back. She hated lying to this woman, but had no choice. "Yes, a bastard," she whispered.

Marsali turned to Jack and opened her arms. "So how can I help, Jackson?"

"Just don't mention Louise to anyone."

"Does this have anything to do with the stowaway the whole island is buzzing about?" Marsali asked.

"Yes," Jack replied. His jaw tightened, which by now Claudia knew meant he wasn't happy. "I didn't know that was common knowledge."

"Americans are such gossips," Marsali said with an offhand wave. "Do you want to move in with me, *cherie*? He couldn't find you at my house."

Claudia blinked back unexpected tears, experiencing a rush of gratitude that this woman, a stranger really, would be so kind. But of course Marsali didn't know what she was offering, the danger her generosity would bring down on her household.

"No," Claudia whispered. "I couldn't do that. But thank you."

Marsali nodded. "Then you must remain here, Jackson. If this man is managing to get aboard the ferry, you must personally guard Louise all night." She turned back to Claudia. "Jack is an expert in martial arts, a black belt."

"Thanks for the security advice," Jack said.

"You are quite welcome." Marsali moved to her fur, took a pink business card from a pocket and returned to Claudia. "This is my cell number. Call me anytime. Even if you just want to chat."

Claudia looked down at the card, which contained Marsali's first name and a phone number in a lovely, flowing script. The same fragrance emanating from its owner floated up from the card.

"Thank you," Claudia said.

"But of course, *cherie*. We women must stick together."

Claudia glanced at Jack. He watched Marsali with hands on his hips and narrowed eyes.

"Now, I really must be off or risk being late," Marsali said. "Do you require something else, Jackson?"

"Just your promise not to mention Louise."

"Oui." Marsali placed an expertly manicured hand over her heart and said, "I promise to tell no one about Louise."

Jack held up the fur, and Marsali slipped her arms into the sleeves.

"Thanks for coming, Marsali."

"My pleasure." She patted Jack's cheek with her long, graceful fingers, and exited in a sweep of expensive perfume.

Jack moved to the monitor, and Claudia followed him. Marsali appeared on the screen and gracefully entered a long, black limo just outside the gate. Of course she wouldn't drive around in a golf cart. Not Marsali. A uniformed chauffeur—complete with a hat—closed the door and disappeared.

When the limo drove out of sight, Jack relocked the gate and armed the security system.

"Don't worry about the chauffeur," Jack said. "He's been with the Winthrops for years and is very well paid."

Claudia nodded. "Do you believe her?"

"Yes," Jack said. "She didn't mention you to anyone. And she wouldn't forget. She's not that kind of woman."

"So you know her well?" Claudia couldn't resist asking. *Even I'm entranced by her, for heaven's sake. She's like a force of nature.*

Jack smiled. "Let's just say I know what kind of woman she is."

Part of Claudia longed to pursue that comment, but now was not the time to worry about Jack's relationship with the enigmatic Marsali. He wasn't her boyfriend. Just someone she hoped would help her. Would he?

"So how did they find me?"

Obviously deep in thought, Jack stared into the monitor, which now only showed the gate. "Could they have planted a tracking device somewhere?"

"I didn't take anything from my apartment. I even destroyed my old cell phone."

"What about your car? I got the impression you've had that vehicle awhile."

She nodded. "I can't afford a new one, but I looked for a bug if that's what you mean. I even crawled underneath with a flashlight."

"Did you have the car swept?"

"Swept," she whispered, horror dawning. *Oh, my God. The demon car.*

"Electronically searched." Jack shook his head. "Bugging your vehicle is the most obvious way to track your movements. Don't you read the paper?"

Claudia narrowed her eyes at his sarcastic tone, knowing he was parroting her words about the government. "I don't have a bug sweeper. I wouldn't even know where to get one."

"Fortunately, I do. Where is the vehicle?"

"In Mr. Santaluce's garage."

"This will take some time. I'll have to retrieve the device from the security office. Arm and rearm the security system each time I buzz."

Clutching her elbows, Claudia nodded and resisted the urge to beg him not to go. Despite all her precautions, Carlos had found her. Terror clawed at her insides, and Jack's presence calmed her fear. Which made no sense.

At the monitor, she watched him exit the gate and immediately rearmed the system. She moved away and began to pace. Now that Jack was gone, she needed to think.

How could she trust a man she didn't know? Sure, he seemed honorable, had been nice to her, but she knew nothing about him. And why should he trust *her*? She'd lied her way onto the island, and he'd quickly sniffed out her deception. He'd seen right through her disguise and even the second lie, yet was still willing to help her.

Why? Carlos had taught her everyone had a motive for everything they did. What was Jack's?

Of course he didn't understand why she wasn't in protective custody, but Jack had no idea what life was like with Carlos. No one did. Her husband had warped her somehow, created an inability to trust. He'd taught her a lot—mainly to rely on nobody. *Nobody but myself.*

Too bad her brilliant plan had put her in a corner with nowhere to go.

You are under my protection. She remembered

Jack's words, and they gave her hope. But the US Attorney had said the same thing, and his office had a leak.

So why did she believe in Jack and not the feds? Because he was all sexy and gorgeous? Was her lustful nature about to do her in again? She didn't dare trust herself when she'd made so many mistakes in the past. She had completely misjudged Carlos.

Was she misjudging Jack?

Right now she had no choice. She had to accept his help even if she didn't trust him.

And, yes, she wanted him to stay the night with her as Marsali had suggested he do…but only for protection. If he was with her, he couldn't report to Carlos.

She just needed to get over her attraction to Jack.

JACK RAN THE sweeper wand around the body of Claudia's rusted car and got a hit almost immediately. No question, this was how the Warriors had tracked her to Collins Island.

He shook his head at Claudia's ineffective method of cleaning her car. A visual search? She wasn't a pro and wouldn't know what she was looking for.

Jack went through his options quickly. If he left the tracking device in place and got her off the island in a different vehicle, the Warriors would believe she remained here and still try to get to her. That solved nothing. If he destroyed the bug, they'd wonder why it had stopped transmitting and keep attempting to breach security.

The best way to protect both Collins Island and Claudia would be to drive the car off the island with the device in place and working. He'd abandon the vehicle and let the Warriors track it down. The safest plan would be to drive it into one of the many canals in south Miami-Dade County so they couldn't plant an explosive device that might injure some innocent citizen on detonation.

Another option would be to inform the US Attorney's Office and let them handle the mess they'd created. But how long would it take the feds to act? Would they require an act of Congress to amend the budget? He wanted that bug off his island ASAP and the Warriors looking elsewhere for a while.

At least until he could figure out what to do with Claudia.

His associates could destroy the car once off the island, but an explosion would attract too much attention, including law enforcement, and Claudia wanted to remain under their radar. He couldn't help but think that was a mistake; she should be in protective custody. But the most important thing right now was to relocate the bug and misdirect the attention of her ex's people. He'd tighten security and persuade Claudia to accept federal protection.

Jack placed a call to Lola and detailed the situation. "I want you to send two operatives," he told her. "One to drive Claudia's vehicle off the island, get rid of it, and the other for transport back. Tell them to be ready for anything."

"Excellent plan, Jack, but I'm short of people tonight. For God's sake, it's Saturday night in our busiest time of year. Everyone is on assignment."

"What about you?" Jack asked. He waited through a long pause, wondering how she'd react to his suggestion. Lola didn't go into the field anymore. No one knew why, but in his analysis this scenario warranted an exception.

"Be on the eleven o'clock ferry with that damn car," she said. "I'll be waiting on the Miami side to follow you."

"Thanks, Lola."

"This won't stop the Warriors," Lola said. "They're crazy. And my sources tell me Carlos Romero is a certifiable psychopath."

"Understood."

"Could there already be a bomb in the vehicle?" Lola asked.

Jack stared at Claudia's demon car. "I've swept for explosives. It's clean but for the tracker."

"We need to harden security on the ferry."

"Handled. I'm confident they won't get on the ferry, but I want you to assign operatives to patrol the island 24/7 in our ocean cruiser until this situation is resolved. There's already been one landing on the beach. There could be another or an attempt to dock at the marina."

"Done," Lola said. "The boat patrol will start at daylight when I have people."

"We probably have a day or two," Jack said, moving out of the garage back to the cabana. "But when the Warriors realize what's happened, they'll come back here to pick up her trail."

"The Warriors for Self Rule," she said wonderingly. "Your instincts were right on, Jack, as usual."

"I wish I'd been wrong."

After a pause Lola said, "What are you going to do about Claudia Romero?"

"She's divorced," Jack said. "Her name is Goodwin now, and I don't know what I'm going to do about her yet."

"She's the feds' problem, Jack. You should turn her over to them."

"Can't do that. She'll rabbit and get herself killed."

"Why would she run?"

"She doesn't trust anyone to protect her," Jack said. *Not even me.* "She believes the US Attorney's Office has a leak. That's why she came to Collins Island. She thought she'd be safe."

Lola cursed.

"My priority is to get the Warriors' attention away from Collins Island for a while, redirect their focus," Jack said. He'd arrived at Claudia's front door. "I'll decide about Ms. Goodwin later."

"Don't take too long," Lola said. "Or I'll make the decision for you." She disconnected.

Jack took a deep breath. Would she do it? Lola

had contacts everywhere. Would she alert the US Attorney's Office to where their witness was located? With Claudia in the wind, the prosecutors were likely frantic with worry.

Lola's warning sharpened his dilemma into focus. What the hell was he going to do about Claudia?

He definitely knew what he wanted to do with her lush body, but now wasn't the time to start extracurricular activities with her. He needed to stay alert to thwart the danger she posed to Collins Island. *That* was his job. And he didn't need any distractions.

He knew one thing. He wasn't going to abandon her to the Warriors. It took a lot of courage to step up and provide evidence to convict Romero. She was a good woman, doing the right thing to bring her murdering ex to justice.

But damn. He shook his head. How could she have married a psychopath like Romero? Maybe he had promised her a life of ease. Maybe she *had* been looking for a sugar daddy and picked the wrong one.

Her reasons weren't his problem. Protecting the residents of this island was, and Romero's dangerous followers had tracked her here. They wouldn't give up until they'd silenced Claudia, no matter how many innocent citizens they killed in the process.

He whirled at a rustling near the pool, going for his gun.

A tawny cat leaped from a lounge chair into the foliage, no doubt after a lizard. Jack relaxed.

This island had a lot of access points. He couldn't

search each vehicle that boarded the ferry, demand the residents open their trunks, patrol every dock, control every inch of the beach. A skilled, motivated commando could slip onto the island and find Claudia.

No matter how good the security, he'd need an army to protect her.

CHAPTER SEVEN

CLAUDIA STARED AT the actors moving across the television screen, oblivious to the old sitcom jokes. She'd muted the sound, needing to remain alert to the slightest noise. Carlos's Warriors had found her. She couldn't stay here and put all the people on this island in danger.

What was taking Jack so long? Her Glock rested beside her on the sofa, cold and hard beneath her palm. The gun should make her feel secure, but she wanted to scream in frustration. *How could I have been so stupid to believe my car was safe?*

At Jack's prearranged knock, Claudia grabbed the gun and hurried to the door to confirm the identity of her visitor.

By the grim set of Jack's mouth, he didn't bring good news.

She flung open the door, glad to see him no matter what the report.

"Tell me," she demanded.

Jack entered quickly, repocketing a phone. "Just as I feared. They found you with a tracking device."

"Did you get rid of it?"

"No."

"Why not?"

"They already know where you are. What good would that do?"

"Then what—"

"An associate of mine will arrive within the hour to help me take your car and its bug off the island. Hopefully, that will misdirect Romero's people for a while."

"Where will you take it?"

"We'll dump it in a canal near Homestead."

"What? No. That's my car. I *need* my car."

His mouth quirked. "I thought you hated that car."

"But I need to move. It's not fair to the residents to stay here. Can't you just remove the bug and let me—"

"Think about it, Claudia," Jack interrupted. He placed his hands around her upper arms. "They know that vehicle. You can never use it again."

She stared at him. How could he look so calm? But of course his life hadn't unraveled. He wasn't being stalked by terrorists. He didn't realize he was taking away her last link to freedom, to independence. Not only was she homeless, but now she didn't have transportation. She might find another junker with the small amount left in her savings, but that purchase would give away her location.

She didn't dare turn to anyone for help or she'd put them in danger, too.

With a sob, Claudia moved to the sofa. She felt empty, brittle, like she would break if she moved too fast. She sat down carefully. She couldn't think, but she needed to think.

"What am I going to do?"

"Didn't the US Attorney's Office offer you a safe house until the trial?"

"Yes," she whispered, dread consuming her at the thought of putting herself under the control of the federal government.

"Why won't you accept that protection?"

Staring at the tile floor, she said, "I told you. Carlos has someone on the inside that feeds him information about the prosecutor's actions."

Jack sat beside her, making the cushion dip. "You're sure the feds have a leak?"

"Even the prosecutor thinks so. Reese Beauchamps, the US Attorney, told me Carlos knew he was going to be arrested before the FBI came. He knew the time and the place." Claudia raised her head and met Jack's gaze. He looked worried. *Welcome to my world.*

"But Reese hasn't been able to find the leak," she continued. "How do I know the person I contact isn't the traitor or won't tell the traitor? Or what if Reese tells the wrong person?"

He shook his head. "You don't trust anyone, do you?"

"I trust my family," she said softly, moisture flooding her eyes at the thought of her mother.

"Do they know where you are?"

"No. I don't dare involve them. It's too dangerous." Claudia tried to swallow away her tears, but she'd been holding them back for too long. "I know my mother is sick with worry. My dad, too." Her voice broke, and she covered her face with her palms.

"Hey."

"And now I'm putting the people on this island in jeopardy."

"Come here." Jack wrapped an arm around her shoulders and pulled her against him.

She went willingly, resting her cheek against his muscled warmth. She didn't have the strength to resist even if she wanted to. Closing her eyes, she wished she could stay snuggled in Jack's embrace forever and forget she'd ever agreed to testify against Carlos. But she couldn't. She had to get off this island before more people were murdered by her ex's terrorist friends.

She took a deep breath to regain control. This wasn't like her, weeping against the shoulder of a man she barely knew, a man she knew better than to put any faith in. She'd always prided herself on being the strong one, able to remain for hours by the bedside of a frightened, sick child to provide comfort.

Who would have ever guessed that a man built like Jack Richards would try to soothe anybody? His hands appeared too large, too powerful for tender movements, yet he stroked her head in gentle, if awkward, consolation.

"You're okay," he murmured.

She didn't respond. She didn't want to admit to him or herself that being held in his arms did somehow reassure her. His heart beat steadily beneath her ear and his masculine aftershave enveloped her senses. Her sweet gladiator. How bizarre.

"I think you should call your folks," he said.

Of all the things she'd expected to come out of his mouth next, that wasn't one of them.

"But what if they have a trace on my parents' phone?" she protested.

"They probably do, but the Warriors already know you're here, so you're not giving anything away. You can tell your folks you're alive, and that will be one worry off your mind."

She opened her eyes. Yes, that would be one less thing to obsess about. "Okay," she murmured, but not moving. "Good idea."

"Also tell them that you're relocating, but don't say where."

"So the Warriors won't be surprised when the bug moves," she said, grasping his reasoning. "They'll be expecting it and leave this island alone for a while."

"For a while," Jack cautioned. "When they don't find you, they'll come back here to try to pick up your scent."

"I know," she whispered, her voice sounding bleak to her own ears.

"I'm not going to let anything happen to you," Jack said, the certainty of his voice settling over her like a warm blanket, calming her.

She wanted to trust him. She wanted to just let him handle everything. But she couldn't.

She hadn't trusted anyone in a long time.

I'M NOT GOING to let anything happen to her? Have I lost my freaking mind?

Jack wondered what possessed him to make such a promise to this woman. Yeah, she was under his protection while on the island, but she obviously had to go. She knew it, and he knew it.

But he also knew he wouldn't—couldn't—send her off to face the Warriors without his help.

Was it her vulnerability, her earthy beauty? The silky softness of her hair beneath his hand? Her courage for agreeing to testify against a violent terrorist, a man she'd once been married to? Damned if he knew. The clients he protected paid good money to the Alliance. Up front. And the check had to clear first.

But something about this woman had gotten under his skin.

She raised her head and met his gaze. Jack's gut clenched at her tears, but she swiped them away impatiently.

"You don't know Carlos Romero," she said, collapsing back against the cushions.

"I've known plenty of men like him," Jack said. He pulled a handkerchief from his pocket and handed it to her. "Men who are mean and angry for no good reason."

She took the hankie, dabbed at her eyes, then blew her nose. "Thanks," she said.

"So a government safe house is definitely out?" Jack asked her.

"That's a death sentence," she replied. "I might as well hand myself over to them right now."

"Did you have a backup plan if your Collins Island experiment failed?"

"I'm still working on that," she said, lifting her chin, a touch of humor now in her blue eyes. "But if you take my car, it kinda complicates any relocation idea."

"Yeah, I see your problem." Her small attempt to cut the tension made Jack even more determined to help her. She refused to stay down for long, and Claudia Goodwin Romero's spirit fascinated him. Her dark hair hung in a tangled mess around her face. He tucked a strand behind an ear, his fingers brushing her cheek.

Her eyes widened, and her full lips lifted into a hesitant, unsure smile.

Knowing it was a mistake, he captured those lips with his mouth.

He'd intended a light, friendly, reassuring kiss, but Claudia responded with a throaty moan that caught him off guard, had him pulling her closer. She opened her mouth and used her tongue to explore his. She slid her hands across his shoulders, probing his muscles as if testing their strength, then ran her fingers into his hair, bringing his face closer. He felt himself harden.

Not breaking the kiss, he lifted her so she straddled his lap.

She continued to make interesting sounds and

rotated her hips against his straining erection. He placed his palms on her buttocks and guided her to just the right spot. She rocked against him with sensuous, encouraging movements.

He heard himself growl. What was happening?

Maybe he'd started this, but she seemed eager to finish it in a way that he hadn't anticipated. So be it. He'd wanted this woman since he'd laid eyes on her, when he assumed she was a rich man's mistress and off-limits. Her behavior left no question that she wanted him just as much.

Not enough room on this sofa for what was going to happen next.

With Claudia still in place, he rose to move into the bedroom. She wrapped her legs around his waist and deepened their kiss.

He felt a vibration in his pocket a second before his phone buzzed the emergency tone.

She pulled back, staring at him with wild, frightened eyes and swollen lips. Her hands remained behind his head.

She released her legs and stood before him, her palms sliding to his shoulders.

"I—I'm sorry," she said. She dropped her hands to her sides.

"For what?" Jack asked, his voice husky, his thoughts clearing. He needed to attend to business, not to Claudia Goodwin.

She swallowed and broke her gaze from his. "For attacking you."

"I didn't mind."

"I noticed," she said, her own voice a low, sexy whisper.

He smiled in acknowledgment of the obvious, and she grinned up at him, a pink blush staining her cheeks. This woman would be fun to play with, but now wasn't the time. He sobered and doubted there *would* be a right time.

Certainly not while she was under his protection. Not if he wanted to keep her—and himself—alive. She was just as much off-limits now as before.

More, in fact.

And he should be thinking about moving her to a safe location, not ripping off her clothes.

He removed his phone and read the text.

"I need to go," he said. "My colleague has arrived at the ferry landing."

"To take my car," she said, her tone now serious.

"Yes. I'm sorry, but it's the only way, Claudia."

"I understand," she said. "I may not like it, but I get why you have to do it."

"Do you need to get anything from it?"

"No."

"Lock up and rearm the system after I leave."

"Of course."

"This could take a while, but I'll return as soon as I can."

"Thanks." She averted her gaze from his and whispered, "I guess."

"What's wrong now?" he demanded.

She shrugged, staring at the floor.

"If you want my help, you need to communicate."

She raised her troubled blue eyes to his. "How do I know for sure who the bad guys are?"

"You think I'm working with Carlos Romero?"

"No," she whispered, shaking her head. "Maybe. I don't know."

Jack watched Claudia wrestle with whether she could trust him. Oh, she wanted him all right, but that meant nothing. Desire came from a different part of the brain than trust. How could he convince this terrified woman that he was on her side?

"Think about it, Claudia."

"I have. It's all I think about. The thing is history has proved I'm a terrible judge of character."

"Just think about my actions, then. If I were a Warrior, wouldn't you already be dead?"

"Maybe. But why are you helping me?" she asked. "You know I've been lying since you met me."

He sighed. He didn't have time for this right now, but she'd asked the very question he wondered about himself. She was beautiful, sure, no question. But he couldn't and wouldn't touch her. Was he really that bored with life on Collins Island?

"Maybe I'm a better judge of people than you are."

A smile threatened her serious expression, but vanished as she looked away. "I'm so confused."

He cupped her cheek and gently raised her gaze to his. "Are you lying to me about testifying against Carlos Romero?"

"I swear to you that's the truth. Believe me, I want that bastard rotting in prison for the rest of his miserable life."

"Then accept that I'm helping you because I want the same thing. Any rational person would."

She nodded, but remained silent.

He dropped his hand and grinned at her. "Or maybe you don't think I'm rational?"

This time her smile did form. "I think there's serious doubt about both of us."

Jack laughed as he moved to the door. "I don't know how long this is going to take. Lock up, turn on the alarm and stay inside."

"Check," Claudia said. "On the bright side, I'm finally getting rid of that demon car."

"You're welcome." Jack opened the door, his thoughts already on tonight's op. Would it be dangerous? Were the Warriors watching the ferry waiting for Claudia to run?

"Jack, wait."

He looked back and found her staring at him with her fingers tightly clenched. "What?"

"I don't know why you're doing it, but thank you for helping me."

He saluted. "You got it, babe."

Jack relished the chill as he stepped into the dark night. He hoped the cooler temperatures and lower humidity hung around for a few days. The change kept him sharp, alert, and now he had good reason to stay on top of his game. He'd decided to leave

Ike in charge again while he was off island ditching Claudia's car.

But he rejected the idea that the Warriors had anyone surveilling the ferry 24/7. They'd be too conspicuous, noticed and reported by Collins Island staff. And he also doubted that they'd immediately know their bug was on the move. Claudia had been rooted in one spot for a week. They likely figured she'd remain on the island, so wouldn't be monitoring the device around the clock.

But of course he couldn't rely on that assumption. Picard had volunteered Claudia's name tonight, which in Jack's mind was a mistake. A big one. Did that error alert the Warriors? Did they realize they'd given themselves away? If so, would they be looking for Claudia to relocate?

Jack hoped not, but he and Lola needed to be ready for anything.

It took four attempts, but Claudia's devil car finally roared to life. He gunned the motor to charge the battery, and remembered the worry shimmering in her eyes as he left.

She didn't trust him. Well, that was okay.

She was the one who'd married a terrorist. He didn't trust her, either.

CLAUDIA SLAMMED THE dead bolt into place behind Jack, and moved to security central to watch the monitor. When he drove her car out of the villa, she closed and locked the iron gate electronically, activated the alarm and waited until he drove off camera.

She remained by the monitor another minute, five minutes, maybe ten. Just staring. Waiting for something to happen? What? Another car to appear? For Jack to return?

She stepped away. It would take hours for him to drive out west to a deserted canal, sink her car and return.

She'd take this time to call her parents and reassure them she was okay. At least for now. Jack was right. Carlos's people already knew where she was. Making the phone call couldn't make anything worse, and she'd feel better after she heard her mom's voice.

So why was she putting it off?

Claudia moved to the couch and picked up the phone on the side table. After a deep breath, she punched in her parents' number. It was still early. *Please be home.*

"Hello?"

A warm glow replaced her dread when Claudia heard her mom's customary cheery greeting.

"It's me, Mom."

"Claudia?"

"Yes. I just called to—"

"Oh, thank God."

Claudia felt tears form at the relief in her mom's voice.

"Where are you, sweetheart? Are you okay?"

"I'm fine, but it's better if you don't know where I am."

"You're hiding from that miserable ex-husband, aren't you?"

Claudia swallowed hard. "Yes."

"At least you're alive. We've all been worried sick."

"I know. I'm sorry, Mom."

"Bill, it's Claudia," her mom yelled away from the phone. To Claudia she said, "Your father has been in touch with the United States Attorney. He thought they had you under wraps somewhere."

"No."

"That's what they insisted, too. Please let them protect you, Claudia. You can't do this on your own. You're a nurse, for God's sake, not a secret agent."

"I know you don't understand, Mom, but I have to do it this way."

"Claudia?"

When her dad's deep voice roared into the phone, Claudia realized why she'd been hesitant to make this call. Many considered her father one of the best salesmen in Miami. The man could argue anyone into a purchase they didn't want or need, and she knew he'd employ every trick to persuade her to come home.

"You stop this nonsense right now, young lady."

"Can't do it, Dad. I just called to let you guys know I'm okay."

"Where are you?"

"It doesn't matter, and I'm relocating, anyway. By this time tomorrow, I'll be out of the state." Of course, she didn't know if that was true, but if the Warriors were listening, it wouldn't hurt to let them think that.

"This isn't like you. Why are you behaving this way?"

"I don't want anyone else to get hurt."

"I blame myself for this," her father said in a defeated voice. *One of his best tricks. Guilt.*

"Stop it, Dad."

"Claudia, listen to me."

"No, Dad. You listen to me." She took a deep breath. When had she ever cut off her father? "Carlos's people might be watching the house, so please, please be careful. I only called to warn you and let you know I'm still alive."

"We've got this number on caller ID."

"No, you don't. It's blocked."

"I'm sure I can get it with the US Attorney's help."

She closed her eyes. "Maybe so, but I'll be gone by the time that happens."

"I don't know about that. They seem pretty desperate to find you."

"I have to go, Dad. I love you. I love Mom. I promise to be careful."

She recradled the phone and released a sob. She held her breath, waiting for the phone to ring, praying it didn't. Mr. Santaluce promised her he'd blocked this number, but she'd learned the hard way you could never know for sure.

Claudia listened to her ragged breathing for long, long minutes, but the pool house remained silent. Her parents couldn't call her back. The government would probably work some magic with the phone company and find her location, but she'd be long gone by then either with or without Jackson Richards.

Okay. She'd talked to her parents. What was she supposed to do now?

Study? Like she could concentrate on medical procedures and terminology.

Television? She'd rather fling the remote through the screen.

Sleep? Never gonna happen until Jack returned. Besides, she had to stay awake to deactivate the alarm and let him in. They had plans to make.

What she needed was to organize her thoughts, calm herself and figure out her next move. Journaling had always worked in the past—even during the hectic days of nursing school—but isn't that what had gotten her into trouble?

No, keeping track of Carlos's activities hadn't gotten her into this horrible mess. Writing all the weird stuff down had kept her sane, finally made her accept that something very, very bad was going on with her husband.

She no longer had that old journal. She'd turned it over to Mr. Beauchamps, the United States Attorney prosecuting Carlos, for safekeeping. He'd told her it was in some sort of evidence vault.

And maybe *journal* was a bit of an overly dramatic misnomer. She'd purchased a three-hundred-page, college ruled, spiral-bound notebook to make notes about Carlos's strange comings and goings. She'd never let Carlos see the notebook. Until it appeared on the list of exhibits for trial, she was certain he hadn't known her record of his criminal activity existed.

She'd kept it hidden behind a five-pound bag of flour inside the rubber-banded packaging of a corn chip brand Carlos hated in a far corner of a kitchen cabinet, sealed inside two plastic Ziploc bags. She knew it was safe there. Even early in their marriage, the man seldom wandered into the kitchen except for coffee, which she, of course, brewed. She was the "little wife," so she prepared all the meals. And shopped. And cleaned up. And worked more than forty hours a week. On her feet most of the time. Oh, sure, Carlos worked a lot of hours, too, at a manufacturing company in Hialeah that she'd soon wondered about. She never did learn what the hell they manufactured, why he always had so much cash or why she'd always had to leave a voice mail. No one ever answered the phone.

What a fool she'd been. So blinded by lust for a mysterious, intense man that she hadn't bothered to ask any questions until it was too late. She'd never make that mistake again.

So was she doing the exact same thing with Jack? Even if he was trying to help her, she needed to keep tons of emotional distance between her and Jackson Richards. There could be no more kissing.

While gathering supplies for her stay on this fancy-pants island, she'd seen an identical version of that first notebook and purchased it on a whim.

With a renewed sense of determination, she moved into the bedroom. Yeah, she was in a pickle, but she'd figure her way out. She'd write everything that had happened and would happen into a journal just as she'd done with Carlos. She'd include all her thoughts, as well as any theories or ideas on what to do.

She pulled her duffel from under the bed and fished out the still pristine notebook. Back in the living room, she grabbed a pen from security central and plopped onto the couch. Fanning the pages of the notebook, she speculated what would appear on these sheets of paper during the next three weeks.

She had to relocate, but where would she go? Would Jack take her to a new hiding place? And what would she write on these blank pages about him? She wished she could see into the future to know if she could trust him.

Writing hesitantly at first, she began with the night the bastards had killed her cat, describing the condition of her apartment when she'd come home that night. Words for her sense of complete violation were impossible to find.

As she wrote, gaining speed as the pages filled

with black ink, she kept a silent prayer in the back of her mind that Jack didn't turn out to be as crazy and scary as her ex-husband.

Jack made her feel safe, but history had shown she was a lousy judge of character. Hadn't she felt safe with Carlos at first? Trusting Jack could be a bigger mistake than her marriage to Carlos.

CHAPTER EIGHT

JACK SPOTTED LOLA'S huge black Hummer when he exited the ferry on the Miami side. Because of dark tinting, he couldn't see her inside, but the vehicle followed him when he turned right out of the parking lot. Communicating by cell phone, they both scanned for a tail and agreed they got away from the dock clean. Even so, they drove a circuitous route, taking a lot of quick turns, each going a different direction to make certain.

They met up again at Big Corky's, a late-night bar in the Redlands, and waited to see if anyone joined them. No one did. Neither of them ordered an alcoholic beverage as they discussed where to submerge Claudia's vehicle. Lola agreed to a deep canal Jack knew in a deserted area of the far southwestern section of the county.

He didn't want any witnesses.

Gravel crunched beneath the tires as Jack drove to the water's edge and placed the transmission in Neutral. When he stepped out into the cool night, a trillion stars lit up the clear night sky. From the racket they made, at least that many crickets sounded in the brush around him.

Wearing a black leather jacket, black jeans and boots, Lola climbed down from her Hummer and approached.

Without speaking, they shoved Claudia's car down the embankment. It entered the water with a quiet splash and floated toward the center of the canal with water rushing inside through the open windows.

"How long do you think the bug will keep transmitting once wet?" Jack asked as he and Lola waited for the car to sink.

"Depends on the quality of the equipment," Lola answered, hands in her jeans pockets. "Since my sources tell me this group has tech experts, it should stay active until the Warriors find this location."

"Good," Jack grunted.

In less than a minute, the front end of the vehicle tilted down and it disappeared into murky waters. A rusted rear bumper was the last thing to vanish beneath the dark surface. After a second or two, not even a ripple remained to mark the sinking.

Jack climbed into Lola's Hummer, and she drove back to the ferry.

"I suspect come morning the Warriors will discover their bug has moved," Lola said. "They'll likely triangulate this location by noon."

Jack grunted his agreement. He knew where this conversation was headed.

Lola threw him a look and said, "You know they'll be seriously pissed that they've lost their quarry. My gut tells me they'll keep trying to breach security.

They'll want to look for clues as to where she disappeared."

"Agreed."

"I confirmed with my sources that she's on the witness list for the Romero trial."

Jack nodded. He'd made a call himself while waiting to board the ferry.

"You need to get that woman off Collins Island," Lola instructed. "The sooner the better."

"I'm working on a plan."

"The hell with a plan. She needs to go into protective custody."

"She won't do it."

"We could force her hand. Call the feds and give up her location. Allow her no choice."

"And what if she's right?" Jack demanded. "What if the feds have a leak and she ends up dead?"

His question simmered in the Hummer between them. Lola remained silent until she reached the ferry landing and shifted the Hummer into Neutral.

"Why do you care what happens to this woman, Jack?"

"We're not lovers, if that's what you're asking." He shifted in the seat.

"She's not your problem."

"I think she's everybody's problem. She's put her life in jeopardy in order to keep a murdering terrorist from killing others."

"You're such a Boy Scout sometimes."

Jack laughed. *A Boy Scout?* "I guess that's the way my momma raised me."

"You've got twenty-four hours to come up with a plan, Jackson," Lola said in a tight voice. "If Claudia Goodwin hasn't relocated by then, I'm calling the US Attorney's Office and telling them where she is." She motioned with her chin. "Our primary focus has to be the safety of the residents on that island."

"Understood," he said.

Jack boarded the 3:00 a.m. ferry. When the boat departed the Miami dock, he moved to the railing and let the cool ocean breeze rush against his face. He'd caught no shut-eye and should be exhausted, but a strange exhilaration energized him.

Was it because he was back in the field—even if for just a few hours—and tonight's op had gone as well as could be expected considering the lack of planning?

Or was it because he looked forward to seeing Claudia again and exploring the possibilities behind that mind-blowing kiss? He remembered how soft and willing she'd been in his arms, the eagerness in her smoky blue eyes, and felt himself harden.

Disgusted, he blew out a breath. The woman was addictive. He hadn't been able to stop thinking about her since she drove off the ferry a week ago.

And she was still off-limits. Getting emotionally or even just sexually involved with anyone under his protection was taboo. He'd seen matters go horribly wrong too many times when that rule was ignored.

He considered Lola's remark that Claudia wasn't his problem. Why did he somehow feel that she was? Why *did* he care about what happened to her?

He wasn't in love with her. He wanted her, sure. Had wanted her since he'd first laid eyes on her. Any man would. But desire, even desire bordering on obsession, wasn't love. His momma insisted he didn't understand love—and she was right—but he knew that much.

His life was all about his work, and he liked it that way.

A gentle bump brought Jack back to the present. The ferry had reached the other side. He stepped off the boat with Lola's ultimatum about relocating Claudia clanging around inside his head. *Yeah, right. A plan. I'm working on it.*

He didn't like the only solution he'd come up with so far. In fact, he hated it.

He nodded at the two guards manning the security office.

"Need a ride, Mr. Richards?" one shouted.

"No. I'm good," Jack yelled back.

Truth was he *needed* to walk. Even better would be a long, brutal workout to generate some heat and sweat and help him figure out what to do about Claudia Goodwin. He knew his boss wasn't just jerking his chain. She meant every word she said. Lola had no qualms about turning Claudia over to the feds.

No question Claudia's presence on Collins Island

created a danger to the owners who paid ridiculous monthly fees for the peace of mind the tight security on this island gave them. And since a sizable chunk of that money went to the Protection Alliance and paid his salary, it was his job to enforce that promise of safety.

So Claudia had to go, and go now. But where? What would be the safest location to stash her for the three weeks until Romero's trial?

Certainly it had to be out of the immediate area. His thoughts churned as he broke into a jog, considering and rejecting possibilities. Broward County? Too close. Fort Myers or Naples on Florida's west coast? Too obvious, and he didn't have any contacts there. The Keys were a possibility. He'd bought a vacation home in Islamorada that he seldom took the time to visit, but that elevated structure would be difficult to defend and he always liked an escape route.

So where could he take her to ensure the Warriors would never find her?

By the time he arrived at Villa Alma, he knew where she had to go. If he were honest with himself, he'd known all along. Much as he hated the idea, it was the only way.

He rang the bell and waited for Claudia to admit him. She'd hate the idea even more than he did, but she had no choice. She either agreed to his plan or went under the protection of the federal government. Her decision.

THE INSISTENT RINGING of the bell at the front gate awakened Claudia. Disoriented, she stared at the planked ceiling wondering why she was fully clothed and sleeping on a couch.

Then, with a sickening blow to her gut, she remembered. Carlos's people had found her, which threatened the people on this island. Jack had taken her car.

She leaped off the couch and hurried to security central to see who demanded her attention.

Jack stood by the gate glaring into the camera. With a relieved breath, she released the electronic lock, and he strode out of the camera's range.

"What happened?" she demanded when he marched into the pool house wearing a determined expression. Damn. He looked like he was about to do some sort of hand-to-hand combat.

He turned to face her, eyes narrowed. "Nothing scary. We drowned your car."

"Did steam rise out of the water as it sank? Lightning bolts illuminate the deep?"

His mouth twitched. Maybe he was fighting a smile.

"No. It went down without any protest at all."

"The demon probably escaped out a window," Claudia said. "Maybe hitched a ride back with you and *that's* what took so long?"

"We took our time. Made sure we weren't followed."

She nodded, and realized she was clasping her hands so tightly her knuckles had begun to ache. Jack was giving her nothing. Didn't he understand how anxious she was? She had no ride, nowhere to go. Why did she let him take her car? What was she thinking?

Dropping her hands to her sides, she said, "I tried to wait up for you, but fell asleep."

"Good," he said.

"I guess you didn't get any rest."

"I'm fine," Jack said.

"I called my parents. I told them I was relocating in case the Warriors were listening."

He nodded, eyeing her speculatively, but didn't respond. What was going on inside his head? He was tense, distant. Why wouldn't he tell her anything?

"So what happens now?" she asked, unable to stand the suspense any longer.

"You can't stay here."

"I know."

"I think protective custody is your best option."

"I know what you think." She shook her head. "I told you I can't do that. I might as well stream a banner over South Beach announcing my location to Romero's people."

Jack continued to stare at her across the small living room. Was this it? Was this man going to abandon her to terrorists? But why shouldn't he? She was nothing but a problem to him. Her mouth went dry, and Claudia licked her lips. *Where can I go? And how can I get there?*

"Do you want my help?" he asked.

She nodded, unable to form words around a tongue that felt clogged with sand from the nearby beach.

"I'll take you somewhere safe, but you have to be honest with me."

"I have been," she managed to say, her voice hoarse.

"No more secrets or lies."

"I promise," she said.

"And do what I tell you."

"Where?"

"Dunnellon."

She must have looked confused, because he said, "A little town in north central Florida, near Ocala."

"Why there?" she asked, although her relief was so immense she wouldn't have cared if he'd said an igloo in Alaska.

"I know the area. I grew up in Dunnellon and own a small cabin in the middle of fifty acres. If we handle this right, the Warriors will never track you."

"When do I go?"

"Daybreak. I need a couple hours of sleep."

That fast? She sucked in a deep breath, but decided it didn't matter. She needed to transition to the next stage of her exile sooner rather than later. All she needed was logistics.

"How will I get there? Are you going to loan me a car?"

"I'm going with you."

She let that sink in before responding. The gladiator was going with her?

"What about your job here?"

Jack shrugged. "Believe me, my boss will understand."

Claudia nodded. His boss had likely ordered him to get rid of her pronto.

"For how long?"

"As long as it takes to make sure you're secure."

"How will I get back for the trial?"

"We'll worry about that in three weeks."

The dread tightening her gut released a little knowing that she wouldn't be alone in a strange new city. But she didn't know this man. She'd met him— what—a week ago? He owed her nothing.

"I don't know why you're doing this, but thank you," she said.

"You might not thank me when I tell you how you're getting off the island."

"And that's how?"

"Inside the gun compartment of my truck. I hope you're not claustrophobic."

She blinked. "A gun compartment?"

"It's snug, but you'll fit."

Claudia imagined being locked in a dark confined space and shrank from the idea. "Couldn't I just lay down in the backseat with a blanket over me?"

"What if Romero's people are watching the landing? Do you want to take that chance?"

"No," she said on a quick exhale. "Definitely not."

Her legs suddenly weak, she sagged onto the couch, circled her knees with her arms and lowered her face.

"You okay?" Jack asked.

The cushion dipped beneath her when he sat. Claudia raised her head and found him watching her with a grim expression.

"What's going on?" he asked.

"This is just—just crazy." She sucked in a breath. "I guess I'm a little overwhelmed. Either that or I'm numb."

"I'm sorry."

Jack smoothed a hand over her hair, a strangely intimate gesture.

"Don't apologize," she said. "None of this is your fault."

He dropped his hand to her shoulder and gave a slight squeeze. "Truthfully, I expected you to fight me on relocating north."

Hyperaware of the weight and warmth of his hand, she said, "How could I? I'm out of options."

He smiled, his green eyes focused on her lips. "There's always the government safe house."

She shook her head, wishing she could read Jack's mind. He slid his fingers down her arm, pausing close to her right breast. Maybe he was thinking about kissing her, picking up where they left off before he went to drown her car. Did she want him to kiss her again?

More than anything.

His gaze shifted to her chest, and a flare of intense, desperate longing surged through her. So she wasn't numb, after all. Not numb at all. Just crazy. She wanted to be held, to be made love to by Jackson Richards when nothing could be more inappropriate.

She took a deep breath, mentally urging him to slide his long fingers over to cup the swell of her breast.

He lowered his mouth closer to hers, almost touching her lips. "You won't change your mind?" he whispered, his warm breath tickling her chin.

She closed her eyes. What was he asking her? She was only sure about one thing. Jack needed to kiss her. Now.

"You won't go into federal protection?"

The words *federal protection* made her leap to her feet and move away from Jack. What was she doing? She'd find maybe an hour of escape in his arms, but then what? Would he own her? Try to control her the way Carlos had? Dear God, she was behaving exactly as she did with her ex, letting her hormones overrule her brain, eagerly tumbling into bed with a man before she even knew him.

That was what got her into this mess. She couldn't do that again.

She took a deep breath and turned to face him. "We've been over that. I can't go—won't go—into a safe house. I wouldn't survive one night."

Jack rose but didn't speak. Was that disappointment in his eyes?

She looked away. "Please understand."

"I'm trying," he said.

Were they even talking about the same thing? Maybe she'd imagined the sparks between them. No, she hadn't imagined that incredible kiss a few hours ago.

"Do you want me to leave?" he asked.

No! she silently screamed, meeting his intense gaze again. She hesitated. Yes, he should go. She was beyond weak, and he was a temptation impossible to resist.

But the thought of spending the night alone in this pool house, knowing the Warriors knew where she was...

"No," she said across a dry throat. She swallowed. "Please don't go. I—I'd feel better with you here."

His gaze raked her body. She folded her arms over her chest. Was he going to demand sex in return for his protection? Is that what this had come to?

"Okay." He glanced down at the sofa, his lips lifting into a resigned smile.

She blew out a breath. "I'll sleep on the sofa," she said. "You can have the bed."

"I couldn't do that," he said.

"I probably won't sleep, anyway," she said.

They stared at each other across the room. Was he thinking the same thing she was, that there were more pleasurable things they could be doing besides obsessing about terrorists alone in the dark? At least there wasn't much of the night left.

"If you're sure," she said.

"I'm sure."

"There's extra sheets in the hall closet," she said, moving in that direction. "I'll get them for you."

She glanced back to Jack and found him watching her. Feeling another of those delicious tugs on her lower belly, she quickly looked away.

Sex was exactly what she needed, but sex always got her into big trouble.

WHEN JACK WOKE, the sun beat against the window coverings of Villa Alma's pool house. He'd actually slept—and longer than he'd intended, but he needed the rest for the long drive ahead. Uncomfortably aware of the tiny couch, he closed his eyes and stretched his body, his thoughts drifting to the events of the night before, to Claudia, a woman on the run from her crazed ex.

To protect her, he'd agreed to take her to his home.

He hardened as he pictured her last night offering him her bed. He wanted her, and last night he had come close to losing control and taking her. She was more than willing. He wouldn't have to use any persuasion.

But sex with Claudia couldn't happen. Not while he was protecting her.

His number one rule was never to get involved emotionally with a client. Bad decisions were made when you were too close to someone on the job. When he'd been with the Marion County Sheriff's Department, a partner had rushed into a domestic situation he shouldn't have involving his sister. Because of a disastrous snap decision, the sister had died and that cop lost his job. Jack shook his head, remembering. Bad business. He'd learned from that mistake.

Maybe she wasn't paying him, but Claudia *was* now his client. She was on the run from her ex, a crazed terrorist, and he'd agreed to take her home to Dunnellon to protect her.

If he wanted to keep them both alive, he needed to remember lessons from the past.

And who the hell was Claudia, anyway? Why was he willing to put his life and career on hold for her? She pulled at him with an insistent tug that he didn't understand, brought out all his protective instincts.

But what kind of a woman falls in love with a terrorist?

A jarring thought brought him to a seated position. Had she rabbited without him? No. Surely she wasn't that stupid.

Certain he detected the enticing aroma of coffee, he sniffed the air. *Thank you, Miss Claudia.* Everything could wait until he'd had a jolt of caffeine.

When he rose to his feet, he noticed a duffel bag and boxes scattered around the living room floor. She'd been busy with more than morning coffee. The sound of the refrigerator door opening caught his attention. She was in the kitchen. Had she even slept?

Jack wrapped the sheet around his waist and went to find her. They had a lot to talk about, a lot of plans to go over.

CLAUDIA STARED INTO the freezer with cold air chilling her cheeks, hating the idea of leaving all this food behind. But she had no way to keep the frozen meat or vegetables from thawing. She sighed. Why was she worried about a couple hundred dollars' worth of food when Carlos and his friends had found her?

Because she needed to eat. She didn't have enough cash to feed herself for three more weeks, didn't dare access any bank accounts or risk giving away her location and couldn't expect Jack the Gladiator to feed her.

Jack. Oh, God. She closed the freezer door, but left her hand on the handle, picturing him as she'd left him last night, staring at her with those intense green eyes as if he knew what she was thinking. Or what she looked like naked. She shivered.

He'd been asleep on the sofa when she tiptoed past into the kitchen, and the sheets hadn't covered much of his magnificent body. Better he not know what she'd been thinking right then.

She shook her head. She'd hoped she'd come up with a better plan in the light of day. How could she leave this island with a man who was all but a stranger and travel to a new city under his protection? It was freaking nuts.

But what other option did she have?

"Good morning."

Claudia whirled around and gaped at Jack's bare chest as he entered the kitchen trailing a sheet behind him. Wow. And there it was. That incredible pull of attraction impossible to ignore every time she was in the same room with him.

She swallowed and managed to say, "Hi."

"Please tell me I smell coffee."

She nodded, cursing herself for feeling this awkward around him. But how was she supposed to act? She'd told him her deepest secret, that she'd been foolish enough to marry Carlos Romero. No one else on Earth but her family and Mr. Santaluce knew.

"Cream or sugar?" she asked as she poured steaming coffee into a mug.

"Black is fine." He stepped close and accepted the mug, brushing his fingers across hers. Her gaze rose to his, and she wondered if he experienced the same jolt of awareness from their casual touch. He seemed unaffected as he took a sip.

"Man, that's good," he said. "Thanks."

She added hot coffee she didn't want to her own lukewarm brew and suddenly wished he'd take her into his arms and kiss her. How pathetic was that?

"I see you've been packing," Jack said. "That's a lot of boxes."

She faced him again. "They're full of nonperishable food. I've been trying to decide if it's safe to take the stuff that's frozen. Unless you have a cooler, it'll thaw on the drive north."

"Leave it," Jack said. "They do have grocery stores in Dunnellon."

She shook her head. "But I don't have much cash left, and I don't dare access any or risk giving away my location."

"Do you think I'd let you starve after going to the trouble to save you from Romero?"

"But I don't want to leave a mess for Mr. Santaluce after all his kindness."

"I'll have maintenance clean the kitchen and donate the food in the refrigerator to a homeless shelter."

She looked away. "Okay. That'll work."

Jack took a swallow from his mug. "You need to trust me, Claudia."

She nodded. "I know. And I appreciate all that you're doing. This is just—" She shrugged, not knowing what to say. *This sucks?* She stole a look at Jack and found him eyeing her intently. She'd love to know what *he* was thinking.

He placed his mug on the counter. "Talk to me, Claudia."

"You have to understand I've got a lot going on right now."

"You're scared."

"I'm terrified. And then you show up looking all…sexy and gorgeous and complicate my life even more."

He grinned. "Sexy and gorgeous, huh?"

Heat rushed into her cheeks. Had she really said that out loud?

"You've complicated my life a bit, too," he said.

He stepped close. Too close. She looked down at the floor, certain they weren't talking about the same sort of complications. Ceramic tile was safer to look at than Jack.

"Sorry about that," she murmured. But she wasn't. Not really. She breathed in the alluring male essence of Jack. She detected a lingering hint of his aftershave and accepted that she needed Jackson Richards. The flat-out truth was, without him, she'd be all alone at the mercy of Carlos's Warriors. They could have come for her at any time, and she'd have never seen the danger coming. She hadn't even known her car contained a bug.

"Why can't you look at me?"

His words catapulted her back to the present. The danger Jack represented was a different kind of scary than Carlos, but threatened her safety just as much. "What?"

"Are you still hiding something?"

"No." *Not other than my desire to rip off that sheet and attack you.*

Claudia closed her eyes against the heated intensity of his green gaze.

"We need to clear the air," Jack said. "We're going to be spending a lot of time together, and I need to know what's bugging you."

She took a deep breath and stepped away. He was right. She needed to be honest with him.

"The thing is," she said, "I'm afraid of you. I don't know you, and I don't understand why you're helping me."

"Maybe I'm just a nice guy doing his civic duty."

"This is beyond civic duty. Carlos wants me dead."

Jack grabbed his mug again. "Maybe."

"What do you mean, 'maybe'?"

He took a sip before answering. "I've been thinking about that. They knew where you lived, probably where you worked. Why didn't they put a bomb in your car instead of a tracking device?"

She swallowed. "Gee, thanks. What a lovely thought."

"I think Romero wanted to keep track of you, know where you were located, but had some reason to keep you alive."

She stared at Jack. "That's crazy."

"Just a theory." He shrugged. "When you went into hiding, they got nervous. Maybe they want to snatch you, not kill you."

"Snatch me?" She leaned against the counter, suddenly needing some support. "Why? So they could torture me?"

"Or brainwash you."

Thinking her ex had already forced plenty of his poison into her head, she said, "What would that gain?"

"Your silence."

"So would my death."

"So is there any reason your husband needs you alive?"

Claudia shook her head. "I can't think of one."

"Who filed for divorce?"

"I did, but he didn't fight it."

"Could he still have feelings for you?"

She gaped at Jack. "You don't know Carlos. The man doesn't have feelings."

Jack shook his head. "Then why did he marry you?"

"I honestly don't know. Maybe as a cover, you know, a pretend normal life."

"Is he that sneaky?"

"You have no idea. After the divorce, he left me alone. Everything changed when he saw my name on the witness list and learned about my journal. Suddenly I was being followed."

"Did you tell the feds?"

"Yes, and they suggested a safe house."

"Which you refused."

"Until they trashed my apartment and wrote a warning on the bathroom mirror."

"I can guess what it said."

"'Keep your mouth shut.'"

Jack nodded. "That fits. And then you disappeared, which they may have expected. The Warriors believe in a crazy ideology. Maybe they have some twisted idea that as long as you don't testify, you're worthy of saving."

"So you think it's twisted to keep me breathing?"

"You know what I mean."

She looked away, her thoughts churning about Carlos and his possible strategies. "Yeah, I guess I do."

But she rejected Jack's theory. Carlos didn't think she was worthy of anything. Before he got all tangled up with hatred, maybe he'd once loved her in his own chauvinistic manner. But he hated her now. She knew that even if Jack had doubts.

"So why are they trying to broach the island?" she demanded.

Jack remained quiet for a moment. She could practically see his brain working.

Finally he said, "Maybe to have a conversation and reinforce the need for your silence. Maybe they planned on using a little pain for persuasion. Or maybe they did plan to kill you. But here's the thing, Claudia."

Jack's deadly tone forced her to meet his gaze again.

"Once they realize they've lost track of you, they'll get nervous."

"Makes sense," she said.

"They'll be desperate to locate you again, use any method at their disposal."

"Okay."

"If they find you—and I'm not saying they will— they won't take any more chances. To make sure you don't testify against their leader, they'll eliminate you once and for all. Along with anyone else who gets in their way."

CHAPTER NINE

"I DON'T LIKE IT," Lola told Jack when he called her with details of his plan for moving Claudia.

"You ordered me to get Claudia Goodwin off the island, and that's what I'm doing."

"I didn't expect you to go with her."

"Hell, Lola. You've been encouraging me to use my vacation time for months."

"I wouldn't call this a vacation. And you'll need backup. What's wrong with you, Jack?"

"I've got friends I can call on if things get hairy."

After a long silence, Lola said, "I hope you know what you're doing."

"That may be open to some doubt," Jack admitted. "But I couldn't send any woman away to face a ruthless gang alone."

"Damn Boy Scout," Lola mumbled. "I still don't like it, but Brad will arrive at thirteen hundred hours to take over for you."

"Well, at least I've made him happy."

"I'm glad somebody is."

Lola disconnected, and Jack clipped the phone to his belt. She'd get over it. He had weeks of leave time, and she was only angry because he'd screwed up her carefully laid out schedule. Lola didn't like anyone messing with her schedule.

He checked the time. Eleven hundred. He wasn't waiting for his replacement. Ike had proven to be a good man and could handle things for a couple of hours. The Warriors would be occupied tracking down Claudia's car, anyway.

He'd gone home, showered, packed what he needed and returned with his SUV to find Claudia cleaning the cabana as if she intended to use the space to assist a physician during open-heart surgery. He'd moved her luggage outside, placed it with his own duffel and sent her to take a shower. He listened to the water running, and the part of him that refused to behave like a professional ached to join her.

So he was going on a vacation—of sorts. The first one in years. A week ago he'd have laughed at the idea, although because of Lola's bitching he had been considering a fishing trip to the Keys. But a visit to check on his home in Dunnellon was overdue, and a remote structure surrounded by fifty acres of pristine north Florida forest was the perfect place to secrete a witness with a price on her head. The isolation would allow him to keep this three-week visit quiet. He wouldn't contact anyone unless circumstances demanded he ask for help. For sure he didn't plan on letting his crazy momma know he was back in town.

Claudia entered the living room, freshly showered and looking around like a dog who'd forgotten where she'd buried her bone.

"Who were you talking to?" she demanded.

"My boss."

"Everything okay?"

"Just peachy."

She made a face.

"Relax, Claudia. I've got everything under control."

She plopped on the sofa and pulled a throw pillow into her lap. "I won't relax until we get out of Miami. Maybe not even then."

"I haven't told anyone where we're going. You don't even know exactly where the cabin is, so there's no way we can be followed."

She rolled her eyes. "Yeah, well, I thought I'd figured out everything when I came here, too. Turned out I was dead wrong."

Jack sat beside her. Tension vibrated off her body.

"You're not dead."

She met his gaze. "Not yet."

"Are you ready?"

She tried to speak, then cleared her throat. "Can't wait," she croaked.

Jack knew soothing words wouldn't help Claudia at this point. Better to get their escape over with. Fast and clean.

"Come on, then."

They moved outside. Jack clicked open the SUV.

Claudia stared at the huge green plastic gun locker that took up most of the rear compartment. He'd removed all the weapons and placed them in the backseat covered by a blanket.

"It shouldn't be for more than an hour," Jack said. "Two at the most." He narrowed his eyes, evaluating Claudia. Wetting her lips, she looked away from his scrutiny. She clutched her purse as if it were a life raft.

"You told me you weren't claustrophobic."

"I'm not—usually."

"This is the safest way to get you away without being seen," Jack told her.

"How will I breathe?"

"The locker isn't sealed, and I don't plan to lock it."

"But I won't even be able to see if something goes wrong."

"Nothing is going to go wrong."

Claudia rubbed her hands on her shorts. "Right."

"What happened to that trust we talked about? I'm not going to let anything happen to you."

She closed her eyes. "I want to believe you. I really do, but I feel so…out of control. Helpless. I'm not good with helpless."

Jack almost relented at the terror he read in her haunting blue eyes. Shit. He'd hate this escape plan just as much. By trusting him, she was losing all control, blindly placing her life in his hands. And she didn't know him. Not really. But any other method could alert the Warriors.

A body under a blanket would be obvious to anyone watching.

He wished he'd had time to secure a burner phone. With one, he could keep her aware of where they were, what was going on, alert her to any problems.

"You can always climb out if you have to, but I don't recommend it while we're underway."

She nodded.

He handed her a plastic water bottle. "In case you get thirsty."

"Thanks." She placed the water inside the purse and looped its strap over her shoulder.

"And here's a flashlight."

"So I can read?"

"I thought a little light might make you feel better."

She grabbed the small light, dropped it in a pocket, but made no attempt to get inside the SUV.

"Can you do this?" he asked.

She curled her hands into fists, then released them. After a deep inhalation, she nodded once and hoisted her leg to climb inside his vehicle. Jack wanted to hug her when she crawled into the empty gun locker. He could only guess how much courage that took.

She curled up on the blanket he'd provided, staring back at him. He stepped forward to touch her cheek to reassure her.

Claudia grabbed his hand and squeezed, her gaze searching his.

"Promise you won't turn me over to Carlos," she begged.

"I promise."

"And no government safe house."

"No feds. I promise. Are you ready? It's going to be dark, but there'll be plenty of oxygen."

She nodded. "Go ahead."

Feeling like a jerk, wishing there was another safe way, he pulled his hand from Claudia's fingers and stared into her wide, frightened eyes as he slowly closed the lid, making sure air could get inside the compartment.

CLAUDIA BLINKED WHEN the lid of the locker closed. *Oh, God. So dark.*

She fished out the flashlight and clicked it on, but immediately turned it off. She should conserve the battery just in case.

She squeezed her eyes shut and clutched her purse to her chest. Better to just pretend she was somewhere else. Anywhere else. She concentrated on slow, deep breaths, and waited for something to happen. The blanket beneath her felt like plush velvet, soft and comfortable. The locker smelled of gunpowder and the oil used for weapons.

The engine ignited, creating a steady vibration beneath her. Lying in a fetal position on her right side, Claudia's body shifted as Jack pulled forward, so she braced herself with her feet. They motored smoothly for maybe five minutes and stopped. She opened her eyes and realized the brake lights provided an eerie red glow around the edges of the locker. Not much illumination, but something.

She heard muted voices, but couldn't make out words. They must be in line for the ferry. She pressed into the floor with her feet, lifted her buttocks to reposition onto her back and then pulled out her arm to read her watch. The ferry was scheduled to leave in five minutes, so they wouldn't have long to wait before boarding.

She tried to make her mind go blank. If only she could fall asleep. Maybe she should have taken a sedative. No. She needed to stay alert in case Carlos's thugs found her and attacked. She wasn't helpless. She had her gun, but what good would that do her if they fired into the closed gun locker?

But they didn't know where she was. Of course they didn't. They couldn't possibly.

Unless Jack worked for them. Maybe he was taking her to them.

Stop it, Claudia.

She reached inside her purse for the water Jack had provided and lifted her head to take a sip. Cool liquid slid down her throat, helping to calm her crazed ramblings.

Claudia pictured Jack behind the wheel of his SUV mere feet from her position, and that image was strangely comforting. When Jack accelerated, her body shifted again. The road noise beneath her changed as they drove off concrete and onto the ferry's metal deck. She heard more muted voices, clanging, and then Jack shut down his engine. The boat's motor roared to life, and Claudia sensed a difference in the vibration when the boat left the dock.

After what she knew was only ten minutes—but felt like an hour—the boat's motor stopped. They'd reached the other side. Now they'd drive north to the prearranged stop in Pompano Beach where Jack would release her from this dark hole. She'd get into the front seat of his SUV where she could ride like a normal passenger. He would take her to Dunnellon, and he'd keep her safe. *Safe?*

She closed her eyes as the doubts and the questions pounded inside her skull.

Why was Jack doing this for her? He gained nothing from helping her. How could she—how could anyone—possibly believe he was just a super nice guy doing his civic duty? Carlos had taught her no one ever did anything for free; everyone always had an angle. So what was in it for Jack?

For that matter, what was Carlos's angle? Jack believed he had some mysterious reason for keeping her alive. Could he have instructed his thugs to keep her from testifying but not to kill her? Did her ex still want her? If so, why hadn't he contested their divorce? Why hadn't she heard from him in over a year?

Damn Carlos Romero. She hated how her brief

time with him had made her suspicious of everyone's motives. Now she was even questioning her ex's reasoning, for God's sake. As if he were reasonable. She sucked air deep into her lungs, telling herself that this would all be over soon. Carlos's trial was only three weeks away.

But would it all be over after that testimony? How long would she be looking for bad guys in the rearview mirror? For the rest of her life?

As the car accelerated, probably onto I-95, she stared into the dark void around her. She knew better than to trust anyone. Look at the mess she'd gotten herself into by trusting Jack. Her car had been driven into a canal and she was stuffed into a gun locker hiding from the world. Painful pressure built in her chest as her heart raced.

She needed to see the sun.

With asphalt rushing beneath her, she reached out to touch the top of the locker. She stroked a soft felt lining rather than the expected plastic, which reminded her of a coffin. Would this small cavity be her final resting place? If someone rear-ended this vehicle, she didn't even have a seat belt. If Jack rolled the SUV, she'd be flung outside.

Her head pounded. She struggled to inhale. Why had she agreed to climb into this tomb?

Recognizing panic, she shifted onto her side and used her hands to press out against the lid. It opened easily and she could see the taillights. Cool air brushed against her skin.

Sweat ran into her eyes, stinging them, and she blinked it away, aware that her clothing was now damp. Why was she sweating so much when this hellhole wasn't even hot?

She needed to crawl out of this coffin, but she was hurtling down the road at a hundred miles an hour. She didn't dare climb out. She could startle Jack, cause an accident, injure him and other people. She needed to think about something else—anything else other than where she was.

She squeezed her eyes hard, took deep breaths and forced herself to remember why this was happening, why she was torturing herself. She'd married a man who wasn't what he seemed, a man who killed people. She was going to ensure he never hurt anyone else ever again.

Right, she was doing her civic duty, just like Jackson Richards.

But if Carlos had turned into a monster, why couldn't Jack? Hadn't she even turned into someone she didn't recognize anymore? She'd become a paranoid, frightened victim who had to fight off panic attacks. Who was that person?

I'm not that woman, she told herself.

"I'm not that woman," she said out loud.

Her voice sounded raspy, weak. That wouldn't do.

She raised her head and took a long pull from the water bottle. She clutched her purse to her chest. The loaded Glock inside reassured her. She found her flashlight and turned it on.

"I'm not that woman. I'm not that woman." She repeated the words over and over like a mantra.

JACK PULLED INTO the exit lane for the Homestead Service Plaza and applied the brakes. Time to transfer Claudia to the front seat.

He wondered how she was doing, and shook his head. Probably totally freaked out. He'd never forget the cornered look in her eyes when he'd situated her inside the small compartment. She'd barely fit, and her terror had haunted him the whole drive south.

He prided himself on being able to catch a tail, and knew with certainty no one had followed him from Collins Island. Once on the Turnpike he'd set the cruise control at the speed of fifty-five—twenty miles per hour slower than the rest of the traffic, and remained in the far right lane. Vehicles zoomed up on his rear, then swerved around him, often with an impatient honk. Sometimes with a middle finger salute.

You just gotta love the polite drivers in south Florida.

But that was the whole idea. No other vehicle stayed with them. He'd left and reentered the Turnpike at three separate exits to make certain. No one had followed them. Of course he'd swept his SUV for bugs.

He'd gotten Claudia away clean.

By now the Warriors had likely found her sunken vehicle, and would double back to Collins Island.

But Lola had tripled security. With the new boat patrol, Romero's men wouldn't easily gain access. If the Protection Alliance had problems they couldn't handle, Lola would contact the US Attorney's Office and alert them to the situation. Once in Dunnellon, Claudia would contact the prosecutor and let him know she was okay—just not her location.

He still considered that a mistake. Claudia would be safer under the protection of the federal government, but his plan was a good one. It could work. Should work.

He drove to the far side of the service plaza's parking lot, parked and jumped out to surveil any vehicles that exited after them. The gun holster under his jacket comforted him as he raised his binoculars to scrutinize the vehicles entering the plaza.

No vehicle looked familiar. No one had followed them from Miami. But he'd wait ten minutes just to be certain.

Behind him, the SUV's rear door popped open, and Jack whirled to see Claudia's leg swing over the bumper. Couldn't the woman follow instructions? She knew to wait for the all clear from him. Why did she—

She lost her balance, and he rushed forward to catch her before she hit the pavement. Their gazes locked, and he read desperation in her eyes. He evaluated her pale, tear-streaked face and understood. She'd reached some kind of a limit. She'd had no choice but to climb out of her prison once they had stopped.

"I've got you," he told her. "You're okay."

She swallowed and nodded.

"Get into the backseat. Lie down."

She took a step, but faltered again. He grabbed her arms to support her.

"My legs are asleep," she said. "I've been in a cramped position too long."

Jack carried her to the backseat, closed the door and again checked the area. All clear.

Convinced they were good to go, he opened the backseat door and leaned in. Claudia lay on her side, eyes wide open, staring out the window.

"You okay?" he asked.

"Better now that I can see the sky. Can I sit up?"

"Yeah, we're clear. Nobody followed us." Jack extended his arm to help.

She blew out a breath when she was upright. "Thanks."

"You need to know we're in Homestead, not Pompano Beach."

"Why is that?" Her voice sounded sharp, suspicious. She narrowed her eyes on his face.

"A bit of misdirection."

"What do you mean?"

"I want you to go inside the plaza to the ladies' room. I'll point out the surveillance cameras, and you need to make sure your face is captured. Don't be too obvious, but walk back and forth, move slowly, find some reason to linger in front of the lens."

"Because Carlos's people have the ability to hack into the security feed."

"The Warriors are known for their tech team. They're going to look hard for you, and this is a ploy to slow them down."

She nodded. "Got it."

"I'll purchase something for us to eat on the road, and I'm going to gas up. This vehicle has a five-hundred-mile range. Once we leave here, we'll only stop for one bathroom break. I know a rest area where there are no cameras. Then we're not stopping again until we reach my cabin. The only images of you will be right here and, because of that, they'll look south."

Jack was relieved to see Claudia smile for the first time since emerging from the locker.

"You thought of everything, didn't you?" she said.

"I doubt it. You okay to walk yet?"

She rotated her ankles. "I think so."

He held out his arm to assist her down from the seat. "Let's get started. I want to make it to Dunnellon by 8:00 p.m."

Claudia clung to his arm as they walked toward the plaza structure. She'd had a rough time in the locker. She was trying to soldier on, pretend she was okay, but maybe they should talk about what had happened to her during the drive. Women liked to discuss their emotions, right? Might make her feel better.

And he'd like to make her feel better. It bothered him to see her this subdued, so miserable, especially when it was his idea. Even if it couldn't be helped.

Jack glanced down at her troubled face and wondered when he'd developed such a protective attitude about Claudia. Wasn't like him. Definitely not professional to feel that way about a client, even on a pro bono job. Where was his usual detachment?

Worse, he'd experienced a flush of pleasure when she said he'd thought of everything, like some hormonal teenaged athlete praised by his girlfriend after a big game. He knew it was impossible to account for every eventuality that could go wrong. Some new twist could always screw up a plan. He needed to remember that, keep looking for that curve ball, keep his head on straight.

If he allowed himself to care too much about Claudia, get too close, he'd get careless. If he got careless, they were both headed for certain disaster.

CHAPTER TEN

WHEN THEY WERE back on the road, Jack set the cruise control for seventy-five. Claudia remained quiet beside him. She'd retreated to some personal space to lick her wounds, and he let her stay there. They both had plenty to obsess about. Better if he kept his mind off her and alert for trouble, anyway.

They agreed on an oldies radio station, but neither of them listened to the tunes. He paid more attention to her than he should, but she just stared out the window, often twirling her hair.

To keep them alert, he'd purchased two extra-large cups of strong coffee. Claudia didn't touch hers. His had gone cold by the time he took the last swallow.

"Are you hungry?" he asked. "We missed breakfast, and I've got sandwiches."

She shifted her gaze from the road to him. "Not really."

"You should eat," he said. "There's a choice of turkey, ham or tuna fish. Plus chips."

She shrugged. "Whatever."

"Whatever, huh? Love your enthusiasm."

"Well, pardon me."

"Would you mind grabbing me a sandwich so I can eat? I'm starved."

"Oh. Sure." She reached for the bag he'd placed on the floorboard. "You sure bought a lot of food."

"I wasn't sure what you'd want," Jack said. "So I got two of each. Give me turkey if you can find one."

When she unwrapped the plastic covering, the enticing fragrance of fresh bread and tangy pickle wafted into the SUV, making Jack even hungrier. She placed the cut sandwich close to him on the console. He finished the first half in three bites.

Claudia gave a little laugh, which made Jack feel far better than the food.

"I guess you *were* hungry," she said.

"Still am," he said, and scarfed the other half.

She mumbled something that sounded like, "My gladiator."

"What was that?" he asked.

"Nothing." She rummaged through the bag. "Maybe my appetite has returned."

Pleased that she'd roused herself enough to take nourishment, Jack said, "I'll take another. Make it ham this time, please, ma'am."

"Yes, sir."

Claudia opened a bag of chips, dumped a few beside his second sandwich and then opened another sandwich for herself. They ate in silence, although she barely nibbled on her food. Not such a great appetite, after all.

"Something wrong with the tuna?" he asked.

"No. It's fine."

When he'd finished his second sandwich, Jack sighed. It would be a long trip if she brooded the whole way. And they'd be spending a lot of time together for the next few weeks. His one-bedroom cabin in the woods was a long way from a spacious villa on Collins Island. And it only had one bed.

That was a problem he'd yet to figure out.

So why not enjoy a little time between the sheets with her? Claudia wouldn't object. It would only be sex, a release for both of them, right?

Wrong. He had to curtail that kind of thinking pronto. He needed to keep his distance.

But he liked Claudia, enjoyed the challenge of figuring her out. They could be friends, right?

Friends? Who was he kidding? He wanted to rip off her clothes every time he saw her.

"You want to tell me what's wrong?" he asked.

"Seriously?" She shot him a look. "Where do you want me to begin?"

"How about with what happened to you inside that locker."

She rewrapped her sandwich and placed it back inside the paper bag. "Have you ever been locked inside a small dark space?"

"You weren't locked. But, yeah, I experienced something similar once when I was a cop. It's no fun."

"Well, I went a little crazy. I wanted to jump out en route."

"But you didn't," he said.

"But I came close." She gave a visible shudder. "I could have killed you or other people."

"I doubt it. I half expected you to do something strange."

"I had a panic attack." She spit out the words as if they burned her mouth. "But I never panic. I've always prided myself on being levelheaded. That's why I'm a good nurse."

Levelheaded? Jack didn't reply. Considering some of Claudia's crazy ideas, that wasn't the first trait he thought of in connection with her.

"So what's wrong," she continued, "is I don't know who I am anymore, and that's scaring me as much as Carlos's thugs."

"So you reinvent yourself," he said. "You'll be stronger on the other side of the ordeal."

"Easy for you to say. You're not the one being hunted by terrorists." She again lapsed into hair twirling.

Jack didn't reply, but he did know about trial by fire and coming out on the other side stronger.

"And you know what," she said. "I liked who I was. What if I'm never able to work as a nurse again?" Claudia sighed. "I'm not good with change. I guess that makes me inflexible, another unpleasant thing I've learned about myself."

Change could definitely be hard. Considering how he'd altered the trajectory of his career—make that his entire life—a few years ago, he understood her point. And now he was about to revisit his old stomping grounds, something he swore he'd never do.

"So you were a cop?" Claudia asked.

"Deputy sheriff with Marion County."

"Why did you quit?"

"That's a long story."

CLAUDIA SHIFTED IN the seat to face him. "We've got hours of driving ahead of us."

"Maybe I'll tell you someday."

"Ah. You don't like to talk about that. Why?"

When he shrugged, she knew he wasn't going to tell her. So Jack had secrets, too. For some bizarre reason, that made her feel better. Mr. Gladiator wasn't perfect, after all. But he definitely knew how to take care of himself. And her. She still marveled at his ploy of driving south to confuse Carlos's people. She'd have never thought of parading back and forth in view of the surveillance cameras.

Could she trust Jack?

Maybe. So far—from rushing to save her from the intruding pool guy to smuggling her off the island—Jack had done nothing but try to protect her.

But her marriage to Carlos had been such a disaster, and he'd filled her mind with such paranoid poison, she didn't trust her own judgment anymore. How could she?

Maybe Carlos was wrong. Maybe everyone didn't have an angle. Maybe Jack was an exception.

As Claudia studied his chiseled face, the tension

in her belly relaxed slightly. He appeared totally absorbed in controlling the SUV. One thing was for sure, this man was definitely easy to look at. Even better, as Marsali would probably say, he wasn't purely decorative. He possessed skills. Skills that she wanted to learn. Needed to learn.

She couldn't depend on her gladiator for the rest of her life. She needed to learn how to take care of herself.

"Marsali said you're a martial arts expert," Claudia said.

"I wouldn't say I'm an expert."

"She said you're a black belt. That's pretty good."

He tossed her an interested glance. "So?"

"So I want you to teach me how to defend myself."

"You plan on doing hand-to-hand combat with the Warriors?"

Claudia felt her face grow warm and realized her idea sounded ridiculous to him. "Only if I have to. Knowing a few moves would make me feel better."

He nodded, refocused on the road. "I get that, but at this point they won't allow you to get close enough. These guys are cowards at their core. If they locate you, it's more likely a sniper will take you out. Or a bomb."

"Thanks for that cheery thought."

"I'm just being honest."

"Of course you are."

He shot her a quick pointed glare. "Like I need you to stay honest with me."

"You know everything about me."

"I hope so."

"But I'm so tired of feeling like a victim," she said.

"I'll give you lessons in self-defense if you want, but expect a few bruises. The only way to learn is by doing. You'll be tossed around a lot—until you can toss me."

Toss Jack? She returned her gaze to his impressive physique and doubted that could ever happen. "Sounds like a good time."

He nodded. "I'll rig a mat so it won't hurt so much. However, in my opinion your time would be better spent becoming proficient with that Glock."

She liked that idea.

"You brought it, right?" Jack asked. "Is it loaded?"

"Oh, yeah," she said. "Can you teach me how to hit what I'm shooting at?"

"All it takes is practice, and we should have plenty of time for that. I'm not planning on leaving the property once we lay in groceries."

"What about ammunition?"

"I brought plenty."

"Won't we need to go to a gun range?"

"No. As you'll see when we arrive."

What the hell did that mean? Claudia realized she didn't know much about where they were going. He'd said a city in north Florida she'd never heard of, but she had been too agitated to ask for any details.

"Tell me about this cabin."

Jack rubbed his neck. "Well, it's no Collins Island

mansion. One bedroom, one bath, small kitchen in the middle of fifty acres of forest."

One bedroom? So she'd be sleeping with Jack every night. That thought created a pleasant tingle in her belly. Disgusted with her reaction, she closed her eyes. Had she learned nothing from the past? Was she nothing but a giant mass of hormones?

Now was definitely not the time to become involved with any man. Especially Jack. Surely there was a sofa for her to use.

"Sounds great," she said.

"No TV reception," he warned.

"What?" Claudia squeaked.

"No one has lived there for over three years, and we don't want to alert anyone to our presence if we can help it. I have a DVD player and some old movies, plus I can set up a hot spot for internet access."

Like she could go online. "What about phone?"

"No landline, but I have my cell phone."

"So we'll be totally isolated."

"Isn't that what you want, what you tried to arrange at Villa Alma?"

"Not exactly."

Couldn't he see how different this situation would be? She'd be stuck all alone without a car in the middle of nowhere with a man she barely knew. A man she wanted to trust but hadn't quite gotten there yet, probably never would. A man who could break her in half without breaking a sweat. Oh, and she'd actually invited him to practice his skills on her. He'd even warned her about the possibility of bruises.

Maybe worst of all, she was so turned on by this stranger, this way-too-sexy gladiator, she'd been thrilled to learn there was only one bedroom.

Jack laughed softly. "It's only for three weeks, Claudia. Think of all the studying you can get done."

CLAUDIA JERKED AWAKE when Jack turned onto a gravel road. Listening to rocks crunch beneath the vehicle's huge tires, she struggled to awareness, escaping a nightmare where she'd remarried Carlos Romero.

The SUV's wipers swept back and forth across the windshield. Rain pounded on the roof. Headlights illuminated a narrow road full of potholes, but darkness pressed in on all sides. Huge trees loomed overhead, ghostly branches illuminated by lightning, thrashing in a stiff wind.

"Where are we?" she asked, noting they ascended a gentle hill.

"*Casa* de Jack," he said.

So they'd arrived. The right front tire dipped into a huge hole, and she struggled to sit up in her seat. "Are you sure we're not in the Sea of Tranquility?" she muttered.

"Where?"

"You know, the craters of the moon? Never mind. What time is it?"

"Just after eight."

"Wow. I guess I fell asleep."

"I guess," Jack said.

"Sorry. I didn't mean to."

He shrugged. "You needed the rest. You were getting a lot of exercise worrying about the lack of TV."

"Very funny. You're the one who didn't get much sleep last night. I should have helped drive."

"I'm good."

Claudia sighed as she stared at the narrow path ahead. She needed to start doing her share of the work on this journey. "When did it start raining?"

"As soon as we left I-95. Another cold front is sweeping through the state."

"I thought we were going to stop for groceries."

"I decided to wait out the storm. Or the better plan might be for me to go alone tomorrow. We've still got sandwiches if we get hungry tonight."

Or maybe he was too exhausted to go into a grocery store now. Jack probably longed for a bed.

When the SUV headlights swept across the facade of a small one-story structure, Jack cursed and slammed on the brakes, rocking her forward against her seat belt even though they'd barely crept along the gravel road. He shut down the headlights.

"What's wrong?" she demanded.

"There's a light on inside the cabin."

Jack stared at his property, evaluating its appearance and the logistics of his approach. To the left, a large plastic garbage can stood upright, overflowing with trash. He'd left that garbage container inside a storage shed so it wouldn't blow away. Someone had been living here a good while.

Every time windshield wipers cleared rain from the glass, he focused on the light through the closed curtain waiting for movement. There. A shadowy figure crossed the opening.

Someone was inside.

The question was who and how many.

"I thought you said no one lived here," Claudia said in a hoarse, frightened whisper.

"No one is supposed to be here."

"It's Carlos's people, isn't it? Let's get out of here."

He swung his gaze to her when he caught the panic in her tone. She'd placed her right hand inside her purse, probably clutching the Glock. Of course she would assume the intruders were the Warriors, but he'd considered and immediately dismissed that idea. Even if the terrorists had tracked them and managed to arrive first—an impossibility considering the speed he'd driven—they wouldn't wait inside the structure. And they definitely wouldn't leave a light on to alert him.

No. The Warriors would have taken them out on the long driveway through the woods. That's what he'd have done.

"Relax," he told her. "The intruder is likely a squatter who thought the cabin had been deserted."

"How do you know?"

"For one thing, our headlights reflected off the taillight of a vehicle parked behind the cabin. It was too quick to determine the make, but your Warriors wouldn't be that careless."

"They're not *mine*," she muttered. "So what are you going to do?"

Good question. He might not believe the terrorists had found them, but another sort of danger could still be waiting inside. Maybe this was a squatter; maybe an old enemy. He grew up in this little burg, and most inhabitants knew he'd moved away. Plus, he'd been a deputy sheriff for four years. Could any of the perps he'd stuck behind bars think it would be sweet revenge to inhabit his home once released? A motivated felon could find the address easy enough. They might even vandalize the place just for fun. God knew what he'd find inside.

He needed to proceed with caution. And that meant with his weapon drawn.

"Wait here," he told Claudia. He glanced to her lap. Her hand still rested inside her purse. "It's okay to be ready for trouble, but please don't have another panic attack and shoot *me*."

Their gazes locked. Claudia gave a quick nod.

"Be careful," she said.

"Always," he replied, and stepped outside the vehicle into a stiff, chilly wind.

Moving fast and quiet, Jack circled to the back of the structure. He wanted to check out the vehicle first to gather possible information. Cold rain saturated his hair, and he noted a neatly stacked pile of firewood a few feet away from the back door. The shrubbery had been recently trimmed. His old Airstream trailer remained where he'd left it next to the shed.

The car parked on the concrete slab close to the back door was a two-year-old Chevrolet he didn't recognize. He memorized the license tag. Stooping low so he couldn't be seen, Jack tried the car's back door. Locked.

Still hunched over, he moved to the driver's door and edged it open without a sound. The overhead light came on and illuminated a half-full coffee cup with a lipstick smudge in the console facing the driver's seat. A pink sweater and a small collapsible umbrella lay in the passenger seat. A pine-tree-shaped car freshener dangled from the rearview mirror, but didn't mask the unmistakable stink of cigarette smoke.

Behind that lingering tobacco residue, he thought he caught a familiar fragrance. He tried to place the smell, but couldn't. He carefully shut the car door to cut the light, then stood and stared at the cabin's back door a mere five feet away.

After grocery shopping, he always pulled his vehicle back here onto the concrete slab because the small kitchen was just inside that sliding glass door. Maybe the intruder was hiding his—or more likely her—vehicle, or maybe she was taking advantage of that convenience.

One of his reclining lawn chairs—with a new cushion—sat on the slab next to a wrought-iron table. The table contained an ashtray full of rainwater and cigarette butts with lipstick on the filters. The interloper had rolled his gas grill out of the shed, too, as well as his outdoor fireplace. Anger churned deep in Jack's gut. The intruder had certainly made herself right at home in *his* fricking home.

He reached inside his drenched jacket and removed his gun from the shoulder holster. As he approached the sliders, his soaked running shoes squeaked. The rain had eased, but the wind remained strong. A curtain covered the sliding doors, shielding the interior. During the day, *his* view outside to the wooded backyard was one he'd always enjoyed.

He'd rejected the idea of an old lover moving in knowing he was in Miami. He'd never given anyone a key. Besides, all the women in his old life hated this rustic cabin.

He decided to go in the front door hard and fast—take the trespasser by surprise. If the invader was an ex-prisoner out for revenge, she'd definitely have a weapon.

Jack halted midstep when the curtains moved. The porch light came on. The door slid open. He raised his Sig Sauer in a two-handed grip.

CHAPTER ELEVEN

"DOES POOKIE NEED to go pee-pee?" a female voice sang out, as if speaking to a demented child. "I don't think the nasty ole rain is going to stop."

Jack tensed when a small white fluffy dog rushed outside. But the animal stopped, hopped in the air and backed away from him, barking furiously.

A plump female figure materialized behind the dog. "What's wrong with little sweetums?"

Jack recognized that voice.

When the intruder spotted him, she let out a scream that could be heard back in Miami.

"Mother." Jack lowered his weapon.

"Jack!" She raised a hand to her heart. "You scared me halfway to hell and back."

"What are you doing here, Mother?"

She closed her eyes and sucked in a deep breath. "I thought you were going to shoot me."

"I almost did. How did you get a key?"

His mother bent over and scooped up the still yapping dog. "Hush, Pookie. It's okay. This is your brother, Jack." She lifted her gaze to his. "You scared her. She's usually very friendly."

"A dog? Really? You brought a dog into my home?"

"Let's go inside out of the rain. I'll get you a towel."

"Is there anyone else here?" Jack demanded.

She shook her head. The porch light glinted off her hair, and Jack realized she'd bleached it platinum. "I'm alone. I've been living here three months."

A hundred questions tripped on the edge of Jack's tongue, but he held them. The danger was over, but Claudia would have heard his mother's zombielike scream and been terrified.

"I'll be right back," he said. "Wait here."

"I'm not going anywhere."

Jack shot her a look. *The hell you're not.*

He returned to his mother's Chevrolet and grabbed the umbrella. Hoping he didn't get shot for his trouble, he hurried back to the SUV to reassure Claudia.

She remained as he'd left her, wide-eyed with her right hand clutching the Glock.

"Jack," she breathed when he approached her door. "Thank God. Are you okay?"

"I'm fine. Just royally pissed off."

"Who is here?"

"My mother."

She blinked. "Your mother?"

"You heard me."

"Your *mother*?" Claudia repeated, as if she couldn't quite believe he actually had a mother. Yeah, well, Irene wasn't exactly a candidate for parent of the year.

Jack popped the small umbrella and held it up

so Claudia could duck under its shelter. "Come on. Let's go inside. I need to find out what's going on."

HURRYING TOWARD THE cabin now that the scare was over, Claudia realized the temperature had to be forty degrees colder here than in Miami. All she wanted was a bathroom. It'd been a long ride from south Florida with only one quick stop to pee.

She expected to find some sort of übermasculine cave when she entered Jack's cabin in the woods. She'd had in mind a hunting lodge, with the heads of shaggy beasts mounted on the walls, or at least some stuffed fish proudly displayed. Instead she found cheery prints of floral bouquets and glorious sunsets. A sofa and reclining chair were covered by patchwork quilts that appeared hand-stitched. A round wooden table covered with plastic bags of groceries sat outside the kitchen.

Jack glared at the furnishings as if he'd never seen them before. At least it was blessedly warm inside.

A fiftyish woman with bleached hair, wearing tight black jeans and a formfitting red sweater, stood at the back door smoking a cigarette. She turned her head to exhale the toxic smoke out a crack in the door, then leveled her focus on Claudia.

"Who's this?" the woman asked, tossing her cigarette outside. Claudia watched the glow of the still lit butt arc into the night.

"Mom. Please don't do that," Jack said. "You could start a fire, and we're in the middle of a forest."

"Oh, please. It's too wet out there for anything to ignite." Jack's mom closed the slider and stepped forward. She held out her hand. "Don't mind my rude son," she told Claudia. "I'm Irene Richards, the fire marshal's mother."

"Pleased to meet you," Claudia said, grasping Irene's warm, strong hand. "I'm Claudia."

"Jack, did you get married and not invite your momma to the wedding?" Irene asked, a hurt tone in her voice.

"What are you doing here, Mother?" Jack demanded, ignoring her question. "And how did you get in?"

"Would you like something to drink, Claudia?" Irene asked.

Claudia decided ignoring questions must be a genetic trait.

"I have some white wine. Or bourbon. Or I could make a pot of coffee."

"Talk to me, Mother," Jack said.

Irene grabbed a pack of cigarettes from the wooden table, shook one out, and picked up her lighter.

"Don't light that in here," Jack warned.

Irene sighed and slammed down the lighter. "All right. Calm down."

"You'd better not have been smoking inside this cabin."

"I know better than that. I always smoke outside."

"Tell me how you got *in*side. Did you break a window?"

"Getting in was easy. I made a copy of the key years ago."

"Why?"

Irene shrugged. "You're my son. What if you needed me?"

Claudia really needed to pee, but was too fascinated by this conversation to miss a word. Why was Jack being so hateful to his mom? Of course he'd been shocked to find her here—especially considering the clandestine reasons for their arrival and how she complicated their mission—but he ought to be glad to see her. He acted as if she was his mortal enemy rather than his mother.

"If I needed help, you'd be the last person I'd call."

Claudia stifled a gasp, and Irene seemed to deflate at his words. She collapsed into one of the chairs surrounding the table.

"Don't be cruel, Jack. Not in front of your new wife."

"She's not my wife."

Irene glanced at Claudia. Knowing what it felt like to be interrogated by Jack, she gave his mom a nod and a reassuring smile.

"I know you're disappointed in me, son, but I'm still your mother."

"Just tell me why you've moved in to my house without an invitation."

After a long moment, Irene raised her chin and held his gaze. "Because I had nowhere else to go."

That statement hung in the room like a deadly but

odorless gas. The only sound was the steady beat of raindrops on the roof.

Claudia searched Jack's face for some subtle sign of softening, but couldn't get a read on his thoughts. This was a whole new and disturbing side of her gladiator, one not quite so heroic.

Deciding now was a good time to defuse the tension, Claudia stepped forward. "Um, I could really use a bathroom."

"Down the hallway," Jack said in a flat tone. "Door on your right. I'll get our luggage out of the car."

When he jerked open the front door, a cold wind rushed inside the cabin, ruffling the plastic grocery bags on the table and chilling her arms. When the door slammed, the turbulence calmed.

"I guess he's still a bit pissed at me," Irene murmured into the silence.

"It's been a long day," Claudia said. What else could she say? She'd like to give this sad woman a hug, but wasn't sure about Irene's reaction. Whatever she'd done in the past, it had to be horrible. Jack didn't want her here, and her presence definitely complicated their plans.

Irene brightened. "Have y'all had supper? I made my famous chili today. Jack loves my chili."

"Sounds delicious." Wondering about the next surprise the universe would toss at her, Claudia opened the bathroom door and a small white dog leaped onto her legs.

"Well, hello there," she cooed, only then remembering the angry barks while waiting in the car. She'd envisioned a huge Rottweiler, not a tiny mop.

Grinning, she bent down to pet the animal. "Did your mom lock you in here to avoid the fireworks?"

The dog licked her face as if it'd been smeared with a favorite treat, then padded into the living room, ears erect and tail high.

When Claudia reentered the living area, Jack wasn't there, but her duffel bag and a few boxes sat inside the front door. Irene stood by the stove stirring a pot while sipping a glass of white wine. An enticing fragrance of chili pepper, tomatoes and garlic wafted through the room, reminding Claudia that she hadn't eaten much lunch. Homemade chili did sound good.

"You want some pinot grigio?" Irene asked holding up a green bottle. "Finest vintage—made just last week."

"Sure," Claudia said. "Thanks."

"Have a seat, honey." Irene placed a plastic wineglass on the table, scooped up the grocery bags and transferred them to a kitchen counter.

When Claudia sat at the table, the white dog jumped into her lap and curled into a small ball of fluff.

"That's Pookie," Irene said, pouring the wine.

"Quite the watchdog." Claudia stroked the dog's soft fur, and Pookie released a contented sigh.

"Oh, she's ferocious," Irene agreed.

"Where's Jack?" Claudia asked.

"He said he was going to check the perimeter, whatever that means."

"In the rain?"

Irene shrugged. "I don't think he wants to remain in the same room with me, but doesn't have the heart to throw me out. A walk is his way of cooling off."

Walking in this cold rain should accomplish that. Claudia took a sip of the chilled wine and doubted this particular bottle cost anyone ten thousand dollars.

"You two seem to have some issues."

"You could say that." Irene issued such a deep, throaty laugh, it created a series of nasty coughs.

Claudia narrowed her eyes at the sound. Jack's mom needed to quit smoking ASAP.

"Are you okay?" Claudia asked.

"I'm fine." Irene blotted her eyes with a paper towel and took a sip of wine. Then she opened a wooden kitchen cabinet and began stowing her groceries. "My son has a lot of good traits, but he isn't the forgiving type."

"Thanks for the tip," Claudia said. "I'll remember that."

"How long have you two been dating? I'm thinking not long, or you'd already know that."

Claudia took another swallow of wine to give her time to think. How should she answer that question? Of course they had to tell Jack's mom something, but what? Definitely not the truth.

"You can't remember?" Irene asked.

"I haven't known Jack all that long," Claudia said.

"I see." Irene stood on her tiptoes to place a box of shredded wheat on the highest shelf. "The last thing he said to me—in his meanest tone—was not to tell anyone about you guys being here."

"*Please* don't," Claudia said. "That's why he got so mad when he found you here. He didn't want anyone to know he'd come home."

"Why?" Irene stood flat-footed and faced Claudia.

"Don't tell her anything you don't want everyone in the fricking state to know," Jack boomed from the front door.

Claudia started at his harsh tone, and turned to see him remove a yellow rain slicker, shake off water and place it on a hook outside the front door. His hair was dripping, but because of the rain gear he wasn't soaked through as she'd feared.

Irene opened a closet and tossed Jack a dry towel. "Did you find any monsters?"

"All clear," he replied, and used the towel to dry his hair.

"So what's going on here, Jack?" Irene asked. "Is Miss Claudia on the run from something?"

"We came up here for a vacation," Jack said. "To get away. That's all you need to know."

"People don't drive to north Florida in February for a vacation. Especially not during a cold snap."

"Let it go, Mother."

Irene glanced at Claudia. "Most likely you're not running from the law, though. Jack don't truck with nothing illegal."

Claudia waited for Jack to respond. What would he tell his mother about her? Jack folded the towel into neat quarters, then strode across the room and sat at the table between Claudia and his mom.

"Why don't we focus on our real problem?"

"What's that?" Irene asked.

"How I'm going to muzzle you."

Irene placed a palm flat over her heart. "I swear I won't tell anyone you're in Dunnellon."

"I wish I could believe you, Mother, but history has taught me otherwise."

For the first time, Claudia caught emotion in Jack's voice, and she decided his mom had done something really awful to him. She must have said the wrong thing to the right person at the worst possible time for him to behave this way.

He placed the towel on the table. "There's only one way to be sure you don't spread the word to everyone you know."

"What's that?" Claudia asked.

Jack didn't look away from his mom. "Take away her phone."

"My phone?"

"Okay," Claudia said, making a T with her hands. "Time-out. The chili is hot, it smells yummy and I'm hungry."

Irene had set out two bowls, so Claudia ladled steaming chili into them for herself and Jack. Hoping food would put him in a better mood, she set a full bowl and a spoon in front of him, poured more wine for Irene and sat to eat her own supper. She needed energy.

They ate in silence for a few minutes. Irene took long pulls on her wine, staring at the table. Jack concentrated on his meal as if it were the last one he'd ever have.

"This is delicious, Irene," Claudia said finally.

"Thanks," Irene mumbled, and shot Claudia a grateful look.

"Isn't it good, Jack?" Claudia prompted.

He grunted in what sounded like agreement and kept eating.

"You must give me this recipe," Claudia said after another long moment.

"Sure," Irene said. "The secret is fresh tomatoes and lots of garlic."

Jack's spoon clattered into his empty bowl. "If you ladies are done with the business of your society of secret recipes, I'd like to resolve our problem."

"We're here on official police business," Claudia interjected before Jack could disrupt the fragile peace. "We can't tell you any more than that, but lives depend on no one knowing where we are."

Irene's gaze darted from Jack to Claudia and back to Jack.

"You're still a cop? I thought you quit."

"Please believe me, Irene," Claudia said. "We can't give you any details, but the security of the United States government is at stake."

Claudia glanced to Jack for his support, but he only raised his eyebrows and gave her a look that said, "Oh, please do go on. This is a fascinating tale."

She glared at him. What she'd told his mom wasn't a lie. Carlos was a domestic terrorist who *would* blow up more government buildings if her testimony didn't keep him in jail.

"The US government?" Irene asked doubtfully. "You work for the government now, Jack?" Her eyes grew wide. "Oh, Lordy. Does this have something to do with that scandal down at the federal farm bureau?"

Claudia shook her head. "I'm sorry, Irene. We can't tell you. The less you know, the safer it is for you."

"That's like waving a red flag in front of her," Jack said. "She won't stop asking questions until she badgers us to death."

"I can keep a secret, son."

"No you can't, Mother."

"Stop it, you two," Claudia said. "This is not helping."

Jack sat back in his chair and issued a disgusted noise that sounded like a snort.

"Irene, if you tell anyone that we're here—anyone— it could be a disaster. That person could mention it to someone else and so on and so on." Claudia placed a hand over her heart. "That would be dangerous for all three of us."

"No, it won't," Jack said. "Because Mother is leaving."

CHAPTER TWELVE

JACK SHIFTED IN his chair as Claudia leveled questioning eyes on him.

"Where's that bourbon?" he asked his mother.

"In Grandpa Strawn's sideboard," Irene said.

Jack rose and approached the wooden cabinet that had been handcrafted by his mother's grandfather. She'd discarded the piece when she'd moved in with a new lover saying it didn't go with his contemporary decor. Typical of her not to cherish things that had real meaning.

He poured himself an inch of straight whiskey and returned to the table. Might as well get this over with.

"What happened to the little love nest Chuck Wheeler set you up with?"

His mother averted her gaze.

"You know I can ask around," Jack said.

"Not without telling someone you're back in town," his mother spit out.

Jack took a pull on the whiskey and waited her out. A conversation with his mother always went this way. Had since he'd been twelve years old and she'd left his dad for a greener bank account.

"Janie Sue found out about us."

"You knew she would eventually."

"Yeah, but I didn't expect her to ask Chuck to fire me. And I definitely didn't expect him to."

"You lost your job?"

"Six months ago. That's why I'm homeless. Janie Sue spread it all over town that I was a home wrecker and a bad employee—which you know is not true—and I haven't been able to find another job because of her lies."

"They're not lies. You *are* a home wrecker, or are trying to be."

Irene looked away, and Jack shook his head. But of course this was the story of his mother's turbulent life. And the blowback from her disasters always knocked him off course.

That was the story of *his* life. Or it used to be. He thought he'd moved beyond his mother's gravitational pull.

"Wait," Claudia said. "I'm confused."

He shot her a glance. He'd been wondering when she'd interject. What must she think about his mother? During high school he'd never brought a girlfriend home so he didn't have to explain Irene's peculiar way of seeing things.

"Me, too," Irene muttered.

"Yeah, it's like a soap opera," Jack said. "Hard to keep track of all the players. Bottom line is my mother was screwing the county sheriff, who happened to be both of our bosses once upon a time, his wife found out and good ole Mom got the axe."

"And now she can't get a job because his wife spread rumors?" Disbelief dripped from Claudia's tone.

"I guess you don't know small towns," Irene said.

"I guess not," Claudia agreed.

"I've been making my quilts and cleaning for old lady Smithfield to buy groceries and gas," Irene said. "I'm a month behind on my car payment."

"I'll help with that," Jack said. "But you can't stay here. I built this cabin for one person, not three."

"I can sleep on the couch," Irene said.

"No," Jack said. He took the final swallow of whiskey.

"Jackson, I don't know why you—"

"No!" he shouted, cutting off her protests. He slammed the glass onto the table. He was sick of this. His mother never listened to him, but he needed to make her understand she wasn't bulldozing into his life again. Whether she believed him or not, if the Warriors tracked them to Dunnellon, she'd be in danger. He didn't need that additional complication. She had to go.

The question was where. He closed his eyes, trying to think. Why couldn't he think?

"Why don't we all sleep on it tonight," Claudia said into the sudden silence.

She placed her palm on his forearm and gave a

gentle squeeze. Knowing she wanted his attention, he met her gaze.

"Jack didn't get much rest last night and drove all day," Claudia said. "He needs sleep. Maybe we'll come up with a solution in the morning."

"Why didn't you get any rest?" Irene asked.

Jack focused on his mother again. She stroked the little dog curled up contentedly in her lap, oblivious to the controversy swirling over its furry head. Like mother; like dog.

"He had things to take care of last night." Claudia rose, tugging on his arm. "Come on, Jack. You're going to bed."

Jack stood, and realized Claudia was right about at least one thing: he seriously needed rest. Now that his body had used up the jolt of adrenaline required to deal with the intruder—his own mother—he was drained of energy. For sure the shot of whiskey hadn't helped, but whatever the cause he wasn't thinking clearly. What was he doing sitting here trying to have a logical discussion with his mother? Conversations with her always had the same outcome.

"Irene, do you want to get anything out of Jack's bedroom you'll need tonight?" Claudia asked as she all but pushed him toward bed.

"No, I'm good. I'll just wash up these dishes and crash on the sofa."

Jack almost laughed. Typical. His mother was trying to make them feel guilty.

"Thanks," Claudia said. "We'll talk more in the morning."

"Sure thing, hon."

Jack turned back to his mother. "Where's your phone?"

Irene hesitated, but like a guilty suspect her gaze darted to her huge purple bag where it rested on the recliner.

Jack grabbed the purse and fished out the phone.

"Oh, come on, Jack," Irene said.

"We'll talk more in the morning," Jack said, repeating Claudia's words but in a more ominous tone.

WHEN CLAUDIA CAME to consciousness, it was to the sound of birds singing and chirping joyously, obviously delighted with the new morning.

The next thing she became aware of was heat from the large body of Jackson Richards—in full, glorious view since he wore nothing but his briefs—stretched out next to her on the bed. Stretched out extremely close to her because the bed was full size, not even a queen.

He lay flat on his back breathing so deeply she'd almost call it a snore. She supposed it would be polite to avert her gaze, but didn't want to. What she wanted to do was give in to the visceral pull that urged her to straddle him and let instinct take over.

She rolled onto her side and allowed herself to

take a long, admiring look at his well-toned physique. Her gaze lingered on a scar that slashed across his abdomen in the wrong location for appendicitis. Had her gladiator been in a knife fight?

To maintain that body, he had to work out regularly. Karate couldn't create all those muscles. Or could it? Damn, but this guy was hot. Would he sizzle? She reached out a finger, but stopped herself.

Jack needed sleep. When he'd hit the bed last night, he'd gone out so fast it was as if he'd turned off a switch. She'd worried about awkwardness, but after such a tension-filled day, they hadn't exchanged a word. Although rolling around with Jack on this bed might have been a nice release.

Yeah, very nice.

She closed her eyes. *Stop it. Think about something else.*

She recalled the previous evening, meeting Jack's flamboyant mother and Pookie, her sweet dog. Now someone else had seen her face, someone else to worry about telling the wrong person. Irene had surely complicated things, especially since Jack didn't trust her to keep their presence a secret. He'd gone so far as to confiscate her phone. Claudia stifled a giggle, remembering the outraged expression on Irene's face, but quickly sobered.

Really, her situation wasn't funny at all.

The calls of the birds snagged her attention again, and she looked out the window, trying to find them. Must be hundreds to make that much noise. She didn't see anything flying, but in the brightening morning she saw the emerging shapes of trees.

Careful not to disturb Jack, she climbed out of bed and padded over to the window.

Wow.

An immense green forest, full of towering pines, spread out beyond Jack's backyard. She longed to go outside and breathe in the scent.

A few isolated trees had been left in the yard, and that was where she spotted three feeders, where a variety of quarreling birds jockeyed for prime position at the trough. Irene must keep the feeders full of seed, which explained all the birds clamoring for breakfast. This was February. Wild birds needed help this far north to make it through the winter. The patch of grass between the house and the forest was brown, not green.

It'd been dark when they arrived last night, so she hadn't appreciated the beauty of this setting. Of course she'd been too frightened of the supposed intruder to appreciate anything at the time. But the lure of those woods was almost as strong as the pull of Jack's body.

She'd been cooped up for so long, first inside the walls of Villa Alma and then—even worse—inside a tiny gun locker.

By God, she was going to go outside and breathe.

Claudia grabbed her jeans from the chair where she'd draped them and moved to the door. She'd slept in her T-shirt, and that would have to do for now.

Turning the knob quietly, she slipped out. Jack didn't so much as twitch as she closed the door behind her.

After pulling on the jeans in the small hallway, she moved to the living room where Irene, covered by one of her quilts, snored loudly on the sofa. The window behind her displayed more forest extending in that direction.

Pookie, resting at her owner's feet, raised her furry head to eye Claudia with interest. When Claudia stepped to the back door, Pookie leaped to the carpet and followed.

Claudia stood at the door and peered outside. Pookie looked up and cocked her head as if saying, "Open the door already. I need to pee."

Trying not to wake Irene, Claudia quietly unlatched the door and slid it across the track. Pookie bounded outside, and the birds scattered into the trees with outraged shrieks. After squatting to relieve herself, the dog glanced toward the house, probably wondering why the stupid stranger wasn't joining her in this perfect morning.

Still Claudia hesitated. She was tired of living in the shadows of life, but was it safe for her to venture outside? Jack claimed his cabin sat in the middle of fifty acres, so there was no one to see her. No way could Carlos's henchmen find her this fast. Surely she could enjoy a few brief moments of freedom.

With a deep breath, Claudia stepped over the threshold onto a concrete slab, keeping close to the cabin. The cold morning air bit at her flesh, making her wish she had a fur coat like Pookie, who had scampered to the beginning of the tree line and patrolled the perimeter with her nose to the ground.

Yeah, maybe it was cold out here, but the huge expanse of open space soothed her soul. She felt liberated by all this undeveloped real estate.

She shut the door behind her to preserve the interior heat and took a hesitant step onto the deck, which contained one Adirondack-type chair next to a small round table, a gas grill and a clay chiminea. Hugging herself for warmth, she took a long look around. The huge forest surrounding Jack's cabin appeared to be endless, but she knew of course it wasn't. Couldn't be. But it felt vast, knowing, as if it protected secrets she needed to learn.

To her right, at the far end of the cleared land, she spotted an opening into the trees and suddenly longed to take that path. What would she discover? Maybe later. But not alone. With Jack.

To her left she found a sleek aluminum Airstream travel trailer, a storage shed and a stack of firewood. The image of sitting in front of a roaring fire with Jack popped into her head.

Too bad Irene's presence ruined that idyllic fantasy.

With Pookie too far away to worry about, the birds had returned to the feeders, and flitted back and forth from their breakfast to the trees. She couldn't identify them all, but recognized a brightly colored male cardinal and his mate, a more subtly hued female. Fascinated by their activity, she gradually realized each bird remained aware of Pookie, constantly on alert for the return of the dog or the approach of some other hidden danger, scattering back to higher perches at the slightest noise.

Just like she should remain on alert for Carlos's henchmen.

Maybe she should go inside. Someone could emerge from those woods any second. With a weapon. Or they could be lurking behind the tree line with a scope aimed at her. Feeling as if a long-legged spider crept up her spine, she shivered and pressed her back against the cold wall of the cabin.

What a way to live. Would she react this way for the rest of her life, scattering for cover, hiding from every loud noise like a nervous bird?

She should go inside.

No. A few more minutes. Even though now thoroughly chilled, she refused to step away from this little slice of heaven just yet.

Behind her, the door slid open, and Jack stepped outside carrying two cups of steaming coffee.

"Morning," he said.

"Morning," she replied.

He wore jeans and a bulky sweatshirt, looking comfortable, well rested and sexy as hell even though fully clothed. What was it with her and Jack? He pulled her in like the moon created the tides.

Claudia reached to shut the door for him, and Pookie darted inside, brushing her ankles.

ACCIDENTAL BODYGUARD

Her gaze dropped to the second mug.

"Is that coffee for me?"

He handed her a mug. The brew was black, the way she liked it. She smiled, pleased he'd remembered.

"Thank you, kind sir." She took a swallow, and felt the welcome warmth slide down her throat. Well, well. Her gladiator had many talents, and he definitely knew how to make coffee.

"How did you sleep?" he asked.

"Great." She motioned with her head toward the backyard. "This is beautiful, Jack. I know I shouldn't be out here, but I couldn't help myself."

He nodded and took a swallow of coffee, surveying his property over the rim of the mug. "You're okay for a few minutes."

"This place is perfect, completely isolated. No way anyone could trace us."

He shrugged.

She took another swallow of coffee and asked, "When was the last time you were home?"

"Three years. I'm thankful the forest hasn't overgrown the yard as much as I feared."

"Do you ever hike in those woods?"

"All the time. Or I used to."

"Any wild animals?"

"Deer, 'coons, squirrels." He looked at the feeders and smiled. "Of course birds. The occasional bobcat."

"Bobcat? You mean Florida panther?"

"No, a much smaller wildcat, not much bigger than a house cat."

"But no bears?"

He shot her a glance. "Are you worried about bears?"

"Should I be?"

"There are black bears in the area, but I've never seen them on my property. Mostly over in the Forest."

She must have looked puzzled, because he said, "The Ocala National Forest, which isn't far from here. The Florida Trail runs through there, and a branch off one of my trails hooks up eventually with the Florida Trail."

She knew of the Florida Trail, a public path that led north from Big Cypress in the Everglades all the way to Pensacola. In another life, before she'd met Carlos, she'd loved to hike and had once planned to complete at least part of the Florida Trail. Carlos had convinced her the idea was nutso because of the possibility of a bear attack. He'd shown her gruesome photos of hikers mauled by bears, all part of his psychological warfare against her.

"So bears *could* get here?" she asked.

Jack shook his head. "There's too much development between here and there, areas without cover. Could happen, but I doubt it. Their numbers are small, and they have plenty of food and shelter where they are. No reason to leave. It's a different story down by Orlando."

"Good."

"Do you want to take a hike?"

She bit her lip. "Maybe. Something about those trees—I don't know—draws me in. It's hard to resist."

He stared at her. "I know the feeling."

She held his gaze and he gave her a lopsided grin. So they had something in common besides raw animal lust. She looked away when she realized the direction of her thoughts. *Stop it, Claudia. This is how you get yourself into trouble.*

"Is your mom still asleep?"

He snorted. "She's never been an early riser."

Claudia nodded. She wanted to ask Jack about his history with Irene, but decided to wait, suspecting Irene was likely to reveal her side of the story without much prompting. Then she could clarify the events with Jack and get a more complete picture.

She'd once heard an old wives' tale that if you wanted to know how your future husband would treat you, just observe how he treats his mother. Not that Jack was her future husband. And of course she never even met Carlos's mother.

"Have you decided what to do about her?"

His face tightened, but he didn't reply, which was her answer.

"Do you believe she has no place to go?"

"Sounds like her normal pattern."

"And if you kick her out, she's likely to tell all of Dunnellon we're here?"

"I've never been able to stop her from doing what she wants."

"I have an idea," Claudia said.

"What?"

She pointed to the Airstream next to the shed. "Is that trailer functional?"

"It was three years ago. That's my mobile hunting lodge."

"Why not let her move in there?"

He narrowed his eyes, considering.

"She'd be out of your hair most of the time, but you could still keep an eye on her."

"I don't want to keep an eye on her."

"Do you want her on the sofa every night?"

Jack turned to face her. "I want her as far away from here as possible."

She met his gaze again. "You're that mad at her?"

"I am, yes, but that's not the reason." He glanced back toward the house and lowered his voice. "Remember who we're hiding from, Claudia. If your ex's thugs do show up here, everyone near you will be in danger. I won't be able to protect you both."

JACK IGNORED A twinge of guilt at the stricken look on Claudia's face. He'd just thrown her situation in her face, but it couldn't be helped. She'd relaxed in this bucolic setting, maybe too much, and she needed to stay on her guard. She seemed more worried about the unlikely possibility of a wild animal attack than the Warriors.

If it came right down to it, who would he save? His mother or Claudia?

That was a choice he didn't want to make. Another reason why Irene should go.

But Claudia's idea was a good one. He'd load his mom in the Airstream, hitch up the old trailer to his vehicle and drive her over to the state park where he'd pay for a hookup for three weeks. Too bad she'd hate the idea of living in a trailer.

He'd decide what to do with her after that when the time came. Right now he needed to focus on keeping Claudia alive to testify.

The real question was whether his mother would keep her mouth shut about him being home. He needed to somehow impress on her the importance of her silence. Yeah, and when had he ever been able to do that?

"One good thing about my mother being here is we have groceries," Jack said. "Are you ready for some breakfast?"

"At least another cup of coffee," Claudia said.

Inside the cabin, his mother had managed to procure her own coffee and return to the sofa to nurse it. She'd positioned herself in front of the window so she could see out front with her dog at her feet.

"Morning," she called out as they entered.

Jack noted she'd combed her hair and draped herself in an elegant satiny robe. She'd even put on lipstick, which surprised him. She'd never been much of a morning person.

"Good morning, Irene," Claudia said. "How was the couch?"

"Not too bad. Now that you're here, Jack, I hope you're going to arrange for some sort of television reception. I sure miss my *Good Morning America*."

"Not going to happen," Jack said.

"And why not?"

"We don't want anyone to know we're here," Claudia said, stepping toward the couch. "Remember?"

"Oh, poo. They'll think it's just for me."

Jack poured himself and Claudia another cup of coffee and moved into the living room. "There's a television in the Airstream."

"But is there service?"

Before Jack could answer, his attention was caught by the unmistakable sound of tires crunching the gravel on his road. The dog heard it, too, because she placed her paws on the back of the couch, looked out the window and emitted a low growl.

CHAPTER THIRTEEN

"WHAT THE HELL?"

Jack handed Claudia her mug and moved closer to the window to get a better look. Because of the rise of his land, he couldn't see whatever vehicle approached, but dust billowed into the air signaling something was definitely coming.

No one ever came out here.

He shot his mother a glance. She'd placed her coffee on the windowsill and leaned forward. Peering down the driveway, one hand smoothed her hair, one hand clutched her robe.

"You expecting company?" Jack demanded.

"Maybe," she said.

"Who?" he demanded.

"Chuck sometimes comes out in the mornings on the way in to work."

"I thought you two broke up."

"I never said that. We just have to be more discreet now because of Janie Sue."

Jack stared at his mother for a long moment, trying to wrap his head around this new development. Even for his mother, this was unbelievable. So Chuck had evicted his mom, fired her and now used this cabin to continue screwing her.

A black F-250 pickup truck crested the hill, and its hood emerged from the swirling dust.

Claudia moved beside Jack. "Chuck is the sheriff, right? Your old boss?"

"Right," Jack said.

"Do you trust him?" Claudia asked.

"I used to," Jack said.

The truck braked to a stop in the driveway.

Jack considered his options. What a mess his mother had made of his plan to protect Claudia.

"Should I hide in the bedroom?" Claudia asked.

"Yeah, why don't you do that," Jack said as a tall, powerful figure jumped down from the huge pickup. "I don't want him to know you're here."

"Got it. *Please* don't tell him," Claudia said to Irene, and scurried down the hallway.

Chuck removed his hat, tossed it in the front seat and slammed the truck door. As he had for over twenty years, he wore the tan uniform of the Marion County Sheriff's Department, complete with personalized Glock and handcuffs on his hip. His pant creases still came to a point crisp enough to cause damage to careless small children. Maybe he'd packed on a pound or two in his belly and his graying hair had thinned a bit, but he still looked damn good for a man bucking sixty.

To think he'd once considered Chuck Wheeler a mentor.

Jack jerked open the front door and pointed at his mother. "You wait here."

Chuck halted in his quick steps when he spotted Jack. Surprise flickered over his face, quickly replaced by what Jack could swear was pleasure.

"Well, as I live and breathe," Chuck said, holding out his arm. "Jackson Richards."

Jack clasped his hand and squeezed hard. "Morning, Chuck. Can I help you with something?"

Wheeler darted a look toward the house. Jack almost laughed. The sheriff had just realized he wasn't going to get his morning nooky.

"When did you get here, son?"

"Last night," Jack said.

"You here to stay?"

Jack shrugged as if he wasn't sure. "Just a short visit to check up on things."

"Well, I'm sure your momma is glad about that."

"Oh, she's overjoyed."

Chuck narrowed his eyes. "I hope you're treating your mother with the respect she deserves."

"About as much respect as you do," Jack said.

The sheriff's mouth tightened, as if he'd tasted something bitter. "Come on now, Jack. You know how I feel about your momma."

"Yeah, I get it, Chuck. I guess that's why you fired her and left her homeless."

"Hey. I don't know what Irene told you, but I did not have a choice."

"We all have choices, Sheriff. Always."

"There's no need for this kind of talk, son."

"I'm not your son."

Chuck stood up straighter, as if Jack had just landed a punch. Good, Jack thought. He won't come back. *At least not while I'm here.*

"Now, is there anything else I can do for you?" Jack asked, folding his arms. "Or have we about covered it?"

The sheriff gave him a long, assessing look and said, "I guess we're done. Tell your momma I stopped by."

"Yeah, I'll do that," Jack said.

Wheeler stomped back to his fancy truck, did a one-eighty and drove away, leaving clouds of dust in his wake. Jack stared after him for a long moment, hoping the unpleasant scene would keep Chuck away from his mother. If they didn't see each other, there was a better chance his mother wouldn't reveal Claudia's presence.

But if he knew those two lovebirds—and did he ever—their separation wouldn't last. His mother would never stop praying for the day Chuck left his wife, although that would never happen. Why couldn't she see that? Damn, but she was the oldest cliché in the book. He remembered when he'd first learned of their affair, the crude jokes of his fellow deputies, his mother's lack of remorse in the face of his humiliation.

The fact that she'd continue their tryst in his home after all that had happened three years ago—Jack turned back to the house. No sense in rehashing old news. His mother would never change, but he couldn't help but wonder just exactly who had tipped off Janie Sue.

He wouldn't put it past Irene to tell Janie Sue herself to force Chuck to make a decision. If so, that brilliant ploy backfired and somehow, once again, he suffered the consequences.

Inside the house, Irene remained on the sofa with a hard look on her face. She glared at him with furious eyes. She'd heard his conversation with Chuck.

"Thanks a whole hell of a lot, Jack."

Jack executed a crisp salute. "You're welcome."

He continued down the hall to the bedroom and knocked. "You can come out now," he told Claudia.

She opened the door holding a spiral-bound notebook against her chest. She'd made the bed, and her Glock lay on the comforter. One thing about Claudia, she liked to be prepared.

"Is he gone?" she asked.

"Yeah. Come on. Let's have some breakfast."

"I'll be right there."

CLAUDIA STUFFED HER journal back inside her duffel bag, hiding it beneath clothing, and followed Jack. The sheriff's unexpected arrival had catapulted her back into terror, and she'd decided to calm herself by entering the latest events into her journal. But Jack had sent the man away so fast, she had barely written a word.

"How did you get rid of him so quick?" she asked when they'd entered the living room.

"By insulting him," Irene stated, coming to her feet.

"They're not insults if they're the truth," Jack said.

"Why did you do that, Jack?" Irene demanded.

"Because I wanted him to leave."

"Now he won't come back."

"That was the idea."

"You had no right," Irene said, placing her hands on her hips. "This is *my* life."

"And this is my house."

Claudia watched mother and son hurl angry, hurtful words at each other with a growing sense of unease. This was not how family treated each other—at least not her family, so to her this behavior was beyond weird. She couldn't fathom any of her siblings fighting with her parents in such a manner. She wanted to put her hands into a T again and call time-out.

Pookie didn't like the conflict much, either, as she began to issue little hiccup-like barks.

Irene snatched her dog from the sofa and shushed her. The dog licked her master's face.

"You know how much I love Chuck," Irene said.

"But he's married, Mother."

The two glared at each other until Irene grabbed her purse and marched toward the back door still holding Pookie in her arms. "Excuse me," she said with dignity. "I need a cigarette."

Jack stepped out of her way.

"Welcome to my world," Irene told Claudia when she moved past.

Claudia didn't reply, but was surprised to note a glimmer of tears in Irene's eyes.

"Damn her," Jack muttered. He grabbed a jacket from a hook by the front door and slammed out, leaving Claudia alone in the house.

Well. Claudia took a deep breath. A morning that had started out so peacefully had certainly turned poisonous. Villa Alma might have been boring, but at least it was calm. Most of the time.

Shouldering on the jacket, Jack disappeared down a path that led into the forest. So much for her breakfast. Was he checking the perimeter or escaping from his mother? She wondered how long he'd be gone.

Claudia slid open the back door. Irene sat in the plastic Adirondack chair drawing so hard on a cigarette it appeared as if she was mad at the tobacco. She turned her head away to blow out smoke, and gave a half smile.

"Sorry about all that." Irene plunged the cigarette into an ashtray and ground it out. Claudia couldn't help but think Irene was using the butt as a substitute for Jack's head.

"Come on," Irene said. "Let's go to the shed and get you a place to rest your bones."

Irene slid open the cabin's door, reached inside and returned with a key ring. Claudia followed Irene to a wooden storage shed that looked handmade, probably by Jack. She inserted the key in a padlock and turned, then opened the shed door to reveal a variety of objects Claudia assumed Jack had stashed in here when he left three years ago, including garden tools, a riding lawn mower and three stacked plastic chairs that matched the one on the deck.

She and Irene each took the arm of one and marched back up the small rise to the deck. Irene didn't speak on the way, probably because she was having too much trouble breathing. Claudia knew it was none of her business, but the nurse in her couldn't help but think Jack's mom needed to quit smoking before it was too late. Maybe it already was.

When they dropped the chair, Claudia said, "Thanks. We should get one for Jack, too, while we're at it."

Irene hesitated so long Claudia thought she would refuse, but finally said, "I suppose."

When they'd returned with a second chair, Irene lit another cigarette and collapsed in her seat. Claudia went back inside to warm her coffee. Returning outside, she took a seat upwind of Irene's smoke and another long look at the surrounding forest.

"This is beautiful," Claudia said to break the awkward silence. "I've lived my whole life in Miami, and we don't have trees like this anymore. Or not very many of them, anyway."

"So you're a Miami gal?" Irene asked.

Claudia held up her mug. "Born and raised."

"I was born in Ocala."

"Was Jack born here, too?"

After a drag on her smoke, Irene nodded. "I know I'm not supposed to ask any questions about what you're doing here, but is it just work or are you and my son, you know, involved?"

Heat rushed into Claudia's face as she remembered just how involved they'd almost become two nights ago. Was she really having this conversation with Jack's mother?

Irene laughed softly. "Honey, I haven't seen a blush like that in years. You don't have to say a thing."

"It's complicated," Claudia said.

"Ain't it always," Irene muttered.

"Amen, sister." Claudia and Irene clinked mugs, and Claudia decided to let Irene think what she wanted about her relationship with Jack.

"What about you and Sheriff Wheeler?"

"Chuck loves me."

"You're sure?"

"I'm sure, and he's everything to me. I love that man too much."

Claudia nodded. That much she'd figured out. "But I'm not sure I could forgive a man who fired me and threw me out of my home."

"Yeah, you'd think not," Irene agreed. "But he didn't have a choice. His wife threatened to make political trouble."

"What kind of political trouble?"

"Being sheriff is an elected position, and it's real important to Chuck."

Claudia nodded, but didn't verbalize the thoughts swirling in her head. He might love Jack's mom, but the sheriff's career was more important than the woman he professed to love. Just like Carlos's hate was more important than his supposed love for her.

"I know what you're thinking," Irene said. "You're worried about his wife."

Claudia remained silent. That wasn't what she was thinking at all, but Irene didn't know how similar their situations were. In a bizarre convoluted way, they'd both been betrayed by men they loved. Or thought they loved.

"Well, don't you worry your pretty head about Janie Sue," Irene continued. "The woman is a cold-hearted bitch who only wants to play tennis. She does not care one thing about her husband's happiness."

Claudia took a deep breath. She ought to keep her mouth shut, but she couldn't. She had to say it.

"Isn't that what married men always tell their mistresses?"

"So you figure he's just stringing me along?" Irene asked, seeming not to take offense. "But why? And at my age? Look at me. I sure don't look anything like you anymore, honey, and Chuck is one fine-looking man."

"You deserve better," Claudia stated. "Are you happy to let things stay as they are?"

"Not happy, no." Irene ground out her cigarette. "But he'll retire in a few years and then we can be together. I've just got to figure out how I'm going to live until then. Jack coming home kinda ruined my plan."

Claudia buried her face in her coffee mug. She hoped she never became so dependent on a man that she'd just tread water waiting for him to do something. Her philosophy—partly learned from her ex— was to depend on no one but yourself. Never trust anyone else to steer your life.

Yeah, and look at the pitiful mess you've got yourself into, Ms. Claudia. Hardly Ms. Independent.

"So why are you and Jack so mad at each other?" Claudia asked. Time to unearth what she really wanted to learn. "It has to be more than you dating his married boss."

A strange look passed over Irene's face, and she gazed out into the trees. "Not my finest hour," she said with a sigh. "You know what. We need something to eat. Let's go scramble some eggs."

WHEN JACK REACHED the clearing for his cabin an hour later, he found Claudia out on the deck scribbling so intently in a spiral-bound notebook that she didn't notice his return. Wearing a bulky sweatshirt, she sat cross-legged in a chair, her thick dark hair all but obscuring her face as she bent over her work.

Unexpectedly stirred by the sight, he watched her for a moment from the edge of the woods. For a woman who yesterday had been obsessively paranoid about leaving the confines of Villa Alma, Claudia seemed a little too comfortable out in the open. She'd make an easy target right now. A skilled sniper could take a bead on her from the camouflage of the trees and plant a bullet in her brain, but she sat oblivious to anything but whatever she was writing.

Did that careless behavior mean anything? If so, what?

He wanted her. More than he'd ever wanted another woman. If he was honest with himself, part of the reason he was angry with his mother was because her presence forced him to sleep in the same bed with Claudia. How was he supposed to resist her?

But with his mother in the small cabin, it would be all but impossible to explore Claudia's lush body. He was in for weeks of pure torture if he didn't move Irene.

Just who was this woman who had entered his life and forced him to deal with his mom again? Lola had confirmed Claudia's name on the Romero witness list, along with her journal, so she'd told him the truth about that. But she'd been lying to him from the moment he met her.

She could still be lying to him. Maybe she'd been a terrorist herself, although that didn't fit what he knew of her personality. That's why he needed to remain professional. He had to stay on top of his game and prepare for any eventuality.

Which meant no sex with Claudia, much as he might want it. Until he could make arrangements for his mom, he'd take the couch and let the women have the bed.

Someone had been busy while he'd been on his recon mission, as a couple of chairs had been re-located from the shed. Surprisingly, Pookie lay at Claudia's feet on the concrete. When Jack took a step into the clearing, the dog raised her head and issued a bark that sounded more like a hiccup.

Claudia looked up, spotted him and gifted him with one of her stunning smiles, which loosened the tension churning in his gut.

"I was getting worried about you," she said as he approached. She clipped her pen to the page and shut the book.

She ought to be worried about her own safety.

"I needed to blow off some steam," he said.

"Feel better now?"

"Not really."

"Would food help? We ate, but made you some eggs and grits. I can warm them up and make fresh toast."

"You don't have to do that," Jack said.

"I don't mind." Claudia put her notebook on the table. When she rose, he noted she'd tucked her Glock in the front pocket of her sweatshirt. At least she hadn't totally let down her guard.

"Do you want coffee?" she asked.

"Yeah, that'd be great. Thanks." He pointed to the notebook. "What's that?"

"I've started a new journal," she said as she slid

the door open. Pookie darted inside. "I'm keeping track of everything that's going on."

Jack nodded. His focus still on the book, he sat in a chair on the other side of the table. What exactly had she written? He wouldn't mind knowing her take on his mother. Not to mention her secret opinion of him. But he wouldn't read her journal. That would be an invasion of her privacy.

Not that either of them would have much privacy as long as his mother remained. Yeah, there it was, the million-dollar question. Jack stretched his arms high over his head, relishing the pull on his tight muscles.

What was he going to do about his mother?

He'd been debating exactly that for the last hour as he hiked his property looking for trespassers. Some jerk had abandoned a broken-down ATC near the southeast corner that he'd have to haul off, but other than that, all remained as it had been three years ago.

No sign of any intruders.

He gazed out into the trees, and despite the unsettled questions that trampled through his head, that old sense of peace washed over him. Even while wrestling with the unexpected complications created by his mother, he'd enjoyed surveying his property, revisiting favorite places like that sinkhole in the east. It'd contained at least three feet of water last time he saw it, but today only a small puddle from yesterday's rain. No one had disturbed his gun range. The hawks' nest remained, and it appeared larger, as though still in use by the pair. He'd forgotten how much he loved this land.

No, he hadn't forgotten. He just chose not to think about his losses. No good ever came from dwelling on the past.

Claudia poked her head out. "Breakfast is ready."

"Thanks."

When Jack entered the cabin, he spotted his mother sitting in the recliner with eyeglasses perched on the end of her nose working on a patchwork quilt. She nodded at him, but didn't speak and returned to her needlework.

Claudia sat beside him at the table nursing a mug of coffee. The dog sat at his feet, its little nose in the air, twitching furiously trying to scent his food.

"We're out of eggs," Claudia said. "And there's not much bread left."

"I'll go to the grocery later."

"I can do that for you," his mother offered from the chair.

"No need." He took a huge bite of scrambled eggs, and realized he was famished. "This is delicious," he told Claudia. "Thanks."

"Your mom helped," Claudia said.

Jack flicked a glance to Irene, nodded and continued eating without further comment.

His mother rose, grabbed her cigarettes and exited the sliders. "Come on, Pookie," she said, waiting for the dog to join her.

Pookie stretched back on her haunches, surely a

delaying tactic, and followed without much enthusiasm. She sniffed the floor around the table as she passed, searching for a dropped morsel.

When his mother slid the door shut, Claudia said, "I think you hurt her feelings."

"I doubt it."

"Jack, come on. You two can't keep at each other like this."

"Yeah?" He bit back the impulse to tell Claudia she didn't know the history, to mind her own business. But he didn't want to start up with Claudia, too. And, hell, she had a point. Truth was, he was sick of the tension in the cabin.

"All the bickering is not...healthy," she said.

"Do you think it's good for *your* health to sit outside in the open?" he asked, keeping his voice low so his mother couldn't overhear.

"Oh." Her shoulders slumped. "I thought it would be okay if I had Pookie with me," Claudia said. "She's like an early warning system. And I had my gun."

"I stood at the tree line for almost five minutes and neither of you noticed me. If I'd had a scope, you'd be dead."

She flinched as if he'd truly just shot her. Fear washed through her eyes.

Finished eating, Jack eyed Claudia's reaction. He hated to frighten her, but she'd been lulled into a false sense of security, and he couldn't allow that to happen. Not to either of them.

Or maybe she knew she wasn't in danger from anyone. Could her fear be a giant charade? But to what purpose?

He had some decisions to make.

"I've been cooped up for so long," Claudia said, shooting a wary glance out the sliders. "And it's so beautiful here, magical, like the mysterious woods in fairy tales. When I sit out there for very long, I feel like nothing can possibly go wrong in the world."

He sat back, surprised by her words. He frequently had that experience when he allowed the serenity of the natural world to seep into his bones. She'd had that feeling twenty minutes ago on the deck, and he'd had it in the forest. But Claudia was the first woman to voice a similar perception. Every other woman he'd brought out here developed hives at the thought of coming back.

"I wonder how can there be whacked-out terrorists looking for me in a place as peaceful as this."

"I admit the odds of the Warriors finding you here are low."

"But they could."

"What bothered me more was how oblivious you were to your surroundings. Whatever you were writing must have been good."

Her cheeks colored, and he again wondered about the journal.

"While outside, you need to remain alert for trouble, constantly vigilant."

"I know you're right," she said with a deep sigh. "Maybe I'll stay inside."

"Just a few more weeks," Jack said.

"So much for my hike in the woods."

"Oh, I think we can still manage that."

"But I thought you…"

"I'll be with you, and we'll be loaded for bear," Jack said. "We're going to do a little target practice today."

"Bear?" Claudia stared at him, blue eyes wide. "I thought you said there weren't any bears."

CHAPTER FOURTEEN

CLAUDIA TOOK A DEEP, pine-scented breath as she followed Jack into the canopy of his forest. The light immediately dimmed. She looked up and saw only patches of blue sky between the towering trees overhead. The path was narrow, hardly wide enough for Jack's shoulders; the ground beneath her feet was flat and soft, full of pine needles.

All around her, the ever-present birds chirped, cawed or sang. The only other sound was Jack's boots crunching the trail ahead of her.

She could also hear Jack's voice in her head telling her to remain vigilant, but found herself seduced by the peaceful beauty surrounding her. Mother Nature in all her glory. Funny, she'd always considered Miami the most naturally gorgeous place on Earth, but hiking in this forest tempted her to change that opinion. For one thing, Miami didn't have near enough shade—especially in the summer.

The woods around her didn't appear threatening, but sheltering, as if they afforded protection to its inhabitants. Like those chattering squirrels scampering on the branches overhead, twitching their bushy tails.

She noticed something else, too. After only fifteen minutes her breathing became labored. Some big hiker she was.

Since she normally worked on her feet for twelve hours, she assumed she was in good physical shape. But she couldn't keep up with Jack, and the weight of her pack pulled on her shoulders. He'd found an old backpack for her in the shed, which he'd loaded with ammo, water and their lunch. Plus she wore her gun in a snug shoulder holster, and despite the cool air, the T-shirt beneath her sweatshirt had become damp from sweat.

She needed to peel off the sweatshirt. And she also needed hydration.

She stopped moving and shouldered off her pack, staring at Jack's pack ahead of her on the trail. His was larger and heavier and also contained various provisions, including more ammo. She knew the gun in his shoulder holster was loaded, as was the one in his boot.

But his guns were loaded for target practice. She took a nervous glance around her. At least she hoped they wouldn't meet a bear. Or a terrorist.

"Try to keep up," Jack barked back at her.

"What's the hurry?" she yelled.

He halted and turned. "Sorry. I guess there isn't any big rush. This is just my normal pace."

Claudia took a gulp from her water bottle. "I need a breather."

He nodded, scanned the area for activity and joined her. "I forget your legs aren't as long as mine."

She glanced at his powerful legs, which were, unfortunately, currently covered by faded denim. He did wear a long-sleeved T-shirt that fit snugly, outlining his gladiator muscles.

"Where exactly is this gun range, anyway?" she asked.

"In the center of my property so no stray bullets can injure anyone. It'll take us another fifteen minutes to get there. Correct that." He grinned. "Better make that twenty-five minutes."

She made a face at him. "Smart-ass."

Claudia pulled the sweatshirt over her head and stuffed it in the pack. The cool air on her bare arms revived her. She stretched her arms high over her head, relishing the freedom of movement and the quiet beauty of the trail. When she reached for her pack, Jack grabbed it with one hand to take part of the weight.

After adjusting the load on her back, she set off down the trail, determined to do better. "Try to keep up," she shouted back at him.

Claudia timed it, and in twenty-one minutes they arrived at a clearing maybe a hundred feet by a hundred feet. A small, obviously man-made hill bordered one end of the area. In front of the rise sat a series of wooden posts displaying battered metal targets with the bold outline of a human head and chest. Concentric circles spread out from the center of the silhouette. Multiple bullet holes indicated previous sessions on the range.

So much for the serenity of the forest. They'd come here so she could practice her aim in case she needed to shoot at a real, breathing human being. Before that human could shoot her.

Looking up, she gazed at an intense blue sky overhead. A soft breeze filtered through the trees, rubbing branches together and ruffling her ponytail. As she removed her pack, she noted a couple of fallen trees had been cleared to one side and that the rotting logs had been charred by fire.

"What happened here?" she asked Jack. She had to raise her voice since he had moved off to scout the area beyond the hill to make sure no one was down range.

"Lightning strike," he said. "It's part of the natural cycle of the forest."

She nodded and took a cool, refreshing swig from her water bottle. Lightning from a thunderstorm had felled a tree, which knocked down another one or two, and probably started a small fire. Rain likely put out the flames before they got too intense, but an opening in the canopy had been created, and from the looks of it later enlarged by Jack.

Jack joined her and took off his own pack. "See how the clearing allows the sun to reach the forest floor here? That encourages the growth of new vegetation, and then it's a race to stay taller than your neighbor so it can't block out the sun, which would mean a slow death."

"Sounds like *Wild Kingdom*," Claudia murmured and sat on a fallen log covered by some type of green spongy moss. She sighed, glad to sit down for a bit. Keeping up with Jack had been a challenge, but for some strange reason her pride wouldn't let her fall behind.

"Exactly," Jack said. "Nothing is wasted in the forest. Small animals will set up housekeeping in that log. Lichens are feeding off the rotting wood. Birds, especially woodpeckers, will colonize a dead tree snag. Recycling at its best, all very efficient."

She closed her eyes and lifted her face to the sun, allowing its warmth to push away the chill that had crept in after she quit moving. "Do you think this clearing will fill back in with trees?"

"Eventually, but it will likely take a hundred years, maybe two hundred. But that's only if the land isn't developed first."

She shot him a look. "You're not thinking about selling, are you?"

He shrugged. "The thought crossed my mind. This is the first time I've visited in three years."

"If I owned this land, I could never sell it."

"But remember I don't live here anymore."

Claudia nodded, ridiculously stung at her mental image of this idyllic setting paved over with slabs of concrete and supporting steel.

After a long drink from his water bottle, Jack said, "Tell me what you know about guns."

"I know they can kill people."

He nodded. "That's a good start. Have you had any instruction?"

"I took the course you need to get a carry permit in Florida. And I went to the range twice to practice."

"Show me. Take your gun out of the holster."

Claudia unsnapped the holster and withdrew the gun, finding the motion awkward since she usually carried the Glock in her purse. Remembering what the instructor had hammered into her, she kept her finger off the trigger and pointed the barrel down. Maybe more *The Wild Wild West* than *Wild Kingdom*.

"You're holding your weapon as if it were an egg and might break," Jack said. "You're afraid of it, aren't you?"

She met his gaze. "It's loaded."

"A gun won't do you much good if it isn't. You don't like guns, do you?"

"Not really."

"Break your weapon down for me."

She demonstrated her ability to remove the magazine, racked the gun three times and visually checked that there wasn't a round in the chamber. She glanced at Jack, then fired into the ground to make certain. Next she took the gun apart as if she were going to clean it, and reassembled the mechanism.

He scrutinized every movement. Apparently satisfied she understood how the gun worked, he asked, "Are you ready for some target practice?"

"I guess."

Jack grabbed his pack and moved them to about twenty-five yards from the targets. He produced ear and eye protection for them both.

"Aim for the center mass of the target on the left. I want to watch you."

Telling herself she was here to learn, Claudia spread her feet and faced the target. She took a two-handed grip, making sure her fingers were clear of the slide, and raised the gun. Holding her arms steady, she aligned the front and rear sights, focused on the front one, positioning it in the center of the target's chest, allowing the rear sight to remain fuzzy as she'd been taught. She shot twice, the sound startlingly loud even under the ear protection.

She missed both times.

"Grip the gun tighter," Jack said. "You don't have enough control."

He moved behind her to assist, and she tensed, not at all certain such proximity to Jack's body would help with her control. Recent history had shown quite the opposite.

"Relax." He said the word close enough to her ear that she could feel his breath. "I won't bite."

She willed herself to ignore his warmth and how good he smelled as he extended his arms forward to realign her grip on the gun. Pulling his hands back, he touched her arms. "Straighten your elbows."

Claudia tightened the muscles in her arms. *Concentrate on the target—not Jack.*

"Good," he said. "Try it again."

She fired three more times, and hit the target once.

"Better," he said. "Pull the trigger more evenly."

Jack turned out to be a patient teacher. He helped her with her stance, explained how the muzzle would rise each time she fired and how to correct for that motion. Occasionally, he demonstrated lessons by taking shots himself, always hitting the target right where he wanted, but she sensed he was trying to help her, not showing off.

But of course Jack never felt the need to prove himself, wouldn't understand how she'd struggled to maintain his pace on the hike.

"Your grip, your stance and your trigger pull all affect your aim," he told her. "Time the shot with your breath, pulling on the exhale. That's the steadiest part of the cycle."

She looked back at him. "I won't have time to wait for an exhale if Carlos finds me."

"But by then you'll have built muscle memory and you'll be more accurate on a regular basis."

On the fourth magazine, she hit the target every time. Not the center, but each loud "pling" against the metal told her she'd made contact.

"Good job," Jack said.

Rather pleased with herself, she lowered the Glock, which had become heavier as the morning progressed.

He high-fived her left hand, seeming genuinely pleased by her improvement, and removed his earpieces. "Your muscles are fatigued by now."

She took off her own ear protection, let them dangle around her neck and rotated her shoulders. Definitely sore, but she didn't want to quit. Not when she was actually making progress. "Yeah, but I'm okay."

"No. That's enough for today."

She nodded, accepting he was right, and removed the clear goggles.

"Muscle memory is what'll make you a good shot," he told her again.

She grinned, thinking of an old cliché. "Practice makes perfect?"

"You got it. Won't happen in one day. Come on. Let's eat before we go back to the house." Jack snatched his pack from the ground and strode back to the log she'd rested on earlier.

So they were going to have a picnic. A week ago if someone had told her she'd dine alfresco out in the middle of piney woods with Jackson Richards, security director extraordinaire, she'd have choked.

She watched his easy, confident strides and shook her head at how much she enjoyed the sight. God, but Jack was easy on the eyes, all rugged and masculine. She might as well quit worrying about her reaction to him. The way he made her feel—well, it just *was*, and she couldn't do anything about it.

She'd be fine as long as she remembered to keep her hands off him.

After loading another clip so she'd be ready in case of attack, she placed the gun in her holster. She'd clean the Glock when they returned to the cabin.

For sure Jack's mood had improved since this morning. Was it the shooting? Firing round after round was oddly stress-relieving. Not to mention empowering. Or maybe he liked teaching. Some people were natural-born educators, although she wasn't one of them. Or was it being away from civilization out in the center of his forest?

Most likely his mood had everything to do with the fact that they'd left Irene in the cabin.

Claudia still needed to learn the reason why mother and son constantly sniped at each other.

She'd been surprised when Irene handed her four carefully wrapped sandwiches as they'd set out for the woods just before 11:00 a.m.

"Here," she'd said. "If I know my son, he'll starve you to death."

"What is it?" Jack had asked suspiciously.

"Peanut butter and strawberry jam on whole grain bread."

Claudia had shot Jack a look and grabbed their lunch. "Sounds delicious. Thanks."

Now she joined Jack on the log, removed the sandwiches from her pack and handed him one.

"You made good progress today," he said, and took a huge bite.

"Because of you. Thanks for the lessons."

He nodded and ate without speaking. Peace had returned to the clearing, and she could again hear the wind rustling through the trees overhead. When the shooting started, all birds had fled, but their cheerful chirps now gradually returned.

"Making us lunch was sweet of your mom, don't you think?" she prompted to get a conversation started.

Jack grunted and took a bite.

She wished she knew what he was thinking.

Chewing thick homemade bread generously slathered with creamy spread, she silently blessed whoever had come up with this combination. Peanut butter and jelly had to be the most delicious food ever. Or maybe she was just hungry. Since learning Carlos had tracked her to Collins Island, she could barely keep anything down. Her appetite had definitely returned.

"Jack," she said.

"What?" He swallowed the last of his sandwich and reached for another.

"Thank you for bringing me here," she said softly.

She could tell her words surprised him by the way he paused. Their gazes met and held.

"I can't tell you how grateful I am for all your help," she said.

A soft light came into his green eyes. "You are very welcome, Claudia."

"I know you didn't expect your mom to be here."

He snorted and opened the second sandwich. "That's for sure."

"She kind of spoiled your plan, huh?"

"In more ways than one."

What did he mean by that comment? "She could find her cell phone and make a call while we're gone."

"I've got all the phones with me, but I've been watching for smoke signals."

Claudia laughed. "I hope not. She might burn down the cabin."

"She might do that anyway with all her cancer sticks."

"She needs to quit smoking."

"She needs to do a lot of things."

"Are you going to let her stay?"

Jack heaved a frustrated sigh. "I don't know. The thing is, if the Warriors do find us—and I'm not saying they will, I don't expect them to—she'll be in danger, too. I may be furious with her, but I don't want her harmed."

"She's your mom."

"Yeah, so she says," he said, but his words held a touch of tenderness.

"And that's why you sent away the sheriff," she said, relieved that he actually did love his mother. She'd known he had to, but Jack could be stubborn.

She ought to remember that. "You don't think he's good for her."

"There's more to it than that."

"What?"

"Let's just say my mother is a liar and leave it at that."

"It can't be just that she's having an affair with a married man."

"It's not."

"You don't want to talk about it?"

"Not really."

Those two words sounded so final, Claudia decided not to push. Gazing out into the trees, she said, "I wish I could talk to my mother."

"You talked to her two days ago."

"For about ten seconds. I hate that I'm putting my parents through this nightmare."

"It will all be over soon, Claudia."

"Will it? Will it really? Let's say Carlos is convicted thanks to my testimony and sent away for the rest of his life. That's great. Wonderful. But do you think his followers will just forget about me? Will Carlos, rotting in prison?"

Jack narrowed his eyes. "So you're worried about retribution?" he asked.

"Carlos will have a lot of time to think about who put him behind bars." She closed her eyes, picturing her ex festering in a prison cell, cursing her with his every breath. "God, he'll hate me."

"And you think the Warriors might still look for

you, wanting revenge for their fallen leader," Jack continued.

"Maybe," she said. "What if he retains control of the group from prison and continues directing their activities?"

"Believe me, he'll have a lot more to worry about than you," Jack said. "Prison is not a fun place. And the group could fall apart without his guidance."

"One can hope," Claudia murmured.

"Or the Warriors could turn on their fallen leader. They might worry Romero could give them up for a lighter sentence or cushier treatment, and he damn well might. It happens all the time."

Claudia shook her head. "Carlos will never turn on his followers. They were always more important to him than me."

"Men like Romero gather disciples for their own selfish purposes. It gives them a feeling of power, but they aren't usually loyal when their needs change."

"Whatever happens, this nightmare won't be over as soon as I testify," she said. "I'll be looking over my shoulder for the rest of my life."

CHAPTER FIFTEEN

JACK COULD HEAR the damn dog yapping when he and Claudia were a quarter mile from home. What was wrong with the mutt? Not liking the frantic—no—desperate sound of those barks, he picked up his pace.

Had something happened in the cabin? Was his mom in danger?

For all his assurances to Claudia that no one could track them here, had the Warriors arrived at the cabin in his absence?

He glanced back to Claudia.

She nodded. "I hear it, too. Go on."

Jack broke into a jog. When he reached his backyard, he dropped his pack. He remained at the tree line, observing the roof of his home. Nothing looked out of place. He'd built the cabin on a rise, but couldn't yet see the dog. Pookie continued to bark, obviously outside.

He removed his primary weapon, aiming the barrel at the brown grass.

Staying out of sight, Jack jogged the tree line to the front of the cabin to check for vehicles. None.

But someone could have left their car by the highway and hiked up his private driveway.

He returned to the rear and dashed to the cover of a closer tree. He had eyes on Pookie now. The dog paced the perimeter of the concrete slab, still barking. No sight of his mom or any intruders. Pookie began to issue a pitiful whine, almost a howl.

Why didn't his mom shut the mutt up?

She would if she could.

Behind him, he heard Claudia arrive at the edge of the trees. He motioned for her to stay put. She nodded and faded back into the forest.

Tensed for gunfire, he sprinted from tree to tree, moving closer to the deck. He wanted to keep the advantage of surprise.

He darted a quick look, then pulled back. Whining pitifully, the mutt nosed a lump on the deck.

Jack looked again and focused on the lump. What the hell?

His mother.

Jack cursed and ran to the deck. His mother was down. Her eyes were closed. She didn't respond to his approach.

He knelt beside her. Holstering his weapon, he searched for blood, saw none.

She lay on her right side, right arm flung over her head. He felt for a pulse on her throat, relieved to see her chest move. She was alive. Her heartbeat sounded strong, steady.

What happened?

A broken plate lay on the slab next to her, a peanut butter sandwich scattered beside it. The small round table had been knocked over. The ashtray and its cigarette butts had spilled over the concrete, as well as a mug of either coffee or hot tea.

Jack turned his head and yelled, "Claudia. Get up here." She was a nurse. She'd know what to do.

"Mom," Jack said. "Can you hear me?"

No response.

She'd fallen. How badly was she hurt? What if she died? His mother couldn't die. His last words to her had been sarcastic and mean.

"Mom," Jack said again, wanting to shake her, knowing that wasn't a good idea. He felt helpless, a new experience for him. Where was Claudia?

"Wake up, Mom."

She moaned, and rotated her neck as Claudia arrived.

Claudia knelt beside him and felt for a pulse on Irene's neck. "Did she fall?"

"Looks like it," Jack said.

"Irene," Claudia said in a calm voice. "Wake up."

His mom moaned again and blinked her eyes open. She blinked again and raised her head. "What—what happened?" She pushed her hands on the deck and struggled to rise.

"Don't move," Claudia instructed.

"Whatever you say." His mother lowered her head and closed her eyes again.

"Tell me where you hurt," Claudia said.

"Oh, shit," Irene said on a ragged breath.

Claudia brushed hair out of his mom's face and said again firmly, "Where do you hurt, Irene?"

"All over."

"Was she unconscious when you arrived?" Claudia asked Jack.

"She didn't respond when I spoke to her."

Claudia removed her sweatshirt and placed it over Irene's legs. "Get your flashlight and some blankets. I want to keep her warm in case she goes into shock."

Grateful for Claudia's calm, take-charge manner, Jack hurried into the house and returned with two thick quilts and a flashlight.

"What hit the ground first?" Claudia asked as she gently tucked the blankets around his mom's legs.

"My right hip, I think." Irene lifted her hand and touched a discolored bump on her forehead. "Ouch."

Jack noted the skin was abraded, beginning to seep a little blood.

"I flung out my arms to break my fall," she said. "My lunch went flying, and my head hit that stupid table."

"Hold still a minute," Claudia said. She switched on the light and flashed it in his mother's eyes.

"Hey." His mom closed her eyes and turned away.

"Open your eyes, Irene. I need to check for something."

When she complied, Claudia flashed each pupil, looking for signs of a concussion. He glared at the bump on his mom's forehead. Could her brain be swelling inside that thick skull?

Claudia sat back, obviously thinking, also staring at his mom's wound.

"Do you even know what you're doing?" Irene asked.

"I'm a registered nurse," Claudia said. "I work with trauma all the time."

"Yeah?" Irene shot Jack a look.

His mother's suspicion made Jack's anxiety crank down a notch. She was sounding more like herself every second.

"Have you been experiencing any dizziness lately?" Claudia asked. She picked up Irene's wrist and looked at her watch.

"No more than normal," Irene said.

"What does that mean?" Jack demanded.

"It means sometimes when I get up too quick, I feel a touch light-headed. Been that way most of my life."

"Sounds like low blood pressure," Claudia said, releasing Irene's hand. "Pulse is normal. That's good. Does the vertigo pass quickly?"

"Vertigo?"

"The dizziness when you get up too fast."

"Yeah. I sit back down, take a few breaths and I'm fine."

"Probably caused by smoking too much," Jack said.

"Can you identify where the worst pain is now?" Claudia asked.

"Yeah." Irene swallowed hard. "My left foot throbs something awful."

"Uncover her feet, Jack."

Jack pulled away the quilt, and sucked in a breath when he saw the disfigured left ankle, swollen to twice the normal size. His mom had lost her right shoe, but the left foot remained encased in a glittery torture device with a towering stiletto heel. Shaking his head, he gently removed the shoe. Why would she wear that? For Chuck Wheeler.

"See that?" he asked Claudia.

"Yeah, I see it. Can you wiggle your toes?" Claudia asked.

Irene grimaced as her toes moved. "Please don't ask me to rotate my ankle because that isn't happening."

"I'll get some ice," Jack said.

When he returned with an ice pack, Claudia had gotten his mother into a chair with her injured foot elevated on the table. The mutt had curled up in her lap.

"Any pain during that transition?" Claudia asked.

"Just in my ankle."

"How does your hip feel?"

"There's nothing wrong with my hip," Irene insisted.

"Any nausea?"

"No. And how do I even know you're a nurse?"

"You can take my word for it," Jack said, placing the ice over her ankle.

When the cold touched her flesh, his mother cursed and made a face. But he couldn't hold on to any anger. He was too relieved that she was alive and able to react.

"And why should I take your word for it?" his mom demanded.

"Because I looked her up on the internet," Jack replied.

"Do you want to see my license?" Claudia asked. "I have ID in my purse."

"Maybe," Irene grumbled.

"Do you think she needs to go to the emergency room?" Jack asked. "That's a nasty bump on her forehead."

Claudia folded her arms and stared down at her patient. "An external bump isn't always a sign of an internal bleed. I don't see any signs of a concussion. But she ought to get an X-ray of that foot, and then the ER staff can assess for head trauma."

"Agreed," Jack said.

"Do you think an ambulance will come out this far?"

Jack shook his head. It would be quicker if he took Mom himself, and why take the chance that the paramedics would see Claudia.

"I'll drive her in."

"I don't have insurance," Irene announced. "Lost it when I got fired."

"Don't worry about it, Mom," Jack said. "I'll take care of it."

"Thanks, son. You know I'll pay you back when I get on my feet again."

Jack motioned for Claudia to follow him inside out of his mother's earshot.

"Stay inside the house while I'm gone," he told her.

Claudia nodded. "I'll clean the Glock, reload it and keep it by my side."

"Don't open the door for anyone. Pretend you're at Villa Alma." He handed her his mother's phone. "Call me if you need me."

"Thanks." Claudia heaved a sigh. "I'll be fine."

"I know you will." Jack reached out and cupped her cheek. "Hey, thanks for keeping my mom—and me—calm."

Claudia placed her hand over his and met his gaze, her eyes soft. "You're welcome."

He pulled her into an embrace and hugged tight. Holding her close felt good. "I can't send Irene away when she can't even walk."

"Of course you can't."

CLAUDIA RETURNED HIS HUG, her arms barely meeting around his back, and drank in his warmth and strength. Jack had been worried about Irene. That reaction to her accident had been solid proof that he loved his mom, although he might not admit it. Sometimes it takes an emergency for people to realize how they truly feel.

He stepped back, leaving his palms on her shoulders. "We'll figure everything out when I get home."

She nodded, wishing he would kiss her.

"Claudia," Irene yelled from outside. "Could you fix me another sandwich before Jack takes me to town? I never got to eat my lunch."

"We'll stop at the Burger Giant drive-through," Jack yelled back, shaking his head. "Give me strength," he whispered.

Claudia stood on her toes and kissed his cheek. "Hurry back."

Jack couldn't have been more careful with his mom when he loaded her into the passenger seat of his SUV, but she complained every step of the journey.

Claudia watched until the dust from the retreating SUV settled in the driveway, then went out on the deck and cleaned up the mess from Irene's fall. Pookie helped her by gobbling the bread and licking the peanut butter.

Once back in the cabin, she locked all the doors and pulled the drapes, wanting to make it appear as if no one was home.

Next she broke down her gun, cleaned it and then reassembled the parts. She made sure the magazine was full of bullets, then shoved it in with a satisfying click.

After that, the silence in the cabin became deafeningly loud.

Well, good. Lack of noise meant she could easily hear the approach of any intruder.

"We're loaded for bear now," she told Pookie, who cocked her head. Claudia sighed. Maybe she wasn't actually "loaded for bear," which Jack had explained was some sort of colloquial saying used by the old-timers when there were actual bears in the nearby woods, but her gun was ready.

She rose, approached the sliding door, and moved the curtain to take one final peek at the backyard. All clear. Not even any birds at the feeders, which she realized dangled empty of seed. She'd ask Irene where she kept the food and refill them this after-noon.

So now what? She should study, but was too agi-tated from all the excitement, so she decided to catch up in her new journal. She gathered the gun and Irene's phone, and set out for the bedroom. A nap also sounded like a good idea. She'd exhausted her-self this morning with all the hiking and target prac-tice.

As she sat on the bed, Irene's phone warbled, "We've Only Just Begun," a ring tone for true ro-mantics if there ever was one. Claudia checked the caller ID and saw Chuck Wheeler on the readout, no doubt calling to arrange a hookup since the morn-ing plan had failed. She let the call go to voice mail for Irene to hear later.

Claudia stared at the phone as an idea generated. She needed to check in with the US Attorney in charge of Carlos's trial and let him know she was still alive. She'd always intended to call, but hadn't managed to get that done. She'd sent an email the day she went underground, letting him know she planned to disappear, but nothing since. He had to be worried about her and the status of his case.

She trusted Mr. Beauchamps, but didn't know beans about his office staff and who the leak might be. So she wouldn't call now, not in the middle of the day. She'd call him later on his cell And she shouldn't use Irene's phone. It could be traced to Dunnellon. What if Carlos's tentacles reached that deep?

She familiarized herself with Irene's phone and punched in Jack's number. He answered immediately.

"What's wrong?"

"Nothing. Do you think you could pick me up a phone while you're out, one that can't be traced? I need to call the US Attorney and let him know I'm okay."

"Maybe," he said. "That might take some doing. If I can't get one locally, I'll get Lola on it. I need to check in with her anyway and see what's happening on Collins Island."

"Thanks." Before Claudia could disconnect, she heard the roar of an arriving vehicle.

She reached for her gun and folded her fingers around the grip of her newly cleaned and loaded Glock.

Pookie raced down the hall into the front room, barking like a demented demon.

"What's going on?" Jack demanded.

Clutching the weapon and the phone, Claudia dropped to the floor. She crawled to the wall. She didn't dare follow the dog to see who had arrived.

She leaned against the wall next to the window so no one could see her if they came around back and peered inside.

"Someone is here," she whispered into the phone. She drew her legs in close to her body, making herself as small as possible.

Out front, the powerful engine shut down. She heard a vehicle door open and slam shut.

CHAPTER SIXTEEN

"Where are you?" Jack asked.

Claudia pressed the phone hard against her ear. Her pulse pounded so loudly she could barely hear him.

"I'm in the bedroom. I locked all the doors and pulled the curtains."

"Stay there. I'm on my way. Have you got your gun?"

"Yes."

Someone banged on the front door and rotated the knob, which caused the dog to growl. Claudia closed her eyes and held her breath. Jack had been gone nearly an hour. It would take him that long to return. Had Carlos found her? Would she really be able to shoot someone—even in self-defense?

Or would they plant a bomb and blow up the cabin—their usual pattern? *With me and Pookie locked inside.*

"Irene! Baby, it's Chuck. Open up."

"Wait," Claudia whispered to Jack. "It's the sheriff."

"What's he want?"

"He's yelling for your mom."

Jack cursed. "That old bag of wind."

"He called a few minutes ago. He's checking to see if she's home."

Pookie switched from snarling to whining, apparently recognizing the sheriff either by voice or scent. Claudia remained still, her heart beating frantically, although everything else seemed to unfold in slow motion. *Just go away, Mr. Sheriff.*

She listened to his footsteps move to the rear of the house. Sure, this was an officer of the law, and maybe he was even an honest one, but no one else could know she was here. No one. That was the only way to be sure.

"Irene!" Chuck Wheeler knocked on the sliders, calling for his girlfriend again, then moved back to the front, slammed the door to what she assumed was his truck and rumbled away.

"You still there?" she asked Jack.

"Talk to me, Claudia. Tell me what's happening."

She blew out a huge breath. "He's gone. Take care of your mom."

"Are you sure?"

"Yeah, he drove away. You don't need to come home."

When they disconnected, Claudia remained where she was for a few deep breaths. Would she have to live in fear of every unexpected knock on the door for the rest of her life?

When her pulse returned to normal, she moved to the bed and positioned herself against the backboard. She picked up her notebook and flipped to the last entry. Her hand shook as she wrote, forcing her to write slowly as she brought the journal up to date, intending to go all the way through her latest scare with the reappearance of the sheriff.

She'd be lucky if she didn't have a heart attack before this adventure was finally over.

As always, the telling calmed her. While married to Carlos, recording his bizarre activities helped her make sense of what was going on, allowed her to put everything into perspective and face the horrible fact that her husband had become a danger to society. As she wrote about Jack and his mom, she realized the dangers were very different this time.

Oh, she doubted that Irene was a serious threat to society, even if the woman was sheer murder on Jack's mood.

Jack was the risk, and a big one. He might not be a problem for the general populace—in fact the world needed more men with Jack's code of honor—but he posed serious peril to her. The more time she spent around him, the more she liked him, wanted to be with him. Liked him? Yeah, right.

She was in danger of losing herself to him, just like she had with Carlos. She needed to put some distance between her and Jack before she lost her heart. But she couldn't do that. She was trapped.

Like a wild animal in the forest hiding from a predator in their lair.

JACK DIDN'T WANT to be in this overheated hospital room. He didn't want to be sweating and not able to see the outdoors, to breathe fresh air. But they'd rolled his mom off in a wheelchair for X-rays two hours ago, so here he waited. He didn't like waiting.

But no one did, especially not in a hospital. A hospital was full of sick people. And most likely the trip had been unnecessary since the head trauma assessment had proved negative. All that remained was making sure his mom hadn't broken a bone. At least he wasn't listening to her constant chatter. He ought to be grateful for the peace.

Instead he worried about Claudia and what Wheeler had been doing out at the cabin.

But he knew. The sheriff had been looking for his mistress. He probably got worried when he couldn't reach her by phone. Well, too bad, lover boy.

With a snort of disgust, Jack removed his phone and called the Protection Alliance office. He needed to find out what was happening in Miami.

"Security," Lola answered.

"It's Jack."

"Well, well. The Boy Scout."

Jack ignored her. Lola loved to jerk his chain. "What's going on down there? Any more attempts to breach Collins Island?"

"Nothing so far," Lola said. "But we're ready."

"Good," Jack said. What were the Warriors up to? Had they found Claudia's car?

"Brad has settled in nicely as the security chief," Lola said.

Brad was a good man, and Jack relaxed a bit, picturing his colleague relishing the good life. That seemed like another world to him now, something from a long time ago. Had he only left Collins Island yesterday?

"When are you coming back, Jack? I'm already shorthanded, and with you gone..." Lola trailed off, letting Jack imagine how hard she was having to work without him. One of her favorite ploys.

"Sorry, Lola. Things have gotten complicated."

After a long-suffering sigh, she asked, "You're going to stay with your beautiful witness until the trial, aren't you?"

"Maybe. I don't know yet. Like I said, things have—"

"Yeah, yeah—it's complicated. I know."

Jack heard his mother's laughter in the hallway, so maybe she was done with her tests. Time to get out of here.

"Listen, Lola, can you get me a burner phone and ship it up here? You've got the address on file."

"Sure, Jack. I'll take care of it. But just so you know, I'm not happy."

"Yeah, I get that, boss. Later."

"All right, Irene," the female orderly said, pushing his mom into the small room. "Here's your son."

"They say it's just a bad sprain," Irene announced,

waving a sheet of paper. "Here are my discharge instructions."

Before Jack could ask any questions, he heard determined footsteps marching up the hallway.

A female voice said, "Sheriff, wait. You can't—"

Sheriff Wheeler pushed into the examining room. "Irene."

Jack leaped to his feet. Someone from the hospital staff must have alerted Wheeler when Irene showed up at the ER. Everyone in Dunnellon knew about the sheriff's interest in his mom. Nothing like small-town gossip.

"Baby, are you okay?" Wheeler asked. "What happened?"

"Chuck." His mother grinned as if she'd been handed a million bucks. "What are you doing here?"

"This is still my town," Wheeler said, kneeling before Mom's wheelchair.

Jack snorted, thinking Wheeler sounded like a pompous fool.

"And there are *some* people who treat me with respect," the sheriff continued.

Wheeler didn't so much as glance at Jack, but he knew the dig was directed at him.

"What happened to your foot?"

"Oh, you know how clumsy I can be," Irene said. "I fell going out the sliders. Jack brought me to the ER to get checked out."

"Are you okay?"

Irene took the sheriff's hand. "I'm fine now that you're here."

"Why aren't you answering your phone? When Jack wouldn't let me in this morning—"

Wheeler paused and looked around the room, suddenly realizing he had the attention of a rapt audience. He shook his head and rose.

Jack noted it took more time for the sheriff to get back to his feet than it took him to go down. Wheeler might have aged well, but his body was no longer in its prime.

"Could I please have a few minutes alone with Irene?" Wheeler asked, his voice formal.

The orderly hurried out of the room without a word.

Jack crossed his arms and stared at his former boss. "Does your wife know where you are?"

"Come on, Jack," Irene said. "Give us a minute."

Jack glared at her and raised his eyebrows. Would his mother even remember the danger he'd tried to impress upon her? Would she tell her married lover about Claudia just for the fun of it?

"Son," Wheeler said, "I'd appreciate just a moment, and then I'll let you take your momma home."

With her gaze boring into his, Irene nodded almost imperceptibly. Jack hoped it was her way of saying she'd keep her mouth shut. But with Irene, you could never be certain.

Yet what choice did he have at this point? How could he prevent them from talking privately? He couldn't without making a scene.

What decided him was realizing how he'd feel if someone tried to keep him from talking to Claudia if he ever needed to make things right with her.

Yeah, that would be ugly. Maybe violent. And that insight rocked him. He cared too much about Claudia.

"I need to get back to the cabin," Jack said. "So you've got five minutes. I'll be in the hallway."

He closed the door behind him and leaned against the wall. Would Irene tell Wheeler about the lie Claudia had concocted about the security of the US government being at stake? He crossed his legs. Yeah, his mom would say something. She wouldn't be able to help herself. She'd never been able to keep a secret. Never. Spreading gossip was her favorite hobby.

Maybe he ought to just tell Wheeler about Claudia, explain the situation and make the need for silence clear. Chuck Wheeler had been sheriff for decades. He might be a rotten husband, but he'd always been a fine lawman.

What the hell was Wheeler doing here, anyway? He'd made his choice. He'd chosen his wife, which is what all married men did. Did he feel the need to keep Jack's mother on some kind of string? The man needed to leave her alone or she'd never get over him.

The door opened, and Wheeler exited, his face unreadable. He nodded once at Jack, but didn't hang around for a conversation. He stomped down the hallway and didn't look back.

Jack stared after him. Apparently that reunion

hadn't gone precisely the way Sheriff Wheeler had planned. *Well, good for you, Mom.*

When Jack reentered the room, his mother stared at the floor with slumped shoulders, her excited grin replaced by a set jaw. He wanted to ask her what was going on, but had another unexpected realization. His mother's private conversations were none of his business—unless the topic included Claudia. And considering his attitude toward her lover, his mom wasn't likely to be in a sharing mood.

"Are you ready to go?" he asked.

She looked up. Her eyes were dry but sad. She tried to smile. When that failed, she nodded.

Jack moved behind the wheelchair. "You got everything?"

"Don't worry," she said in a tired voice. "I didn't mention Claudia. Chuck doesn't know anything about her."

Jack released the brake on the wheels and pushed. His mother sounded sincere, and he wished he could believe her. Unfortunately, history wouldn't allow him to take that chance with Claudia's life.

He needed to have his own private conversation with Sheriff Wheeler. The sooner, the better.

CLAUDIA MET JACK and his mom at the front door when they returned home from the ER. Wearing a thin smile, Irene hobbled into the house on crutches without speaking, a real switch from the normally talkative woman. Assuming the lack of communication was due to her injured ankle, Claudia decided to have Irene quantify the pain with a number like she did with her patients in the hospital. Doing that sometimes made a patient realize things weren't all that bad.

"Anything broken?" she asked.

"No," Jack said, watching his mom arrange herself on the sofa. "But it's a bad sprain."

Pookie sniffed at the bandages on Irene's foot, sneezed, circled three times and then settled on the cushions beside her master.

Irene would be more comfortable in a bed. Should they let her take the one in the bedroom? But then where would she and Jack sleep? No way could they both fit on the sofa. Claudia's thoughts wandered to the camper, which had to have a bed. But Irene couldn't make it up the steps.

"Did they give you any pain meds?" she asked.

Jack nodded. "I'm going back out now to pick up the prescription."

"I wanted to stop on the way home," Irene said. Her first words.

"And I wanted to make sure Claudia was okay first," Jack replied.

"Why wouldn't Claudia be okay?" Irene asked with a decided edge to her voice. "*She* didn't fall."

Claudia shot Jack a look. Was that the pain talking or had something happened to make Irene more testy than usual?

Jack motioned with his head for them to move outside.

"Oh, that's great," Irene yelled after them. "Real nice, Jack. You can have a private conversation with your girlfriend but I can't have one with Chuck."

"So Chuck showed up at the ER?" Claudia asked when Jack had slid the door shut.

"Yes, and they spoke without me in the room. I don't know what Mother told him, and I need to clarify the situation for him."

"I thought you didn't trust him."

Jack met her gaze and held it. "If Irene told him about you—which she denied—I haven't got much choice. Depending on the results of our conversation, you and I may need to relocate."

Claudia nodded. "So the trip to the pharmacy is just an excuse to go speak to the sheriff."

"Not exactly."

Claudia caught her breath as Jack pulled her in for a quick hug. She all but stumbled into his chest, but didn't care because of the warm glow that started in her belly and spread up her neck to her face. She wrapped her arms around him and buried her face in his neck, allowing herself to enjoy the physical contact. It felt good—too good—to be in Jack's arms.

"I really did want to make sure you were all right," he said softly. "I didn't like leaving you alone."

"Thanks," Claudia said, although she wasn't sure why she was thanking him. For caring about her? For hugging her? And maybe for taking care of his mom.

"Stay inside," he said, stepping back. "I'll be back as soon as I can."

"Do they have pizza in Dunnellon?" Claudia asked.

He raised an eyebrow, his expression so comical it made her laugh.

"We're not that small of a town."

"Assuming you and your mom like pizza, how about picking one up for dinner?"

He nodded. "Good idea. Anything else we need?"

"I made a list."

After Jack roared away in his SUV, once more sending dust swirling into the air, Claudia went to check on Irene. She remained on the sofa with her legs extended and her back propped against multiple pillows. Pookie raised her head as Claudia approached.

"How are you feeling?" Claudia asked.

Irene shrugged. "Jack's gone to get my painkillers?"

"Yes. Are you in a lot of discomfort?"

"They gave me a pill in the ER, but it won't last all night."

"On a scale of one to ten, ten being the worst, what's your pain level?"

"Maybe you are a nurse," Irene grumbled. "That sure sounds like nurse talk."

"I swear I am a registered nurse," Claudia said, raising her hand as if taking an oath. "Although I usually work with children."

"Oh, yeah? Are you and Jack thinking about having kids?"

Claudia opened her mouth to speak, but nothing came out. She blinked. *Kids? Good heavens!*

Realizing she was gaping at Irene, Claudia stood straighter and managed to squeak out, "No."

"Too bad," Irene said with a sigh. "I'd like to be a grandmother. Two."

"You want two grandkids?" Claudia asked.

"No, my pain level is a two."

"Oh. Well, that's pretty good."

Irene glared at her bandaged ankle. "But it'll creep up if Jack doesn't get back quick."

Claudia nodded. "Are you hungry? Jack's bringing dinner, but I could fix you something in the meantime."

"What's he bringing?"

"Pizza. Is that okay?"

Irene smiled. Her first one since returning home. "My boy knows how much I like Gino's pizza. I'll wait." She released a heavy sigh. "Chuck likes anchovies on his. Not that that matters anymore."

Claudia pulled a dining room chair closer to the sofa. "Jack told me the sheriff came to the hospital."

"Yeah." Irene lowered her gaze. "He came to make sure I was okay."

"I guess he got worried. He called earlier and left a voice message."

"He told me. Chuck couldn't understand why I didn't call him back." Irene shook her head. "I always call him back."

"What excuse did you give him?" Claudia held her breath. Would Irene admit she'd told Chuck

Wheeler she couldn't return the call because her son had taken away her phone? If so, that would prompt more questions. Had she made something up or told the truth?

When Irene didn't answer right away, Claudia closed her eyes. Great. A confession was coming, which meant she'd have to find a new burrow to crawl into and hide. She didn't want to leave this cabin.

"I told him what I should have told him three years ago," Irene said. She sucked in a deep, shaky breath. "And now we're finished. For good this time, I imagine."

"Finished?" Claudia opened her eyes and found Irene swiping away tears with an angry motion. "What in heaven's name did you tell him?"

Irene looked down at her hands. "Would you mind getting me a tissue?"

Claudia hurried to the bathroom and returned with a box of Kleenex.

"Thanks." Irene blew her nose with a loud honk.

Claudia waited, but Irene seemed to be having a hard time knowing where or maybe how to start.

"Would you like a beer?" Claudia asked. *Oh, that's a good nurse, Claudia. Ply your patient with drinks to get her talking.*

Irene looked up and nodded. "Hey, that would be great."

Claudia returned from the refrigerator with two beers. Irene popped her can and took a long swallow.

"Aren't you gonna drink?"

Claudia stared at her can. Since Jack wasn't here, she hadn't intended to drink it. But what could she tell Irene? That she needed to stay sharp in case a terrorist showed up? Deciding to nurse the brew, she opened it and took a small sip.

"Did you ever wonder why Jack is so mad at me?" Irene asked. "I mean, it's not normal for a son to treat his momma the way Jack treats me, is it?"

"Not in my family, anyway," Claudia replied. "I figured it had something to do with your—" she searched for the right word, *affair* sounding too harsh "—liaison with the sheriff. You know, because he's married and all."

"Well, yeah, that's part of it. Did you know Jack was a deputy sheriff, worked for Chuck for close to four years?"

Claudia nodded. "Before moving to Miami."

"Did he tell you why he quit?"

"No." Claudia leaned forward. So she was finally going to hear that story.

"Well, it's because of me."

"Because of your relationship with his boss?"

"Because I lied about when some stupid reports were turned in. Now, believe me, I didn't know Jack was the deputy involved until later, or I wouldn't have done it." She shook her head and took a long pull on the beer. "Or maybe I would have."

"Why would Jack quit over late paperwork? Doesn't sound like him."

"Well, I screwed up and was too much of a coward to admit it. One day at work I'd gone outside for a smoke—which I'm not supposed to do except on my break. The reports landed on my desk while I was gone, so I didn't see whose case it was."

Irene closed her eyes, probably remembering, and gave a defeated sigh.

"It was late in the day, and I didn't want to start entering all that in the computer, so I stuck the file in a drawer and forgot all about it. Two days later Chuck comes looking for the paperwork, and I don't know what he's talking about. I insisted I never got any such-and-such file with so-and-so reports. Chuck went ballistic and Jack got a reprimand in his file over the whole mess. I figured it out later."

"So why didn't you just tell the sheriff what happened?"

"I should have done just that, except that meant I'd be the one in trouble with Chuck, and by then we had something going on." She met Claudia's gaze, but quickly looked away. "I didn't want to mess that up."

Claudia stared at Irene in horror. So Irene let Jack take the fall for her mistake, and he refused to rat out his own mother. No wonder Jack was angry at his mom. That was so not how a mother should treat her son.

Irene looked away from Claudia. "Like I said, I didn't know until later it was Jack. He quit and moved away right after that."

"You confessed all this to Sheriff Wheeler today?"

"That, and I also told him I wasn't going to be his second banana anymore." Irene fiddled with the pop-top on the can. "I told him he had to decide between me and Janie Sue, that he couldn't have us both."

"Wow." Claudia took a swallow of beer.

"Yeah, wow."

"How did that feel?"

"Scary." A small smile tugged at Irene's lips. "But you know what—it felt good."

Claudia scooted forward and clinked her can against Irene's. "Good for you."

"I don't know how good it is, but it's done." She rolled her eyes. "And now I'm done with men."

Claudia laughed, remembering those were her exact words to Marsali Winthrop a week ago, but decided not to ask if Irene had decided she liked women better than men. What other words of wisdom had Marsali preached that night?

"Never in your darkest hour think you're done with men," Claudia said. "You just need one that's not a water buffalo."

Irene choked midswallow. "What?"

Claudia shook her head. "There'll be other men for you."

"The thing is, I don't want anyone but Chuck." Irene sighed and looked out the window.

Claudia also looked out at the long gravel driveway and noted how the approach sloped down, away from the house. A vehicle had to get close to be seen, which is why you heard something coming before you saw it.

There was nothing coming right now, but what

if someone showed up? Like the sheriff had earlier today.

She set her beer aside. She'd only taken three swallows, but Jack was right. She'd let her guard down too much. What was it about this cabin?

The sun had begun its descent toward the horizon, and she hoped Jack would return before dark. But that wasn't likely. Even in Florida, dark came early in the winter.

Irene turned back to Claudia. "Are there any more beers in the fridge?"

CHAPTER SEVENTEEN

JACK FOUND CHUCK WHEELER exactly where he knew the sheriff would be—in his Ocala office where the decor hadn't changed in the last three years. Dusty awards and commendations covered the walls. Two worn leather chairs sat before the same heavy oak desk piled high with paper. A police scanner squawked in one corner.

Chuck slumped in the swivel chair behind the desk, obviously deep in thought.

Jack rapped on the door. When Chuck looked up, the expression that crossed his face could only be described as pained.

"How'd you get back here?" Chuck demanded. He sat up straighter, but didn't rise.

"Ralph Munroe was on duty and let me in," Jack said, entering the office. "I need to talk to you."

Chuck stared at him with a hard look. "I know why you're here. Irene told me."

Disappointment shot through Jack sharp as the twist of a knife. He'd expected his mother's betrayal, but couldn't she have kept her mouth shut just once? And why did she have to lie so emphatically to him about her blabbing?

"Exactly what did she tell you?" he asked.

"That she lied about those reports, that you had turned them in on time."

"What reports?"

"Come on, Jack. The Crawley murder three years ago. The reprimand, the reason you quit and moved away."

Jack dropped into one of the leather chairs. "She told you about that *today*?"

"A little too late, I know." Chuck shook his head. "A lot too late. Your momma sure has got some issues."

Stunned into silence, Jack didn't reply.

"She claimed she didn't know it was your paperwork until after. Anyway, I'm sorry, Jack."

Jack nodded.

"But you should have said something, son. You didn't need to resign over something that wasn't your fault."

Jack cleared his throat. "It would have been my word against hers."

"And you didn't want to get into a pissing match with your momma."

"She needed the job worse than me. Plus, I didn't want to take the chance of something similar happening again."

"Your momma sure is a pistol," Chuck said on a sigh. "I guess she told you she broke up with me."

"She did?"

"Told me I had to choose between her and Janie

Sue, which basically means between her and my job as sheriff."

Jack nodded. "And you've been sheriff a long time."

Chuck shifted in the chair. "Maybe too long."

Of all the surprises thrown at him this evening by Sheriff Chuck Wheeler, the fact that he was considering retirement was the most shocking. Jack almost laughed, remembering how he'd once intended to follow in Chuck's footsteps and run for sheriff when he stepped down.

"Anyway," Chuck said, "I figure you're here to discuss removing that reprimand from your record. Consider it done."

"Thanks. But what's the point?"

"Aren't you thinking about coming back to work for me?"

"Uh, no," Jack said.

Chuck frowned. "Isn't that why you came home?"

Jack hesitated. Based on that comment, his mother hadn't blabbed why he'd come to Dunnellon, after all. The purpose of this visit was to clarify Claudia's situation and ensure Chuck's silence, but apparently there was no need to clarify anything.

"I'm just here for a visit, Chuck. To check on my property."

"Then why are you in my office?"

"It doesn't matter anymore."

The sheriff snorted. "I get it. You came to tell me

to stay away from Irene. Maybe ask what my intentions are?"

"Like I said, it's irrelevant since you two are done." Jack rose.

Wheeler's gaze bored into his. "Your job's open if you want it. You were the finest deputy I ever had."

"Thanks, but I've got a job." And right now it was protecting a witness. One he'd grown too attached to.

The sheriff made another dismissive noise. "What? Private security? You need to wear a badge, son. It's what you were made for."

"That's your opinion."

"Maybe so." The sheriff nodded. "But I know you, Jack, and I'd bet a passel of prize-winning bird dogs that you miss that badge."

"I'll see you around, Chuck."

Jack left the office with the sheriff's words echoing in his ears. Did he miss the badge? The authority, the power that went with it?

No way. He loved his job in Miami, the constant party that was South Beach, the thrill of bright lights, the media exposure around Protection Alliance's clients. Although, of course not every gig involved a celebrity. Some assignments could get boring. But a deputy's work could also become mind-blowingly tedious at times. Yeah, Miami was too hot in the summer, but summers up here were no cruise to Alaska, either.

He pulled into the parking lot of the general store, still debating the pros and cons of a career choice.

What was that about? He'd never even considered a move back home before. The idea was ridiculous. His life was in Miami now.

Working for Lola paid a lot more than working as a deputy sheriff in Marion County. But, man, maybe he did miss the badge. Working for justice instead of just cash could be a lot more satisfying.

Wasn't that why he was helping Claudia?

CLAUDIA LOOKED UP when Jack pushed backward through the front door balancing two pizzas, three plastic grocery bags and a prescription package. A delicious garlicky fragrance accompanied him inside, reminding her she was hungry. On the sofa, Pookie came to all fours and sniffed the air.

From the tight set of Jack's jaw, things hadn't gone well with Sheriff Wheeler. His gaze lingered on the beer cans beside the sofa, and he shook his head.

"I see you ladies are having a party."

"Oh, it's hardly a party," Irene told her son, reaching for one of the boxes. "Claudia would only let me have two beers until she knew what pain medication I'd been prescribed. Get down, Pookie."

When the dog leaped to the floor, Irene opened the box, and the enticing aroma intensified as steam escaped into the air. "Lordy, this smells good, Jack. And you remembered my favorite."

Claudia moved to the kitchen to retrieve plates and napkins. Was Jack pissed because his mom had a few beers? When she returned, Jack met her gaze and held it.

"Did you even hear me drive up?" he asked.

"Of course we did," Irene said. She removed a slice, melted cheese dripping over the edges. Pookie watched her master with pleading liquid eyes.

"I knew it was you," Claudia added. She handed him and his mom a plate. "I recognize the sound of your engine by now."

"Were we supposed to greet you at the door like some conquering hero?" Irene asked. "Sorry. I've got a busted ankle." Closing her eyes, she bit into the pizza, making small noises of delight. Pookie whined.

Jack placed the second pizza on the table, pulled a chair next to Claudia and sat. "You need to stay aware of your surroundings."

"I am," Claudia said. But of course Jack was right. She should have gotten up to confirm the approaching vehicle was indeed him. Was it the beer? She hadn't even finished one. And, man, she was hungry. Lunch seemed like a long time ago.

She reached for her own slice of pizza. Mushroom, green pepper and extra cheese. One of her favorites, too, but anything would be good right now. She broke off a dangling string of cheese, took a huge bite and decided this was the best pizza she'd ever tasted.

"It's delicious. Eat," she told Jack, and bit into her pizza again.

"Where's your gun?" he asked.

"In the bedroom," she answered. "Locked and loaded."

"Won't do you much good there."

Claudia narrowed her eyes at him over the pizza. Was she supposed to carry it with her in the cabin? Maybe strap on her shoulder holster? Irene would love that.

"Are you expecting some kind of trouble tonight, son?" Irene asked, glancing between Claudia and Jack.

Jack hesitated, then reached for a slice of pizza. "No more than any night."

No one spoke for a few minutes as everyone ate. As Irene chewed, she stared at Jack with an expression that morphed from curious to suspicious.

When she reached for a third slice, Irene asked, "Did you get my meds?"

Jack tossed her a small plastic bag. "I also got everything on your list," he told Claudia. "But I guess I should have bought more beer."

"There's one left. Go get him a can, Claudia."

"No thanks," Jack said.

Chafing under Jack's disapproval, Claudia remained silent. She wanted to know what happened with the sheriff, but that would have to wait until later. Maybe when they were in bed. She took another slice of pizza. Where would everyone sleep tonight? Would she sleep beside Jack again?

"What are you on the run from, Miss Claudia?" Irene asked.

Claudia stopped chewing and looked up, mouth full.

"I know it's got to be something, what with such concern over approaching cars. Not to mention target practice for a nurse."

"Mother," Jack warned.

"You got a mean husband, honey?"

Claudia shook her head and swallowed. "I'm not married."

"Abusive boyfriend, then?"

"It's nothing like that," she said.

Irene nodded. "But it's something."

"Nothing you need to know about, Mother," Jack said.

"I see," Irene said in a long-suffering tone. "I'm just your poor injured momma who has to remain ignorant of what's going on. That doesn't seem fair to me, Jack."

Claudia shot Jack a look. He glared at his mother.

"I told you all my secrets, honey," Irene said softly to Claudia.

Claudia sighed, placed her half-eaten slice on the plate and set it aside. "It's safer for you if you don't know."

Irene's eyes widened, and Claudia realized her mistake. She'd just made an admission. Now Irene would pester her until she'd ferreted out the details.

"I spoke to Chuck tonight," Jack said, surprising Claudia—and Irene, too, from the look on her face.

"What about?" Irene asked.

"Why did you tell him the truth about the Crawley murder reports?"

Irene raised her chin. "I thought it was time."

"Why now?"

She shrugged. "Because we're through, so it doesn't matter anymore."

Feeling as if she were watching a tennis match, Claudia watched mother and son dance around the long overdue conversation they needed to have. Jack didn't seem so much angry at his mom as confused. Irene was defensive, but standing her ground. Now that the truth was out, perhaps they could discuss past mistakes and move on.

Jack leaned forward. "You've broken up before and didn't tell him."

"Yeah, but in the past, I always left the door wide open for him to walk back through. But after talking to Claudia, I realized I deserve something better."

"You do," Claudia said, ignoring Jack's unbelieving glance.

Irene smiled. "Thank you, honey."

"Well, of course you do, Mom," Jack said. "But what if he comes sniffing around again? Then what?"

"What's done is done," Irene said with a note of finality. "I love Chuck, but I've wasted enough time on him."

"Good for you, Irene," Claudia said.

"I know I've made mistakes, but I've finally come clean. And you can thank Claudia for that."

Jack's intense green eyes locked with Claudia's. She shrugged, and he gave her a smile that sent her pulse racing.

Irene sighed. "Can we change the subject? I want to enjoy the rest of this fine Gino's pizza."

"Gino said to tell you hello," Jack said.

Listening to Jack and his mom discuss their old friend, Claudia nibbled on pizza. Still chatting with Irene, he flipped open the second pizza box and took a slice. Claudia smiled, enjoying the simple pleasure of watching him eat.

But Jack was right. She'd let her guard down too much tonight, even to the point of having a beer. He'd been right to disapprove. What had happened to lull her into a sense of safety?

Jack had happened to her, that's what. He made her feel safe, and that was nuts.

With a sickening jolt, the truth hit her. She was falling in love with Jack. Murderers were hunting her, and she was besotted with her bodyguard, a man she barely knew, a man she shouldn't trust.

Or were these fears more of Carlos's insane paranoia? Her ex had messed with her head until she didn't know what was real anymore.

Maybe she *could* trust Jack. Or maybe history was repeating itself and she couldn't trust her own emotions. She tossed her pizza back in the box.

"I'm not feeling so great," she said, coming to her feet. "I think I'll go lie down."

MAKING AS LITTLE noise as possible so as not to wake Claudia, Jack entered the bedroom two hours later. She lay on her side, her back toward the door, and appeared to be asleep. He stripped down to his briefs and stretched out on the bed beside her. She continued to breathe regularly and didn't stir.

So much for his plan to let the women sleep together. Maybe he ought to make a bed on the floor.

On his back, still wide awake, Jack stared at the ceiling. He and his mom had spoken for hours about nothing much at all, really—past mistakes, old friends, neighbors, a lot of gossip—the best conversation they'd had in years. Until her eyes began to droop. He'd called it a night, deciding it was easier to leave her on the sofa.

What had caused the turnaround between them? His worry over her fall? Because she'd told Wheeler the truth about what had happened so long ago? Or maybe it was the softening influence Claudia had on them.

He turned his head to look at the woman sleeping beside him. He hoped nothing was seriously wrong with her. If he had to make another trip to the ER tomorrow, that would force them to relocate. Whatever happened to her sure came on fast, but she seemed okay now.

Although it was dark—no streetlights in the middle of the forest to illuminate the room—he could see the outline of her lush, perfect body, the curve of her spine, the slight bend in her knees. Her dark hair spilled across a white pillowcase. She wore a T-shirt, lacy panties and nothing else. They lay so close to each other in the small bed, he sensed her heat, the gentle movement of the mattress as she inhaled and exhaled.

Maybe she felt the weight of his attention in her sleep, because she shifted, turning on her side to face him, making a small, sweet noise. Her warm breath feathered across his arm, and he felt himself harden.

He longed to touch her. He wanted to smooth his palm down her arm and feel her flesh. He mentally urged her to wake up.

She'd be willing, but he wasn't quite so much of a jerk that he'd awaken a sick woman to satisfy his own needs. Plus, his mom was in the next room. Although thanks to a pain pill, it was not likely she'd wake up anytime soon no matter what sounds came from the bedroom.

Sounds? If only. He sighed and stared at the ceiling again. Sleeping next to Claudia without touching her was a special kind of torture. He could go sleep in the trailer, but he'd be too far away in case of trouble.

He looked at her again and found her eyes open and staring into his.

"Hey," she whispered.

"Hey, yourself," he whispered back. He turned on

his side, careful not to touch her. Doing so would destroy any professional restraint he'd managed to cling to.

"How do you feel?" he asked.

"Scared."

Stung by her tone, he couldn't stop himself from running a finger down her cheek. "What are you afraid of?"

"Myself." She lifted a shoulder. "Carlos. You."

"Me? I don't understand."

"Me, either. How's your mom?"

"You're not afraid of her, are you?"

"Should I be?"

"Maybe. But she's sound asleep. The pain meds put her out."

"Good," Claudia said. "I'm glad you two are getting along better."

"We'll see how long it lasts."

"She loves you."

He sighed. "Yeah, but she loves a lot of people."

Claudia closed her eyes. She remained quiet for so long, he thought she'd fallen back asleep. But her eyes opened again.

"Have you ever been in love, Jack?"

He frowned. "Where did that come from?"

"I guess I'm curious about the man I've trusted my life to," she said, her voice soft, worried.

"I'm not going to let anything happen to you, Claudia."

She held his gaze. "Promise?"

"I promise."

"Thanks," she whispered, and lifted to kiss him.

He lowered his mouth to meet hers. When their lips touched, she made a desperate sexy sound, almost a whimper. A fire raced through his body, consuming any last shred of control. With a groan, he rolled on top of her. The feel of her smooth, warm skin drove him beyond any rational thought, and he pressed his erection into her soft belly as she deepened their kiss, exploring his mouth with her tongue.

He hardened until he was close to pain. A good kind of pain, the kind of pain he wanted every day. He needed to be inside her now. This was a mistake. He knew it and she knew it, but there was no way he could stop now. He wanted her too much, had wanted her for too long. He'd worry about the consequences later.

CLAUDIA THREADED HER fingers through Jack's hair, loving the feel of it, the weight of his hard body pressed against hers. This was finally going to happen. Why had they waited so long? Her gladiator was so strong, his muscled body so perfect. How could she ever be afraid with Jack protecting her?

He broke their kiss and stared into her face with troubled eyes, holding his upper body off of her with his forearms. A sensual tug low in her belly overpowered any other thoughts.

"Jack," she whispered, wanting to tell him how

she felt, that she loved him, that making love to her was okay.

"Yeah, babe?" he answered softly.

Unable to find the words, Claudia pulled her T-shirt over her head, revealing her breasts to him, wanting to reveal everything to him, to give him anything he wanted.

He smiled, and lowered his head to take her nipple into his mouth.

She closed her eyes as he suckled, holding his head in place with one hand. She slid the other into the waistband of his briefs, sliding the cotton away to get a better hold on him.

He groaned and rolled away, reaching to the floor for his wallet while she wiggled out of her panties. He ripped open a foil package with a vicious pull.

"Let me," she said, reaching out. He placed one knee on the bed. She smoothed the condom on, and lay back, admiring Jack's body.

He paused, staring at her. "You're beautiful."

"So are you."

He placed his hands on either side of her and entered her with a long sensual push. Claudia closed her eyes. She'd never felt this complete. She met his slow pleasurable pumps with thrusts of her own, relishing the sweet, sweet pressure as it began to build. *Oh, Jack.* She wanted to shout that nothing had ever felt this good. She didn't care how crazy this was, how dangerous. He felt perfect inside her. She let his power and strength consume her. Her release came too soon. She arched against him and cried out his name again, triggering his own shuddering climax and a ferocious groan.

And then he went still, the room quiet but for their harsh breathing.

She found herself staring into eyes that glittered with mysterious depths. She couldn't read his expression, had no clue what he was thinking. Maybe it was better if she didn't know. She closed her eyes against a sudden rush of confused emotion, of love for this man she barely knew.

Had she just repeated the biggest mistake of her life?

CHAPTER EIGHTEEN

DRYING HER HANDS on a kitchen towel, Claudia stepped outside on the concrete slab and found the backyard shimmering with an eerie coral glow. The sun was setting behind the forest, painting the sky with gorgeous streaks of orange and deep red. She took a deep breath of the cool, pine-scented air, unfortunately mingled with a noxious note of Irene's cigarette smoke.

Jack stuffed wood and kindling into the chiminea, making preparations for a fire. Relaxing in one of the chairs with her foot elevated, Irene gave instructions about where to place each log as she enjoyed her after-dinner coffee and smoke.

Jack glanced up at Claudia and smiled, making her feel welcome, like she was part of his family now. Her heart squeezed as she smiled back, and he returned to building his fire.

She'd been playing house with Jack and his mom for over two weeks now. Sitting out back after dinner to talk around a fire had become their evening's entertainment. Her days had become a delightful blur of hiking into the woods either for morning target practice or just for the pleasure of getting away from Irene for a little privacy.

Her nights were all about making love with Jack.

She shivered and raised her gaze from Jack to the spectacular sunset.

She'd been taking pleasure in simple things, like cooking, cleaning and doing laundry. Not that there was much else to do. Most days she studied for an hour or two while Irene worked on her quilts and nursed a broken heart. Jack disappeared during this time, presumably scouting his property for signs of intruders. He'd strung up some kind of an early warning system that used a trip wire so he'd know about any trespassers, which was what allowed them to sit outside after dark for an hour or two.

Strangely, the last few days would have been the most pleasurable of her life if she weren't falling deeper and deeper under Jack's spell. She tried to resist his pull. She constantly reminded herself she didn't really know him, that she shouldn't trust anyone, that she couldn't be falling in love. Too bad nothing worked.

She knew better than to rely on her own instincts. She'd married a man who turned out to be a terrorist, and she'd had no clue about his true nature. How could she have fallen for a man so twisted? She didn't dare trust her own judgment.

Yet as she got closer to Jack, got to know him, she believed him to be a rare, special man. A man with honor who would never turn his back on a friend—

like her, for instance, a woman he met three weeks ago. He didn't have to help her, but went all in to protect her from the Warriors because he thought it was the right thing to do. He was kind, caring, competent, gorgeous, smart. Everything Carlos had never been and never could be.

But maybe she was wrong again.

She shook her head and placed the dish towel over a chair to dry. There'd been no talk of love between her and Jack. She'd hinted around the subject once or twice, but he'd refused to bite. Jack didn't appear to even believe in love. Good for him. That way he could never be hurt.

He'd never asked anything about her marriage. Why was that? Likely because he didn't want to know. So how did he feel about her exactly? He was a fabulous lover, but maybe sex was part of the protection package and nothing more.

She didn't dare tell him how she felt. She didn't know what was real anymore, how he would react. Her life was nothing but a complicated muddle.

"Just light the damn thing already, Jack," Irene said, bringing Claudia back to the present.

"Yes, Mother," he said in a long-suffering tone, and struck a match. The kindling caught quickly, and soon the chimnea roared with fire, and smoke billowed out the top.

Claudia shivered in the cool night air, looking forward to sitting by the heat from the fire.

"I'm going in for a cup of tea," she said. "Anybody need anything?"

"I'm good, honey," Irene said. "You just come on back out here and sit yourself down. That was a delicious dinner, and you worked hard today."

Jack looked up, and she could see the fire reflected in his eyes. "Hurry back," he said.

Claudia nodded. She still needed to call the prosecutor and let him know she was alive. Jack's colleagues had sent an untraceable phone a few days ago, but she hadn't used it yet.

It would all be over soon. And after the trial, she'd never see Jack again.

"MAKE THE CALL, CLAUDIA," Jack said, handing her the burner phone. They'd moved into the bedroom and sat on the bed. "It's almost ten."

"He'll still be up," she said—a little too confidently.

"How do you know?"

"Reese is the intense type," she said. "Always working. Never stops."

Jack folded his arms, not appreciating her admiring tone. "Sounds boring."

"Oh, he's far from boring," she said.

"So you know him well?"

"Before I went into hiding, we spent a lot of time together preparing for my testimony."

"I see." He didn't like the thought of that at all. How much time? And why was she so hesitant to call this intensely fabulous and far from boring federal prosecutor? She claimed to trust this guy, so what exactly was she worried about? Was there something special between them?

"The trial starts Monday," Jack said. "You need to let him know you're still willing to testify."

She took a deep breath. "Right."

Her eyes on a sheet of paper, Claudia punched a number into the burner phone. "Is that you, Reese? Yes…That's not important…I'm fine."

As Jack listened to the one-way conversation, he relaxed, deducing Claudia wasn't intimate with this man. Far from it. More like she hardly knew him. Telling him she was worried about a bug, she ended the call quickly, but promised to phone the pay phone of a café on Friday, two days away.

"Will he need you Monday?" Jack asked. Was his respite with Claudia coming to an end? An unsettling hollowness bit into his gut.

"No," she said. "Jury selection starts Monday, which Reese says should take a while. He'll put me on the stand a week from Friday at the earliest."

"So we've got another ten days, give or take." Jack relaxed as relief flooded through him. Ten days was a hell of a long time.

She nodded, worrying her bottom lip with her teeth. "Do you have a plan on how to sneak me into the courthouse?"

"First, you should be in disguise," he said. "My mom has got some old wigs, and we'll use one of those. Maybe trick you out in one of her more bizarre dresses."

Claudia's mouth twitched as she fought a smile. "We're not exactly the same size."

"She's a good seamstress and can alter something to fit you."

"I guess that'll work." Claudia nodded again, and looked out the window, her thoughts obviously somewhere else.

"What's wrong?" Jack placed a hand on her shoulder and squeezed. Damn, but she was tense. He repositioned himself behind her and massaged her shoulders, using his fingers to loosen kinks. "You're tight," he said. "Something is bothering you. I can tell."

She shifted to face him, and his arms dropped away.

"You think you know me that well?"

He shrugged. "I can read you like a book."

"Is that right?" she challenged.

"Yeah, that's right, and something heavy has been weighing you down lately."

Her eyes narrowed. She started to say something, but shook her head, changing her mind, making him wish he could actually read her mind rather than just her body language and facial expressions.

"I've been thinking about how you promised to train me in self-defense."

Jack rubbed his chin. He thought she'd forgotten about that. "The Warriors like to detonate bombs from a safe distance," he said. "I don't think they'll get close enough for defensive training to make any difference."

"But what if they do?" she responded. "Can't you just show me some tips?"

"Sure," he said, flipping her onto her back, causing her to shriek in surprise. "We can begin the first lesson right now."

He used one hand to pin both of her arms to the mattress over her head and pressed his growing erection into her pelvis. With his free hand, he traced the outline of her full lips, quite the erogenous zone for Nurse Claudia. Something he'd learned about her in the last week.

She grinned up at him. "Now I suppose you want me to try to escape?"

"If you can," he said. He lowered his mouth to hers and kissed her thoroughly, leaving them both breathless.

"I know all about a knee into the groin," she said when he broke away.

"And you think you can manage that?" He smiled down at her.

She shook her head and provocatively thrust her hips against him.

"I have absolutely no interest in trying," she said, holding his gaze with her clear blue eyes.

THE NEXT MORNING, hiking their way through the forest to target practice, Jack halted suddenly in the path and held up a hand signaling for her to hold in place. He placed the opposite index finger across his lips.

Claudia froze, not daring to breathe. Had he sensed an intruder?

Stepping lightly, Jack worked his way back and stood behind her. He pointed forward to the top of the tallest tree, a mammoth pine.

"Red-shouldered hawk," he whispered.

Claudia exhaled and quickly sucked in more air. He'd seen a bird, not a terrorist.

"A female, working on her nest, getting ready for spring. Do you see her?"

"No," Claudia admitted, her heart still racing.

Jack stepped closer and raised his arm next to her face. "Think of the tree like a clock face, the trunk pointing to twelve and six. Now focus on the large branch jutting out at nine o'clock. Follow that out to the end and up one branch."

Claudia followed the direction of Jack's powerful arm and spotted the bird, which was obvious once you knew where to look.

"How do you know it's a female?" she whispered.

"The females are larger. More powerful." He lowered his arm, joined it with the other one around her waist and squeezed.

"Do tell?" Claudia relaxed into his body, enjoying his strength.

"Wow," he said. "Your heart is galloping a hundred miles a minute. I didn't realize I had such an effect on you."

Claudia closed her eyes. If he only knew.

"You startled me when you stopped so abruptly," she said. "I thought we had trouble."

Just as she said *trouble*, she felt Jack's phone vibrate, alerting him to an incoming call.

Frowning, he checked the readout. "It's Lola. I told her to call if anything changed."

He answered the call with, "Richards," and turned away.

Claudia recognized the name as his boss, or office manager, or supervisor, or something. Jack had never been specific about exactly who this Lola was.

She searched for the hawk again, and found her industriously poking at a large nest made of intertwined twigs and leaves with her beak.

"What?"

The vehemence of Jack's question caused Claudia to whirl. Something had definitely changed.

Jack raised his gaze to hers, and her heart began to pound again. *And whatever it is has to do with me.*

"Are you sure?" he demanded, his tone harsh, unbelieving. "No mistake then," he said, his voice now flat.

After a long pause, during which Jack stared at her the entire time, he said. "Yeah. Great. Thanks, Lola."

"What?" Claudia asked as soon as he'd disconnected.

His face impassive, Jack looked away and glanced up to the hawk.

"Is there trouble on Collins Island?"

He held her gaze again. "Someone tried to break into Villa Alma."

"Tried to?"

"Our security cameras caught them, and the man was arrested."

"Is he talking?"

"No. He lawyered up fast."

"What else?" she demanded, suspecting this security breach wasn't the only problem.

"He used Marsali Winthrop's name to get on the island."

CHAPTER NINETEEN

"MARSALI?" CLAUDIA STARED at Jack.

"She's been calling the PA office trying to get in touch with me." He shook his head.

"Doesn't she have your cell number?"

"Only the one I used on Collins Island."

Claudia nodded. That made sense. "Did Marsali say what she wanted?"

"She's trying to determine our location. I knew Marsali was all about money, but this…" He shook his head again. "I never expected this from her."

The earth shifted under Claudia's feet. She reached out to hold on to a tree. "So she's—she's working for Carlos?"

Looking grim, Jack began to pace. "I gave Lola a tag number of a man trying to bluff his way on the ferry. It didn't seem important at the time, but I had her run it down after we left Miami. Turns out it's the same guy who tried to get inside Villa Alma."

"So Marsali let him on the island."

Jack nodded. "Somehow they got to her."

Feeling sick, Claudia sank to the ground. "But she was so nice."

"She's a con artist, and a good one. That's what they do."

"But how did she know I'd be on the beach in the middle of the night?"

"That could have been a coincidence. Or they told her where you were." He shrugged. "She could have watched for you to leave."

A cold chill traced Claudia's spine. "She could have killed me."

"That wasn't her job. She's not a hit man."

"So she's been working for Carlos all along?" Claudia swallowed. "Marsali is one of his Warriors?"

"Probably not. When they realized they couldn't easily access the island, they found the right person to bribe. Dangle enough money in front of Marsali's gorgeous face, and she'll lunge for it with claws extended."

Nausea churned in Claudia's belly. She sank her head into her hands. Suddenly everything seemed wrong. The forest around her now appeared threatening instead of sheltering. How had this happened? How had she gotten to this place?

Because I'm the world's worst judge of character.

Never, never trust anyone. First Carlos, then Marsali.

What about Jack?

She raised her head to watch him pace, hands on his hips, deep in thought. As if sensing her attention, he paused and knelt before her.

"Hey. Are you okay?"

"When will I ever learn?" Claudia murmured.

"What's going on?"

"Carlos was right. You can't trust anyone."

"Carlos?" Jack's face hardened. "I suppose you're including me in that blanket statement. You don't trust me?"

"I don't know," she whispered.

"I put my life and career on hold, move you three hundred miles away and you still don't *trust* me?"

"I trusted Carlos, and look what happened."

"And now you're comparing me to Carlos Romero?"

She looked away from the white-hot fury flaring in his eyes.

"After the intimacies we've shared, you cannot believe I'm working for your ex."

She swallowed hard, unable to answer. Jack couldn't work for Carlos or she'd already be dead. She was in love with Jack.

But she'd been in love with Carlos, too. Or had she? What she felt for Jack was so very different. So maybe she didn't understand what love was. Maybe she didn't understand anything.

When she didn't respond, Jack rose.

"What are we going to do?" she asked, scrambling to her feet beside him.

"I'm going back to the cabin. You can do whatever the hell you want."

"Jack, wait."

He turned and jogged back the way they'd come.

WHEN JACK REACHED the clearing behind his cabin, he slowed his pace. Breathing hard, he placed his hands on his hips and stopped. The hard run through the forest hadn't helped. He was still pissed.

No, not pissed. Fricking furious.

Claudia couldn't tell a terrorist from a puppy dog. She obviously needed help. Serious help from a good shrink.

How could she equate him with Carlos Romero? The thought of her married to that slick son of a bitch made his skin crawl. He'd seen photographs of the man. Handsome, dark and sophisticated. Jack pushed away a stab of jealousy.

He stared at his cabin. So now what?

She didn't trust him. And now he wasn't sure he trusted her.

But he couldn't leave her unprotected. He'd started this mission so she could provide evidence against Romero—and apparently she intended to testify—so he couldn't send her away.

He could go back to Miami. And why not? The Warriors hadn't found her and probably wouldn't. Claudia and his mom could stay here, and he'd go home.

Too bad Miami no longer felt like home.

When he entered the back door, Irene looked up from her needlework and frowned. "Where's Miss Claudia?"

Wishing he could slam a door shut, Jack motioned with his thumb back out into the woods. "She couldn't keep up."

Pookie raised her furry head and growled low in her throat, reacting to his tone.

Irene patted the dog to quiet her. "What's gotten into you?"

Jack grunted and moved to the bedroom. He needed to pack. But he wasn't going back to Miami. He couldn't leave Claudia and his mother here alone and unprotected. The Warriors could still pick up Claudia's trail. Yeah, she was a much better shot now, but she'd never been battle tested.

Or so she'd led him to believe. Maybe she was a true blue, card-carrying Warrior for Self Rule.

Jack paused from stuffing clothing into his duffel bag. That didn't make sense. If so, why was she on the run from Romero? Why hadn't the feds charged her, too? Why would she agree to testify?

Jack slung his bag over his shoulder and reentered the living room.

"Where the hell are you going?" Irene asked.

"I'm moving in to the Airstream."

"Why?"

He didn't answer.

"You and Claudia had a fight, didn't you?"

Jack ignored his mother and exited the cabin. As he stomped up the steps of the travel trailer, Claudia emerged from the tree line, and he breathed a sigh of relief. He'd been about to go look for her.

Their eyes met across the distance. She'd been crying.

He unlocked the Airstream door and entered a frigid living room. As always, he'd left the trailer neat and ready to roll, but he hadn't used this vintage RV in a while, so the interior smelled musty and felt a little damp. He dropped his bag and turned to find Claudia standing in the doorway.

She stepped inside and closed the door.

"I'm sorry," she said.

"For what?"

"I know I've made a mess of things, but please let me explain," she said.

He advanced on her. "Tell me exactly what I've done to make you doubt me?"

She raised her chin and met his anger head-on. "Nothing. You've been wonderful."

"Wonderful? You sure don't act like it."

"Life with Carlos was—difficult. He constantly put me down, made me feel stupid, doubt my own abilities. When I left him, I could barely tell right from wrong."

Jack turned away. He didn't want to hear the details of her life with another man. He'd been careful not to ask. But maybe he had to know.

"Did he hit you?" he asked over his shoulder.

"He wasn't physically abusive. Just verbally."

Jack nodded, his fury dying. He knew the type.

"Carlos was a terrible mistake. I'm afraid of making another one."

He turned back to her. "You mean with me?"

"Yes. Please don't get mad again. I know it doesn't make any sense."

Jack stared at her tear-streaked face, his anger now simmering at a more manageable level. No, it didn't make any sense, but neither did his actions. He'd gone off on her like a jerk for what reason? He'd always known she had issues with trust.

But her lack of trust in *him* hurt. Hurt badly.

Because he'd allowed her to become important to him. He'd broken every rule and permitted her to get too close. She'd bewitched him, and as a result his judgment was impaired.

And he'd known better.

If he wanted to keep her safe, from now on he needed to keep his distance. No more sex with Claudia. That thought set him off again.

What he needed was a good workout. Too bad he hadn't left any weights here when he moved to Miami, but his old sparring mat was still in the shed.

"I haven't trusted anyone in a long time," she said. "But I trust you, Jack. Please believe me. I even think—"

"Okay," he said, interrupting her before he relented and pulled her into his arms. "I forgive you."

"So we're okay?"

"Sure."

CLAUDIA STARED AT the duffel bag in the middle of the floor. His tone said something different than his words. "So you'll come back to the cabin?"

"No. I think it best that I sleep over here."

She blinked at the harsh edge to his voice. He didn't sound like he'd forgiven anything.

"Why?" she asked.

"I need to keep my head on straight, Claudia."

"But you said you forgave me."

Shrugging his shoulders, he made a noncommittal sound that she interpreted to mean he hadn't really forgiven her. He wanted nothing more to do with her.

"So that's it?" she asked.

"Don't worry," he said. "I'll see that you get to the courthouse to testify."

"Thanks," she whispered.

"Sure thing."

"Okay, then," she said, her voice breaking. She lifted her chin and took a backward step. To think she'd been about to tell Jack she was in love with him.

"Wait," Jack said.

She froze, waiting to hear what he said, not daring to hope.

"Do you still want self-defense lessons?"

"Yes," she said, her voice still cracking. She cleared her throat. "If you're willing."

"Be ready for your first lesson in the morning. Wear comfortable clothing."

AFTER BREAKFAST, WEARING loose-fitting sweats, Claudia watched with Irene on the concrete deck as Jack rooted around in his overstuffed storage shed.

As usual, Irene had elevated her injured foot on a chair.

"What is he looking for?" she asked.

"Not sure. How's your ankle this morning?" Claudia asked.

"Almost good as new," Irene said. "Just a little tender."

"You should get an elastic brace from a drugstore and wear it for a while so you don't retwist the joint."

"Soon as Jack lets me out of prison."

Jack emerged from the shed carrying a large gray mat. Claudia had seen similar mats in gyms.

"What's he doing with his sparring mat?" Irene asked.

"He agreed to give me self-defense lessons."

Eyes wide, Irene leveled her gaze on Claudia. "Do you think that's wise, hon? I mean, considering his god-awful mood?"

"What are you talking about?"

"He's bringing out that mat so he can throw you on your cute little butt over and over again. I imagine he'll feel better after, but you'll be black and blue."

"Jack would never hurt me," Claudia said. As she spoke the words, she knew it was true. How could she ever have doubted him? No wonder he was so angry. Jack had an inner core of honor that wouldn't allow him to harm her. *My gladiator.*

Could she have fallen for two more opposite men? Boy, could she really pick 'em.

And after he dropped her off at the courthouse to testify, she'd never see him again.

Jack also wore a sweatshirt and pants in the early morning chill, but his strength was obvious as he wrestled the huge mat—which from his body language had to be heavy—into the center of his backyard. While admiring his activity, Claudia remembered the biggest reason for her poor choices: she let her hormones do the thinking. But how could she help it? Tall, wide-shouldered and slim-hipped, Jack was one magnificent piece of work.

Why couldn't she fall in love with some nice, boring middle-of-the-road type of guy? *Because I'm an idiot with lousy judgment.*

Yet falling in love with Jack wasn't stupid. It was the smartest thing she'd ever done.

After positioning the mat where he wanted it, Jack turned to Claudia and beckoned her forward with his index finger, wearing a huge grin.

"I hope you know what you're getting into," Irene murmured. "Jack can hold a grudge longer than anyone I've ever met."

Claudia rose and smoothed suddenly damp hands down her sweats.

Pookie jumped into her master's lap and settled down, ears alert, as if preparing for a show. "Yeah, I agree, Pooks," Irene said, stroking her pet's fur. "This ought to be interesting."

With a fluttery sensation in her belly, Claudia walked down the slight incline to where Jack waited with his hands on his hips. She stepped onto the mat and faced him.

Eyeing him warily, she rubbed the back of her neck. "Aren't we supposed to bow?"

Still grinning, Jack leaned over and executed an elaborate bow with a dramatic sweep of his arm. When upright again, he began to circle her.

Claudia shuffled her feet to keep him in sight. What was he doing? Looking for a weak spot? He knew them all.

"What would you do if someone approached and you *knew* they intended you harm?" he asked.

"Pull out my gun."

"Just pull it out? Not use it?"

"Well, I wouldn't shoot if my attacker ran away."

"Good. Always avoid violence if possible." Jack kept circling, his gaze intent on her face. "What if you didn't have a gun?"

Her fingers tingled, so she shook her hands. "Run. Scream."

"What if you couldn't get away? What if no one came to your rescue?"

"I guess I'd—" Before she could finish her thought, Jack grabbed her, positioning his forearm around her throat. She hadn't seen it coming, had no idea how it happened, but knew if he applied any pressure, she'd pass out. Or he'd break her neck.

"That's how fast it can happen," he said, his breath hot on her nape.

With her heart beating a rapid tattoo inside her

chest, she took a deep breath and inhaled the familiar scent of his aftershave.

He released her, giving her a slight shove away as if he didn't want to be close to her.

"Do you remember how you were standing when I made my move?" he demanded.

She shook her head, still rattled by the suddenness of his attack.

"You should have been ready for me. You're right-handed, so stand with your left foot forward, your right leg back."

He demonstrated, and raised hands curled into fists.

"Bend your knees slightly with your weight evenly distributed," he said. "Try it."

Claudia assumed a stance similar to his.

"Keep your hands up so that if you stick out your thumbs, they'd touch your cheeks. Keep your hands relaxed. If you punch, make a tight fist. Keep your wrist straight or you might break it."

Claudia copied everything Jack did, staying light on her feet, her hands fisted close to her chin. They bounced around each other for a few minutes, checking each other out. She got how it wouldn't be so easy for an attacker to take control.

"Now you don't look like such a victim," Jack said. "For the techniques I'm going to teach you, the object is to turn yourself from the victim into the predator."

"I'd have to see someone coming," Claudia said.

"Yeah, you would. That's why you need to stay alert at all times. If you feel you are physically in danger, there are no rules."

Jack stepped toward her again. She raised her right forearm to ward off the assault, but he easily maneuvered himself behind her and placed his arm around her neck.

"The danger in this position, a rear headlock, is you could be choked out quickly. You want to take pressure off your throat."

She swallowed hard as Jack's words rumbled close to her ear, his body hard and unyielding pressed into hers.

"Hook my arm with both of your hands and pull down," he said, "then dig your chin in behind."

Claudia did as instructed, but suspected she was able to slightly move his arm because Jack allowed it to happen. Hopefully any attacker wouldn't be quite as strong.

"That will buy you some time. Maintain your hold on my arm, but widen your legs, lower your hips and drop down slightly."

Realizing what he wanted, she said, "There's no way I can pick you up."

"You're not going to. You're going to throw me."

"Yeah, right."

"Pay attention. If you lean forward, my body will curve, forcing me up on my toes."

Claudia did as he requested.

"Now twist your body away from my elbow around your neck. Maintain your grip on my arm."

Before she could execute his instructions, a shrill alarm sounded. Jack dropped his arm and stepped away.

"What the hell is that?" Irene yelled from the deck.

"The security perimeter has been breached," Jack said. "Someone's coming."

CHAPTER TWENTY

"GET IN THE CABIN," Jack ordered Claudia. "Help my mother."

"Can you tell where the breach occurred?" Claudia asked, looking around wildly.

"Get inside. Lock the front door and wait for me in the bedroom."

Jack rushed to the Airstream to retrieve his weapons and laptop. By the time he got back to the cabin, the women sat next to each other on the bed. Claudia had her Glock beside her. Irene looked angry.

"What is going on, Jack?" his mother demanded.

"I don't know yet," he said.

"Is there any way to tell what direction they're coming from?" Claudia asked again.

"It's not that sophisticated a system. Just an alert."

"For what?" Irene shook her head. "It's probably someone coming to visit."

"Who?" Jack asked. "No one knows we're here but Sheriff Wheeler."

"Well, we know it's not him," Irene said. She dug her cigarettes from a pocket.

Jack snatched them from her hand.

"We're trapped," Claudia said. Her voice remained

calm, but blood had drained from her face. "What are we going to do?"

Jack jerked a throw rug back from the hardwood floor. Claudia gasped when he pulled on a recessed strap and opened a trap door. Wooden stairs led down into a dark space.

"This is my storm cellar," he said.

"For hurricanes?" Claudia asked.

"Not usually. Tornadoes."

"Yeah, this area is a tornado magnet," Irene said.

Claudia peered into the cellar. "There's not enough room for all three of us."

"Just you and Mom."

Claudia shook her head. "No. I'm not going to hide down there and leave you out here to die. Besides, they'll find us and I'd rather—"

"This is just an escape valve," Jack interrupted. "No one is going to die."

"Escape?" Claudia narrowed her eyes at him. "Is there a tunnel?"

Jack whirled at the sound of an engine straining on the incline to the cabin.

"Wait here," he ordered, surprised the Warriors would be so open. Maybe the breach wasn't as sinister as he'd thought. But maybe it was.

He ratcheted a bullet into the chamber of his Sig Sauer. Aiming its barrel at the floor, he moved into the front room.

Dust swirled into the air signaling the approach of a large vehicle that couldn't yet be seen. Still doubting that Romero's people would stage a frontal assault, Jack positioned himself beside the front window so he couldn't be seen and waited.

In less than a minute, Chuck Wheeler's fancy truck rolled into view. Well, damn. He needed to install a gate on the driveway to keep this guy out.

Jack holstered his weapon and called out, "Relax. It's Chuck."

"Chuck?" Irene squeaked.

Claudia appeared at the edge of the hall and peeked out. "Is he alone?"

"Yes. Wait here."

Claudia complied, leaning against the wall. But his mother pushed past her. No longer needing crutches, she limped out into the front room, favoring her injured foot. The hopeful expression on her face made Jack swear under his breath.

"Let me see what he wants, Mom."

The truck door slammed, and they both turned to look out the window. Chuck jumped out of the truck, hitting the ground with a heavy thud.

"He's here for me," Irene said.

"We don't know that," Jack said.

"I do, but I'll stay inside. I just wanted to get a look at him."

Jack went out to meet Chuck. The sheriff looked as if he hadn't gotten a good night's sleep in weeks.

Jack nodded. "Sheriff," he said, reaching out an arm.

"Jack." They shook hands. Chuck looked over Jack's shoulder toward the house. "We've got a situation."

"Situation?"

"Is there anyone else here besides Irene?"

Jack hesitated. "Why do you ask?"

"Because some rough-looking strangers have been asking around town about a woman, showing this photograph." Chuck handed Jack a black-and-white image printed off a computer.

Jack stared at the photograph. Grainy, but definitely Claudia.

"And this one."

Jack accepted another photo. One of him at the ferry landing on Collins Island.

"Shit," he muttered. So the Warriors had traced them to Dunnellon. How had that happened? Claudia insisted the US Attorney's Office had a leak. Had they traced her call to the prosecutor? Had Marsali somehow located them?

"These dudes aren't making any friends with their belligerence," Chuck continued. "Most folks won't tell them squat, but this morning at breakfast one of my deputies overheard a conversation with Cindy down at the Dinner Bell. She said she didn't know the woman, but told the guy asking that the photo looked like you."

Jack nodded. They had to relocate. Fast.

"Won't be hard to find out where you live. Likely they'll show up here before long."

"Likely," Jack agreed. He needed a plan.

The sheriff folded his arms. "You in some kind of trouble, son?"

Thinking hard, Jack stared at Chuck Wheeler. Wheeler met his gaze with steady gray eyes. Circumstances dictated he had to trust the sheriff. He had no choice.

"Do you know this woman?" Wheeler asked.

Jack released a heavy sigh. "Have you ever heard of a group out of south Florida that call themselves the Warriors for Self Rule?"

Wheeler nodded, eyes narrowed. "Bad bunch. Blew up a post office in Broward County as I recollect."

"I suspect the men asking about me belong to that group."

"What do they want with you?"

"This woman," Jack said, holding up Claudia's photo, "is the primary witness in a trial against their leader that starts Monday."

"Carlos Romero. Nasty one."

"The group made threats, and I'm protecting her until her testimony."

Again Wheeler glanced toward the house. "And you're telling me you've got her stashed here?"

Jack took a wary look around his property. Could the Warriors be close, waiting to pounce? "I don't like being out in the open. Come on inside."

WHEN JACK ENTERED the cabin with Chuck Wheeler, Claudia knew by the tight way he held his jaw that something was very wrong.

His eyes intent on her, Jack handed her two photos. "Men have been showing these photos around town."

Claudia glanced at the photos of her and Jack. Unable to respond, she collapsed in the recliner where Irene sat to sew.

Carlos had found her again.

She looked at Jack, who stared back, his face still grim. Now what? Would the sheriff betray them?

Nausea churned in her stomach as she tried to decide what to do next. What she had feared most had happened. She was helpless. A stranger in a small town. No car. No friends. She'd alienated her only ally, the man she loved.

Would her gladiator continue to protect her?

As Jack explained her situation, Claudia watched Sheriff Chuck Wheeler's reactions closely, trying to determine if he was friend or foe. Wheeler's face remained impassive.

Irene, sitting beside the sheriff on the sofa, bounced her knee up and down, kept shooting wide-eyed glances at Claudia and generally looked like she would burst.

Claudia hugged herself. Jack was telling Wheeler everything except the very minor detail that Carlos Romero was her ex-husband. While she appreciated that, she couldn't help but wonder why he did it.

"Dear Lord," Irene exploded when Jack had concluded the sorry tale. "So these Warrior people are trying to find our Miss Claudia to kill her?"

"I can prove Romero blew up the post office that killed two people."

"It was a damn good plan, Jack," Sheriff Wheeler said, "but something went wrong somewhere."

"There's a leak in the US Attorney's Office," Claudia said. "No one believes me, but I've been saying that from the beginning."

"You called Beauchamps on his cell phone," Jack countered. "While he was at home."

"Maybe Romero's people found a way to bug his apartment," Claudia said.

"Who is Beauchamps?" Irene asked.

"The US Attorney handling the case," Claudia told her.

"Do you trust him?" Wheeler asked.

"I do," Claudia said. "Or I did."

"Doesn't matter," Jack said, a sour look on his face. "We've got to relocate. Now."

"Why can't you protect them, Chuck?" Irene asked.

"Well, for one thing, I doubt if Ms. Goodwin would allow it seeing as how she rejected protection from the federal government."

"You're right about that," Claudia said.

"And I don't have the resources to commit to that sort of a mission," the sheriff continued.

"Claudia, go throw the bare minimum in your duffel," Jack said. "We're out of here."

Claudia met Jack's gaze, relief making her dizzy. She shouldn't have doubted him. He was still willing to help her. When would she learn?

"You can't remain here either, Irene," the sheriff said. "It's not safe."

"Agreed," Jack said.

"What do you mean?" Irene looked from her son to the sheriff. "No Warriors are trying to kill me."

"Whoever is in town looking for Claudia will eventually find their way to this cabin," Jack said. "We'll be gone, but you'd be collateral damage."

"Collateral damage." Irene swallowed hard, looking nervously out the front window. Agitated by the tense voices, Pookie jumped into her master's lap, and Irene patted the dog absently.

Wheeler stood. "You two need to get on the road pronto. We don't know how close these scumbags are to finding you."

"Move, Claudia," Jack said.

Claudia rose.

"I'll get my men to provide a roadblock both ways on Highway 40 until you're gone," the sheriff said.

Jack nodded. "Thanks."

Wheeler looked at Irene who remained seated on the sofa. "You're coming with me, Irene."

Irene folded her arms around Pookie. "The hell I am."

"This is not up for discussion."

"Oh, yeah? Well, guess what? You can't order me around anymore."

"Irene—"

"What about Janie Sue?"

"I moved out two days ago."

Any other time, Claudia would linger to eavesdrop on what was sure to be a fascinating conversation between Irene and the sheriff. But not today.

She hurried into the bedroom, surprised at the sight of the open trap door in the center of the room, and stuffed underwear, jeans, T-shirts and her cosmetic case into her duffel on top of the journal. She grabbed her Glock and purse and reentered the living room.

The sheriff, Irene and Pookie were gone, but Jack waited for her, wearing a black baseball cap.

"You ready?" he asked.

She nodded.

"Let's go."

"What's with the hat?" she asked as Jack locked the door.

"Disguise." He shoved wraparound sunglasses onto his nose.

"Where are we going?" she asked once inside the SUV. "Do you have a plan?"

Jack started the engine. "I'll worry about a plan when we get out of town."

She frowned at his answer. "Do you think we'll have trouble?"

He hesitated. "I don't know."

"Jack."

"What?"

"Thanks for sticking with me," she said softly.

He turned to glare at her, but she couldn't see his eyes behind the dark lenses.

"Damn, Claudia. Did you really think I wouldn't?"

Before she could answer, he shoved the transmission into Reverse and backed away from the cabin, tires spinning in the gravel. Dust whirled into the air as he straightened his vehicle and punched the gas.

Too nervous to think, Claudia remained silent on the long, bumpy drive through his property to Highway 40, where Jack braked to a stop.

"What's going on?" she asked.

"We wait until we hear from Wheeler."

Claudia nodded as Jack drummed his fingers on the steering wheel. The sheriff had said something about a roadblock on Highway 40, but what good would that do? Yeah, it would allow them time to escape from Jack's property in case the Warriors were already on their way. But would the police block every side street? And once they got past that barrier—

Jack's phone buzzed.

"Richards," he barked. "Yeah, we're in position. Good. Thanks, Chuck. I owe you."

Jack disconnected and faced Claudia. "Are you ready?"

She swallowed. "Yes."

"As a precaution, Chuck will escort us as far as I-75. I want you to slide down beneath the dash so you're not an easy target."

She hesitated, hating the idea of again not being able to see what was happening.

The sheriff's vehicle appeared on the highway, driving toward them. Claudia watched his approach with dread mushrooming in her gut, her brain scrambling for another way out of this trap.

But there wasn't any other choice. They had to relocate, yet this mad dash for freedom seemed crazy.

"They're out there somewhere. Close. And my truck isn't bulletproof," Jack said.

"What about you?"

"One of us has to drive."

"How did they find us, Jack? Was it Marsali?"

He shook his head. "That's not important right now."

Chuck was almost at Jack's driveway. Only one head was visible, so the sheriff had stashed Irene and Pookie somewhere away from the action. At least Jack's mom was safe.

"What if they know this Navigator?" Claudia wondered out loud.

He pointed to his hat. "Remember my disguise."

"You know that's no disguise if they recognize your vehicle. I don't know about this."

"For once, trust me, Claudia."

With a soft curse, she released her seat belt and curled up on the floorboard. What choice did she have? Her sweats covered most of her bare flesh, but grainy dirt from the sole of someone's shoe pressed into her cheek. Was this her life from now on—never being able to see where she was going?

"Here we go," Jack said, accelerating with a right turn onto Highway 40.

The truck bumped onto the highway. The road hummed beneath her, the vibration increasing as the Navigator picked up speed. Claudia focused on Jack's face, hoping his expression would yield clues as to what was happening. But the sunglasses shielded his eyes, and the black cap covered his forehead. His jaw remained set, his gaze fixed on the road ahead.

"How long do I have to stay down here?" she asked.

"Until we get to I-75." Jack's voice remained steady, which reassured her slightly. She'd been asleep when they'd driven in weeks ago, but knew the interstate was a twenty-minute drive away. Only twenty minutes. Twenty long minutes.

And then what?

"Are we going north or south?"

He didn't answer immediately, then nodded as if coming to a decision. "South. Toward Orlando. There are thousands of motel rooms around Disney. We'll find a dive that will allow me to pay cash for the week."

That made sense to Claudia. She felt a whole lot better that Jack had a plan.

Only one more week. All they had to do was remain alive seven more days. Then she'd testify and this nightmare would be over.

As would any connection to Jack.

His phone buzzed. "Richards...What?...Shit."

He flung his phone into the seat. "Brace yourself."

CHAPTER TWENTY-ONE

JACK FLOORED THE ACCELERATOR. As the Navigator rocketed forward, Claudia pressed her feet and hands against the seat as her body was flung backward. A siren wailed in the distance.

"What's happening?" she demanded.

"A pickup truck breached the west roadblock," Jack said. "They ran down a deputy. Shots were fired."

Claudia's gut tightened. So her nightmare wasn't over quite yet.

"Is the deputy okay?"

"Unknown. But another deputy is in pursuit. They're headed this way."

Claudia heard a horrible screech of tires. Not the Navigator. Its speed didn't alter.

Another siren blared. This one close.

"What was that?" she demanded.

"The sheriff executed a U-turn to assist his men." Jack glanced into the rearview mirror. "He'll meet the Warriors head-on."

Every instinct Claudia possessed urged her to get up from the floorboard so she could see. Maybe she wouldn't be shot down here, but without the protection of a seat belt, she was in just as much danger from a crash or a rollover. Maybe more.

"Hold on." Jack applied the brakes. The Navigator's rear end slid, but the tires held and the vehicle came to a wrenching stop.

"Red light," Jack said, gaze on the rearview mirror.

"Shouldn't we get off the road?" she asked. "Let the sheriff handle this?"

"And do what? Wait for the terrorists to nail us?"

"I don't know, but we can't keep speeding down Highway 40 and hope we make the lights."

"There's only two more."

"We can find somewhere to hide."

"That's exactly what we're—"

Another long screech of tires straining to grip the road halted Jack's words. Claudia sucked in a breath waiting for it—and there it was—the sickening thud of metal against metal. Whose car? The siren stopped.

Jack punched the accelerator, and she was flung back again. His jaw clenched, he again glanced in the rearview. Another siren shrieked a warning.

Claudia sighed in relief. Good. The cops hadn't given up.

"Can you see anything?" she asked.

"No. Chuck is out of sight." He glanced down to her. "But that didn't sound good."

"Let me come up," she begged.

"No. Stay down."

As if to emphasize his words, the sharp report of gunfire sounded in the distance. Then more shots.

Jack cursed.

"Oh, my God," Claudia moaned, terrified for Chuck Wheeler and his deputies. All of this was because of her. Were any police injured in that crash? Wounded in the flurry of shots? Bleeding? Dead?

"Grab my phone," Jack ordered, eyes straight ahead. "I need you to make a call."

Spotting the phone on the seat, Claudia pushed up and took it, catching a quick blur of trees rushing by on both sides of the truck. How fast were they going?

Nauseous from the too-rapid sensory input, she lowered herself back down.

"Press number five," Jack said. "That's the dispatcher."

Because of the motion of the SUV, she could barely focus on the tiny keypad.

"No, no, no!" Jack shouted. He slammed on his brakes and applied the horn in one long continuous blast.

Thrown toward the front of the Navigator, Claudia lost the phone. Her head collided with the floorboard.

Other horns sounded. No telling how many tires screeched.

The Navigator fishtailed, straightened and Jack punched the accelerator again.

"You okay?" he asked when they were back up to speed.

"I'll live." Rubbing her head, she searched for the phone. "Intersection?"

"Yeah. The light changed just as we approached. The other drivers were none too happy."

Claudia located the phone, punched in number five and stretched to hand it to Jack.

"I'm approaching the eastern roadblock without Wheeler," Jack said. "I need to be let through because I'm not slowing down."

After a pause, during which she supposed the dispatcher relayed information, Jack asked, "How bad? Any word from the sheriff? Thanks."

Jack tossed the phone away.

"Is Chuck okay?"

"Unknown."

Before she could ask another question, Jack cursed.

"What?" she demanded.

"They're right on our ass," Jack said.

A gun fired. Close. Too close. What had to be a bullet slammed into the Navigator, the sound more frightening than anything she'd ever heard in her life.

She closed her eyes. This couldn't be happening. Yet it was.

Another noise. A window shattered. Three more bullets pinged into the car's metal.

Jack didn't slow down.

"Stay low," he ordered, his voice strained.

She reached inside her purse and felt for the Glock. She wrapped her fingers around the cool plastic ridges. What good would this do if she couldn't see anything to shoot?

"Not much longer," Jack said. "We're almost to the second roadblock."

"Is there another cop car chasing the Warriors?" Claudia asked.

"I think there's two."

"Why won't they stop?" she moaned, her gaze glued to Jack's grim face. "They can't get away."

"They've got nothing to lose at this point."

"So they intend to die for their stupid cause?"

"And take us with them." Jack grimaced and shifted in the seat. "That's the point."

"Oh, God," Claudia whispered. How could anyone be willing to die for Carlos Romero, a jerk who was nothing but a big bully?

"We're there," Jack said, his voice tight. "This isn't going to be pretty."

Wishing with all her heart that she could see, Claudia stiffened, preparing herself for the inevitable crash she knew was coming. What would it feel like? *Maybe it's better if I don't see the end.*

Jack sucked in a loud breath. Claudia closed her eyes. *This is it.*

But the Navigator kept racing at an ungodly speed. They didn't roll, didn't collide with anything.

Sudden noise exploded—as if a freight train rumbled by next to her ear. But it wasn't a train. It was one hell of a lot of bullets being fired.

It had to be the cops firing at the terrorists chasing Jack. Did they make it through the roadblock?

As if holding on to a lifeline, Jack clutched the wheel with both hands, his eyes focused on the road. She didn't dare distract him with questions.

He flicked a glance to the rearview. "Oh, shit," he muttered, his tone full of awe.

"What?" Claudia begged.

Before he could answer, a vehicle somewhere smashed hard into something solid. Next came an explosion, the sound deafening. Probably a gas tank. She swiveled her head to see out the passenger window. Black smoke mushroomed into the air, along with a strong acrid odor. No one had survived that.

"The Warriors went airborne," Jack said. "Guess they thought they could fly."

Without slowing down, Jack swerved sharply to the right, the motion again flinging Claudia across the floorboard.

"You can get up now," he said. "We're on I-75."

Claudia scrambled onto the seat and clicked her seat belt into place.

Pushing her hair behind her ear, she asked, "What happened?"

"Well, I can tell you that particular truck of terrorists will not be giving us any more trouble."

She turned to look back. Behind them, smoke still billowed into the air, but they were too far away to smell the burning gas. More sirens screamed, and she surmised the fire department now added to the din.

"The fools ran the blockade?" she asked.

"Hit a parked cop car at full speed."

She faced front again and released a breath. Was it over? Were they safe?

"Any cops hurt?" she asked.

"Unknown, but I doubt it. Looked to me as if they anticipated the outcome and stayed clear." He shook his head. "But I was going fast. Hard to say for sure."

She released a breath and offered a silent prayer for the police involved in their escape. Escape? Had they truly gotten away?

Doubtful.

"So are we okay?" she asked.

"For now," Jack said. "It'll take them time to regroup."

"So you think there'll be more bad guys?"

"There's always more bad guys."

She nodded. Of course there was. Even after she testified—assuming she got out of this mess alive—she'd always be looking over her shoulder.

And she wouldn't have Jack to protect her.

She shoved away the memory of their insane wild dash for freedom. It was over. She didn't need to think about it anymore. Somehow they'd made it out safely.

Claudia was relieved that they rode without speaking. Her nerves were frayed into confetti. She suspected even Jack needed some time to recover. They rocketed south on the interstate, pushing the speed limit, putting distance between them and the horror.

This part of the state was lightly populated, heavily wooded. Trees flew by on both sides of the Navigator, calming her, allowing her to consider what would happen next. Would the Warriors locate them again? And how did the terrorists find them in Dunnellon?

"Have you figured out how they found us?" she asked, breaking the silence.

When Jack didn't reply, she turned to look at him and gasped. His face was pale, coated with a sheen of sweat, and he drove with only his right arm. He no longer sat erect behind the wheel.

"What's wrong?" she demanded. "Talk to me, Jack."

He tossed her a look. A look she recognized only too well from her years of nursing. This man was in serious pain.

"There's a rest area coming up," he said, his voice weaker than she'd ever heard it. "You're going to have to drive."

She scanned his body and spotted blood spreading through the gray sweatshirt on his left shoulder and arm. The driver's-side window had been shattered. Damn. He'd been shot.

"You're hit," she accused.

"Sorry about that," he muttered. He moved the Navigator to the far right lane and slowed.

"How bad is it?" she asked.

"How the hell do I know? I'm not a nurse."

"Bull." He didn't want to tell her, which meant the wound was serious.

"Are you still bleeding?"

"Yeah."

"Why didn't you tell me?"

"Thought I'd be okay. Not as if I could stop."

"I need to stop the bleeding."

Jack exited the interstate and brought the Navigator to a stop at the far end of the rest stop, away from any other vehicles. Claudia released her seat belt, jumped out and raced to his side of the truck. He'd slumped against the seat and closed his eyes.

She ripped the cotton fabric to assess the damage.

"Oh, my God," she gasped, then clamped her mouth shut, furious with herself. She knew better than to alarm a patient with her reaction to an injury. But this wasn't just any patient.

She loved this man with all her heart. And he'd just taken a bullet for her.

He'd saved her life.

The bullet had entered his shoulder, exited and slammed into the seat cushion, grazing his huge muscled thigh. His sweatpants had been burned by the friction. That's how close it had come.

If the trajectory had been a mere inch or two to the left—she dismissed the horrifying thought of his femoral artery being hit and spurting blood with every beat of Jack's strong heart.

It didn't happen. *Treat the injury in front of you.*

Yes, he was bleeding, but not badly. The brachial artery had been spared. They'd been lucky. The first bit of luck they'd had since they'd started their journey.

Hands shaking, she ripped open her duffel and dug out her cosmetic case, which contained a tube of antibiotic cream. She gently smeared a coating over both the entrance and exit wounds, an act she'd performed countless times that somehow calmed her. Steadier now, she tore apart one of her T-shirts, fashioned it into a makeshift bandage and secured it around his shoulder with as much pressure as she could manage. Eyes closed, Jack didn't offer any protest while she worked.

"How do you feel?" she asked.

"Like shit."

"Can you walk?" she asked when finished.

"Yeah."

She helped him down from the truck. Supporting his weight, she tried to walk him to the backseat.

"No," he said, resisting the direction.

"What?"

"Up front—with you."

"You need to lie down, Jack, elevate your legs so you don't go into shock. I'm surprised you haven't already."

He shook her off, swaying for a moment. She stepped forward to catch him before he fell, but he collapsed against the Navigator.

A car drove by, its occupants eyeing them speculatively.

"What's wrong with you? Get in the backseat and
lie down."

Jaw set—using what was surely his last bit of
energy—Jack pushed off the Navigator, walked to
the passenger side, opened the door and pulled himself into the seat.

She shook her head but didn't argue. She knew
why. Sure, it was okay if *she* couldn't see what was
going on, but not if Jack couldn't. He had to stay in
control. Stubborn gladiator.

She hauled herself into the driver's seat, adjusted it
so she could reach the pedals and put on her seat belt.

She had one mission now—getting Jack to an ER.
She took a deep breath.

"We need to find the closest hospital," she said.

"Agreed."

That surprised her. She reached for his phone. After
she spent several seconds of fumbling with apps, Jack
took the phone from her hands. His fingers were icy.

"Let me," he said.

While he worked the tiny computer, she eyed her
less than professional bandage, looking for blood
seepage. Nothing yet. Maybe keeping him upright
was better since it would slow down blood loss.
Maybe not.

"Westview Hospital near Winter Haven is the
closest. Get back on the interstate and drive south."

She handed him a plastic bottle of water from the console. Half full. No telling how long it had been there, but in their hurry to flee neither one of them had thought to bring any food or water.

"Drink," she said. "You need fluids."

He upended the bottle and drained it.

"Thanks," he muttered. He turned to look at her. "Drive, Claudia. We can't stay immobile."

CHAPTER TWENTY-TWO

JACK SHIFTED IN the seat, trying to get comfortable. The pain wasn't the worst of it.

True, his whole shoulder and arm hurt badly, but he'd been shot before. He knew how to deal with pain. And they'd caught a break that the bullet had exited cleanly.

It was his fear for Claudia that made him crazy. What would she do once he was admitted to the hospital? Where could she go?

He needed to ignore the pain and figure that out. If the Warriors had tracked Claudia to Dunnellon, they could find her anywhere.

She couldn't remain in an ER waiting room. The ER staff would notify the police of a patient with a gunshot wound. It would be all over the police scanners for anyone to hear.

She would be located again. Quickly.

Did these terrorists have ears in the US Attorney's Office? Or on Lola in the Protection Alliance office? He doubted the latter. Too many safeguards in place. Most likely his mother somehow managed to give away their location. He no longer doubted Chuck—who may or may not be alive. Or maybe

Marsali Winthrop had managed to figure out where they were hiding.

The how of their discovery shouldn't matter now, but it definitely did if he wanted to keep Claudia alive.

Just another week. That's all he needed.

Would she go back to Miami? Allow the prosecutor to stash her in a safe house? After all that had happened, surely the feds would realize how serious the danger was and do everything required to keep her alive.

The bigger question was, would Claudia trust them and go along with it.

Probably not. She didn't trust anyone. Not even him. A sense of betrayal gripped him again, squeezing hard, harder than the pain in his arm. *Hold it together, man. Focus.*

When Claudia braked to a stop, they were on a city street, surrounded by commercial buildings. He blinked. She'd exited the interstate. He must have faded out for a second or two. Not good.

"How are you doing?" she asked, her voice soft.

"Great," he mumbled.

She accelerated. "We're almost there."

He nodded.

"We need to get our story straight," she said.

"What do you mean?"

"We have to tell the ER staff how you got that bullet wound. Something plausible. I wouldn't believe the truth."

"*We* don't have to do anything. You deliver me to the emergency room and drive away."

"What?"

"Listen to me, Claudia." He sucked in a breath, searching for the words to convince her. "You'll be trapped, vulnerable."

"No way, Jack."

"You can't stay with me."

"You expect me to drive away and leave you bleeding?"

"I'll be in a hospital."

"I'm not abandoning you, Gladiator. Forget it."

"Damn it, Claudia. Stay with the plan. Drive to Orlando. Find a motel, something cheap, out of the way. I'll give you cash."

"Shut up, Jack. It's not happening."

She pulled under an overhang and braked. To his right were glass doors with Emergency Room in huge block letters.

"I'm not getting out of this truck unless you promise to drive away."

"Don't be ridiculous. You need medical attention."

"I won't get it unless you leave."

"I'm not leaving you," she said. "I can't."

"Yes, you can." He struggled to hold on to his anger, and realized he was struggling to hold on to consciousness.

"I love you, Jack," she said softly. "I'm not leaving you."

She loved him? When did that happen? He shook

his head, trying to focus. She'd called him *Gladiator*. What was that about? His eyes drifted closed, and he forced them open. He had to stay alert. He had to convince her. She had to listen to him. But his thinking was so damn fuzzy he wanted to tell her he loved her, too.

"If they find me, they find me," she said. "I don't care anymore. You're more important."

"No," he said.

"You've done all you can, all anyone could do." Shaking her head, she said, "Don't you see I *can't* leave you here alone? I couldn't live with myself. Because of me, you're vulnerable now, too."

Jack knew if she went in that hospital with him, she'd die. He knew it in his bones. Or was that more fuzzy thinking?

Why couldn't he think straight? Must be all this crap about love and gladiators.

"I'm getting out of the car now," she said, her hand on the door handle. "I'm coming around to help you inside."

"You'll have to fight me."

"Jack, please. Be reasonable."

"Could you stitch me up?"

She paused. "I could, yeah. The bullet passed through cleanly, didn't do a lot of damage. But I don't have anesthetic. Or nothing strong enough, anyway."

"Doesn't matter."

"I know you think you're Rambo, but come on."

"Yeah, that's it." He closed his eyes. "I'm Rambo." Too bad Rambo was slipping under.

"It'll hurt like hell," she said. "And there's the risk of infection."

"Antibiotics are easy to get."

"Yeah, they are." She sighed. "Too easy. I have some tetracycline."

Relief flooded him as he realized she was wavering.

"Maybe we could try it," she said, obviously thinking aloud. "Considering what we've been through so far..."

"Drive away, Claudia. Find a cheap motel. There's cash in my wallet."

JACK AWOKE WITH a start. He grunted, jerked upright. What the— His left side throbbing with pain, he began an assessment. A dark room. Unfamiliar. Musty.

He reached out with his right arm, searching for his weapon.

"Shhhh." A calming sound. A cool hand cupped his forehead. He looked into the most beautiful blue eyes he'd ever seen. Kind eyes, worried. Claudia.

And everything came slamming back.

Cursing, he collapsed back onto the lumpy bed. They were in a motel. Kissimmee. Definitely a dive from the smell of things. He closed his eyes, remembering the haze of Claudia helping him out of the truck, wrestling him into bed, making him swallow pills, drowning his arm in alcohol.

God, that had stung, but much worse came next. She'd sutured his wounds with amazingly steady hands.

She'd been right. It *had* hurt. Still did.

The mattress dipped as Claudia sat beside him. He opened his eyes.

"Take this," she said, and held out a glass of water and a capsule. Suddenly parched, he popped the pill and drank every drop, recalling that sometime during the night she'd lifted his head, softly encouraging him to drink cool water.

He lay back down, relishing the feel of the cool sheets, and realized he was naked but for his briefs. She'd stripped him.

"How do you feel?" she asked, taking the glass.

He held up his hand and made a rocking motion, surveying the darkened room. The blackout curtains were drawn tight, light barely filtering in around the edges. She'd propped a chair underneath the doorknob to prevent anyone from breaking in. A small microwave sat atop a mini refrigerator. Coffee machine. Television. Your standard cheap motel room.

To his right a digital clock on a cheap nightstand read 10:45. Had to be a.m.

"Is it Saturday?" he asked, his voice rough.

"Yeah. You slept through the night. Fitfully, but you slept. Best thing for you."

"Did you sleep?" he asked.

"Not much."

He noted she'd strapped on her shoulder holster,

the Glock in place. His own weapons were laid out on the opposite nightstand. She'd created an arsenal and stood ready to defend him.

He hoped that wouldn't be necessary. At least not until he regained his strength. How much time did they have before the Warriors found them?

"Are you hungry?" she asked.

"Too soon to tell."

"What's your pain level?"

"You don't want to know. Bring me up to speed. What's been going on?"

"I registered under Louise Clark with my fake ID," she said, shoving uncombed hair off her forehead. "Paid cash for five days in advance. I told the clerk me and the hubby planned to do all the theme parks, but you had food poisoning."

He grunted. Good cover story.

"I went out once for groceries, and parked the Navigator in a location hidden from the street maybe a half mile away. I walked back. They'll have to look hard to spot our vehicle."

"Good."

"I talked to the prosecutor, but called the pay phone at a coffee shop near his office. I got the number before I went to Collins Island."

"In case something like this happened," Jack guessed.

"The trial still starts Monday, but Reese won't need me until Friday at the earliest. I'm supposed to check in again on Thursday."

Jack nodded. Thursday. Could they hole up in this room until then?

"I picked up a copy of an Orlando newspaper. The shoot-out in Marion County is front-page news. As we suspected, two people in the truck died. Chuck is banged up, but okay. He went on camera for the evening news last night. One of his deputies is in critical condition."

"Damn," Jack muttered. "Who?"

She shook her head. "I don't remember the name. I think it's in the article, though. I saved it for you. I'm so sorry, Jack."

"Any mention of you?"

"Not me or Carlos. Or you or your mom."

"Chuck managed to keep it quiet."

"For now," Claudia said. She yawned, but tried to hide it with a hand.

Jack reached out with his uninjured arm to touch her leg and was rewarded with her first smile. Even in the dim light he could see her eyes glittered with tears.

"You did good, Claudia."

CLAUDIA CLASPED HIS cool fingers with both of her hands, hating the pitiful little sob she couldn't suppress. She stared down to where they were joined. Her two hands couldn't cover his one big one.

Every muscle in her body tingled with exhaustion, as if stretched beyond breaking. Last night had been horrible, never-ending. She'd been terrified that Jack wouldn't regain consciousness, that she'd made the worst mistake of her life by not forcing him into the ER. Worse than marrying Carlos.

But he was okay. A tear dropped onto her wrist.

She blew out a breath. *Get a grip, girl. You fall apart now when the crisis is over?*

"You should get some rest," Jack whispered.

"I'll sleep after I change your bandage. I need to check for infection."

Reluctantly, she released his hand and rose. "Close your eyes." She turned on the lights, wincing at the sudden brightness.

When she returned to Jack, he asked, "Where did you get medical supplies?"

"A pharmacy next to the grocery. Sorry, but this will hurt."

"Do it," he said.

Trying to be gentle, Claudia removed the bandage. She'd seen neater sutures, but these weren't too bad. The wounds were healing nicely. No sign of infection. Plus, Jack wasn't feverish. No doubt her gladiator had the best immune system in the known universe.

On a good day, he could probably deflect bullets. That thought made her smile as she rebandaged his shoulder.

"Something funny?" he asked.

She looked into his green eyes. "I was just thinking what an amazing body you have."

His mouth twitched. "Sorry, honey. Not tonight. I've got a headache."

She laughed. A real laugh, the first one in months, God, maybe years. It broke some tension wound tight deeply inside her, became a release that she couldn't control. She kept hooting until her stomach hurt, until her eyes swam with tears.

Jack narrowed his eyes. "It wasn't *that* funny."

But his words only made her laugh harder. She collapsed sidewise on the bed. *Oh, my God.* She was cackling like a witch and couldn't stop.

"What exactly are you laughing at?" Jack demanded.

She rolled onto her back and tried to control her mirth, but chuckles kept hiccupping out. "I don't know."

"Claudia," he said quietly.

She inhaled deeply and pushed herself up to face him, trying to suppress another fit of giggles.

"Come here." Jack extended his good arm, and she crawled across the bed to snuggle up on his uninjured side.

"Sorry," she murmured, her head on his shoulder. But she wasn't really. Her ludicrous laughing fit had turned off a stress switch, if such a thing existed. Right now she didn't care if Carlos's Warriors found her. Curled up next to Jack, touching him, everything seemed okay.

After a moment, she asked, "Am I hurting you?"

"You're fine." He laid a hand on her hair and

stroked lightly. Her eyes drifted shut, his breathing steady under her ear.

"So are you," she murmured. *Oh, so very fine.*

She smiled at her thoughts, but the giggles didn't return. As she drifted off she thought she heard Jack mutter something, but was too sleepy to struggle to comprehend.

She awoke in darkness. No light was visible around the edges of the curtains. Jack slept beside her, his breathing regular. She touched his arm. Cool. No fever. Thank God. He had to be better because he'd gotten up at some point to kill the lights.

She turned to read the digital clock. Nine thirty. She'd slept away the day beside Jack, not even bothering to remove her holster.

Careful not to disturb him, she climbed out of bed and stretched. She found a soda in the refrigerator and took a long cool drink. Refreshed, she grabbed her journal from her duffel and moved to a chair close to the door where she could angle the light away from Jack. They'd missed the six o'clock news, but maybe they could learn something at eleven.

For now, she'd make sense of her feelings by writing them out. Journaling had made her realize what a good person Jack was, which allowed her to trust her own judgment again. Too bad it had taken so long. Jack would never forgive her for doubting him.

After writing for a short time, she got that eerie feeling of being watched and glanced up. Jack's eyes were open and staring at her. Sporting a two-day beard, he looked more intimidating than usual.

He swung his legs over the bed.

Claudia tossed the book aside and moved to help him, but he rose effortlessly.

"How do you feel?" she asked.

"Like I need to piss," he growled.

"Go for it." She stepped aside and brightened the lights.

When he returned from the bathroom, he opened the refrigerator and peered inside with a sour expression. "Didn't you say something about groceries?"

"How about some chicken soup?"

"I'd rather have a steak."

"Me, too. Can we risk going out?"

He shook his head. "Soup's fine." He rummaged in her grocery bags, found a bag of potato chips and opened it with a vicious snap. Cramming chips in his mouth, he returned to the bed.

Ignoring his grumpy mood, Claudia added water to cardboard cups, stirred the contents, and placed the mixture in the microwave. Jack had reached that point of recuperation where the patient became ill-tempered, which would make their already tense situation worse. But big deal. He was alive.

"Time for an antibiotic," she said, handing him a plastic water bottle and two pills.

"What's the other one?"

"For pain."

"Just the antibiotic," he said. "I need to stay alert."

She hesitated. "What's your pain level?"

He rolled his eyes. "I'm fine."

She knew better, but removed one of the capsules. He swallowed the remaining pill, downing all of the water in one long pull.

"What were you writing?" he asked, nodding toward the chair.

"I was bringing my journal up to date."

"Why?"

"It helps me make sense of things to write them down."

He raised his eyebrows. "Yeah? Maybe I should start a journal so I can understand you."

She nodded. She definitely deserved that jab. "Putting the words on paper made me realize that I can trust you."

"About damn time."

"I'm sorry I doubted you."

He shrugged and stuffed more chips into his mouth.

"You're the best man I've ever met, Jack."

The microwave pinged. Their dinner was ready. Claudia rose and removed steaming soup from the microwave. As she stirred, she knew Jack would never understand why she found it so hard to trust. He'd never lived with Carlos's poison.

"Do you still love your ex?" he asked.

She whirled. "What? How can you ask that?"

"Sometimes we love people even though we shouldn't."

Wondering if there was hidden meaning in his words, she picked up the soup cups with terry-cloth towels. "I despise Carlos Romero."

"Maybe he still loves you."

"Oh, I'm sure." She placed Jack's cup on the table beside him. "That's why he sent those goons after us."

"Maybe the goons are no longer taking orders from him. Maybe they're worried he's going to flip on them for a reduced sentence."

Claudia seated herself in the chair facing Jack. "That's a lot of maybes."

"You must have loved him once."

She shook her head. "I don't think I ever did."

"So why did you marry him?"

Well, there's a question. To delay her answer, she reached for the soup, but it was still too hot. "I have bad judgment when it comes to men. If I'm attracted, I let my hormones do the talking."

He folded his arms. "What happened with me?"

"I was terrified of you," she said. "Because I wanted you from the moment I saw you."

"You're a good actress. I thought you were Santaluce's mistress."

"Oh? I suppose women usually rip off your clothes ten seconds after 'hello'?"

"Usually," he agreed.

"Wipe that smirk off your face and eat."

"So when did you fall in love with me?"

CHAPTER TWENTY-THREE

WATCHING CLAUDIA'S REACTION, Jack rubbed the stubble on his face.

She raised her gaze and met his direct stare. "You remember me saying that?"

He nodded. "I remember." The question was why he wanted to talk about it.

Claudia placed her soup on the table. "I thought you were too out of it."

"Almost, but not quite."

She looked away.

"How can you be in love with someone you don't trust?" he asked.

"One of the great mysteries of the world," she murmured.

He remembered their first meeting, her cool reserve and his own vicious pull of attraction. Yeah, a total mystery.

She sighed. "As ridiculous as it sounds, despite everything, I was happy living with you in that cabin. Happier than I've ever been."

He blinked and reached for his soup. "You like the cabin?"

"I felt like I belonged there."

Jack let those words dangle in the air as he scarfed down the soup. *What? Three bites?* He scraped the bottom of the cup, doubting any chicken had died for this thin broth.

"How about a turkey sandwich?" Claudia suggested.

"That would be awesome."

Jack remained silent as she prepared the food. He liked watching her efficient movements, probably developed from years of nursing. Hard to believe she'd felt comfortable in his cabin. He'd never met another woman who could stand the place, yet she claimed to have been happy there. And now she was taking care of him, even refusing to abandon him at the hospital. While he'd vehemently objected, deep down he'd been touched by her courage.

She claimed to love him. Could such love be real? Or just a result of forced togetherness and his protection?

What would it be like to move home and live in the cabin permanently with Claudia? Nurses were in demand everywhere, right?

He shoved away those thoughts.

"Maybe this will improve your mood." Claudia presented him the sandwich.

"Another big maybe." He took a huge, satisfying bite.

She aimed the remote at the television. "I want to watch the news."

She climbed into the bed on his good side, leaving

distance he didn't like between them, and arranged pillows to lean against.

The lead story dealt with worries over a possible freeze and damage to orange groves. The shoot-out in Marion County came next. A police spokesman—not Chuck—claimed the roadblock had been designed to catch fleeing felons. But the reporter dangled questions about who these mysterious felons were.

The section ended with, "Dead men can't answer questions."

"Amazing." Claudia muted the sound. "They act like they feel sorry for the bad guys."

"Because of the mystery surrounding who they are. Chuck bottled it up tight, giving us time to get somewhere safe."

She shook her head. "The media will keep digging until they unearth something."

"By then you'll have testified."

"Maybe," she whispered.

"Are you getting cold feet?"

"No. Definitely not." She looked toward the window. "But I am sick of hiding."

Jack followed her gaze. Nothing to see thanks to the curtains. Yeah, he was tired of hiding, too, but some sick part of him didn't want this journey to end. After he delivered Claudia to Miami, would he ever see her again?

"And what if the Warriors find us?" she asked.

"Come here." He raised his arm, inviting her to move closer, pleased she didn't hesitate.

With her head resting on his shoulder, he said, "It's unlikely they'll find us by Thursday. They suffered a huge loss and have to start over."

"I'm sorry, Jack," she said softly.

He closed his eyes and breathed in the fragrance of her hair. "For what?"

"Getting you involved, getting you shot, not trusting you. For everything."

"I'm not sorry."

"You're not?"

"Not for everything."

"Yeah." He felt her smile even though he couldn't see it. "Some things were great."

As he stroked her hair, he knew by her tone that she alluded to their lovemaking—which, no question, had been beyond spectacular—but he was thinking more of hikes through the forest to the gun range, easy conversations about nothing special, quiet evenings they'd shared with his mother and how Claudia had helped repair that bond. Her willingness to help around the cabin. Her courage.

Was that love? His momma said he didn't know what love was.

Did he even believe in love? Had he ever seen a relationship work out?

With a sigh, Claudia raised the remote and turned on the sound.

AT FIRST LIGHT Thursday morning, her ever-present holster hidden beneath a sweatshirt, Claudia hurried toward the Navigator, constantly surveying the area for trouble. When she got close, she breathed a sigh of relief. Although covered with dust, the SUV remained where she'd parked it. The engine turned over on the first try. Had her luck changed?

Alone in the sparse motel room, she'd endured four tense days with her gladiator, hoping he'd forgive her, maybe admit he loved her, too. But that was a pipe dream. They played a lot of cards, read, watched horrible TV, suffered through restless nights, but didn't do much talking.

What was there left to say? She loved him, but he didn't love her. He was her protector, her bodyguard, and that's as far as it went. So there wasn't any hope for them. He hadn't made love to her, but he'd been shot. Or at least that's what she told herself. She'd been too afraid of rejection—or too proud—to initiate anything herself.

He'd watched her constantly with those intense green eyes, making her feel nervous and wonder what he was thinking. She didn't ask. They were like polite strangers.

But they weren't strangers anymore.

He was healing nicely, although he wouldn't be swimming any laps or performing marathon push-ups for a while yet.

When she backed up the Navigator to their motel

room, Jack tossed their meager possessions inside before she'd come to a complete stop.

"I'll drive," he said.

Claudia slid to the passenger side and snapped on her seat belt.

"Any trouble?" he asked as he accelerated onto the all but deserted highway.

"Nothing," she said.

"We've seen the last of the Warriors," Jack said confidently. "At least for a while."

"Maybe." After the shoot-out in Marion County, the story had remained on the evening news for days. Her name had emerged, and law enforcement had stomped down hard on the Warriors, bringing in at least twenty members of the group for questioning. Two had been arrested for obstruction of justice. In Miami, a jury had been seated in Carlos's trial. Opening arguments started today.

All she had to do was make it through one more night. Then she could start her life again.

A life without Jack. Whenever she remembered that, a hollow space inside her grew larger.

If only she'd realized what a good man he was sooner. She released a sigh. But would that have mattered? She couldn't make him love her.

"What?" Jack said.

Snapped out of her depressing thoughts, Claudia noticed they were headed south on the Florida Turnpike. "How should I disguise myself to enter the courthouse?"

He shot her a glance, a smile playing on his lips. "Is it true blondes have more fun?"

"I wouldn't know."

"You're about to find out."

IN ANOTHER NONDESCRIPT motel room, this one in North Miami, Jack stepped back to admire his handiwork.

Unsmiling, eyes wide, Claudia stared into the bathroom mirror at a woman with short blond hair.

He couldn't tell if she liked it or was horrified. The cut might be a little ragged, but not bad. He'd picked a dye to make her hair as light as possible. He wasn't sure how he felt about the change himself. She was Claudia, but somehow different.

With glasses, even her ex wouldn't recognize her.

She turned her head one way, then the other. "If you get bored with the protection racket, you can always start a new career as a hairstylist."

"You think?"

"You're a man of many talents, Jack," she said, meeting his gaze in the mirror.

A knock had them both whirling toward the door. Jack approached with a weapon drawn and moved the curtain.

He tucked the gun in his waistband.

"Pizza," he reported, opening the door. They'd decided to splurge on hot food for the first time in almost a week, but elected to order in. Just in case.

He placed the warm box in the center of the bed

and lifted the cover. Steam floated into the air, releasing the fragrance of garlic and sausage.

Grinning, Claudia approached. "That smells divine."

Jack grabbed a slice, took a bite and nodded.

Still not used to the strange blonde he'd created, he watched Claudia as they scarfed down the pizza. He'd heard of men getting turned on when their wives or girlfriends changed hair color, but not him. He preferred the old Claudia and wondered how long it would take for her natural color to grow back. He hoped not long.

Then, with a stab of pain to his gut, he realized he'd never know.

His appetite gone, he tossed his slice back into the box and glared at her.

Claudia raised her eyebrows. "What?"

"I need some air."

He was out the door before she could object. He needed to move. That was the way he always made sense of things. She wrote; he moved. He waited until she resecured the lock before walking toward the warehouse area behind the motel.

The night was cold, but he began to jog, causing the holster to thump against his side. He'd be sweating before long.

He and Claudia danced around his need to forgive her. Why couldn't he let it go? Some bit of pigheaded male pride? She'd apologized countless times, and the truth was he understood why she hadn't trusted him. Carlos Romero had made her afraid of everyone, not just him. He'd made her fear life.

Why couldn't he tell her, make things right between them?

His mother claimed he was the most stubborn person on the face of the earth. Maybe she was right. Hadn't it taken him three years to forgive her?

Claudia wouldn't wait three years. No woman would. So he'd lose her, and the thought of living without her made him want to break something. He'd gotten used to her smile, having someone to think about, work with, *be* with.

Maybe it was because he'd never been in love before and didn't know how to handle the power of that emotion. So he ran like hell from it.

He'd never felt this way about any other woman. Was he afraid of those feelings?

Damn right he was afraid. And running.

He stopped, placed his hands on his knees and inhaled deeply. She called him her gladiator, like he was brave enough to fight lions barehanded.

She was wrong.

He didn't even have the courage to fight for their love.

"I'LL BE AT the courthouse in an hour," Claudia told Reese Beauchamps, her gaze on Jack, who paced the room, obviously ready to go, anxious to finally be rid of her.

"Someone will meet me, right? And you'll have the clothes, size eight? Thanks." She disconnected and handed Jack his phone.

"Security is in place?" he demanded.

"He claims an army of FBI agents will meet us."

Jack nodded. "Good. Are you nervous?"

She placed a hand on her uneasy belly. Nervous? She was a pathetic wreck, but not about testifying. She'd be in a room full of people and safe for the first time in weeks. But Jack would drop her off at the courthouse and drive away. She'd never see him again.

"I just want it over with," she whispered, unable to meet his penetrating gaze.

He stepped toward the door. "Then let's get moving."

"Right," she said with a quick nod.

The morning was cold and dark when they exited the motel. They rode in silence. Claudia tried to plan what she'd say on the witness stand. That was what was important, why she'd met Jack in the first place. Hyperaware of him alertly navigating the streets of Miami, constantly checking the rearview mirror, all she could think about was how empty her life would be without him in it.

She'd been nourishing a faint hope that he'd say something to her about what would happen after the trial—but what? He simply didn't love her enough, or maybe not at all. Not the way she loved him.

She surely didn't want to suffer through some embarrassing conversation about what a great gal she was, but how she just wasn't the right woman for him, how he wished her all the best.

So it was better this way. The break should be clean and quick. No last minute recriminations. He couldn't help who he was. She'd get over it. Or anyway, she hoped so.

He'd been her bodyguard, and he'd completed his mission. She was still alive to testify. That's all he signed on for. She should be grateful to him for that.

The sun hadn't yet risen when Jack braked to a stop in front of a boxy seven-story building. Seven or eight suited unsmiling men and women waited on the sidewalk.

"Do you see Beauchamps?" he asked.

"Yes," she answered. Willing herself not to cry, she turned to Jack and took a deep breath. "Thanks for everything."

"You're welcome."

"I'll never forget you, Jack," she said, her voice breaking as she spoke his name.

He smiled. "I know."

Claudia gripped the door handle, a prick of anger breaking through her regrets. Arrogant, insufferable male. *He knows? Damn him.*

Reese jerked open her door as Jack said, "Good luck."

FBI agents surrounded her and escorted her into the courthouse. She watched the Navigator drive away, but events didn't allow time to feel sorry for herself. She was introduced to two female agents who swept her into a bathroom where she changed into the clothing they provided as they barraged her with questions about where she'd been and what she'd been doing. She met with Reese to review her testimony until it was time for court to begin. She was his first witness.

Even waiting for her testimony in a chilly conference room, the agents kept at her with questions about the Warriors, her time on Collins Island and how she knew Rodolfo Santaluce.

Then everyone looked up at a knock on the door. It was time.

Claudia's first impression of the courtroom was that every seat was filled. And every pair of eyes watched her as she walked up the center aisle toward a black-robed female judge who sat behind a huge elevated desk, her dark hair pulled back into a neat bun. After a clerk swore Claudia to tell the truth, she seated herself in a comfortable chair, took a deep breath and stared into the handsome, angry face of her ex-husband who glared bullets at her. Big bullets.

She raised her chin and glared back. She wasn't frightened of Carlos anymore. Because of Jack, she knew what real love was, and she'd never loved this black-hearted terrorist.

Reese rose from his chair and strode to a lectern. She followed his movement, her gaze flickering over the crowded courtroom, landing on a tall man standing in the back.

Jack.

Her stomach lurched. He met her gaze and gave her a thumbs-up.

Jack had stayed to watch her testify. He hadn't driven out of her life.

As that wonderful knowledge registered, Reese said, "Please state your name for the record."

She did so, still holding Jack's gaze as he mouthed, "I love you." Her heart slammed against her chest. Had she imagined that, wishing the words into existence? She narrowed her eyes, trying to be sure.

"Do you recognize the defendant sitting at the defense table?" Reese demanded.

Claudia switched her focus to Carlos, took a deep breath, and said, "That's Carlos Romero, my ex-husband."

JACK LISTENED TO Claudia's testimony for over three hours. She answered Beauchamps's questions clearly and without hesitation. The jury believed her. Even the judge seemed impressed with the details in her journal.

Two hours in, the defense team looked ready for a three-martini lunch. He got it why the Warriors wanted her dead. Claudia's testimony booked Romero a seat in prison for the rest of his life.

Beauchamps flipped his notepad shut. "That's all I have, Your Honor."

The judge checked her watch. "Now is a good time to break for lunch. Bailiff, please escort the jury to the cafeteria. Everyone back by one."

Her gaze glued to his, Claudia stepped down from the witness stand. Jack moved to meet her, but was blocked by a burly uniformed guard.

"Hold it there, pal."

"No," Claudia said, hurrying toward him. "Let him through."

And then she was in his arms. He gathered her close, breathing in her sweet fragrance.

"I thought I'd never see you again," she said, her voice muffled by his embrace.

He pulled back and cupped her flushed face between his hands. "No way. I still owe you a karate lesson."

She gazed up at him questioningly, her blue eyes swimming with tears. "Only one?"

Wanting to kiss her, he traced her full lip with his thumb. "One won't be enough."

Still searching his eyes, she asked, "Can we go back to the cabin?"

"If that's what you want."

"Say it, Gladiator," she whispered.

Of course he had to say it. He glanced around the room. At least twelve suited men, no doubt FBI agents, watched their reunion. Jack placed his mouth next to her ear.

"I love you, Claudia 'Louise Clark' Goodwin. I

love you no matter what your name is, and I want
to spend the rest of my life with you."

One month later

TEMPTED TO PINCH herself to make sure this wasn't
a dream, Claudia smiled at the reflection of Jack's
mother in the mirror. Dressed in wedding finery,
hair perfectly coiffed, they both looked absolutely
fabulous.

She and Jack were getting married in the cabin's
backyard—by none other than Sheriff Chuck
Wheeler—in two minutes. Her family waited out
back with the other guests, but she'd chosen Jack's
mother for her matron of honor.

Irene's expertly made-up face crumpled, and she
collapsed onto the bed. Pookie, wearing a pink se-
quined sweater, jumped into her lap.

Claudia turned. "What's wrong?"

"It was me," Irene said, pushing the dog away.

"What?"

"I gave away your location. I couldn't help myself
and told my friend Alice about you. She's the biggest blabbermouth in the state."

Claudia sighed. *Irene had to pick my wedding day
for true confessions?*

"There's no way to know that, Irene. These guys
were very good." And done for. After Romero's con-
viction, any remaining Warriors had dispersed.

Irene dabbed her eyes with a tissue.

"And it could have been Marsali Winthrop." Marsali had been questioned, and it turned out she'd cooperated with the Warriors because they were blackmailing her, threatening to tell her husband about past indiscretions, some of which would affect her prenup agreement.

"I almost got everybody I love killed," Irene said.

"But you didn't." The haunting sounds of a harp began to echo through the cabin. Claudia held out her hand to Irene. "It's time."

"You forgive me?"

"Of course," Claudia said. *Forgiveness is the most wonderful thing.*

"No one is perfect, you know," Irene said, fluffing her hair.

"That's what I keep telling your son."

When Claudia stepped into the festively decorated backyard, her gaze zeroed in on Jack standing by the sheriff. She caught her breath. Wow. She'd never seen him in a suit.

Maybe no one was perfect, but her gladiator came awfully close.

* * * * *

*Be sure to check out
the first installment of Sharon Hartley's*
THE FLORIDA FILES *miniseries,*
THE SOUTH BEACH SEARCH,
*available now from
Harlequin Superromance.*

And look for the next book in
THE FLORIDA FILES
*from Sharon Hartley,
coming in 2017!*

LARGER-PRINT BOOKS!
GET 2 FREE LARGER-PRINT NOVELS PLUS
2 FREE GIFTS!

HARLEQUIN®

Romance

From the Heart, For the Heart

YES! Please send me 2 FREE LARGER-PRINT Harlequin® Romance novels and my 2 FREE gifts (gifts are worth about $10). After receiving them, if I don't wish to receive any more books, I can return the shipping statement marked "cancel." If I don't cancel, I will receive 4 brand-new novels every month and be billed just $5.09 per book in the U.S. or $5.49 per book in Canada. That's a savings of at least 15% off the cover price! It's quite a bargain! Shipping and handling is just 50¢ per book in the U.S. and 75¢ per book in Canada.* I understand that accepting the 2 free books and gifts places me under no obligation to buy anything. I can always return a shipment and cancel at any time. Even if I never buy another book, the two free books and gifts are mine to keep forever.

119/319 HDN GHWC

Name   (PLEASE PRINT)

Address   Apt. #

City   State/Prov.   Zip/Postal Code

Signature (if under 18, a parent or guardian must sign)

Mail to the **Reader Service:**
IN U.S.A.: P.O. Box 1867, Buffalo, NY 14240-1867
IN CANADA: P.O. Box 609, Fort Erie, Ontario L2A 5X3

Want to try two free books from another line?
Call 1-800-873-8635 or visit www.ReaderService.com.

* Terms and prices subject to change without notice. Prices do not include applicable taxes. Sales tax applicable in N.Y. Canadian residents will be charged applicable taxes. Offer not valid in Quebec. This offer is limited to one order per household. Not valid for current subscribers to Harlequin Romance Larger-Print books. All orders subject to credit approval. Credit or debit balances in a customer's account(s) may be offset by any other outstanding balance owed by or to the customer. Please allow 4 to 6 weeks for delivery. Offer available while quantities last.

Your Privacy—The Reader Service is committed to protecting your privacy. Our Privacy Policy is available online at www.ReaderService.com or upon request from the Reader Service.

We make a portion of our mailing list available to reputable third parties that offer products we believe may interest you. If you prefer that we not exchange your name with third parties, or if you wish to clarify or modify your communication preferences, please visit us at www.ReaderService.com/consumerschoice or write to us at Reader Service Preference Service, P.O. Box 9062, Buffalo, NY 14240-9062. Include your complete name and address.

HRLP15

LARGER-PRINT BOOKS!

HARLEQUIN

Presents

GET 2 FREE LARGER-PRINT NOVELS PLUS 2 FREE GIFTS!

PASSION
GUARANTEED
SEDUCTION

REQUEST YOUR FREE BOOKS!
2 FREE WHOLESOME ROMANCE NOVELS
IN LARGER PRINT
PLUS 2
FREE
MYSTERY GIFTS

☆☆☆☆☆☆☆☆☆☆☆☆☆☆☆☆☆☆☆☆☆

HEARTWARMING™

❀❀❀❀❀❀❀❀❀❀❀❀❀❀❀❀❀❀❀❀❀

Wholesome, tender romances

YES! Please send me 2 FREE Harlequin® Heartwarming Larger-Print novels and my 2 FREE mystery gifts (gifts worth about $10). After receiving them, if I don't wish to receive any more books, I can return the shipping statement marked "cancel." If I don't cancel, I will receive 4 brand-new larger-print novels every month and be billed just $5.24 per book in the U.S. or $5.99 per book in Canada. That's a savings of at least 19% off the cover price. It's quite a bargain! Shipping and handling is just 50¢ per book in the U.S. and 75¢ per book in Canada.* I understand that accepting the 2 free books and gifts places me under no obligation to buy anything. I can always return a shipment and cancel at any time. Even if I never buy another book, the two free books and gifts are mine to keep forever.

161/361 IDN GHX2

Name   (PLEASE PRINT)

Address   Apt. #

City   State/Prov.   Zip/Postal Code

Signature (if under 18, a parent or guardian must sign)

Mail to the **Reader Service:**
IN U.S.A.: P.O. Box 1867, Buffalo, NY 14240-1867
IN CANADA: P.O. Box 609, Fort Erie, Ontario L2A 5X3

* Terms and prices subject to change without notice. Prices do not include applicable taxes. Sales tax applicable in N.Y. Canadian residents will be charged applicable taxes. Offer not valid in Quebec. This offer is limited to one order per household. Not valid for current subscribers to Harlequin Heartwarming larger-print books. All orders subject to credit approval. Credit or debit balances in a customer's account(s) may be offset by any other outstanding balance owed by or to the customer. Please allow 4 to 6 weeks for delivery. Offer available while quantities last.

Your Privacy—The Reader Service is committed to protecting your privacy. Our Privacy Policy is available online at www.ReaderService.com or upon request from the Reader Service.

We make a portion of our mailing list available to reputable third parties that offer products we believe may interest you. If you prefer that we not exchange your name with third parties, or if you wish to clarify or modify your communication preferences, please visit us at www.ReaderService.com/consumerschoice or write to us at Reader Service Preference Service, P.O. Box 9062, Buffalo, NY 14240-9062. Include your complete name and address.

HW15

LARGER-PRINT BOOKS!
GET 2 FREE LARGER-PRINT NOVELS PLUS
2 FREE GIFTS!

H HARLEQUIN®

INTRIGUE
BREATHTAKING ROMANTIC SUSPENSE

HILP15

Her Lips Tingled With Wanting His . . .

Her fingers itched to bury themselves in his wavy black hair. The hammering of her heart sounded so loud to her that she was sure he must be able to hear it. They stood that way for a long moment, staring into each other's eyes.

Brad held his hand out to her then, and she paused only a moment before putting hers in it. His fingers tightened, sending a current of excitement through her. It was asking too much for her to remember that he was someone she probably shouldn't get involved with. All her instincts told her to believe him. Those other matters could sort themselves out later; right now all she wanted was to be held in his arms.

Dear Reader:

Nora Roberts, Tracy Sinclair, Jeanne Stephens, Carole Halston, Linda Howard. Are these authors familiar to you? We hope so, because they are just a few of our most popular authors who publish with Silhouette Special Edition each and every month. And the Special Edition list is changing to include new writers with fresh stories. It has been said that discovering a new author is like making a new friend. So during these next few months, be sure to look for books by Sandi Shane, Dorothy Glenn and other authors who have just written their first and second Special Editions, stories we hope you enjoy.

Choosing which Special Editions to publish each month is a pleasurable task, but not an easy one. We look for stories that are sophisticated, sensuous, touching, and great love stories, as well. These are the elements that make Silhouette Special Editions more romantic...and unique.

So we hope you'll find this Silhouette Special Edition just that—*Special*—and that the story finds a special place in your heart.

The Editors at Silhouette

ELIZABETH NEFF WALKER
Paternity

Silhouette Special Edition
Published by Silhouette Books New York
America's Publisher of Contemporary Romance

For Miranda Coffey and Kay Turner,
with thanks.

SILHOUETTE BOOKS
300 E. 42nd St., New York, N.Y. 10017

ISBN: 0-373-09251-2

First Silhouette Books printing July, 1985

10 9 8 7 6 5 4 3 2 1

America's Publisher of Contemporary Romance

Printed in the U.S.A.

BC91

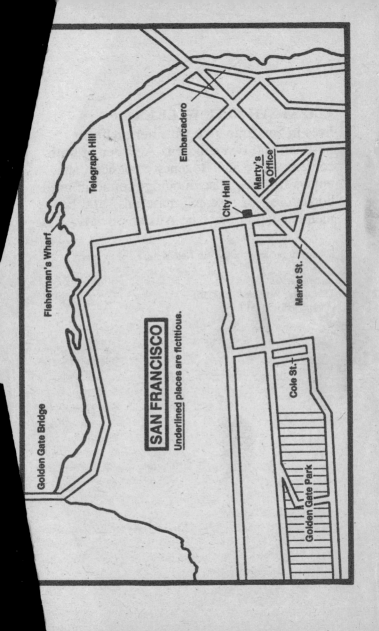

ELIZABETH NEFF WALKER
lives in San Francisco with her architect
husband and two children. A writer of bo
contemporary and Regency romances, she
enjoys traveling, "scrounging around in use
bookstores for research materials" and her
membership in the Jane Austen Society.

Silhouette Books by Elizabeth Neff Walker

Antique Affair (SE #122)
That Other Woman (SE #176)
Paternity (SE #251)

Chapter One

*W*hat the *hell* is the meaning of this?" the man demanded as he slapped the Summons of Complaint down on Marty's desk. She was more startled by the smacking sound than by his voice, which was a nicely controlled growl. Looking up, she was almost surprised that the growl could have come from him. He wasn't all that big; perhaps five seven, wiry and solid. His jet black hair was under control, though barely, but his wild eyebrows weren't. They scattered like unruly twigs from the main branch, climbing jaggedly toward his hairline. Beneath them his eyes were an intense blue and there was an expression in them compounded of annoyance and disbelief.

Marty pulled the summons toward her, noting that her card was still firmly attached: Marty Woods, Investigator, Paternity Unit, Family Support Bureau. He should have called. That was really why the card was attached, but some of them just showed up. It wasn't the first time; it wouldn't be the last. Her eyes dropped to the name on the summons. "Mr. Macintosh? Please sit down."

For a moment he looked as though he'd refuse. Then he changed his mind and took the chair beside her desk. "There's a mistake," he said firmly. "You've gotten the wrong man."

Marty opened the drawer where she kept the files on her paternity cases. Maybe there *had* been a mistake. She didn't usually run into men in her job whose eyes made her doubt her own expertise. Each case was carefully documented; there were seldom errors of identity. She shoved the drawer closed with a heavy thump and set the folder carefully in the center of her desk, opening it to the detailed sheet on Brad Macintosh.

"Brad Macintosh, thirty-five, owner of Macintosh Building Supplies. Divorced, joint custody of one thirteen-year-old daughter. Lives on Liberty Street and drives a Volvo (blue) which is several years old. Plays tennis, hikes, swims." Marty looked up from the file questioningly. "Is that you?"

He looked incredulous. "Where did you get all that information?"

"From Lydia Brown, of course."

"I don't know any Lydia Brown," he insisted, hiking the chair closer to her so he could impress her with his earnestness. Almost all the men denied the charges.

"Well," she said, trying to sound just as straightforward, "Lydia Brown obviously knows you, Mr. Macintosh. In fact, she has stated quite positively that you are the father of her child."

He disrupted the smoothness of his thick, wavy hair

by raking strong fingers through it. Disordered, it looked as wild as his eyebrows. He took a deep breath, possibly trying to rein in his frustration. "I don't know anyone named Lydia Brown. I've never known anyone named Lydia Brown. I wouldn't be likely to forget someone whose child I'd fathered, would I?"

Though he made it sound the most perfectly reasonable statement in the world, Marty grinned. "Men do it all the time. After all, they have no way of knowing they've fathered a child. Lydia told me she'd never informed you of the pregnancy or birth. However, she's applied for Aid to Families with Dependent Children, and in order to be eligible, she had to come to this office so that we could obtain child support from the father, which in this case is you."

Brad leaned forward in his chair. "You're not listening to me. I have never heard of this woman."

"I'm listening," she retorted. "You're only saying the same thing almost every other man says when he's sued for paternity, Mr. Macintosh."

"But I'm telling the truth! How can I get you to believe me?"

"You don't have to convince me. You have to convince the court. At this stage you can do one of three things: voluntarily agree to child support; do nothing, in which case a judgment will be entered against you after thirty days; or deny the paternity charge and request a blood test. I presume you intend to deny."

"You're damn right I do!" He again raked his fingers through his hair. "This is preposterous. I'm not going to let some woman falsely accuse me of fathering her child."

"Then I'd suggest you get a lawyer, Mr. Macintosh,

to guarantee your rights." Marty pushed her chair back slightly to indicate that the interview was over.

Brad Macintosh didn't budge. His deep blue eyes, like icy lake water, continued to regard her intently. "I don't want to get a lawyer. They're immoral bloodsuckers, and I haven't done anything that I should need one for."

Marty's lips twitched. "I take it you've had a bad experience. Still, in your position I'd recommend getting one."

"I'll think about it."

He rose abruptly, his eyes still fastened on hers. Though he wasn't particularly tall, he was a great deal taller than her five feet. She watched him take in her short, curly hair, her snub nose and her wide gray eyes. Probably deciding, as they all did, that she hardly looked like an investigator in paternity cases. Marty didn't offer her hand. There was a resoluteness to his expression that warned her he'd ignore it. She shrugged inwardly. It was difficult for men charged with paternity. Even when they knew they were responsible, they didn't want to accept the burden of child support. It was up to the district attorney's office to see that they did. Marty was only doing her job.

"Why didn't someone contact me before this?" he asked.

"You mean, before you were sent the summons?"

"That, or when the child was born. Sometime. Anytime."

"Because most men deny paternity, and the blood test can't be done on the child until it's six months old."

"Why not?"

"Because some of the antigens aren't fully developed until then, and sometimes the child's veins are too small to get a good sample," she said matter-of-factly.

He grimaced. "What does a blood test show?"

"It eliminates men who couldn't be the father. Blood tests are very sophisticated these days, Mr. Macintosh. If you're not the father, in all likelihood you'll be excluded immediately. They don't just check red blood cell factors anymore. They do an HLA, serum proteins and enzymes. By the time they're done they can get a ninety-nine point five or better percent statistical certainty that a given man is the father."

"Good," he said, a smile for the first time transforming his face. "Then I have nothing to worry about."

When he turned to go, she reached down to pick up the summons. "You'll need this, Mr. Macintosh. It's essential that you give an answer to the court within thirty days. You can do it on your own or have a lawyer do it for you."

Brad turned back and accepted the summons with a frown. "What happens then?"

"After the blood tests have been completed, they'll set a date for a hearing. If the hearing goes against you, there will be a trial later, say in nine months or a year. With a preponderance of evidence at the hearing the judge can order temporary child support."

"You think that's what will happen, don't you?" His eyes flashed with anger. "If these blood tests are so great, you must have men excluded all the time."

"You're assuming the mothers lie," Marty said gently. "Actually, we only have a fifteen percent exclusion rate, Mr. Macintosh."

Brad glared at her, stuffed the papers in the pocket of his green parka and headed for the exit. Marty

studied his energetic lope until he was out of sight.
There was a great deal of controlled wrath in that
stride. She imagined he'd do something to let off
steam now—perhaps a few sets of tennis, or swimming a couple of miles in some pool.

What had he expected? she wondered. Did he think
coming in and telling her it wasn't true would convince her of his complete innocence? Did he think
that she would say, "Oh, well, then, we'll just tear up
the summons, Mr. Macintosh"? Marty grinned at the
thought. If he was not, perhaps, the swaggering male
she often encountered, his approach to the situation
was very little different. The alleged fathers could
rave and badger and bulldoze as much as they wanted.
She had the facts in hand, and the facts indicated that
they were the fathers of her cases.

But Brad Macintosh had somehow gotten through
to her more than the others did. There was some
quality about him, some inherent honesty in those
startling blue eyes, that gave her pause. If she had met
him somewhere else, she would possibly have labeled
him constitutionally unable to lie. It might simply
have been that he reminded her of someone who
fitted that description; heaven knew there weren't
that many of them. Still, he had disturbed her, and
she leafed through the file on her desk, as though that
might restore her confidence.

There was no reason to doubt the mother. She was
young, of course, only nineteen. She had told Marty,
with the usual prompting, that she'd left home at
eighteen with a girl friend and had hitchhiked to San
Francisco. Lydia's friend had drifted off north after a
few weeks, leaving Lydia alone and frightened in the
strange city. With no job skills, no friends, and no
money left, she had taken a waitressing job in the

Mission and found a minuscule apartment on Valencia Street. The landlord wouldn't bother with the repair of a broken faucet, so she had eventually gone to a building supply store to find a replacement.

That was where she had met Brad, or so she said. It certainly made sense. Lydia said he'd helped her find what she needed and had offered to install it for her. Not really having the first idea how to do it herself, she'd agreed. A dangerous thing to do, perhaps, but not unheard of. Their relationship had lasted for two months. The only slight weakness in her story had been its abrupt termination. "And then I never heard from him again," she'd said, staring defiantly at the corner of Marty's desk.

"Had you told him about the baby?" Marty asked.

"I didn't know then."

"Well, didn't you call him when you found out?"

"No. It's my baby. He'd just have yelled at me for getting pregnant. I was going to take care of everything myself, except that when I got real big they fired me at work, and no one else would hire me."

"What about after she was born?"

"I didn't want someone else taking care of her. I would have supported her, except that I can't make enough to pay for her care and still have money left over to feed us and all. I tried one time but the sitter wasn't any good, and when Cheryl got sick a couple of times and I took off from work, they fired me."

No, Lydia was legitimate enough. Marty had seen her with the baby, too—fiercely protective and loving. When the child was a little older, maybe Lydia could be trained for some kind of work that would pay well enough to get them out of this circle of poverty, but this was probably not the time. Marty's own job at the moment was simply to see that Brad Macintosh paid his share of the child's support, so that Aid to Families with Dependent Children didn't have the full burden.

If it seemed strange to her that Brad would have picked an eighteen-year-old, well, men were sometimes like that. Lydia was not a street-smart kid; she was incredibly naive and rather helpless, in addition to being pretty. That combination would be fatally attractive to some men. Marty closed the folder and returned it to its slot in the drawer. There was nothing more she could do with it now.

She looked up to find Virginia Rodrigues standing beside her desk, regarding her curiously. "An alleged father?" Virginia asked, nodding her head in the direction Brad had disappeared.

"Yes. One of the ones who vehemently denies it." Marty stood up, trying to shake off the slight feeling of anxiety that still clung to her. "Ready for lunch?"

"Sure." Virginia removed a pair of glasses she used only for reading. "Don't let it bother you, Marty. He looks like he can afford a good lawyer. That parka he was wearing must have cost a hundred and fifty dollars. There's one just like it in the L. L. Bean catalog. I was thinking of getting one for Pablo for his birthday."

"Apparently he hates lawyers. He called them immoral bloodsuckers."

Virginia laughed. "Clever fellow. And good looking, too. You're going to have to look out for that one."

Marty slung her purse over her shoulder. "That's what I'm afraid of," she said.

Brad emerged from the building at Tenth and Folsom more disgruntled than he could recall feeling in a long time. Imagine that little snip of a woman not believing him! As if it hadn't been bad enough when he'd walked toward the door of his business to find a nondescript man coming up to him and handing him the Summons of Complaint. Several of his employees had been there at the time and he was convinced they now thought him a hardened criminal. His waving aside their curiosity with the comment that it must be a mistake had not appeared to alleviate their suspicions one bit. Well, in a similar position he supposed he wouldn't have believed himself, either.

But *she* should have. Miss Woods. He pulled out the crumpled summons and stared at her name. Marty. Short for what—Martha? Martha didn't suit her at all. She looked like a counselor at a Girl Scout camp—wholesome, energetic, cheerful and whatever else those women had to be to take care of a bunch of rowdy ten-year-olds. She had no business looking like that and holding the kind of job she did, where she tracked down innocent men to squeeze child support from them.

Brad hunched his shoulders and zipped up the parka against the nippy April morning. His business was only three blocks away, and he had walked to the Family Support Bureau, hoping then, as he did now, that a vigorous walk would ease his rage. What could be more infuriating than being falsely accused of anything, especially being the father of a child whose mother he'd never heard of?

He had told Marty the truth, for all the good it had done. As he loped along the sidewalk, his mind was working with its usual speed and efficiency. The first thing to do was check the employment records of Macintosh Building Supplies to see if Lydia Brown had worked there. How else would some unknown woman have found out so much about him? He

frowned as a bicycle messenger swept past, dangerously weaving in and out of the Folsom Street traffic.

Offhand Brad couldn't think of anyone except an
employee who could put together so much information on him, not that most of his employees could,
unless they purposely went after such details so they
could sue him for paternity. If someone had told him
he would receive a summons this morning, the last
thing in the world he'd have imagined it would be for
was paternity. Hadn't he practically been a monk
since Karen divorced him?

He considered the possibility that Karen had something to do with all this. It seemed highly unlikely. She
wasn't the least bit vindictive. She had, after all, been
the one to request the divorce—to change her life, to
"realize" herself, to get away from the building supply
business, for a hundred different reasons, it seemed,
most of them having to do with his supposed inflexibility. Brad was personally convinced now, as he had
been then, that there wasn't an inflexible bone in his
body.

He liked coming home to a hot meal. Hadn't he
sent her home from the store in time to be there when
their daughter got home from school, with plenty of
time to make dinner and do any necessary cleaning?
They had a maid who came in once a week, didn't
they? What was so tough about picking up a little
around the house? Brad had mulled these things over
so many times in his mind that just the thought of
Karen seemed to set off the whole refrain again. Well,
he didn't have time to go through the complete litany
now; there were more important matters to be considered.

The store sat like a squat peacock, taking up about
a third of the frontage of the block. Karen had said it

needed to be colorful to attract customers. It was colorful, all right, bright yellow with splashes of red, blue and green but tastefully done, of course. Everything Karen set her hand to was done tastefully. There was parking to one side, an essential facility in the city. His own Volvo sat in the lot. He would have called it blue-gray rather than blue, but Lydia Brown obviously didn't let such details bother her.

The side door to the building was kept locked, and he let himself in with the key. Ordinarily when returning to the store he would walk through the main floor to see if everything was in order, if there were a good number of customers, if the sales and stocking people were doing their jobs well, if there were any problems only he could handle. But he was in a hurry now, and almost uninterested in the state of business. The hallway was inelegant, with scruffy linoleum floors and walls continually banged by materials being brought through to the floor display. Karen had not convinced him that sprucing up the back areas would in any way increase his profit. Their profit, she would have said.

Their divorce had damn near bankrupted him. In order to buy her share of the business he had been forced to borrow money, just when it looked as though Macintosh Building Supplies was really going to take off. The only thing that had saved him at all was Karen's agreeing to take part of her share in continued ownership of the business. *That* was the lawyer's suggestion. *His* lawyer. Oh, the hell with both of them.

Brad unzipped the green parka and hung it on the scrubby coatrack outside his office. Karen had said if he didn't appreciate the antique one, she'd replace it with something more serviceable, which she had.

Brad sometimes kicked it out of sheer frustration. He was frustrated a lot these days. And to think he'd always considered himself the most easygoing of fellows. He felt as though he hadn't laughed in a million years. Karen said . . . oh, forget it, he told himself sternly as he brushed his windblown hair down with his hands and nodded to his secretary. In the doorway of his office, he paused.

"I want the personnel files for everyone who's ever worked here, Kerri," he said. "Right away."

Kerri blinked at him. "All of them? Do you have any idea how many people that is, Brad? And I'm not sure they're all easily accessible."

"I don't care how accessible they are. I want to see every one of them."

Kerri shrugged. "Whatever you say, boss."

Brad hated it when she called him boss. Mostly because he knew she'd picked it up from Karen, who only used the term when he'd annoyed her by ordering her around. He didn't think of it as ordering her around. He thought of it as taking charge of things in the most efficient way possible, which was the only way he ever did things. After being married to him for thirteen years, she should have known that.

When the files eventually came, an hour later, they were not complete. "Personnel says some of them are in storage and they don't know exactly where." Kerri looked uncomfortable. "They said Karen would probably know, though."

Brad silently gritted his teeth. There was nothing he liked less than calling Karen about work-related matters. It was perfectly all right to talk to her about their daughter; that didn't bother him at all. But asking her about business matters somehow always made her laugh and say, "You see, Brad, I was more involved in the business than you thought." He could, of course, have Kerri call her, but Karen would see that as cowardice and tease him about it the next time he had to talk to her.

"All right," he sighed. "I'll call her."

"She may be in school now."

Brad glared at her. "If she's in school," he growled, "I'll call her again later. That will be all, Kerri."

Damned if the girl didn't grin at him as she swung the door shut behind herself.

Karen's answering machine was on. Brad didn't care much for leaving messages on answering machines; it seemed so silly to talk to a machine. But he wanted the information as soon as possible, so he forced himself to say, "This is Brad. We . . . I need to know where the old personnel files have been stored." And because he was feeling particularly cross, he added, "You should have given them all that information when you left."

He was about to hang up when there was a click and Karen's amused voice said quite clearly, "Should I? Well, I'm quite sure I did, you know, but they've probably lost it. Why do you need the old personnel files, Brad? The ones in the office go back more than a year."

"Why is your answering machine on if you're at home?" he demanded.

"Because I'm studying and I didn't want to be bothered for anything unimportant. Since you never call about anything unimportant, I felt in all fairness I should pick it up. It's called monitoring calls and it gives me a wonderful sense of power."

"I'm flattered you accepted my call," he said,

sounding sardonic rather than appreciative. "I won't keep you from your studying, if you'll tell me where to find the files."

"They're in a file cabinet in the smallest storage room, second drawer, clearly marked. Those go all the way back to the day the store opened, when it was on Potrero. There aren't any current addresses for any of the employees, so I hope that's not what you're looking for."

"It's not. Thanks for your help."

"No problem. Andrea said she had a good weekend with you."

Their thirteen-year-old daughter had spent most of the time reading novels Brad considered far too sophisticated for her, but he didn't remark on this. "We always have a good time together," he said, more defensively than he'd intended.

"She's looking forward to going to Disneyland over spring vacation. I really appreciate your doing that. It'll give me some extra time to catch up on my course work."

Brad wanted to insist that wasn't why he was doing it. Instead he said, "She's arranging the whole thing with the travel agent—airline tickets, hotel, rental car. She said maybe she'd be a travel agent when she grows up."

His former wife laughed. "She changes her mind about what she wants to be almost every other week. Fortunately, she has plenty of time to decide. Look, I've got to go, Brad. If they have any trouble finding the files, let me know."

Brad found the files himself, without any difficulty. It took him several hours to go through each of the records, and when he was finished he hadn't turned up one single bit of useful information. Macintosh Building Supplies had never hired anyone by the name of Lydia Brown, or anyone resembling her. He crumpled the empty paper cup from the soda Kerri had brought him with his lunch and tossed it at the wastepaper basket across the room. He missed.

Chapter Two

$\mathcal{M}$ arty awoke from the dream feeling disoriented. It had been very hot wherever she was, in Mexico or Hawaii, perhaps. The sun sparkled off miles and miles of gorgeous blue water, and off the dazzling white sand as well. There were only the two of them on the beach, lying side by side in their swimming suits. The sunlight had crept beyond the shade of the umbrella and rather than move the canopy, the two of them had raced for the cool water, diving in and surfacing moments later in each other's arms. The experience was both languid and exhilarating. Marty could feel her heart pounding.

A furry head nudged against the small of her back and she groaned. "All right, Misty, I'm getting up. Your nose is cold." She gave the lhasa apso a cursory pat on the head and inched her legs over the side of the bed. Her clock radio hadn't gone off yet, and the dream still clouded her mind with a vague euphoria. Not a bad way to start the day, she thought ruefully.

Just then the radio jarred her by clicking on with headlines of daily disasters. What was worse, it jarred her into realizing that the man in her dream had been none other than Brad Macintosh, alleged father in a paternity suit.

"Humph," she snorted, jamming one foot into a woolly slipper. "That's all I need—having a sexy dream about some bozo I'm likely to end up fighting in court." She worked her other foot into the remaining slipper and padded across the room to the window. Marty had a row of different shapes of crystals hanging there, forever hopeful that the sun would be shining. Today a beautiful spring morning was developing, the sun cascading through the glass and breaking up into prisms on the walls. The rainbows scattered over rows of books, framed prints, her bureau and bed.

Well, that explained the dream. Probably one of the rainbows had settled across her face while she slept, bringing with it images of sun, surf and sensuousness. Since there was no man of the least romantic interest in her life, her mind had brought forth the only man who was on her mind at all, even though he was merely a work-related problem. Not a strictly Freudian interpretation, perhaps, but then who cared? It was a good enough explanation for her.

She splashed water on her face and blinked at her reflection in the mirror. In the mornings her eyes looked more black than gray because they were so heavy with sleep. She wasn't an instant riser. It took her a good half hour to bring herself to the reality of a new day, and that included a cup of strong, hot coffee and a couple of frozen waffles with syrup, preceded by a glass of cold grapefruit juice. Even at the best of times, Marty wasn't handy in the kitchen. There were people who'd been horrified at the extent of her frozen food supply, but cooking didn't hold much interest for her. She was great at finding new, good, cheap restaurants—Mexican, Chinese, Indonesian, ribs. If a disproportionate amount of her salary was spent in eating out, well, what was money for?

The kitchen was in the back of the apartment, where the sun didn't reach in the mornings. Sometimes, if Marty felt really out of it and needed to absorb a little vitamin D from natural light, she put her plate, cup and glass on a small tray she had purchased for the purpose and climbed the stairs to Jim's deck. The furthest corner of it was not shadowed by the building, and he had set up a redwood table and bench there. Though they owned the building together, the deck was not part of her holdings. He had had it built at his own expense and generously allowed her to use it on occasion. Never on Saturday or Sunday mornings, because he might have brought someone home with him, and he didn't want her to mess up his romantic setting with her ratty robe.

On a weekday morning, though, he didn't mind, so she went through the ritual of trying to find the tray and hoping she remembered all the necessary utensils so she wouldn't have to shuffle back down the stairs. He said it annoyed the hell out of him when he saw her from his kitchen, wandering up and down the stairs with a fork or a glass or her coffee pot. Frankly, she couldn't see why it would make any difference to him. If she was dumb enough to keep forgetting things, that was her problem. He always cooked himself a real breakfast and he'd shown her, on several occasions, that his freezer contained nothing in a package. Big deal.

She could see him now, puttering happily around his kitchen, frying bacon and beating eggs in a copper bowl with a whisk. He knew she was out there, but he wouldn't look out. Seeing her scurry back down the stairs would put him in a bad mood for the rest of the day, he said. Jim was famous for thinking any number of things put him in a bad mood. Actually, there was probably no more even-tempered man in San Francisco. When Marty had first met him, five years before, she felt sure she was going to fall in love with him; he was just that kind of man. Tall, good-looking, intelligent. He worked for the district attorney's office as an assistant D.A. and he had been attached to the Paternity Unit for a while, which was something they did with assistant D.A.s who refused to toe the line. After a little stint there, most of them were willing to shape up and fly right. He had gotten out of there quicker than any other one she'd run across since. She could tell he was bucking for D.A., but so were most of the other hotshots.

That was the main thing Marty didn't like about him—that and the women. He was a little too ambitious about both. Every woman she'd ever seen him with had been some kind of goddess, as though mortals weren't good enough to catch his attention. However, he was thirty-two and had never married one of those beauties. So either he didn't think any of them were good enough for him, or he still had some doubts about whether they'd make good long-range partners.

When she was halfway through her waffles, Jim kicked open the door, his hands full, and nodded at her. It was a myth with him that he was too unsociable in the mornings to talk, except when he made a supreme effort because one of the beauties spoke to him and it would have been impolite not to respond. This always lasted for about three minutes, while Marty stared mesmerized at him, watching his elegant way of attacking an omelette, pondering whether this was one of the herb or cheese ones. She couldn't really tell the difference, since they both had herbs and cheese, but he had explained to her that there was an important distinction between them. Apparently it was all in the taste but he'd never offered to make her one, which was perfectly all right, because she couldn't face an egg at that hour of the morning.

"Cheese this morning?" she ventured.

He grunted his incredulity. "Does this look like cheese, Marty?" he demanded, stabbing here and there with a fork at the bits of green herbs. "I have salsa with it when it's a cheese omelette, remember?"

"Not always." There were three pieces of bacon on his plate. Though he had never actually said so, she knew that one of them was for her, because he always ate only two pieces himself. He cooked bacon perfectly, so that all of it was crisp, and it wasn't all gnarled the way it got when Marty tried it. Possibly he put a plate down on it. Marty didn't know because no one was allowed in the kitchen when he cooked. She helped herself to "her" piece, savoring the crunchy, fatty pleasure of it. He didn't even glance at her.

"So," she said, when she had finished the bacon and was cutting up the waffles again. "How are things at the D.A.'s office?"

"We have criminals to spare," he said. That was Jim's idea of a joke. He did better than that later in the day, but not a whole lot better. "How's the paternity business?"

She shrugged. "The same as usual. They didn't do it; they never met the mother; someone is out to get them. We had a maternal exclusion the other day."

Jim's head bobbed up, and he frowned at her. It was a rarity, to be sure. In giving the blood tests, they expected a given number of men to be excluded as possible fathers. Certain characteristics had to be passed on by either the father or the mother of the child, and in this case it was clear that the woman could not possibly be the mother. A maternal exclusion. Jim picked up this fork again and asked, "So did you find out what the story was?"

"Yes. Presented with the evidence, the woman explained the circumstances to us. It was her niece's baby, but the niece had taken off after it was born, and she wanted to raise it."

"But didn't she understand about the blood tests, what they would tell? Didn't you explain it to her?"

Marty felt impatient with him. "Of course I did. Look, Jim, blood test results are all a lot of hocus pocus to some of the mothers. They look at a test tube full of their own blood and don't believe for a minute that we can actually break it down into a lot of significant factors, no matter what I say to the contrary. Or they think, somehow, that because they're related, the blood has to be alike. You were there long enough to know that."

He shuddered. "More than long enough. All those poor jerks who were going to have to shell out their hard-earned money for some kid for the next eighteen years."

"I don't feel the least bit sorry for them. They're just as responsible for what happened as the women. Why do they think they should get off scot-free?" She could tell she was getting ruffled, but she couldn't stop. "She's going to have the daily burden of raising the child; the least he can do is come up with some child support. Otherwise, the state is going to have to pay the whole price tag."

"I know, I know." He waved his fork at her, grinning. "It's just so much fun to get you riled up in the mornings. Think how much more alert you'll be at work because your adrenalin is already flowing."

"By the time I get to work I'll be having arguments with you in my head," Marty declared. "Which isn't going to make me alert." There was only a sip of coffee left in her cup, and she polished it off, frowning at him. "You just pretend to be a devil's advocate, Jim. I'm convinced it's exactly what you *do* believe. You don't think much of women or you'd look for a little more in them than beauty."

As a parting shot, it didn't have quite the pizzazz she would have liked, but it was as good an exit line as she was going to come up with at that hour of the morning. He was still grinning as Marty gathered up her tray and stalked down the stairs to her own apartment.

Marty couldn't help but wonder if the whole point of his taunting her was to put *her* in a bad mood for the day. Everyone constantly accused her of being perpetually "up." She couldn't help it; she just got a kick out of life. She would have thought that other people would appreciate this, but no, they usually seemed to think it was almost an indictment of them for not being the same way. When Virginia and Marty first started working together, Virginia couldn't believe Marty was really that cheerful. "It's Pollyanna gone mad," she announced about a week after Marty started. "Don't you read the papers?" she'd demanded. "Don't you know there are awful things going on in the world?"

"Sure," Marty said. "It makes me really sad. But look, Virginia, I figure I've only got one life, and I might as well make the most of it." Steve Yu, who worked with both of them, had come along just then and said, "This job will get you down after a while. You haven't been here long enough."

Not that either of them seemed to Marty to be particularly browbeaten by the work. She supposed it could have been considered a slightly unsavory type of work, but all of them simply did what was expected of them. Women were always going to have babies, and somehow they had to be supported until the kids were old enough and the women could be trained to support themselves. It would be nice if nobody needed help, but that just wasn't the way things were. No one lived in luxury on the minimal AFDC and food stamps in San Francisco. The child support the Paternity Unit got from the fathers simply went to reduce the amount the state had to pay. They were lucky if they got $100, $150 a month from the paternity settlements. Still, it kept the cost to the state down, and that was why they were there.

By the time Marty got to work she'd shucked off Jim's comments—what did *he* know? He'd probably let the mother and child starve if he had his way. It was a good thing he wasn't with the Public Defender's office.

Her boss beckoned to her as soon as he noticed she'd come in. Ralph Hall had been director of the unit since long before her time and he'd been skeptical of hiring her, at first. Who could blame him? Here was this short, bouncy woman who was supposed to tell some bus driver he had to support a child he didn't even know he had. Ralph hadn't thought she'd be able to stand up to the pressure. But she had known he was wrong, so she'd set about convincing him by looking tough. He just laughed. It was hard to manage a really mean look when her hair curled all over her head like a demented angel's and she didn't come up to some guy's collar bone. Ralph was sixty at the time, with grizzled gray hair and a bit of a paunch, a no-nonsense person who expected a lot from his investigators. He shot questions at her right and left, trying to catch her out in snap judgment errors. After about half an hour, he raised his brows, sat back in his chair, and said, "Okay, we'll give it a try, Marty." That was four years ago.

His office wasn't very big, and most surfaces were covered with file folders or photos of his family. Maybe he needed the photos to remind him there were standard family units left in the world. His, of course, had grown to grandchildren by this point, about eight of them. As often as not, when he waved her into the office, the first thing he did was show her the newest picture he had received. Today he merely waved her to a chair and dug around on his desk until he came up with a message pad.

"This man called," he said, squinting at his own writing. "Brad Macintosh. One of your alleged fathers."

Marty nodded.

"Seems he doesn't want to get a lawyer, and he wanted to be sure you were capable of handling the paperwork to respond to the summons." He cocked his grizzled head at her. "Maybe you put his back up?"

"Probably I did. He denies any knowledge of the mother."

"I see." Ralph crumpled the note in one of his big hands and tossed it into the wastebasket. "It's always possible, you know."

"Unlikely," she retorted. Then her eyes narrowed. "Did he try to pull some influence with you?"

Ralph's eyes twinkled. "You bet he did. Seems he knows three or four really important people in San Francisco. He'd had lunch with the mayor once. A while back, of course, when she was President of the Board of Supervisors, you understand, but she'd remember him."

Marty burst out laughing. "How could anyone forget him? He came in here yesterday all righteously indignant. When I told him about the blood tests he got very cocky, saying they'd prove he wasn't the father."

"Which you don't believe?"

"Well, it happens sometimes, of course, but Lydia is very convincing. She can give page and verse of their relationship and insists he's the only man she's seen since she came to the city a year and a half ago. She doesn't have any physical evidence—pictures or letters—but she can describe his office, knows all about his family situation, what kind of car he drives, where he lives, what he does in his spare time."

Ralph pursed his lips. "Is the guy married, then?"

"No, no. He's divorced, but she knows all about the arrangement. The kind of thing a man might talk about with her. She's very young and not very bright, but pretty."

The information seemed to satisfy him. He stood up and said, "Okay, everything sounds in order. I told him you were perfectly capable of handling it, of course. Don't mess it up, Marty. We don't want one of his influential friends shaking their fingers at us."

"I'll do my best," she said, rising, and matching his mock gravity with her own.

"What you might do," he suggested, as an afterthought, "is go by his office and see if it really is the way the woman described it. She could have made something up, thinking we'd never check it out."

Marty didn't like the idea of visiting the building supply company, but it was a reasonable request and she agreed. "It can't do any harm."

He seemed to sense her hesitation and smiled. "You're not likely to run into any of his influential friends there, Marty. Don't let that bother you."

It wasn't the "influential friends" who bothered her; it was Brad Macintosh himself. She was uncharacteristically annoyed by his going to her superior, while at the same time amused by his gambit of trying to use influence with Ralph. A lot of good that would do him. The description of his office was noted in her file, and she read it over carefully before jamming the file in her purse and putting on her coat.

"I'll be gone about an hour," she called to Virginia as she headed for the door.

Her co-worker looked up absentmindedly, but her gaze sharpened. "You look a little anxious. Need a bodyguard?"

"I could wrestle this one to the floor myself." She sniffed.

"Ah, the one with the parka," Virginia guessed, smiling. "I wouldn't lay odds on it, sweetie. That man has a streak of macho in him, and he doesn't like getting caught one bit."

"He should have thought of that a long time ago," Marty retorted as she stalked off.

The store wasn't at all what she expected. Not that it didn't fit Lydia's description, but Marty had a rather different expectation of what a building supply company would look like. She had thought Lydia's description was an exaggeration: "It's more like a boutique from the outside than a place where you buy wrenches." Marty had always bought wrenches at stores that had cluttered window displays and crumbling exteriors. This one was classy, with its colorful paint job and wide expanse of sliding glass doors. Inside she could see the rows of shelves neatly stacked with merchandise that ranged from small packets to large tools. Lydia had told her there was an entrance at the side that led through a hall to the business offices.

The door on the side was locked, as Lydia had said it would be, so Marty rang the bell and waited. After a while a young woman came to the glass door, eyed her speculatively, and pushed the door open a few inches. "Can I help you?"

"Yes. I've come to see Mr. Macintosh. If you'd tell him Marty Woods is here . . ."

"Sure." The young woman pushed the door open wider. "Just follow me. I think he's around somewhere."

Marty followed her into the hallway with its worn linoleum and pockmarked walls. "It's real grungy," Lydia had said. "Not like the front area at all." Well, she was quite right so far. The contrast between the snappy entrance and store and this back area was almost alarming. Didn't his suppliers visit his office?

"There's a coatrack there, like the kind my grand-mother had when I was a kid," Lydia had said about the area inhabited by Brad's secretary. Marty saw it immediately, with the green parka draped carelessly over it, and a woman's light jacket hung by the tag.

"I'll page him," the secretary announced. She punched a button, and even from the cubicle Marty could hear her voice booming all over the building. "Mr. Macintosh. Mr. Brad Macintosh." She turned to Marty with a grin. "I like to do it that way, like they do at the airport. It drives him crazy. Every once in a while I'm tempted to say, 'Red Courtesy Telephone, please.'"

Obviously the woman was not the least bit intimi-dated by her boss. She waved Marty to a straight-backed wooden chair, grimacing slightly. "Karen tried to get him to buy some decent furniture, but he never would. He said we didn't have visitors often enough to make it worth the expenditure. Maybe he'll change his mind." She looked wistful as she settled back at her typewriter and rolled in a purchase order form.

There were a few magazines on a formica-topped table beside Marty's chair, and she picked them up to see if there was anything interesting. Two of them had to do exclusively with tools and another two were business magazines. She returned them to the table and amused herself counting how many dead leaves there were on the grape ivy plant that hung by the window. It was dusty, too, and she felt an urge to carry it into a bathroom and give it a good bath, but of course she didn't. Brad showed up at the doorway just as she was debating how long the plant had to live.

He was dressed informally in a pair of tan corduroy pants that had an unusual number of pockets and a blue chambray shirt. They had heard him coming before he appeared in the doorway because he also had on a pair of heavy work boots, as though he were headed for a construction site. Maybe he was in the habit of dropping weighty tools on his feet, Marty thought. The boots would certainly have protected him. He glared at the secretary for just a moment before he noticed Marty in the corner and quickly replaced his frown with an engaging smile.

"Ah, Miss Woods. There was no need for you to come here; I'd have made an appointment with you at your office. But I appreciate your effort. Why don't we go into my office?"

"Thank you," Marty murmured as she rose from the chair, wondering whether it had been as dusty as the plant and if she should inconspicuously brush off her skirt. But he was already loping into his office, where he turned at the door and waited expectantly for her to get a move on. So she followed him meekly and watched as he closed the door firmly behind her. Obviously he didn't want his secretary to overhear their conversation. He waved her to an old armchair that was in desperate need of recovering. At least it was a great deal more comfortable than the chair she'd just deserted.

He dropped into an old wooden swivel chair that groaned under this assault and squeaked when he swung it around. "Your boss said you'd be able to handle filing my denial with the court. Did you bring the papers for me to sign?" He gave no indication that there had been anything arrogant and underhanded about his action of consulting her boss.

"Yes, I have them with me," she admitted, "but I really came here because I wanted to check a few things." If he thought this was an encouraging sign of her imminent conversion to his point of view, she quickly disillusioned him. Pulling his file from her purse, she opened it on her lap and read: "A squeaky swivel chair and a dark wood desk with a sheet of glass on it. He keeps pictures of his daughter Andrea stuck under the glass."

His arm moved almost involuntarily to cover the pictures, and she smiled at him. "I already noticed them, Mr. Macintosh. Don't you want to ask me how I got my information?"

"No," he said emphatically. "It's more of the garbage that woman gave you."

"Right. She also listed a high school trophy for diving, a couple of dead plants, an orange shag rug that should be thrown away, a glass-fronted bookcase, and a couple of old-fashioned tools." Marty looked around the office, with Brad following her gaze as it lighted on almost every one of the items. "I guess you got rid of the dead plants, but that one out in the reception area is going to die soon if you don't take better care of it."

"That's Kerri's responsibility." Though he was doing a good job of controlling his temper, she could see that he was really upset about something. Probably that she had such good evidence of Lydia's having been in his office, which pretty much destroyed his assertion that he'd never met her.

"Are you sure you want to deny paternity, Mr. Macintosh?" she asked softly. "It would save a lot of time and energy if you'd sign a voluntary agreement."

The wild black eyebrows seemed to bristle over his sparking blue eyes. Through clenched jaws he said, "I have never met anyone named Lydia Brown. There is no way I could be the father of her child. I wish you could bring yourself to believe that, Miss Woods. She has never been in this office—at my invitation, at least."

The folder started sliding off Marty's lap, and she grabbed for it with a jerky movement. Something about him rattled her, just as it had the day before in her office. There was a persuasive sincerity in his confidence, and it was almost impossible not to be influenced by him. While she squared the papers up, keeping her eyes on them instead of him, she said, "You can't see the trophy or the bookcase from the reception area."

"I know you can't!" He ran a hand distractedly through his hair. "Why do you think I'm so confused? I've never had an employee with her name or even one who sounds like her." He waved a hand at a stack of file folders that rested precariously on the corner of his desk. "I don't know who she is. I don't know how she got into my office. I don't know why she's doing this to me." He shrugged and stood up. "Look, I want to think about it a while, okay? Maybe talk to a lawyer or something." This very grudgingly. "I'll call you in a day or two."

"You have thirty days to make a decision," she told him, feeling almost sympathetic. What was there about this man, anyhow? She felt mysteriously drawn to him, affected by his presence even when he was aggressively denying any involvement in the paternity suit. He radiated a masculine tension that ruffled her composure but made her want to remain in his vicinity, to see what would happen next, to find out what the upshot of this subliminal excitement would be.

Something had to come of the strong current he projected. It had to move things, to change them, to invest them with energy or rob them of resistance.

Somehow she could not believe things remained static around Brad Macintosh. She was intrigued, no doubt about that.

Before she could do anything unwise, she made a quick exit. After all, prudence was the better part of valor—wasn't it?

Chapter Three

In thinking back over their confrontation, once she returned to her office, Marty realized that what had really gotten to her was his use of the term "confused." There hadn't been a whole lot of men in her life who'd been willing to admit anything confused them. Men seemed to think it wasn't masculine to be confused about anything. And yet it was the first time in their acquaintance that Brad had said or done anything that wasn't tinged with a "Me Tarzan" attitude. Had he been trying to win her sympathy? Well, he'd won a bit of it, she admitted to herself. What if he was, indeed, the victim of a misunderstanding, or a conspiracy?

Marty shook her head to clear it of such an outrageous thought. In the course of her work at the paternity unit, she'd certainly run across women who'd had ulterior motives for accusing men of fatherhood, but even when it was a vengeance of a sort, they knew the men. As Lydia Brown obviously knew Brad. After all, she'd been amazingly correct about his office, down to noticing what the trophy had been for. She wouldn't have picked that up on a casual visit there; the writing on trophies is small and obscure. There was no getting away from the fact that Brad was lying about knowing her. Lydia hadn't been an employee. The building was kept locked, and there was no way she could have been in his office without his permission.

If Brad was lying about knowing her, Marty shouldn't feel the least compunction about prosecuting the case to the fullest. It was Lydia who needed her sympathy, not Brad. Lydia with her six-month-old daughter, no job, a crummy apartment, not enough money to do anything but survive. Besides, Marty had her job to do. Against all those points, the only one in Brad's favor was a certain indefinable aura that made her want to believe him.

That, my dear, has nothing to do with truth, she told herself. It has to do with sex appeal. Every time you're within five feet of him, you can feel the tug of his sexuality, like a magnet. And what he's projecting isn't even his masculinity, it's his tension. He doesn't like the spot he's caught in, and you're feeling the "fight or flight" reaction in him every time you meet. So what if he has incredibly intense eyes? Probably lots of men have the same kind of eyes, and you just haven't noticed. Maybe they're that intense because he feels trapped. Some men are very convincing liars. And so are some women, another voice in her urged.

Marty reached for the phone and dialed Lydia's number. When the phone was answered, she could hear the baby crying in the background. It seemed an imposition to ask to come over at such a time, but Marty was driven by an inner necessity to get to the truth of the matter. Usually an in-depth interview took place only after the alleged father had officially denied paternity; it would do no harm to conduct it now.

"Well, sure," Lydia said. "Cheryl will probably fall asleep before you get here. It's her nap time. She's usually fussy just before."

Marty stopped at a bakery on the way and picked up a couple of pieces of a rich-looking chocolate cake. There probably weren't many occasions on which Lydia could afford to indulge herself. Marty would have liked to take something for the baby, too, but it seemed unprofessional. Right from the start Ralph had warned her not to get too involved with the mothers, or the fathers, for that matter. Taking a piece of cake to eat while they talked was merely a gesture of thoughtfulness. Lydia wasn't likely to have anything to offer her, nor would Marty feel right in accepting any of her meager stores.

The building on Valencia was run-down, with paint peeling from the stucco. Most of the windows were dirty or cracked, the lower ones with iron bars across them. There was a security gate at the entrance, but its lock had been broken. It swung in the wind, collecting debris that blew from the street. Originally the building had probably been divided into four units per floor on each of the three levels, but there were twenty-four bells lined up in rows now. Marty rang the one beside L. Brown, a number on the third floor, and the door was released with a long buzzing.

The entry hall was dirty, the stairs were narrow, and the banister looked about to collapse. Old cooking odors permeated the stairwell, as though no fresh air ever reached it. Marty climbed quickly, catching her foot once in the worn carpet. Dangerous. A woman carrying a baby down these stairs could trip on it and fall. . . . She shuddered at the thought and hurried down the dim corridor to 309.

Lydia was already standing in the doorway, her hair brushed and fresh lipstick applied. At nineteen she still had the fresh skin of youth, but her complexion was paled slightly by being indoors a lot, and possibly by not eating as well as she should. Her thinness seemed natural to her, though, and with her long brown hair she looked waiflike. Actually, the first time Marty had seen her, she'd guessed Lydia's age to be about fifteen. The younger woman had a nervous mannerism, which she used now, of brushing the long hair back from her face and using a finger to roll a long strand up like spaghetti on a fork.

"Come on in," she said, her voice lowered. "Cheryl's asleep now."

Marty followed her into the cramped apartment. There was only one major room, which served as both living room and bedroom. The baby's crib was in the far corner, away from the window. Marty caught only a glimpse of the top of Cheryl's head before Lydia led her into the small kitchen. There wasn't space here for a table, but Lydia had pushed two stools up to a counter, where a pot of tea and two cups rested. Marty produced the pieces of cake, saying, "I couldn't resist them. By this time of day I'm always starving."

"Thanks." Lydia took two plates and forks from a drainer and carefully set a piece of cake on each plate. Marty looked around her, noting with interest that Lydia was obviously house-proud. Despite the general condition of the building, the apartment was clean.

The windows had been washed recently, and the cabinet fronts were wiped. The tiny stove shone, and the linoleum had been scrubbed. A discouraging job when it was so worn, Marty imagined.

"I didn't see a bathroom," she said as Lydia set the cake in front of her.

"It's down the hall. I share it with a couple of other apartments. Do you need to use it?"

"Oh, no. I just wondered. That's a bit inconvenient with a baby."

Lydia shrugged. "It was the cheapest place I could find when I came to San Francisco. Then with the baby I couldn't afford to move."

Marty nodded and took a bite of the cake. There was a layer of filling that tasted like chocolate whipped cream or mousse that melted sensationally in her mouth. "Wow. I think I'll pick up a couple more pieces of this on the way back," she murmured.

"My mom used to make one like this." Lydia put down her fork and pushed the plate of cake away. "You'd think a mother would be happy when her daughter had a baby, wouldn't you?"

"Yes." There were other answers, but Marty knew that was what Lydia wanted to hear.

"I didn't run away from home because they were mean or anything. I just left with my friend because my folks wouldn't treat me like a grown-up, you know? Lukeville is such a backwater, where everybody knows what everybody else is doing. It's not like that in the city."

"No."

Lydia sighed. "Nobody cares about you at all in the city. You'd think there'd be some middle place, wouldn't you?"

"Yes." Marty just wanted her to talk, so she took another bite of her cake.

"When I ran away, I didn't make them worry. I called every couple of days to let them know I was okay. Julie wouldn't call her folks at all, but that didn't matter because mine let them know. It was okay here until she took off up north with some guy she met. My folks sent me some money to come home, but I used it to get this place." She gestured narrowly with a thin, long-fingered hand. "I couldn't go back there then. And I can't go back there now."

"Why not?"

Lydia grimaced. "Because of the baby, of course, and not being married. They don't want unwed mothers in Lukeville. Everybody raised a big stink when some group tried to start a home for unwed mothers a couple of years ago. I think they'd rather the girls starved to death."

"Probably they just don't want to face up to the problem," Marty suggested.

"It all comes out the same in the end, doesn't it? They treat you like some kind of creep if you have an illegitimate baby. My parents won't have anything to do with me now, but all they ever told me I should do in life was raise a family. Isn't that two-faced of them?"

"I guess they meant you should have a family when you were married."

"Well, I thought s . . . see, I thought Brad would marry me."

"Did he ever say he would?"

Lydia made an impatient gesture. "Not in so many words. After Julie left I was real lonely, you know? But I didn't want to go back home; it would've been the same thing all over again. So then I met him at the store. He was real helpful and he seemed to like me and all."

"He's a good bit older than you are."

Lydia looked surprised. "He's not that old. Maybe he just looks younger. I mean, he doesn't have any gray hair or anything. That's how you tell when they're old."

It was perfectly true that Brad had no gray hair, and he did look young for his age, probably because his build was so wiry. His face, too, was youthful, though something about the eyes spoke of a life less than carefree. Marty wasn't sure Lydia was old enough, or perceptive enough, to notice the disparity between his eyes and the rest of his face. But she was observant, as she'd proved from the detailed description of his office.

"Did he ever take you to his house?" she asked.

"No. But that doesn't mean so much, really. I mean, he came here all the time. I used to see him a couple times a week. It wasn't just a one-shot thing, you know. He talked to me, confided in me, all the time. Sometimes I was so sleepy I could hardly hold my eyes open, and he'd be talking away a mile a minute. I wanted to listen to him but the waitressing job was exhausting. I'd nod off, but then his voice would wake me up again."

Marty could imagine Brad talking. She didn't like to imagine it, but she could.

Lydia continued in a bland voice, her face tightened with concentration. "I think the reason he didn't take me to his house must have been because of his daughter. She doesn't live with him, but she spends most weekends there. Maybe he thought it wasn't a good thing for the neighbors to see some woman going in and out of his house. I think maybe men are funny that way."

"Maybe. How long did you continue seeing him?"

"Well, it must have been more than two months. We went out to movies sometimes, and sometimes we went to bars. They always asked for my I.D. in the bars, and I didn't have a fake one, like Julie did. Lots of times we just stayed here, and I cooked for us. He bought me an old tv, and we watched that a lot, too. He liked my cooking. I was learning a lot at the restaurant; I never did much cooking when I lived at home. He'd talk about how maybe I'd learn to make Mexican dishes and Chinese ones. That's the kind of thing I mean, where he acted as though sometime we'd get married. He talked as though we'd be together a long time."

Marty nodded. They often did. Sometimes it meant something, most of the time it didn't. You couldn't expect an innocent of eighteen to know the difference. Women a whole lot older couldn't tell the difference. "Why didn't you take birth control precautions, Lydia?"

A flush stained the pale cheeks, and she shrugged uncomfortably. "I don't know. Everyone seems to think people my age know all about birth control. Well, they sure didn't say anything about it in the school I went to in Lukeville, and it was against my folks' religion. I just didn't really think about it. I mean"—the flush became darker—"I didn't really know all that much about . . . sex. Sure, maybe I should have bought a book or something, but I didn't. All the other girls ever talked about was petting, you know, not about . . . what you really do. Of course, I knew," she said defiantly, her chin tilted up. "I figured it out. But I hadn't done it before."

"Brad was the first?"

"Yeah. Oh, he didn't force me or anything. In fact, we went out a whole bunch of times before we went to bed. Then I did it, I guess, mostly because I liked him. It wasn't very exciting for me."

Not very difficult to seduce an eighteen-year-old who was lonely and in love, Marty thought, feeling a band of anger toward Brad tighten in her chest. Many a young woman, even today, thought it was the best way to prove her love, even though she didn't get much out of it. Subconsciously there was often the desire to get pregnant, to have a baby, to get on with the important part of life. Having babies meant you were grown-up, meant you were not a child anymore. Getting pregnant sometimes meant the man would marry you. So many issues getting all intertwined. It was impossible to sort them out.

Marty pushed aside her empty plate. "Why didn't you tell him about the baby?"

"He'd already left when I found out I was pregnant."

"Left?"

Lydia pushed her hair back from her face and wrapped a strand around one finger. "One day he just said it wasn't going to work out between us, you know? He said he had too many other . . . responsibilities and that I was pretty young. I didn't hear from him again after that."

"You could have called him when you found out about the pregnancy," Marty said insistently. "He was responsible for that, too."

The younger woman looked sulky. "I didn't even want him to know. She's my baby. I was going to manage it myself, everything, and I would have if I hadn't gotten fired when I got so big. Do you know I didn't have the slightest idea where to go then? It was this woman I worked with who told me I should apply for help. But they wouldn't give me anything if I didn't come to your office and tell you who the father was."

"Yes, I know. It's required for eligibility." The street-smart ones knew how to get around it, but Lydia wasn't street-smart. Marty decided to push things a little farther. "Mr. Macintosh has been served with the summons. He denies any knowledge of you."

This bombshell didn't seem to distress her particularly. She let go of the strand of hair and curled her hand into a fist, which she tapped impatiently against the countertop. "Men are creeps."

A unique point of view, Marty thought, barely able to suppress a chuckle. "What's likely to happen now is that he'll deny paternity and request a blood test. I've explained to you about the blood tests."

"Yeah. You said they couldn't actually prove he was the father, but that they'd show if it was likely."

"Right. However, they can prove that he *isn't* the father, if certain elements don't match with the baby." Marty could tell Lydia was bored and uninterested in this recapitulation, so she went on to other matters. "We can always use as much corroborating evidence as possible. You've already told me you don't have any pictures or letters from him. Would any of your neighbors recognize him?"

"People around here keep pretty much to themselves. I don't think any of them noticed him, but they wouldn't want to come to a hearing even if they had."

Marty knew that was perfectly true. "When was it he took you to his office?" she asked.

"Oh, I was in the office a couple of times, after business hours, when the store was closed. He'd have to go in for something, you know." Lydia uncurled her fist and regarded a chipped nail with chagrin. "He was real wrapped up in his business."

The baby began to fuss in the other room, and Lydia rose. "Do you want to see her?" she asked.

"Sure." Marty followed her into the combination living room and bedroom and watched as the young mother stooped to pick up her baby.

There was a tender expression on her face as she cuddled Cheryl against her shoulder and spoke softly to the yawning child. "This is Miss Woods, Cheryl. She brought me a piece of delicious chocolate cake. I'll give you a bite later on."

The child's hair was darker than her mother's, and had a decided curl to it. Her eyes were more green than brown like Lydia's. Cheryl smiled at Marty and thumped a chubby fist against her mother's shoulder. "She's beautiful," Marty said.

"She's a wonderful baby. I can take care of her better than anyone else. He can't come to see her if they say he's the father, can he?"

"He's not likely to want to," Marty replied dryly. "But if he asked the court for permission, they might grant it."

Lydia held the child with fierce protectiveness. "She's my baby. I don't want him to have anything to do with her."

"In my experience, I'd say you have nothing to fear. We're lucky if we can make them keep up the support payments." Marty gathered up her purse and jacket.

"I've got to be off now, Lydia. I'll be in touch with you."

"Thanks for the cake."

Marty had several other business matters to attend to, and it was late afternoon by the time she returned to her office. On the way back she considered what Lydia had told her and wondered if she'd learned anything new. Lydia's story sounded so entirely reasonable. Though Lydia spoke of Brad in a bland, distant way, Marty found that eminently understandable.

To Lydia, Brad was a figure in the past, someone she had loved briefly because she was lonely, and would just as soon forget now that she had a child to love and care for. He had, after all, left her with very little explanation. Lydia's hopes of his marrying her had been illusions even then. For all her youth, Lydia had a certain practicality which would soon have convinced her that men who own successful businesses don't usually marry girls who have run away from home and taken waitressing jobs in San Francisco.

Still, Marty had a great deal of empathy for women who were manipulated by men. She knew that men frequently talked women into doing things they didn't particularly want to do, just because men seemed to have a lot of authority. Someone as naive as Lydia could be convinced that it was simple generosity to give herself, even if she wasn't ready.

It's not that women weren't at fault for not respecting their own principles. When a man was bigger, more experienced and richer, and he *expected* you to behave in a certain way, it was difficult not to think maybe he was right. He was certainly the first one to tell you he was. It took more courage than many women had to defy a bulldozer of a man.

Marty was familiar with men who expected their own way and with the awful feeling that somehow she'd become wrong just because she had a different opinion than theirs. Men tended to treat someone as small as she like a doll who didn't have to be taken seriously. Too often she hadn't had the strength and perseverance to keep them from getting away with it. Going along was easier than constantly fighting against someone. Except in the long run. In the long run you had to stand up for what you believed, otherwise you couldn't live with yourself. . . .

There was a note on Marty's desk asking her to call Brad Macintosh. She stared at it for a long time before she glanced over at Virginia, who had put it there.

"Did you tell him I'd be back this afternoon?" she asked.

Virginia shook her head, her thick black hair bouncing exuberantly. "I said you might not be back for the rest of the day, so you might not call until tomorrow morning. Is this guy getting to you?"

Disgruntled, Marty sighed. "I don't know. He's very credible, Virginia, but so is the mother. What they have to say is in direct opposition to one another. He says he's never even met her; she says he's the only one who could be her baby's father."

"I don't see why you're letting it bother you. The blood tests are going to sort out the whole mess."

"I know." Marty tucked the note with his phone number under the blotter on her desk. There was no sense in trying to explain to Virginia the effect Brad had on her; she couldn't even explain it to herself. No doubt it would do her some good to let her thoughts about Lydia really seep in before she contacted Brad again. Both the anger and the distance would be useful weapons against whatever was drawing her to him. "I'll call him in the morning," she said, and turned to other work on her desk.

Out of the corner of her eye she could see that Virginia watched her for a moment before shrugging and picking up the phone.

Chapter Four

$\mathcal{B}$rad waited at his office until almost seven o'clock, hoping Marty Woods would call. It was an unreasonable thing to do. People who worked for the city didn't keep hours like that. However, he had nowhere more interesting to go before he picked up his daughter. He took her to dinner once a week, in addition to having her stay with him two weekends a month. He hated picking her up, though, climbing the stairs of the house he'd lived in for so long with Andrea and her mother. Andrea was good about answering the door herself. There was never any need to speak to Karen if he didn't wish to. He especially hadn't wanted to tonight.

The outfits Andrea wore made him nervous. They weren't particularly outrageous, not punk or anything like that. Well, perhaps a little like that. The colors were just a bit off, like the avocado gauze skirt she wore tonight. However, that was nothing compared

with the salmon-colored net tank top she wore over a
solid-blue tank top that looked rather like a T-shirt.
He had no idea whether she wore a bra under all of
this, or whether it wasn't necessary for her.

She was definitely developing, which also made him
nervous. Only to be expected in a thirteen-year-old,
of course, but still, how did you treat a teenage
daughter? It had been a great deal easier when she
was five. In those days you could brush her hair when
it looked like it did right now. When he'd suggested a
comb a few months ago, she'd stared at him as though
his intelligence were suspect. "This is the way it's
supposed to be," she'd said haughtily. Wouldn't other
people think she was some kind of nut? Windblown
hardly described the effect she created.

"Any place special you want to go tonight?" he
asked as she climbed into the Volvo. He noticed she
had short knit leggings on under the gauze skirt,
which was probably all to the good. Why did her
mother let her buy these outrageous clothes?

"Mexican, I guess. A tostada would be okay for my
diet."

Brad clamped his teeth together. They'd been over
the diet business before, on which occasion Andrea
had informed him, in a very knowledgeable tone of
voice, that she had no intention of becoming anorexic.
She merely had three pounds to lose. She always
seemed to have three pounds to lose. Of course,
he'd seen her eat when she wasn't on a diet, and there
seemed no chance of her becoming anorexic then. If
there weren't soft drinks and snacks in his house when
she came to stay with him, she was disappointed.

"Mexican sounds good," he agreed as he climbed in
on the driver's side. "The Little Fiesta?"

"Sure." She tugged at the salmon mesh scarf that

was tied around her head like some parody of a
washerwoman. It was wretchedly inappropriate in the
masses of black curls and one end of it kept drooping
over her eye. "You can wear it as a belt, too," she
explained as she shook her head free of it and undid
the knot. "We went to the outlet yesterday, but Mom
said I didn't need another pair of shoes, so I couldn't
get a pair to match it."

Thank God for small favors, Brad thought.

"We were getting my clothes for next week's Disneyland trip. You don't think I'm too old for Disneyland, do you?"

Andrea loved Disneyland. She'd loved it from the
first time they took her there when she was three. Just
the thought that she might be getting too old for it
made Brad shudder. "Of course not," he said reassur-
ingly. "If I'm not too old for it, you certainly aren't."

She had managed to tie the mesh scarf around her
waist. To him, it looked terrible against the avocado-
colored skirt, but he said nothing. He supposed it was
the sort of thing her friends wore, and he reminded
himself of peer pressure at that age. "How's school?"
he asked, and listened absently as she told disturbing
tales of teachers who showed rock-music videos during exams, who didn't allow makeup of work from
absences due to sickness, who always gave open-book
tests. Andrea was seldom at a loss for words and had a
refined sense of justice. Brad wondered if her teachers
found her difficult to handle, with her feisty integrity
and her disconcerting blend of being childlike and
precocious at the same time.

His mind, though, was more than half given over to
the paternity matter. Not that he was going to tell
Andrea about it. You didn't tell children about adult
problems like that, and he certainly wasn't going to

tell his former wife about it. It would have been a relief to talk about it with someone, though. He seemed to have gotten himself rather isolated since the divorce. Whether that was the reason Marty kept coming to mind, or whether it was because she was the symbol of his problem, he couldn't be certain. He did know that there was no possibility of her being neutral in the matter, which depressed him. He thought he was doing a good job of hiding the depression until Andrea cocked her head at him and asked, "Hey, what's the matter, Dad?"

Brad forced a wry grin to his lips. "Weighty matters, chickadee. Nothing for you to worry your pretty head about."

She gave him a scornful glance. "That's a chauvinistic thing to say. Mom tells me when things are bothering her."

"Your mother's . . ." No, he wasn't going to say anything derogatory. "Your mother's a different sort of person than I am."

Andrea giggled. "She sure is."

Brad didn't even want to know what his daughter meant by her giggle.

Marty called Brad first thing in the morning. Not that she felt any better about the whole situation, but there was his note stuck under her blotter, and he deserved to have his call returned. Otherwise he'd probably have complained to Ralph about her. She called early, in the hope that he wouldn't be at his office yet, but he answered the phone himself.

"Look, Marty," he said, just as though they'd been old friends for years, "I want to come in and get this thing settled. Would eleven o'clock be okay?"

A man of action. She agreed to make room in her tight schedule for him at eleven and hung up.

Actually, it was sort of a down time at work. There was a trial the next day with some loose ends she had to tie up, but other than that it was mostly a time of waiting for information to come in. Every job had its moments like that, with everything on hold. They were times she hated, and sometimes she'd work on a little project of her own then. However, today she didn't feel inclined to update the job requirement information or study the text on presenting in court the results of blood tests. The latter was really the assistant district attorney's job, anyhow. It never hurt to know more than the assistant D.A.'s did, because they could botch cases if their loads were heavy. Today, though, she couldn't get too excited about increasing her knowledge. Just before Brad was due she hurried off to the women's room and brushed her hair, put on fresh lipstick and straightened her skirt. This was not her normal procedure before one of the alleged fathers was due at her desk.

He never seemed to just walk like anyone else. That lope of his was becoming familiar to her. The contained energy it suggested always made her feel a little . . . edgy, or something. He appeared from the hall when she just happened to be looking in that direction, and his eyes immediately found hers. Marty could have sworn he winked at her. Now what's he up to? she wondered as she nonchalantly moved his file from her IN box to the center of her blotter. If he thinks being charming is going to help him the least bit, he has another think coming.

Brad had dressed up for the occasion: chocolate-colored wool slacks with a brown and beige plaid button-down shirt and a camel-hair sportcoat. What was really astonishing was to see a tie on him, and such a conservative one, solid brown and narrow. Probably he was trying for dignity, and Marty had to admit he looked prosperous, respectable and handsome, not someone who would lie about whether he was the father of some young woman's baby.

But it was the way all the men dressed—if not as expensively—when they came to the hearings. Marty refused to let it impress her. She smiled formally and nodded to the chair beside her desk. Brad seated himself casually, as though he'd just taken a seat at the movies, and crossed one leg over the other. His gaze swept quickly over Marty and returned expectantly to her face.

"I have the papers ready for you to sign," she said, withdrawing them from the folder and sliding them toward him. "Read them carefully, and sign where it's indicated. There's no reason you can't get an attorney later in the proceedings if you aren't excluded by the blood test, but this will take care of responding to the Summons of Complaint."

She was relieved to see that he did indeed read the document thoroughly before pulling a pen from his sportcoat pocket and signing with a flourish. "What happens now?" he asked.

"I'll call the lab and schedule you for a blood test." Marty drew the phone closer and tapped out the number she knew by heart. When she'd given the extension number and reached the technician with whom she regularly worked, she asked for an appointment. Turning to Brad, she asked, "How's Tuesday at eleven?"

"Fine, fine. The sooner the better." He looked very

confident. They didn't usually look that confident. In fact, they usually looked a little worried, though they tried to appear blasé.

Marty wrote the time and the lab's address on a sheet of paper. Their fingers touched when she passed it to him, and she quickly withdrew her hand. He grinned at her. "I'll schedule the mother and child for a different time, unless you'd prefer to see them," she said. "We used to have everyone go at the same time, for purposes of identification, but that got a little hairy on occasion."

"I can imagine. No, I don't want to see them."

Maybe he was too confident. Did he have some idea of sending someone in his place? It had been done before. "They have what they call a 'chain of custody' at the lab so the right donor's name is on each tube," she explained. "They also photograph all parties."

There was a sardonic gleam in his eyes. "Do they give us all lie detector tests, too?"

"No, Mr. Macintosh. They only test your blood."

"Brad. I want you to call me Brad." The blue of his eyes gleamed with something entirely different now, a blend of mischief and enticement. "I call you Marty, after all."

"Yes, I noticed."

"You don't mind, do you?"

Marty hesitated. "No, I don't mind."

"Good. How about lunch?"

The invitation came as a complete surprise to her. Not once in the whole time she'd been with the Paternity Unit had an alleged father invited her out to lunch. She was sure it wouldn't be allowed, even if no one had ever actually said so. Probably they'd never considered the possibility, either. Already she could feel her head shaking, and she added quickly, "I'm afraid that's not possible . . . Brad."

"Why not?"

She plucked nervously at the jacket of her olive-colored suit while his eyes mocked her. Maybe he was just doing this to make her uncomfortable. Not something she was going to let him get away with, of course. She folded her hands tidily on her desk and met his gaze. "Because you're one of my cases and it wouldn't be proper to accept lunch from you."

"You mean someone would consider it a bribe?" His wild eyebrows twitched with amusement. "Come off it, Marty. Either the blood test excludes me, in which case I won't be one of your cases any more, or it doesn't. I'm sure the district attorney isn't going to drop the case because you ask him to do it."

"Of course not!" she said indignantly. "That's not the point at all."

"Sure it is," he insisted, getting up and standing over her. "If having lunch with me can't be considered a bribe, then it can't be improper, right? Where's your coat?"

"I don't *have* a coat."

He regarded the light suit jacket skeptically. "Well, there's probably some place close enough so we won't have to walk far."

To her chagrin, she found she'd risen. But she didn't move an inch from behind her desk. "I don't want to have lunch with you." It was what she should have said in the first place.

"That's not very kind," he said, pretending to look hurt. "Consider all the trouble you've put me to in the last few days, and you won't even go out to lunch with me."

"I've only been doing my job." Her voice was defensive, even though she tried to keep it neutral. "It has nothing to do with going out to lunch with you."

"I'm a busy man, Marty," he informed her. "If I'm not going to get a lawyer to handle this matter, I'm going to need a little more information. We can discuss it over lunch; that way neither of us will lose any time. Remember, your boss told me you could manage all this for me."

"It's already been managed."

"But I have more questions."

Virginia was smirking at Marty from her desk. "You'd better go," she said.

"Bring along some stuff about blood tests," he suggested. "It'll make great conversation."

Just to spite him, she searched through her file drawer and pulled several examples of paternity test results which she stuck in a folder and jammed into her purse. If he thought haplotypes over hamburgers was such a great idea, that's what he'd get.

Naturally Marty knew all the restaurants in the area. She was a restaurant freak, after a fashion. Since she did more than her share of eating out, it was no wonder. At first she thought she'd take him to some real dive, but once they were headed down the street, she found she couldn't do that. He'd just think she had bad taste. Instead she headed for The Half Shell, which was pretty expensive as lunches in that neighborhood went. If he was going to coerce her into having lunch with him, he might as well pay through the nose.

Marty couldn't keep up with his long, easy strides, and he kept forgetting to set his pace to hers. She was wearing high heels; she almost always wore high heels. Short women did. Brad controlled himself for a minute or two, then forgot and surged ahead. She made no attempt to match him, but continued strolling along at her own pace. Eventually he found he was talking to thin air and swung around to find her. After he waited for her to catch up, the whole process began again with him forgetting and charging ahead only minutes later. He did all of the talking, mostly about his business and how hard it was to find and keep good employees.

The restaurant was largely glassed in, with an entryway through an arbor and courtyard. He looked around him with interest, commenting, "I'd never have guessed there'd be a place like this down here." Down here was well south of Market Street, but a lot of good restaurants had been springing up in the area over the last few years. He should have known that, since his own business wasn't that far away. Marty decided he was probably one of those men who had his secretary bring him a sandwich every day from the local greasy spoon.

They were seated at a small table toward the end of the room, where only one other table was within hearing distance—not that it mattered. It was obvious Brad didn't know anyone there, and Marty certainly didn't. The Paternity Unit investigators only went to places like The Half Shell for special occasions. Brad ordered a martini, Marty ordered a wine spritzer. Awful stuff, but it was better for keeping a clear head. She had a feeling she'd need a clear head with him.

"Isn't your job sort of depressing?" he asked, with a kind of complaisant sympathy.

"Not particularly. It has its rewards, like making fathers take some financial responsibility for their children." Marty knew it was a purposely provocative thing to say. He was coming on cocky again, though, and cocky men irritated her.

"I've never met that woman," he insisted. "And supporting a kid for eighteen years is a hell of a price to pay—"

"Is it? I don't think so. I think it's exactly the price every man should know he might have to pay for careless coupling. After all, the woman usually has to pay a great deal more than he does, doesn't she? She has the child with her twenty-four hours a day for eighteen years, and she doesn't live on welfare for more than a couple of years, statistically. She goes out to work at some menial job where she's paid a pittance, in order to provide for the two of them."

"But she *wants* the kid!"

Marty nodded. "Usually. But no parent, certainly not a welfare mother, has any idea of how difficult it is to raise a child until she's had one. She thinks a baby is going to provide love in her loveless world; she doesn't understand about the other side—the responsibility, the drudgery, the worries, the expense. It's never easy to be a single parent, and being a poverty-stricken one is the pits, Brad."

He glared at her. "I'm sure it is, but it doesn't mean I have to support some kid who isn't mine."

"Of course not. No one has any intention of making you do that. That's why we use the blood tests."

Their drinks arrived, and he lifted his in a silent toast before taking a healthy sip. "Let's change the subject," he suggested. "Tell me about yourself."

"What do you want to know?" Marty asked, wary.

"Everything."

"Do you know how corny that sounds?"

"Does it?" He looked genuinely surprised. "I thought that's what everyone said."

"It is what everyone says. That's why it's corny." She smiled at him. "You don't want to be like everyone else, Brad."

"It's hard to get used to going out again after you've been married for a long time," he grumbled. "The women don't seem the same as they were when I finished college."

"Times change. You have to keep up with them."

"No, I don't. I'm still a man; they're still women. That's all I have to know."

"Then what's your problem?" she asked, trying to control the twitching of her lips.

"I don't have any problem. I just don't like all the petty formalities."

"You're a straight-to-bed man, huh?" Now she really couldn't help laughing, but she did her best to smother it with the wispy cocktail napkin.

"That's not what I meant!" He frowned at her, aloof now. "It's more comfortable when you already know someone, instead of having to find out everything. Like, if we'd known each other for two months, we wouldn't be sitting here making small talk. We'd be planning where we were going to go this weekend, or something like that."

"Would we?" She thought about it a moment, and added, "Where would we go?"

"To Yosemite, maybe, or Mendocino. Someplace where I could hike or fish or get into a softball game."

"What would I be doing while you were hiking or fishing or playing softball?"

He looked shocked. "You'd do them with me, of course. Don't you like sports?"

"A little tennis, a little swimming. Walking, not hiking." She shook her head sadly. "I guess we weren't made for each other, Brad."

"Hell, Karen didn't like them either, but she went with me. At least we were together."

"So where did you go for her to do what she wanted?"

"She could do the things she liked right here in the city. We couldn't get away from the store all that often."

"No wonder you're not married anymore."

His body stiffened and his eyes became decidedly belligerent. "What's that supposed to mean?"

"It means that women get tired of making all the compromises. They get a little fed up with letting the man have his way all the time."

"Oh, boy. Another one." He noisily set his glass back on the table. "Why do I always run into the ones who're into equal rights for women?"

She asked as graciously as possible, "Why do I always run into the ones who aren't?"

It would have made a good exit line; she was getting better. However, they'd already ordered their meals, and it would have been a rotten thing to do, getting up and leaving the male chauvinist to pay for two expensive meals. Instead she took a small sip from her wine spritzer and allowed her eyes to wander around the restaurant. It was filling up quickly now, as lunch hour really began. With its wooden tables and hanging plants, the place looked festive in the abundant natural light. The only thing she could find to feel happy about, however, was that there would be no need to get to know Brad any better. She already knew enough to stay clear of him, given her penchant —with men—for becoming a doormat.

Brad hadn't said anything all this time. He finished off his martini and looked around for a waiter but seemed to change his mind when he got the man's attention. "Look," he said finally, "a woman likes a man she can lean on."

"For what?"

"All sorts of things. A man's got to be strong."

"For what?" she asked again. "Digging ditches? Fighting off dragons?"

"Come on, Marty. We're not talking about that kind of thing. He has to be both dependable and exciting. He has to take charge of things. Otherwise he's a wimp."

"And you called it taking charge of things when you insisted on weekends where you could do what you wanted, and your wife couldn't? That's not taking charge; that's being selfish."

"I can see we're not going to hit it off," he said, as though this were news to her. "I like my women more feminine."

Marty recognized the ultimate put-down: you're not feminine enough. Men thought you'd just knuckle right down if they threw terms like that around. Well, she'd had her fill of macho jerks who thought they could manipulate her by trying to make her feel guilty for some supposed lack of femininity. She batted her eyelashes at him, with a sweet smile, and said, "That's a real shame, honey. Here my heart was just pitter-pattering away because you're such a masculine hunk."

The waiter arrived just then with Brad's sautéed shrimp and her monk fish. Though monk fish sounded odd, someone had told her that it tasted like lobster, and she was game to try it. She spread her napkin on her lap and picked up her fork; he was watching her closely. "Looks delicious," she said brightly.

His shrimp smelled better but he made no move to taste it. "Okay, I shouldn't have said that," he admitted. "You just made me so damn mad, taking my wife's part and all. You don't even know her. You don't even know *me.*"

"It doesn't matter. Forget it." The monk fish was okay but nothing to write home about. He still hadn't tried his shrimp. "How about if we just concentrate on the paternity suit? It's the only thing we have in common, Brad."

"Hell of a thing to have in common," he grunted. "All right, tell me about blood tests."

It wasn't the most stimulating conversation Marty had had in her life, but it got them through the meal and back to her building. Then an unfortunate thing happened. As he handed the paternity test result samples back to her a gust of wind swooped around the corner of the building and took hold of them. They both gave chase at the same time, but from different positions, and managed to crash into one another as they lunged to retrieve the papers. The breath was knocked out of her, and she wobbled for a moment. He spent the same fraction of a second deciding whether to rescue the papers or her. His foot thrust out to trap the reports, and his arms went around her.

They remained that way far too long. A spark of physical excitement charged between the two of them in that moment. She'd been supported before in similar circumstances and no such thing had happened to her. He grinned as she stepped hastily from his grasp. When he bent to pick up the papers, she clutched her purse against her chest, not looking at him. He pressed the papers into her clenched fingers, whispering, "Pitter-patter?"

"You're a tower of strength," she muttered, and turned to walk into the building.

Chapter Five

Steve Yu, one of the other investigators, rode up in the elevator with her. "You look a little rumpled, Marty," he said. "You didn't get mugged on your lunch hour, did you?"

"Not exactly." She tried to smooth out the papers and loosen her grip on her purse at the same time, but only managed to drop both. She got to them before Steve did and once again pressed the whole bundle protectively against her chest. Steve walked off with a puzzled frown.

Virginia looked up as Marty passed. "Really, Marty, I expected more reserved behavior from you on a first date."

"It wasn't a date, and I had a small accident."

Virginia looked as though she didn't believe Marty. "Nothing serious, I hope."

"Not at all," Marty said primly, setting the purse

and papers down on her desk as though nothing had happened.

Something had happened, all right, but she wasn't quite sure what—yet. Just because she felt a physical attraction for someone, that didn't mean anything had to come of it. Especially when she knew very well he was an inappropriate partner for her. Not only an alleged father in a paternity suit, but a male chauvinist to boot. The paternity part could conceivably be dismissed in a few weeks, but the other was a permanent fixture with those men who had it. If she saw any more of him, she'd soon be wandering around in a daze, going off on fishing trips with him, scraping together inedible meals. Ugh.

"I don't cook," she muttered to herself.

Virginia's lips twisted into a rueful expression. "How well I know! Are you practicing telling him?"

"I was just thinking out loud. Have you ever had monk fish? I tried some at The Half Shell."

"You're changing the subject, Marty, and monk fish doesn't sound very appetizing."

"It wasn't bad." She shoved her purse into her bottom drawer and smoothed out the papers. They looked like they'd been stomped on, which they had been.

"Have you set him up for a blood test?" she asked.

"Yes. Next week."

"Well, you'll know soon enough, then."

"It doesn't matter—except to the case," Marty assured her with a dismissive toss of her head. "I knew he was a 'Me Tarzan' type the first time I saw him."

"Yeah, just the type you're always attracted to."

"I am not! I like warm, sensitive, considerate men."

Virginia laughed. "Sure, Marty. That's not exactly how *I'd* describe Harry."

"I admit it took me a while to uncover Harry's less admirable traits, but I've learned my lesson. No man is going to walk all over me again. It's only too evident that's what Brad tried to do with his wife. I don't need that kind of man in my life."

"Well, good luck," Virginia retorted, turning back to her work.

Marty was determined to put Brad entirely out of her mind. There were several things she had to do during the afternoon, and she didn't need the distraction. She might have been successful, except for remembering the wild black eyebrows and the laughing blue eyes when he whispered, "Pitter-patter." Really, that was uncalled for. It was the first evidence she'd seen that he had a sense of humor, and it was a dastardly one. But then, maybe it wasn't so bad for a man charged with paternity, not a particularly laughable matter.

He seemed very sure that the blood tests would exclude him. Though he didn't perfectly understand the test results she'd shown him, he did grasp the fact that there were several different tests run, any one of which could eliminate him as a possible father of Lydia's child. She knew that subconsciously he'd already convinced her of his not being the father because she was thinking of ways in which Lydia might be mistaken. Someone might simply have used Brad's name, mightn't he? The first thing she'd have to do was show Lydia the picture of Brad that would be taken at the lab. Perhaps that would clear up the mistaken identity.

Since that was settled in her mind, Marty should

have been able to get down to work. But Virginia's reference to Harry nagged at her. There was no similarity between Brad and Harry. None. Except, each of them expected to have his own way. Brad had assumed his wife would go off camping with him even though she didn't enjoy it; Harry had assumed Marty would cook even though she was a total failure at it.

She had tried to cook for him. Instead of appreciating her effort, he had always wearily shaken his head, and she'd let him get away with it. She had let him suggest how she should dress, where they would go out to eat and when they would see a play together. She had yielded to his opinions on a variety of subjects because she'd found that arguing with him merely made him disagreeable.

Why? Why had she let him treat her like a doormat? Was it because he was handsome, intelligent and charming—when he felt like it—and he professed to admire her? She'd thought she admired him, too. Because he was so sure of himself and so authoritative, she was sure he must be right. You could depend on a man like that, couldn't you?

She'd ended up feeling like a paper doll that he could manipulate in any way he chose. After a few months she hadn't felt quite real. She would look in the mirror and wonder who this woman was. She didn't dress like Marty Woods, she didn't wear her hair like Marty Woods, and she didn't have a sparkle in her eyes like Marty Woods. The image was a creation of Harry's, not a real person.

Once she'd realized the problem, Marty had spent hours trying to make Harry understand. Nothing she could say seemed to get through to him. Finally she had given up, simply saying, "I'm not going to see you any more." He had acted as though she were crazy, throwing away a gem like him. Marty felt as though she'd barely escaped with herself intact.

It had been a difficult experience and had left her badly shaken. She had no intention of duplicating it. Brad might have convinced her he wasn't the child's father, but he wasn't going to convince her of anything else. She wasn't going to think about him, or Harry, for one minute longer.

When it was time to leave for the day she made a point of telling Virginia how much she'd accomplished during the afternoon, but Virginia just raised her brows in her usual die-hard skepticism. It was still reasonably warm and sunny when Marty walked out of the building, dreading the crowded bus ride home. She heard a car horn honk but thought nothing of it. Horns were honked all over San Francisco at rush hour, and they had nothing to do with her. Her mind was on other matters.

"Marty!" a voice called as she trotted off down the sidewalk.

She recognized the voice. Really, she shouldn't, when she'd only seen him three times in her life. She seriously considered ignoring it. There was no legitimate reason on earth for him to be parked in front of her building in his blue Volvo. None. If she just kept walking, he'd never be able to catch up with her because his car was pointed in the wrong direction— unless he came after her on foot.

"Marty!"

The voice came from directly behind her. So he'd abandoned his car in a no parking zone to come after her. Naturally she couldn't ignore him now. She turned with an aloof expression on her face, though her heart was thumping uncomfortably in her chest.

Why does he have this effect on me? she asked herself.

"I'll give you a ride home," he said.

"Why do you presume I don't have my car here?"

"Because it's expensive to park downtown and you can't make that much money."

That really irritated her. "I make quite enough money to park down here if I wish," she informed him in her most haughty voice.

"But you don't, do you?"

"As it happens, no. The bus service is adequate and more economical."

"You could park in my lot every day. It's only a short walk, and a whole lot nicer than riding the bus at rush hour."

Tempter! There wasn't a soul she knew who wouldn't give a right arm for a free parking space downtown and within a few blocks of work. She knew people who wouldn't work for a company unless it provided parking. It was a perk worth a small fortune. "That's very kind of you, Brad, but I'm afraid I couldn't accept."

His lips curled, as though he were trying to still an almost unbelievable urge to laugh. "Another bribe, huh? Well, we can discuss it after I've been excluded in this case of yours. Come on. I'm going to get a ticket if I don't move my car."

Marty had not agreed to go with him, but he took hold of her arm. When he took her arm, that jolt of physical response raced through her again. The cad. He knew that would happen. It was not easy to deny that kind of chemical reaction or pretend it hadn't happened. She'd never figured out why this made some men feel superior. After all, *she* wasn't the only one who felt it. It was just as obvious that he did. Did she go around feeling superior to him? There was something wrong with the male mind, she decided.

Brad gallantly bundled her into the Volvo, chucking a finger under her chin before he locked and closed the door—all this with the widest grin on his face. She set herself to thinking of ways to wipe it off, and then she started to wonder if anyone from the Paternity Unit had seen their little dance on the sidewalk. There was no one in view who seemed to be taking the least notice, but somehow she felt sure Virginia would have managed to witness the whole episode.

The car nosed slowly into the stream of traffic. "Where do you live?" Brad asked.

Somehow she was surprised that he didn't know. Not that her card had the information, and she didn't put her address in the phone book. "On Cole Street, near Carmel. Is that very far out of your way?"

He glanced at her slyly. "You know where I live."

She hadn't thought about it, but of course she did—from his file. The exact address she couldn't remember, but it was on Liberty Street. Her place was quite a bit out of his way. Well, that was his tough luck. If she'd lived across the Bay it would have served him right.

When she said nothing, he maneuvered the car from the far left lane into the far right one. It was a tricky piece of driving at that hour of the day, but he appeared to enjoy the challenge. When he'd turned right, he said, "I thought you could make me dinner, since I bought you lunch."

"I don't cook."

He swung slightly toward her, startled. "I beg your pardon?"

"I don't cook."

"Every woman cooks. They may not be good at it, but they all do it."

"Well, I don't. I've never had the least interest in learning."

He considered that for a moment. "What do you eat?"

"Sometimes frozen dinners. Usually I eat out."

"That's very expensive."

She smiled sweetly at him. "I told you I make a good salary."

"Yes, and you also take the bus."

"That's so I can eat out as often as I like."

He turned the car onto Duboce. "I didn't have anything fancy in mind. Toasted cheese sandwiches would be all right."

"I've never made a toasted cheese sandwich in my life." It was true, though she didn't expect him to believe her. Her best friends didn't believe her.

"Nonsense. Everyone's made toasted cheese sandwiches. There's nothing to it. You just butter some bread, put a few slices of cheese between the bread and heat it on a grill. You do have a grill, don't you?"

"I think so."

He shook his head, still thinking this was a joke. "I'm sure you have bread and cheese and butter in your apartment."

"I may have butter," she said.

"For God's sake, a grown woman doesn't live without bread and cheese in her apartment!"

She nodded sagely. "It's because I'm not very feminine, I guess."

"I said I was sorry about that," he muttered. "Look, we can stop and get some bread and cheese."

"I don't really think it's a good idea for you to come

home with me. If you like, I'll buy you dinner at Bambino's. It's Italian, in my neighborhood."

"I don't let women buy my meals."

"You just let them make them, huh?"

"It's not the same thing."

She snorted. "No, I suppose it isn't. If they make them, they have to go to a lot of effort for you. Much more satisfying to the ego, I'm sure."

"Has anyone ever told you you're a very difficult woman to talk to?" he demanded, zipping out onto Market on the yellow light.

"Lots of people have told me." Maybe that wasn't precisely true; a few people had told her.

Cars coming from the opposite direction blared their horns at him for blocking the intersection, but he wasn't the least perturbed. Marty dissociated herself from the scene, thinking that if a man's home was his castle, surely his car was his charger. Men didn't seem to worry about inconveniencing other drivers, the way women did. They assumed their right to be on the road allowed them to do precisely what they pleased. It was a short tie-up and he talked all the way through it.

"When I used to date before I married my wife, women were more considerate of a man's feelings. They didn't try to antagonize me the way you do. They wanted me to like them."

"Maybe that's the difference," she said.

He glared at her. "Even when they didn't care whether or not I liked them, they were polite."

"It isn't polite to contradict you?"

This was apparently too ridiculous a question for a response. He was silent until he'd gotten them onto Seventeenth Street, and they were climbing the hill past renovated Victorians and freshly painted later-era houses. "What it is," he said finally, "is that you're fighting your attraction to me."

Probably very close to the truth, but it wasn't the sort of thing she was willing to confess at the moment —not in a way he'd accept. She allowed a heavy lacing of sarcasm in her voice when she said, "I'm sure that's exactly what it is."

He'd gotten a red light at the top of the hill and turned to study her. His tone softened. "Look, there's nothing wrong with being attracted to someone, Marty. It happens. Forget about the paternity case. I didn't father that kid. I'm not married. There's no reason you have to put up barriers against me."

"The light's turned green," she said.

With a cluck of annoyance, he drove ahead, making a second gear stop at the next corner. At Cole, though, he made a complete stop. "To the left?"

"My apartment is to the left, Bambino's is to the right." He turned to the right.

"I'm paying."

"Then you might as well take me home."

"Why do you have to be so difficult, Marty?" he asked as he pulled over to the side of the street, blocking a driveway, and stopped the car. "I can afford to buy you dinner as well as lunch."

"It's not a question of whether you can afford it. I can afford it, too. You bought me lunch, so it's my turn. You're the kind of man who's going to consider me 'obligated' to you if you pay for both."

"How can you make such crass generalizations?" he demanded. "You don't know what kind of man I am."

Marty sighed. "I'll tell you what, Brad. Would you go dutch?"

He hesitated, his wild eyebrows twitching in and out

of a frown. She saw his hand clench slightly on the steering wheel. Then the fingers flicked out in a gesture of resignation. "All right."

She reached out to press his hand briefly. "Thank you."

"You don't have to thank me for something like that," he grumbled, starting the car.

The sensation she'd felt on touching his fingers remained with her. To counteract it, she said, "You just tell me when I *should* thank you, so I'll know. I wouldn't want to be impolite."

"It's a wonder any man even talks to you."

"I know."

But they had very little trouble conversing over their shared pizza. Brad told her about growing up in Colorado, and Marty offered her experiences in San Francisco. They were both one of two children in their families, both graduates of state colleges, both animal lovers. However, Brad tended toward horses and big dogs, while Marty liked small, fluffy dogs like Misty. Hardly enough on which to build a relationship, Marty told herself as Brad's hand enclosed hers where it lay on the table. The feel of his warm skin on hers made her want to shudder, a pleasurable shudder, but she repressed the urge.

Against her better judgment, she left her hand where it was, even when he started to rub his thumb along the tender skin. Such a very simple contact, surely. Ridiculous to protest against it. Yet that simple touch made her whole body come alive. What was it with him, anyhow? She'd felt a physical response to other men in her life, of course, but nothing like this instant and powerful tension from the slightest contact. Marty was beginning to believe that Brad was a very dangerous man.

There was no protest when she paid for her share of the meal. He put his arm around her waist as he guided her from the restaurant and into the gathering dusk outside. They'd been fortunate enough to find a parking space in the same block, so she didn't bother to protest his hold. He unlocked the passenger door and pulled it open, but remained blocking the way. Marty looked up at him questioningly.

"Are you still determined not to let me come in when I take you home?"

She nodded. "I think it would be better not to."

"Then let's drive up to Twin Peaks. I'm not ready to leave you yet."

"How about Tank Hill? It's closer and the view's just as good."

"Never heard of it."

"It's just above where I live, but with a car you have to drive a few blocks out of the way."

"Okay." He stepped aside so she could get into the car, his hand just brushing her cheek.

As soon as they parked on Belgrave, Marty knew it was a mistake. On Twin Peaks there would have been dozens of other people and cars around; on Tank Hill there was no one. The path up the hill was almost invisible in the dim light, and it was rough with loose stones. Unfamiliar with the hazardous footing, Brad stumbled twice, exclaiming finally, "Are you some kind of mountain goat, Marty? I thought you didn't like hiking."

"It's not far," she said, scrambling in her high heels to the top. Why had she done this? He was going to think she'd deliberately chosen a secluded place so he could . . . had she? Had that tightening of her body subconsciously urged her mind to this private spot? It would have been better if she'd let him come in for a cup of coffee.

"Hey, this is great!" He stood beside one of the huge boulders at the crest, gazing out in a westward direction where the sun was just setting. The final blaze of color held his rapt attention for several minutes, and then he turned to take in the rest of the city, which was catching the last rays of light, each of its hills crowned with glowing buildings. "Damned if I know why anyone would want to live anywhere else," he muttered.

"I know." She'd been keeping her distance, but moved closer to him now. "Mostly I come up here during the day when you can see all the details—the houses clustered in the valleys and perched on the hills, the parks and green spaces, the downtown highrises, the sailboats on the bay." She wrapped her arms around herself to keep away the cold. "It's almost always windy up here, though."

He put his arm around her shoulders and drew her closer to him but kept his eyes on the view. "Where do you live?"

When she moved forward to the left of the first boulder, he moved with her. "Right down there. The beige pair of apartments. I have the lower one."

"Cul de sacs are great places to live. You probably don't have any traffic at all."

"Just the neighbors." His arm tightened around her somewhat, and she felt her body tense. "We should go back down before it's too dark to see."

"There's no hurry. Once my eyes get adjusted to the dark, I can see like an owl."

"Yes, but I can't," she protested, turning toward the path.

"Marty."

His hand was still on her shoulder, locking her against him. She frowned at him. He reluctantly released her, but his eyes held her motionless. There was such intensity in his gaze. So much need, and sincerity, and longing. Her body ached with the desire to respond to all that emotion. She licked her lips and swallowed, trying to think of something to say, trying to decide what she should do. Her lips tingled with wanting his on them, her fingers itched to bury themselves in his wavy black hair. The hammering of her heart sounded so loud to her, she was sure he must be able to hear it. They stood that way for a long moment, staring into each other's eyes.

Brad held his hand out to her then, and she paused only a moment before putting hers in it. His fingers tightened, sending a current of excitement through her. It was asking too much for her to remember that he was someone with whom she probably shouldn't get involved. All her instincts told her to believe him. Those other matters could sort themselves out later; right now all she wanted was to be held in his arms.

He folded her hand under his, drawing her closer to him. His lips just brushed hers the first time, like a nibble of food reminding one of how enormously hungry one was. When they met her lips again, they lingered, but softly, almost tentatively. She returned their wistful pressure. His hands went around her waist, and she raised hers around his neck, where she could just feel the edges of his rough black hair. This languidness was like a seductive dream, pulling her in slowly but inexorably. His lips were magic: they spoke of erotic pleasures, they tasted of romantic dreams, they had the firm authority of knowledge. It was almost as if the two of them had done this before, been this close, closer.

The sense of déjà vu was heightened by the play of his hands on her back. His fingers seemed to know every inch of her flesh under the green suit jacket and blouse. Somehow it was as if she wore nothing at all, and felt his touch on her bare skin. His touch was as familiar as her breathing, as necessary as sunlight. She had never felt this way before, and it almost frightened her.

Shaken, she drew back from him slightly, putting a hand on his chest to separate them. His face was still there, right in front of hers, his eyes bold with his need, his lips still parted. It was almost dark then, but she could see him perfectly. His aggressive chin, his unruly eyebrows, the strong column of his neck. Do I know you? she wanted to cry. Where are these feelings coming from? She raised a finger to trace the line of his cheek, bringing it down to wander over his lips. He caught it into his mouth and sucked on it, making her insides melt.

Then he crushed her against him, holding on more tightly, his lips on hers, urgent now, demanding. His tongue eagerly tasted the oval of her lips and slid inside with an ease that startled her. She felt the tip explore along the ridge of her teeth, before it twined with her tongue. His heated breath seemed to sweep through her body. Like a fire-breathing dragon, she tried to tell herself, in a desperate effort to counteract his powerful influence. She was on fire all over and clung to him, pressing against his solid frame to ease the incendiary impact he was having.

His body, too, felt heated, radiating a more subtle,

enticing warmth. His fingers stroked invitingly at her nape, pressing her gently toward him, supporting the fragile balance between them. Her hips and thighs touched his, and the hardness of him made her feel unbearably soft and vulnerable. She clasped her hands behind his back, hanging on for dear life. He stroked the column of her back with one hand, merging them more closely, until she felt almost a part of him. When he cupped her buttocks and strained them toward him, she thought her legs would give out. She had never been so aroused that she thought she would faint, but her head felt fuzzy, spinning out of control.

The only thing that saved her from asking Brad home with her right then was the dog. At times dogs have a most disconcerting way of greeting strangers. There Marty was, clinging to Brad and thinking she might faint, when this cold, wet object was thrust between her legs. She squeaked her surprise and objection, only to have Brad abruptly release her, growling, "Go away!"

She was about to tell him precisely that, until she saw the dog. It was a golden retriever, jumping merrily around the two of them, giving short, sharp, ecstatic barks. Marty was so relieved she couldn't help laughing. Brad looked annoyed for a moment, before a rueful smile worked its way onto his lips. They were grinning at each other when the dog pounced on him in a most painful way. He tried to pretend nothing awful had happened, but she could tell because of the way his face paled. It was no laughing matter, of course, so she caught her lip between her teeth and bit down hard to prevent the hysterical burst of inappropriate mirth that swelled inside her.

"Dusty! Here, Dusty," a voice called from not very far away.

The dog bounded off, and Marty put a steadying hand out to Brad. "Are you all right?"

He drew a deep breath before he answered. "Yes."

"I think we'd better go, then."

She headed toward the path, and he followed more slowly. It was hazardous in the dark, and they didn't talk, concentrating instead on negotiating the uneven footing. She stumbled twice, due to her inappropriate shoes, but he was too far behind to be of assistance. When they reached the car he seemed okay again, just not very talkative. She chattered a bit as she directed him to her apartment. He got out to see her to the door, but he didn't press to come in.

"How about Saturday?" he suggested.

By this time reason had completely reasserted itself. "I don't think so, Brad. Let's see how this whole paternity thing comes out."

He stared at her, trying, she thought, to remind her of what had happened up on the hill. When she remained silent, he shrugged in a very macho manner, and loped back down to his car. Marty let herself into her apartment with a sigh of relief.

Chapter Six

"Turn that down a little, would you?" Brad asked his daughter. No matter how often he heard the current rock music, it sounded raucous to him. He wasn't able to understand any of the lyrics, which was probably all to the good.

"Sure, Dad," Andrea agreed, though her voice had a long-suffering tinge to it. She was sprawled on the sofa and used her toes to work the volume knob, accidentally making it much louder before turning it down. "Sorry."

"Does your mother let you have it that loud?"

The girl's face screwed up in thought. "She doesn't seem to notice it. Sometimes, if she's on the phone, she'll tell me to turn it down."

"You mean she can study right through that noise?" Brad didn't believe it for a moment.

"Carl says it's distracting, but Mom says it's just background noise. She says women learn to live with that kind of distraction better than men do because they have more experience with it."

Brad didn't want to hear anything about Carl at all. As a rule, Andrea seemed to realize this because she seldom brought up his name. Usually at this time on Sunday, Brad would be getting ready to take his daughter back to her mother, but he had Andrea with him for the whole week of her spring vacation. It was probably a good thing Marty hadn't agreed to Saturday night. What would he have done with his daughter? He hadn't thought of that at the time. All he'd wanted was to see her again. He'd waited for her after work the next evening, but she'd never come out of the building. She could have left early, or very late, but Brad felt sure she'd simply left the building by another exit to avoid him.

"Tell me something," he said to his daughter now, looking up from the doorbell buzzer he was trying to repair. "How old are most girls when they learn to cook?"

Andrea frowned at him. "I don't know. Most girls my age help out in the kitchen sometimes, but they don't know how to put a whole meal together."

"So why do you?"

"Because I was interested. Mom would get real wrapped up in her studying sometimes and forget to start dinner until seven. Carl and I got hungry."

Let Carl starve, Brad thought. "How often do you do the cooking?"

"Two or three times a week, I guess."

"That doesn't seem fair . . ." Brad began, but his daughter was eyeing him with thirteen-year-old disdain. "Well, I know you do most of the cooking here when we don't go out, but I don't know how to cook much of anything."

"You could learn. It's not that hard."

"I don't have time to learn." It wasn't Brad's only objection, but it would do.

His daughter turned back to her book, but as she lowered her eyes to the print she said quite clearly, "Jane's dad is a terrific cook."

It was the end of the discussion. Already he could see that she was immersed in the novel, having given her parting shot every bit as effectively as her mother might have. Jane, Andrea's best friend, lived with both of her parents in a house just down the street from Andrea's. Jane's mother was an executive at IBM, and her father was an electrical contractor. Jane's father was also a marathon runner and a soccer addict, of the playing, not viewing, variety. In other words, an actively masculine man, not to be confused with a wimp, and he was a terrific cook.

After being on his own for more than a year now, Brad had learned to fix himself two items: spaghetti and tacos. He seldom ate out at a restaurant because he hated eating alone. He did pick up carryout food for himself, and he bought frozen tv dinners and pot pies. He hated every bit of it. Karen had been a good cook. See how she'd degenerated since she'd abandoned him! She let her own daughter cook for her instead of doing the motherly thing and providing a warm meal for her poor young innocent.

The poor young innocent was lying there giggling over some passage in a Judith Krantz novel. Really, it was too much, what Karen let her do. When he'd asked Andrea why she read that stuff, she'd said, "I'm picking up pointers." What could you do with a child like that? She was far too young to be interested in sex, and if a man ever laid a hand on her . . .!

Karen had once, in a moment of complete frustration, told him he was a Neanderthal. She had apologized, of course, but the sting remained with him. "So it's all right with you if your child's abused?" he'd yelled. Karen had leveled one of her most devastating looks at him and replied, "Unfortunately, Brad, you lump all sex together. There will be a time when Andrea welcomes sexual attention from a male. Your assumption that any male interested in her will abuse her is not a healthy attitude."

Well, he hadn't been talking about that kind of situation, had he? It would be years before Andrea was in that kind of situation. Karen thought of herself as progressive; Brad thought she didn't care enough for time-honored traditions. She thought women should be able to take care of themselves. What good was a man to them if they could do that?

Brad shoved aside the doorbell buzzer and leaped to his feet. For more than a year now, he'd been more restless than he could ever remember being, even as a teenager. It wasn't exactly that he was in need of sexual release, though that might have been a part of it. Nothing seemed to give him the kind of pleasure he'd experienced when he was happily married. When he'd protested to Karen that he *had* been happily married, she'd said, "Maybe *you* were." It never helped when she softened the blow of some remark like this by adding, "I was, too, Brad, for a lot of years. But I've changed, and you haven't changed with me."

What did she expect, for God's sake? No one was ever one hundred percent happy one hundred percent of the time. They would have gotten over the rough spots; they'd done it before. When she'd insisted on working at the store—nagged him for months about it—instead of doing the books at home, hadn't he let her come? As soon as Andrea had started school, he had let her work at the store. That was the kind of compromise at which any two reasonable adults would have arrived. Brad had always wondered if Karen would have agreed to having another child if he'd let her come back to the store sooner. He suspected she didn't want another one because she would have had to wait until *that* child was old enough for school.

What was so exciting about the store, anyhow? Brad didn't find it of much interest these days. Karen had been free to go anywhere with Andrea, or to stay at home and enjoy herself. Compared to that, the store was hard labor. Probably that was why she'd gotten so excited about going to law school. It wasn't at all true that he hadn't wanted her to go because she'd end up making more money than he did. He just wanted her to wait until Andrea was older, maybe out of high school, and not in need of constant supervision. Was that asking so much?

Brad found himself in the kitchen, staring at the paperback copy of *Joy of Cooking* that Andrea had presented to him on his birthday. It had seemed a tactless gift at the time. He'd just moved into his own house because Karen wanted a divorce. He'd always thought Karen must have suggested it to Andrea to somehow make him feel ridiculous. The pages of the book were still almost pristine, although Andrea used it occasionally when she cooked for him. Brad flipped absently through the book, meaning to slam it shut and return it to its shelf. But the pages stopped moving at a recipe for cheese soufflé. It had been years since he'd had a cheese soufflé.

Brandishing the book like some kind of talisman, he loped back to the living room where Andrea was still engrossed in her novel. "Could we have cheese soufflé tonight?" he asked.

She blinked up at him. "We're having barbecued chicken. You said you'd do it on the hibachi if I got it ready for you."

"Couldn't we have cheese soufflé, too?"

Andrea held out her hand for the recipe book, and Brad relinquished it to her. After skimming the recipe, she snapped the book shut. "You don't have any cheddar cheese and I doubt if you have a soufflé dish. Besides, I've never made a soufflé before."

"I know you could do it."

A calculating look flickered in her eyes, but she shook her head. "Not tonight, Dad. We'd have to go out and get stuff. I'll tell you what. Tomorrow I'll get everything we'll need, if you promise to help me make it."

Why were they always trying to trap him? Wasn't life supposed to be more placid than this? You'd think a thirteen-year-old would have more respect for her father, even if her mother didn't. He tapped his foot impatiently against the worn gray carpet that had come with the house. Andrea didn't show the least sign of backing down. Brad really wanted a cheese soufflé. "Oh, all right, but I don't know the first thing about it."

"You'll learn," she said. "It's easy."

Later, when she was already in her bedroom for the night, she called out to him. "Don't forget you're going to take me to the travel agent in the morning."

Brad had been thinking about Marty, and the paternity suit, and the blood test. His hand with the screwdriver paused above the doorbell buzzer, which was almost fixed. "What day are we going to Disneyland?"

"Oh, Dad, I've told you a million times. We're going on Tuesday and coming back Thursday night."

"Damnation!" he muttered, not loud enough for her to hear, and hurled the buzzer into the wastebasket.

"I need to talk to you, and I don't want to do it here," he said, bending earnestly over Marty's desk. "Couldn't you just come outside with me for a few minutes? We'll walk around the block."

"Brad, I told you I think it's better if we don't see each other until this paternity suit is settled." Marty ran her fingers nervously through her hair. Seeing him again did strange things to her breathing.

"It's *about* the paternity suit."

Marty stared at him, a sinking feeling seizing her. Without further hesitation, she rose from her chair and shrugged into her suit coat. Virginia looked up from her work, and Marty said brusquely, "I'll be back in a few minutes."

He was going to admit that he was indeed the child's father. Marty could tell by the defensive look in his eyes. He was going to say that it needn't come between the two of them. He would accept responsibility, and they could get on with their lives. He didn't want this to drag out any longer, since the blood test would prove it anyhow. Marty stared at the elevator door as they rode in silence to the ground floor.

They walked quickly toward the door, and he put his hand on her elbow. She moved so it was impossible for him to keep it there. Outside it was a chilly, gloomy day. Marty started walking slowly toward the south. Brad walked close beside her, his fists shoved in the pockets of his green parka.

"Look, I know you're going to be angry about this and think all sorts of wrong things about me," he finally blurted, "but I can't keep the appointment for the blood test tomorrow."

It was not what she'd expected to hear. Possibly it amounted to the same thing. "Why not?"

"Because I'm taking my daughter to Disneyland. It's something that's been arranged for weeks. I just forgot about it when you made the appointment for me."

"It's easy enough to set up another one," she said. Her voice seemed to have developed a frost.

"Anytime's okay. I'll be back Thursday evening. Even Friday would be fine."

"You should have told me in the office. I could have called right away." Marty had seen many men put off the blood test again and again. First this thing came up and then the other. She had never seen one of those men excluded. Abruptly she turned back toward her office.

Brad planted himself in her way. "Don't go back yet. This is why I didn't want to tell you there. I knew you wouldn't believe it was an honest mistake."

"It doesn't matter what I believe. What matters is that you have the blood test."

"I'll *have* the blood test, as soon as I get back." He put both hands on her shoulders and stared into her eyes. "I want you to believe me, Marty, without the evidence of the blood test. It's not asking so much."

Marty felt as brittle as a November leaf. "You're forgetting how long I've been in my job, Brad. I see men do what you're doing all the time, and they turn out to be the fathers every time."

"Not this time! My daughter made all the arrangements with the travel agent. I just didn't pay attention to which day we were leaving because it really didn't matter. The store runs itself most of the time. My secretary's only twenty years old, but she could handle just about any emergency that came up."

"I'm glad to hear it." Marty edged around him. "You don't have to walk back with me. I'll make another appointment for you and call your secretary with the information."

He kept pace with her brisk stride. "You're going to feel foolish when you get the results of the tests, Marty."

"I can live with that." What she wasn't sure she could live with was the realization of how much this had upset her. She hadn't realized, until that moment, how strongly she wanted to believe him. Oh, she'd hoped almost since she'd met him to discover some mistake, but ever since the night he'd kissed her on the hill she'd somehow started believing him. An impulsive, unfounded belief, absolute suicide in her job. Maybe she'd been there too long. Maybe it was time for a change.

"Look at me!" he demanded. His eyes were angry, making the black brows look almost menacing. "Do I look like someone who would lie about something like this? Do I?"

"Right now, yes," she said evenly. "Brad, it doesn't make any difference what you look like. Men lie about this sort of thing the way they lie about their taxes, because it's going to cost them money."

"I don't lie about my taxes, either!" The wind was tossing his wavy hair into little horns all over his head, but he wasn't aware of it. "Has it ever occurred to you, for even the briefest second, that maybe this *woman* is lying?"

"Of course it has. I went to see her again after we'd talked a few times."

"And?"

Marty shrugged a shoulder. "And she said the same things she'd said before."

"Why? Why is she doing this to me?"

There was no answer she could make that wouldn't further antagonize him. They were almost at the door of the building, and, against her better judgment, she laid her hand on his sleeve. "Brad, I think you should get a lawyer."

His eyes had gone cold and he shrugged off her hand. "I don't need a lawyer. I haven't done anything wrong, and I'm not going to waste my money."

"That's up to you, of course." She tried to smile to ease the tension between them, but the muscles in her face refused to respond. "I'll call your secretary with a new appointment time."

"Sure, you do that. Don't worry, I'll keep it."

He had become completely remote from her. There was no way to reach him now, unless she was prepared to say she believed him, and she didn't believe him, much as she wanted to. The physical attraction she felt for him warred with her rational mind, but he had shrugged off her touch, her attempt to reduce the gap between them. Marty could think of nothing further to keep her there. "Good-bye, Brad," she said softly, and walked up the steps and into the building. She didn't look back, and he didn't answer her.

Always curious, Virginia looked up inquiringly when Marty returned to her desk and removed her suit coat. "That didn't take long."

"No. He simply wanted to explain why he couldn't keep the blood test appointment."

"Uh oh. One of those, huh?"

"I'm afraid so."

"Still protesting his innocence though, I take it."

"Definitely, and very antagonistic toward me because I don't believe him." Marty sighed as she settled into her chair. "Well, it wasn't a good idea to see anything of him in the first place."

"I don't know. There's something about him," Virginia admitted, drumming her fingers lightly on her cluttered desk. "Maybe he really is the victim in this case."

Marty drew her phone toward her. "Maybe, but it's unlikely."

"The blood test will settle it once and for all."

"Yes, but as far as anything between us goes, it's already been settled. He made it pretty clear that if I couldn't accept him on faith, he didn't want anything to do with me."

Virginia frowned. "Men certainly do expect a lot, don't they?"

"More than they give, usually," Marty replied, punching out the lab number on her phone. When she had canceled Brad's appointment and set up a new one, she dialed his office number and gave the information to his secretary, saying only that he would understand. Marty felt sure Brad hadn't confided his situation to anyone else, least of all an employee.

Immediately after finishing this task, wanting to be alone for a minute, she left her desk to get a cup of coffee. Virginia was a rock of support whenever Marty needed her, but right now she wanted to think about what had happened during those few minutes with Brad. Whether or not she chose to admit it, she

had been greatly affected. She felt torn by her response.

Rationally, there was nothing else she could have
done or said. Of course her job experiences colored
her outlook on the situation. Men who started to skip
the blood test appointments were almost invariably
subconsciously declaring their responsibility in the
paternity matter. It was possible, certainly, that Brad
had not realized ahead of time that his two commit-
ments were scheduled for the same time. But he
didn't strike her as a disorganized man, one who
ordinarily let that sort of thing happen to him. The
fact that it had happened probably signaled the unac-
knowledged wish not to be able to keep the appointment. It was all very psychological, but Marty had
been a psychology major in college. It made a lot of
sense to her.

Emotionally, she had wanted to reach out to him,
had wanted to touch him and admit to the effect he
had on her. However, when she had literally reached
out, he had shrugged off her hand. In essence he was
saying he'd have nothing to do with her if she
wouldn't make the gigantic leap of faith that believing
him entailed. It was expecting too much. He had no
right, at this early stage in their relationship, to ask for
unquestioning loyalty. Especially when it went directly contrary to her experience.

He had asked too much; she hadn't given too little.
All very well, but then why did her insides feel
frozen? There *was* something about Brad, something
she'd responded to very strongly. If that something
was merely physical, perhaps it was better that their
connection ended now. However, Marty had thought
it might be more than that, had felt it inside. Those
blue eyes had told her about depths under the macho

exterior; his grin had assured her of his sense of humor.

No.

That was just what she'd *wanted* to see. Marty had hoped to see those qualities in men before, and had imagined they were there. She'd been mistaken. Obviously she was mistaken about Brad, too. It was far better that she learned that now.

She filled her cup with coffee and returned to her desk.

Brad stared at the white soufflé dish, his hands jammed in his pockets. "I thought you meant you'd buy one. I didn't want you to borrow it from your mother."

"It wouldn't make any sense to buy you one, Dad," Andrea protested. "It would just sit around here and gather dust."

"Was your mother there? What did you tell her?"

"I said we were going to make a soufflé, of course. Why else would I borrow it?"

It was the "we" that bothered Brad. Had Karen laughed at the thought of Brad helping to make a soufflé? He didn't feel he could ask Andrea any more about it. She was gathering together the ingredients— the eggs, cheese, milk and flour—and setting them out on the counter. He'd meant to do something about the counter. The ancient white tiles were scarred and chipped. It would have been easy enough to retile. It would have taken no more than a weekend, probably, and all the materials were right there in the store. He simply hadn't had the inspiration.

Andrea set several pots, a mixer and bowls on the counter along with the ingredients. "You don't have a double boiler," she said, "but we can manage with one pot inside the other. The first thing you should do, Dad, is read through the recipe.''

For something that was supposed to be so tricky, the recipe didn't sound particularly difficult. ''Seems like a lot of eggs, though,'' he said.

''Mom suggested we cut it in half, for just the two of us. She didn't give me the biggest soufflé dish.''

Even now she had to have her own way, he thought disgustedly. Brad was beginning to wish he'd never thought of having cheese soufflé. ''What do you want me to do?''

His daughter regarded him speculatively. ''You do the part in the double boiler; I'll grate the cheese and beat the yolks and whites. Remember, we're cutting it in half.''

He felt awkward at first, measuring the butter, flour, salt and paprika, but decided after a while that it was something like carpentry. Andrea had offered him an apron, but he recognized it from their former kitchen, and refused it. Besides, men didn't wear aprons. What they did do, he learned, was get flour and milk on their shirts and jeans, globs of melting cheese on their tennis shoes and ruin perfectly good dish towels.

''What does it mean, 'fold'?'' he asked at the critical moment in making the delicate dish.

''Do you want me to do it?''

Brad was tempted. Andrea would do it right, and he might mess it up. However, the result wouldn't be his if he let her do the tricky part. ''No, just show me.''

There was a gleam in his daughter's eyes, but she said nothing until the soufflé was in the oven. Then she gave him a quick hug, grinned, and said, ''You're going to make a terrific cook, Dad.''

"Thanks," he said gruffly, forgetting for the moment why it was he'd even agreed to help. He remembered then that it had something to do with Marty, who didn't cook, who had refused to believe him, but who made his pulse beat faster just thinking of her. Well, she'd lost her chance. Let her find out how many other men would take a crack at cooking because she couldn't be bothered.

Brad had no intention of getting involved with another woman who didn't appreciate him. He got a beer from the refrigerator, snapped it open and announced to his daughter, "I'll be in the living room until dinner is ready."

"Oh, no you don't!" Andrea stood with hands on hips, looking remarkably like her mother. "You said you'd help with dinner. You can fry the sausages while I make the salad."

Since when did thirteen-year-olds order their fathers around? "Where's the apron?" he asked.

Chapter Seven

There wasn't time for Marty to think much about Brad during the next week. Two paternity trials and one hearing were taking place, and she had to prepare the women in each of the cases. She also had to make an appointment for Lydia and her baby to have their blood tests, whether or not Brad managed to make the new appointment she'd scheduled for him. Maybe she worked harder on each of the cases because she didn't want to think about Brad. She was good at her job, and this was one of the times when all her hard work came together. All the photos and blood test results and corroborating evidence had to be gone over with the assistant district attorney so he would know exactly how to proceed when he had the various parties on the stand.

Some people found her kind of case embarrassing, because of the sexual evidence that was presented. They didn't have to go into detail on the subject of

sex, just ascertain when it took place and with whom.
Years ago, any lingering discomfort she might have
felt had been swept away by the necessity to cover this
ground quickly and thoroughly. It was, after all, at the
heart of any paternity case, and her major goal had
always been to see that justice was done and responsibility assumed for irreversible actions. The most important individual under consideration was the child,
not the mother or father. If the state thought she was
there to protect the government's interest, that was
fine. Marty could do that at the same time she
protected the child's.

Although there were patterns to the cases, each one
seemed to have a personality of its own. As she
walked through the rotunda at City Hall on Friday
afternoon, she was wondering what the judge would
think of the case they were about to bring before him.
The Domestic Relations actions were under the juris-
diction of the superior court and were held on the
fourth floor. Marty headed for the elevator on the
other side of the building. She had been staring at
the back of a man's head for a moment before she
realized why her heartbeat had quickened. There was
no mistaking the way he walked, even when viewing
the lope from behind. What was he doing here?

She was torn between quickening her pace to catch
up with him and slowing it to slink behind some
column. It was Friday, and she had known he'd be
back from Disneyland by now. However, she hadn't
been able to schedule his blood test until Monday,
and this was not where blood tests were given anyway.
It seemed too coincidental that he would appear in
City Hall just when she was headed to a paternity
trial. How often did any given San Franciscan enter
these exalted portals? You could get a marriage

license or look up information on property taxes, but it wasn't the sort of place most people came for a little excursion on a Friday afternoon.

Without realizing it, she'd quickened her pace and almost caught up with him. "Brad," she said distinctly. The word echoed through the high-ceilinged space like an announcement over a loudspeaker. He spun around with the agility of a quarter horse, not looking particularly pleased to see her.

He'd gotten some sun in Anaheim. His face looked good with a tan complementing the black hair and blue eyes. He was in a three-piece suit, a brown tweed that fitted him exceptionally well. He wasn't smiling.

"So this is one of yours, is it?"

For a second she didn't understand what he was talking about. "The paternity case at two? Is that why you're here?"

He'd had a haircut, too. The tops of his ears were no longer covered by the riotous black hair. It made him look endearingly naked. His voice was distinctly cool. "I wanted to see just what went on at a paternity trial."

"How did you find out there was one today?"

He shrugged and dug one hand into his pants pocket. "From a court reporter I know. She looked it up for me."

"If you'd asked me, I'd have told you."

"It wasn't necessary." He might as well have said, "I don't need your help."

Marty started walking toward the elevator, and he hurriedly straightened from his negligent pose and followed her. There were several other people waiting, and she kept her head slightly averted from him. She was trying so hard not to see anything that she didn't notice the assistant D.A., Harry Mills, standing right beside her. Harry was not just an assistant D.A.; he was the man with whom she'd been involved two years previously, the man who'd made her feel like a doormat. He'd since married, and his wife was pregnant, which seemed to give him inordinate pleasure, as though he were the first man on earth to impregnate a woman. His attitude had always seemed strange to her considering the work he did, prosecuting alleged fathers.

"Not speaking, Marty?" he asked now, a wry twist to his lips. Harry was always ready to believe that Marty had lost a great thing when she ended their association. She suspected he'd even convinced himself that *he'd* ended it.

"Sorry, Harry. I didn't see you." She had spent the better part of the morning with him, going over the evidence. "Do you know if court's running on schedule?"

"Miracle of miracles, I understand it is. We shouldn't be more than fifteen minutes in getting on."

The elevator doors opened, and she walked in, followed by Harry and Brad and several other people. Brad was not looking at her, though he ended up right at her elbow. In the crowded space both men were touching her, though she was really only aware of it on Brad's side. She kept her head turned toward Harry.

"How's Sara doing?"

"Terrific! Only three months to go. We start prenatal classes soon. She quits work a week from today so she can get things ready. We decided on the sunroom for the nursery, even though it's smaller than the second bedroom."

For the remainder of the elevator ride, he discussed the merits of the sunroom versus the second bedroom.

Marty nodded when appropriate, though she wasn't paying much attention. Brad kept shifting restlessly, as though trying to avoid contact with her. First both hands were dug in his pockets, then he folded his arms across his chest. When two people exited on the third floor, there was more room, and he moved slightly forward, breaking their forced connection. Although he got off the elevator before them, he stood to one side, waiting for them to lead the way. Harry was too wrapped up in his monologue to notice. Marty got a better grip on her briefcase and marched off beside Harry, giving Brad no more than a cursory glance.

Footsteps ring in those halls, and she could hear Brad's very clearly behind them. He was not loping. If he had, he'd have overtaken them because Harry walked very deliberately, and she set her pace to his. Outside the courtroom the mother was waiting for them, looking young and frightened. She kept fingering the folds of a black wool dress with nervous fingers.

"Oh, Miss Woods," she cried. "I feel as though I'm going to faint, I'm so scared. I've never been in a court before. And I saw *him*," she added, dropping her voice to an awed whisper. "He's already in there, sitting in the back. When he saw me, he looked really mad, just like Bobby does when he doesn't get his way."

Probably an apt analogy, Marty thought. "Don't let him bother you," she said soothingly. "He's perfectly aware that he's the father of your child; he's just trying to save himself money and ignore his responsibilities." She forced herself not to glance at Brad at this point. "You've met Mr. Mills. If you have anything more you want to discuss with him, you should do it now before we go in."

Brad was listening to all this with a faraway expression on his face that didn't fool her for a minute. Not knowing who Brad was, Harry didn't pay the least attention as he gave instructions and encouragement to the mother. Her case was among the strongest they'd had in months, with tons of supporting evidence and witnesses to back her up. The only thing Marty was worried about was the mother's tendency when nervous to talk too much. A lot of witnesses thought they had to answer every question in the fullest, rather than the most succinct, way. Usually Harry was good at keeping them on track. When they dawdled over an answer, his look of impatience ordinarily brought them back to the point.

In a few minutes they slipped into the courtroom, with Brad right behind them. He took a seat in the back, right next to the alleged father, but of course he didn't know that. Marty had her hands full trying to keep the mother from becoming unbearably nervous. She couldn't pay any attention to how the proceedings struck Brad. Once Harry was presenting their case, she also had to make sure he was covering everything. The assistant D.A.s weren't given enough time to prepare a case properly because of the heavy case load they carried.

It was the defense attorney who started the problems. He was trying to impress the jury with his flair, instead of simply challenging any and all evidence brought forward. He had made the common mistake of trying to confuse the jury over the complex, scientific evidence of the blood tests. This almost invariably backfired, as Marty knew, because the jury thought *he* was confused, rather than that the blood tests didn't prove the case. Most jurors had trouble with statistics, and it was better to challenge the

Hummels "Likelihood of Paternity" chart, claiming that terms such as "practically proved" and "extremely likely" had no admissibility in a court of law. That kind of objection was usually upheld.

Instead, the defense attorney tried to take on the mother, in order to gain sympathy for the father. It was the sort of thing of which this particular father would have approved, and Marty could see that he'd chosen his attorney not for his ability but for his point of view that women were always at fault. It was a drastic mistake. The question before the court was not who was right or wrong but the paternity of an existing child.

The mother was getting more nervous under the hostile questioning. Her voice shook slightly, and she glanced over at Marty, who smiled encouragement, trying to look as firm and supportive as a small woman could look. It was one of the few times Marty actively wished she were larger, so her very bulk would carry authority. The mother had lost the thread of the questioning and was rambling a bit, but the defense attorney didn't have the sense to stop her.

When she dribbled to a halting finish, he regarded the jury with one of his See-what-a-foolish-woman-she-is looks before swinging back to pounce on her again.

His voice thundered in the courtroom. "If what you say is true, why didn't you take birth control precautions?"

You're going to regret that question, Marty thought, amused.

"Well, I did," she protested, close to tears. "I went to a doctor and got a diaphragm. He said I shouldn't take the pill because I'm a smoker. I've tried to give it up, but I just can't seem to do it. I get nervous, and a cigarette is the first thing I think of. If there aren't any in the apartment, I'll go out and buy a pack. I wish I had one now."

"I'm sure you do," he replied smugly, thinking he'd latched on to a good point for comparison. "Are you as careless about using the diaphragm in your various sexual activities as you are about keeping cigarettes around the house?"

Harry was going to object to that kind of loaded question, but Marty quickly shook her head at him. He looked puzzled but dropped back into his seat, trusting her judgment. She'd spent more time with the mother than he had.

The attorney had touched a sore spot with the mother. "I wanted to use the diaphragm," she insisted. "I mean, otherwise why would I have gone to the bother and expense of getting it? *He* was the one who said I shouldn't." She waved an expressive hand toward the alleged father. "He said making love with a diaphragm in was like taking a shower in a raincoat!"

A titter of laughter ran through the courtroom. If the defense attorney hadn't already lost the case, he lost it then. Harry turned to Marty with a wink of approval; he understood now why she hadn't wanted him to object. In this particular instance, the mother's wayward tongue had done her nothing but good. It was impossible for a jury member not to believe such a surprisingly frank declaration. That ring of truth continued to reverberate through the rest of her testimony, try as the attorney did to shake her. Marty knew, when the jury went out to deliberate, that they'd have no trouble reaching the right verdict.

The mother was flushed and apologetic when she came up to Marty during the break. "I didn't mean to say that," she whispered. "It just sort of popped out; he made me so mad. It was just the sort of thing Bob said when I got pregnant, that it was all my fault. I don't know how he figures that. Does he think you keep yourself from getting pregnant by wishful thinking?"

"No, he just thinks the world should be the way he wants it to be," Marty replied, knowing that Brad was walking past her at just that moment. "The jury's going to find against him, though, so he'll have to live with reality."

There was a tug at her sleeve, and she glanced up to find that Brad was still there. "Do you have to stay any longer?" he asked. "I want to talk to you."

Her part in the trial was finished, and the mother had already turned to Harry, planning to apologize to him, too, Marty supposed. Brad's face was completely closed, no telling what he was thinking. "If you can wait two minutes for me out in the hall. I have to get all this stuff back in my briefcase."

"I'll wait for you."

Naturally it took longer than two minutes, but not much. He was leaning against the opposite wall, one hand in his pocket. She kept telling herself he was only an alleged father, someone who had a right to ask her questions about the procedure he'd witnessed.

"You sewed him up like a bundle of burlap," he said.

"He fathered her child. There was never any doubt about it. He just wasted everyone's time and money trying to weasel out of it." She wouldn't have used a term like "weasel," except that she could feel his hostility.

"Well, you don't have that kind of evidence against me." His jaw was set rigidly. "You can't, because I don't even know the woman. There can't be letters, or photos, or any of that other stuff. It's just her word against mine."

"There will be the blood test," she said softly.

"I'm tired of hearing about the damned blood test! What would happen if I refused to take it?"

"You should speak to Mr. Mills about that."

He glared at her. "I'm asking you."

"I'm not sure what would happen. The blood tests are given for the man's protection, after all. There's the possibility of exclusion. The action doesn't go any further if that happens." She backed away from him, wanting any distance she could get. "If you don't keep the appointment on Monday, I'll have Mr. Mills give you a call. He can tell you what to expect."

"I'm going to have the stupid test, and it's going to prove I couldn't be the child's father. Then what are you going to do?"

"Drop the action against you, of course." She bit her lip, but still couldn't keep from blurting, "And be happy to do it."

"Sure you will."

His sarcasm was the last straw. She turned away from him and headed for the elevator. It was hard enough maintaining a professional detachment in his case, without his adding to her discomfort at every turn. Maybe she should turn the case over to Virginia. However, that would mean Lydia would have to get to know a new investigator, and that was hardly fair. She had managed to keep a rigid division between her work and personal life when she was seeing Harry, for heaven's sake, and he *worked* with her. Why was it so much more difficult with Brad?

Because you're so much more attracted to him than you were to Harry, she heard an inner voice say, which was perfectly ridiculous, since she hardly knew him at all.

The elevator door opened just as she arrived, and she stepped right in, watching it close before Brad could reach it. He had taken his time in following her, and she wasn't willing to hold it for him, though she could have. She drew a deep breath, letting it out slowly as the elevator descended. So much for Mr. Macintosh and his sulks, who needs him? It was only a few days ago that she'd been a happy-go-lucky woman who enjoyed her job and found life a perfectly worthwhile and interesting adventure. With a little perseverance, she could be that way again.

Two other people had gotten on the elevator on lower floors, and she was the last to get out. Since Brad might have gotten another elevator shortly after hers, she was hurrying a little as she moved toward the Polk Street side of the building. For a small woman in high heels, carrying a briefcase, this was not an easy maneuver.

As she was passing the enormous staircase, she heard feet pounding down quickly. He was lucky the security guards didn't notice him. As he flashed past, the people around him stared curiously, wary of anyone moving at that speed in the sedate climate of city hall. He didn't look like a maniac, of course. He looked like he was going at his ordinary pace and they were slow-moving snails. His eyes searched the people below, looking for her.

What he announced when he finally reached her side was, "I'm tired of apologizing to you."

"Maybe if you acted like a reasonable human being, you wouldn't have to," she flashed back.

"I'm *not* a reasonable human being where you're concerned. Can't you see that?"

"I thought it was your natural personality. In fact, I'm quite sure it is, maybe slightly exaggerated when you're on the prowl, but essentially what you are, Brad."

"On the prowl!" he yelped. "On the prowl is when you pick up women in singles bars, which is not something I'm interested in doing, whether you believe it or not."

She stopped walking and turned to face him. "You might as well. It's the only place you may find your macho image of any use these days. I'm sure you're a nice guy, Brad, but I don't want another man in my life who things I exist for his convenience or that I'm the one who's supposed to make all the leaps of faith. We're not right for each other. Thank your lucky stars we found out this soon."

"You can't know we're not right for each other. You don't know me that well."

"I know enough to think twice. That's really more than I need to know. If someone can't learn from experience, she deserves to repeat her mistakes. I'm not interested in repetition."

"I'm not a mistake."

He startled her then by reaching out to brush his thumb along her lips, a peculiarly intimate gesture right there in city hall. Two people walking by grinned at them, thinking "young love," she supposed. She would have been irate, except that his touch electrified her—as usual. Although she tried to say something, her throat suddenly felt swollen shut. She did manage to keep him from grabbing her briefcase, though she knew he meant it as an act of gallantry. Why did all their acts of gallantry result in making women look like weak, helpless creatures?

Her lips were so dry she had to moisten them

before she could speak. "You can call me if you want to," she murmured. "*After* we get the test results."

"But that's more than two weeks away."

"If I'm lucky," she said, "by then you won't want to call." She waved good-bye with her fingers, so he wouldn't try to follow her again. The last glimpse she had of him, he was standing there with one hand stuffed in his pocket, his wild black eyebrows raised and a knowing grin on his lips.

Chapter Eight

*B*rad had no intention of waiting another two weeks before he saw Marty again, but he felt fairly certain she'd hold to her decision. He had to find some means of contact other than calling her. It took him the rest of the afternoon to come up with a solution, and then he had to wait until evening to carry it out.

When he had called the court reporter, Jessica Thatcher, about when a paternity trial was scheduled, she'd agreed to find out for him. She had left the information on his answering machine while he was away, but he'd called to thank her. Jessica was a sociable soul who gave parties with unnerving frequency. He and Karen had gone to quite a few of them—in the old days—but he hadn't been invited to any since they'd split up.

Jessica had been hesitant about asking him, he could tell by the long pauses between her words. "I'm having a . . . sort of a . . . party, you know? A week from Saturday. And I've invited Karen. But, well, you two are . . . on good terms, right? And she wasn't sure they could make it. So, maybe you'd like to come?"

Brad had not felt civilized enough to attend a party at which he might see his former wife—and the rat Carl. He was civilized enough to thank Jessica for the invitation. He worded his answer in such a way that it would be possible for him to show up if he felt like it and found out from Andrea that her mother was definitely not going.

It had occurred to Brad during the afternoon that Jessica would almost certainly know Marty. Since he could not remember ever seeing her at one of the parties, though, it was important that he do a little arranging, if he wanted to find her there. He tried calling Jessica several times over two days before he caught her at home.

If he'd thought ahead of time about how difficult it would be to phrase his request, he might have had second thoughts about making it. Two weeks was not, after all, an impossibly long time. Because he had tried so many times without getting hold of Jessica, he wasn't particularly careful about which phone he used when he called. He found himself talking with her while his daughter sat in the next room.

"Jessica? It's Brad Macintosh here. I wanted to thank you again for getting me the information on the trial." He paused to listen to her question and replied, "Yes, it was interesting. There was a woman there— Marty Woods. Do you know her?"

Jessica assured him that she did, though Marty's cases weren't handled in her courtroom.

"Well, I was wondering if you'd invited her to your party." He couldn't be much more blunt than that, could he?

"Why no," Jessica admitted. "As I said, I don't know her very well. But look Brad, if you want to bring her, that's great."

"No, no, I don't . . . know her well enough to ask her, but if she was there. . ."

"How well do you have to know someone to ask them to a party?" Jessica asked amused. "Just call her up. I bet she's in the phone book."

Brad didn't like the idea that Andrea was overhearing his half of this conversation. He lowered his voice when he said, "I don't think she'd go out with me. If you were to ask her to the party, and we just happened to meet there . . ."

Jessica's tolerant sigh wafted over the phone. "All right, Brad. I'll invite her."

"And don't tell her I'm coming."

He could picture her shaking her head, but she agreed. Certainly waiting two weeks would have been easier than this he decided as he wandered back into the living room. Andrea, whose head had been in a book when he left, was now staring straight at him.

"Who's Marty Woods?" she asked. "And why wouldn't she go out with you?"

She sounded offended that any woman would refuse to go out with her father, and Brad felt like hugging her, but didn't. "She's a woman I met a few weeks ago, and *maybe* she'll go out with me, just not right now."

"Why not?"

Brad had no intention of telling her the story, though he realized how much he'd like to confide in someone. "We're involved in a kind of . . . negotiation right now, and she thinks it would be better if we didn't see each other until it's settled."

"What kind of negotiation?"

"It isn't something I can explain."

"So what's she going to do when you turn up at the party?"

Brad sighed and rumpled his daughter's hair. "Probably walk out, if she runs true to form."

Andrea offered her most mysterious smile. "She sounds just right for you, Dad."

The remark startled him. "Why?"

"Oh, I don't know," Andrea said, burying her head in her book again. "She just does."

Brad knew he wouldn't get any more out of her. "I'm supposed to take you home in an hour. You should probably start getting your things together."

Marty had felt nervous all weekend, afraid Brad would call and her resolution would crumble. In an effort to be out of her apartment as much as possible, she'd taken the dog for long walks on the beach, which managed to exhaust both of them. She had gone to a movie alone on Sunday evening, just to fill up the remaining hours before bedtime. If she could just make it to work in the morning, she knew she could handle any call from Brad with conscientious firmness—under Virginia's inquisitive gaze.

However, he didn't call, at least not when she was at home, and he didn't call her office when she started the new week, either. This was a relief, of course. She didn't want him to call—yet, maybe ever. Although one part of her wanted him to call, the other was obstinately wary. Even if he was vindicated by the blood test, there were other things about him that set off jangling warning signals in her mind. Too bad her body paid no attention.

Marty was slightly surprised by the call from Jessica Thatcher inviting her to a party. She was aware of the fact that Jessica gave parties frequently. The court staff often mentioned them, but Marty had never gotten to know Jessica well enough to be invited. Once she had almost gone to one with Harry, but in the end he'd been tempted by the closing performance of a play he'd intended to see.

When Jessica called, though, Marty accepted the invitation with a certain eagerness, telling herself it would be good for her to get out and possibly meet someone more appropriate than Brad. Hadn't Jessica actually said there would be a few extra men around? With a rather choked giggle, to be sure, but Marty hadn't thought much about that. Maybe Jessica always giggled at the possibility of extra men; it didn't happen all that often.

On Monday, Marty had to appear in court for a hearing, but as soon as she returned to her office she called the lab to find out whether Brad had shown up for his blood test appointment. When she was told that he had, she felt as though a weight had been lifted from her. "Will you call me the minute you get the results?" she asked.

"Sure thing, but the mother and child aren't scheduled until tomorrow, and we're running a little behind. It could take the whole two weeks."

"I understand. Thanks for your help."

Well, he'd done it. He'd said he would, and he had. Now all Marty had to do was wait to find out whether the tests proved he couldn't be the father, excluded him with no possibility of a doubt. Marty wondered what possible reason Lydia could have for falsely

accusing him. She had known about his office. Brad
had checked out former employees, and she hadn't
been one. That left Marty right back where she had
started: wanting to believe Brad, but having no
rational basis for doing so.

She concentrated on her work, trying not to think
about him. Fortunately, it was a busy week, with
several new cases to investigate and information to
prepare for a hearing and a trial. The week went
faster than she'd dared hope, but she felt restless,
rather than tired, by the time the weekend came.

Friday evening, she ran errands and ate out at a
small neighborhood restaurant before returning to her
apartment to sit down with a good book. Instead of
putting the book down at a reasonable hour, she read
until she finished it, long after midnight. In the
morning she slept until ten, waking with a feeling of
grogginess and hunger. She padded into the kitchen in
her ratty robe, remembering she'd bought frozen
croissants the previous evening. While she was waiting for them to heat, and for the coffee to finish
perking, she sat down at the kitchen table and almost
fell asleep again.

A tapping at the rear door startled her, and she
thought for a moment it was the timer. Stumbling half
awake to her feet, Marty lurched toward the oven,
only to have the tapping continue with great impatience from the other direction. She turned and
blinked at her upstairs neighbor, Jim Friedman, who
smirked at her through the glass. With a certain
reluctance, she retraced her path and opened the door
to him.

"A little sleepy this morning, Marty?" he asked as
he followed her into the room, looking very alert.
"I'm not interrupting anything, am I?"

"Only my breakfast. It's a weekend, Jim. I sleep in on weekends. For that matter, what are you doing up at this hour?"

"Looking for sustenance. There's not a thing to eat in my apartment. When I heard you staggering around down here, I thought, 'Marty would probably love to feed me breakfast.' Wouldn't you?" He beamed on her with enough good cheer to make her wince.

Marty smothered a yawn. "That depends on whether you're willing to have frozen croissants."

"Not much of a breakfast." At her sardonic expression he hastily added, "But it will do. It will do."

"Pour yourself a cup of coffee while I put another one in. You could pour me one, too. I seem to need it."

She managed to come up with a cantaloupe and some orange juice as well as the croissants. After all, she owed him for the occasional slice of bacon he made for her. "How come you didn't just go out and get something to eat?" she asked.

"I lent my car to someone."

Marty stared at him. His Porsche was his favorite toy, status symbol and sex symbol wrapped into one. He spoke of it more lovingly than she'd ever heard him speak of a woman. "I don't believe it."

"Well, it's true, just until this afternoon." He refused to meet her incredulous stare.

"But why? You're always so terrified you'll get a ding in it. Surely you wouldn't trust someone with it."

Jim lifted his shoulders in a careless shrug. "It's only a car."

Not for a moment did Marty accept his nonchalance. "Who did you lend it to?"

"A woman I know. Her father was in town, and her

car broke down yesterday. She was going to rent one, but I told her she could use mine. He leaves on a noon flight."

"Wow. This must be serious."

His face became stern. "What do you mean?"

"It's totally out of character for you to lend your Porsche, Jim, so this woman must be something really special. Have you been seeing her long?" Marty hadn't noticed any one beauty in prominence recently.

"I don't *see* her," he said haughtily. "She's a friend; I've known her for years."

"Someone you work with?"

"She works at the Hall of Justice, but not in the D.A.'s office." Jim brushed the crumbs from his hands with the napkin Marty had provided. "She's a law librarian, actually, very intellectual and efficient."

"Then she's probably a good driver," Marty suggested, not sure if that was the point he was trying to make.

"Who knows? In any case, she's not likely to drive wildly with her father in the car."

Marty couldn't help needling him. "Oh, yes, but there's the drive back from the airport, whizzing along 101 with all that aggressive traffic. Maybe she'll decide to zip off on 380 and roar over 280 back to town. Slipping in and out of all those weekend drivers, she could really lose her restraint in that Porsche."

To her surprise, he grinned and said, "I wish she would. She's the most restrained woman I've ever met. I think she believes the myth of Marian the Librarian. She wears her hair in a very stern French twist and dresses like an undertaker."

"And you'd like to introduce her to the hedonistic life."

He contemplated his steepled fingertips. "Sometimes. I can't help thinking there's a great well to be tapped there. Oh, she's a perfectly congenial person to talk to over lunch, but there's always this incredible reserve, not icy, just distant. You can't get very close to her."

"Maybe it's just you."

"I don't think so. Some of the others have mentioned it, too. One of the guys was so mad that she wouldn't go out with him, he was going to try to get her fired."

Marty stared at him. "That's ugly, and it's sexual harrassment."

"I know. We put a stop to it pretty fast. The D.A. told him if he didn't get his consciousness raised, he'd be out on his ear."

"One of my alleged fathers could stand a little consciousness raising. I swear he's from the dark ages." Marty realized that wasn't a completely fair way of describing Brad and tried again. "With him it's maintaining a sort of macho image, and expecting women to fit into some kind of fifties view of the sex. We're not talking about some uneducated redneck, either. This guy has been to college and runs a successful business. How can he not have noticed there have been a few changes in the world since then?"

"He probably doesn't want to recognize it." Jim pushed his plate aside, looking thoughtful. "A lot of your mothers are living a kind of fifties view of life, too. It's not surprising some of the fathers do."

"I suppose not, but Brad is thirty-five, not eighteen." She hadn't meant to let his name slip out and immediately changed the subject. "I've been thinking about buying some planter boxes and putting flowers out on the front stoop. Want to share the expense?"

"How much will it cost?" he asked suspiciously.

"I don't know yet. This afternoon seemed like a good time to visit a few nurseries."

"It would make the place look better," he conceded as he rose. "Okay, as long as it doesn't cost me more than fifty bucks. Thanks for breakfast, Marty. I should straighten up my apartment before she returns the car—just in case I can entice her inside."

Marty grimaced at his lecherous wink. "You have a few fifties attitudes yourself, Jim."

"I'll let her talk me out of them," he retorted as he let himself out.

Marty dragged a lot of plants and containers around during the afternoon and was a little tired by the time she fixed herself a frozen dinner. Not only was she tired, she was discouraged with the condition of her fingernails, which were cracked and dirty from working with the potting plants. She almost convinced herself that she didn't want to go to Jessica's party, until she found herself daydreaming about Brad over her second cup of coffee. It would be better to get out of the apartment and keep herself busy than to waste her time fantasizing about him.

A shower restored some of her missing vigor, and choosing a dress she hadn't worn yet made her positively eager to get out and show it off. The open weave was rather daring, for her, and she experimented with various combinations of underclothing until she was satisfied that it was provocative but not openly revealing. The flowing lines and natural color needed a touch of contrast, so she wore a cinnabar necklace and bracelet she had recently purchased.

Jessica lived in the inner Sunset district, where she had a ramshackle but large house on a block where the parking was already becoming impossible at 8:30. Marty's aging Chevette wasn't very large, but she couldn't find a space for it closer than two blocks away. As she walked back toward the house, she was following an attractive couple who she decided were probably headed toward the party, too. The man carried a bag that obviously held a bottle. Jessica had not said anything about bringing liquor, but Marty immediately realized it would be a good idea. After all, a woman couldn't hold as many parties as Jessica did and not need a little assistance with the drinks.

There was a corner grocery at the end of the block, and she decided to pop in and pick up something. She had gained on the couple, though, and almost regretted crossing the street. They were so delightful to watch. They held hands as they walked, their fingers brushing back and forth against the woman's blue silk dress with a soft swish. They were talking to each other in animated voices, as though they'd just jointly discovered the secret of happiness. From behind, Marty could see their faces only when one turned to make a point to the other, but even from that slight angle, Marty could see they were smiling, fascinated with one another.

Well, she would meet them at the party, she told herself as she detoured across the street. Even the smallest grocery in San Francisco carried a selection of wine, and she took her time figuring out whether to buy a large bottle of something decent or a small bottle of something bettter. Deciding a party was not the place someone was likely to appreciate the finer points, she chose the former. Quantity with sufficient quality, as long as it was chilled, would be best for this kind of gathering.

By the time she left the store, she could see several other people climbing the front stairs to Jessica's house. They were laughing as they reached the sagging porch, and she could hear energetic music drifting from the partially open window. There were times when you could tell a party was going to be good: everyone was in a mood for a great time, the people were interesting, the music touched a special chord in you, and you felt you looked your best. It was one of those nights. Marty skipped up the steps just as the door opened to let in the group ahead of her. Jessica greeted each of them by name, introducing Marty to the others, and shepherded them all into the hall.

Several of those she could see in the living room were people she knew, and others looked vaguely familiar. The music was fairly loud but the buzz of conversation rivaled it. Only a few people were dancing, in the dining room, where the table and chairs had been pushed back against the walls. Marty stuck her coat in the closet Jessica indicated and followed her back to the kitchen to deposit the wine and get a drink.

The kitchen was a bright glare compared with the rest of the house. After the dusk outside and the dimness of the hall, everyone in the kitchen seemed spotlighted. Jessica stood at a counter on the left with the group who'd just arrived, warily surveying a trio on the other side of the room. Marty, ever alert to human drama, gazed in their direction, too.

The couple she'd first seen on the street were standing close together. She recognized them because of the woman's blue dress, but they were no longer smiling. She was a strikingly attractive woman, though not in a conventional way. Her shoulder-length blond hair softened an otherwise slightly angular face. She had a prominent nose and chin, full mouth and wide-set blue eyes. The man with her was different from what Marty had expected. He was rather ordinary looking, but his face had character. There were deep furrows above his brows, and a noticeable cleft in his chin. He looked much more serious than she'd expected from their behavior on the street, and he was a little older than she'd expected—maybe forty.

They were facing her, and the third person had his back to Marty. The woman looked sad, in contrast to her excitement of a few minutes earlier. Her partner looked as wary as Jessica did, and Marty saw his hand creep up to tighten around the women's waist. Marty stood poised in the doorway, too fascinated by the scenario to move, but knowing she should join Jessica at the counter. It wasn't until she forced herself to look away that the horrible realization struck her. The third person in the trio was Brad.

She knew that if she had any sense, she would simply turn around right then and leave, but she was too startled to prevent his name from escaping her lips. He swung around, a pained expression giving way to a very real relief and a very phony exasperation.

"What took you so long?" he muttered, coming over to claim her free hand. "You should have let me drive you, Marty." He glanced briefly at the frozen couple, and said coolly, "I don't suppose you know my former wife and her husband."

Chapter Nine

$\mathcal{I}$t would have served him right if Marty had exposed his little game right then, she thought, but she couldn't do that to him. Emotions were running too high, and he had too much to lose by her not helping him save face. Already the man and woman had relaxed slightly, she putting on a tentative smile and he looking as though it were of great interest to meet Brad's "new woman." So Marty said nothing, just waited to see what would happen.

Brad introduced them. "Karen and Carl Nash, Marty Woods."

Karen stepped toward her and extended her hand. "Actually, I'm not using Carl's name. It's Karen Baker. How do you do, Marty?"

"Fine, thanks," she said automatically as she gripped Karen's hand. Her skin felt cool compared to Marty's, and her nails were cut short. She had a charming smile, slightly off center so that it looked a bit rueful. Marty liked her immediately.

She liked Carl, too. He shook her hand with a firm grip while he met her eyes squarely. There was something kind about his eyes: they said he'd suffered a lot and learned to live with it. He commented that he thought he'd seen her somewhere before.

Brad relieved Marty of the bottle of wine as she replied that she thought Carl looked familiar, too. She wasn't sure where she might have seen him, but probably around court. Most of Jessica's guests were somehow associated with the courtroom. "I'm with the Family Support Bureau," she said, thinking that might help him place her.

Obviously this was more information than Brad wanted them to have. He became very solicitous, saying, "I should get Marty a drink. If you'll excuse us?" He didn't wait for a reply, but as he nudged Marty toward the drink counter, she saw Karen shake her head the way one does when wondering, "Will he ever change?" Marty couldn't remember how long they'd been married, but she assumed it was about a dozen years. Karen must know him very well, she thought.

Only when Marty had a glass of wine in her hand and was following Brad into the dining room did it occur to her that he'd arranged for her to be there. On top of the scene he'd just drawn her into, it seemed like the vilest treachery. He had—more or less—promised not to contact her again until after she received the blood-test results. There were people all around them, watching the three couples who were dancing. She lowered her voice and whispered directly into his incorrigible ear, "You're a cad, you know that?"

He looked hurt—not apologetic or embarrassed, she noted—just hurt.

"And don't give me that wounded look," she hissed. "It doesn't impress me one bit. You had Jessica invite me tonight, didn't you?"

Marty had observed that when you asked someone like Brad a direct yes-or-no question they got an "I cannot tell a lie" look on their face. She had known from the first time she saw him that he'd have trouble dissembling. It was why she'd never been able to quite believe that he was the father of Lydia's baby. He'd denied it so convincingly.

It was more than that, though. He didn't use the little lines that would have won him favor with her, because they wouldn't have felt right. There was a basic integrity to him that she had responded to from the start. He was an obvious failure at lying. He could stretch the truth, in a pinch, but he couldn't manufacture it. Now he looked martyred when he answered her. "Well, yes, I did. But it's not the same thing as calling you, is it?"

"Yes," she insisted, "it is. You knew perfectly well that I meant we shouldn't see each other at all. Now, not only are we seeing each other, but you're claiming me in front of your ex-wife. You're using me, Brad."

"It wasn't like that, I swear. I'd just forgotten that Karen might be here. When I saw her with that . . . her husband, it bugged me. I've made a point of never seeing him." He glanced around to see whether anyone could overhear them and apparently decided not to take a chance. He took hold of her elbow and steered her toward French doors that led onto a deck.

There was no one out there because it was quite chilly. Marty had no intention of freezing. "I'm not going out there. Have you forgotten how cold it is outside?"

He had the door open, and a gust of frigid air rushed past them. With a gesture of irritation, he stripped off his sports jacket and slung it around her shoulders. "That will keep you warm enough," he said, dragging her out onto the redwood planks and closing the door firmly.

The jacket was warm from his body heat and enveloped her with his scent, a rather unnerving experience. It reminded her of having his arms around her that night on Tank Hill, and she didn't want to be reminded of that. She wanted to stay righteously angry with him for manipulating her. She could tell he wasn't thinking about amorous possibilities; he wanted urgently to explain things to her, to clarify his position. The first thing he said was, "Do you know who Carl Nash is?"

It wasn't what she expected, but she made a stab at an answer. "My guess is that he's a lawyer. I think I've seen him around the courts."

"He's a lawyer, all right. He was *my* lawyer—in the divorce case."

Marty stared at him. "I don't understand."

"What's there to understand? He was my lawyer, and he stole my wife."

"There has to be more to it than that," she reasoned. "You wouldn't have gotten him as a divorce lawyer unless you were already getting a divorce."

Brad moved to lean against the railing, staring out over the ragged back yard. Though he never glanced at her, she knew he expected her to move beside him and listen to the whole story. Despite herself, she wanted to hear it. Underneath his bitterness was a great deal of pain, which brought out a broad streak of tenderness in her. He looked so alone slumped over the railing, as though his last friend had deserted him. They didn't call Marty Pollyanna for nothing.

"It's hard to know where to start," he said after a moment. "It goes back further than the divorce. Maybe I should begin with how Karen and I met Jessica originally. We lived next door to her for a few years." He waved a hand toward the house on the right. "Karen was the one who got to know her, and after a while we were invited to the parties. There are always all these legal people at the parties. I find most of them stuffy and boring; Karen found them fascinating. I think it was from meeting them that she got the idea of going to law school."

"When was this?"

"Oh, she first started talking about it years ago, when we still had to invest all our energies in the store to make a go of it. She'd say, 'Some day I'm going to be a lawyer.' A kind of pipedream, I thought, and I always assumed she'd forget about it. But she didn't. Two years ago she announced that the store was doing well enough that I could do without her help there. She was going to start law school."

"And was the store doing well enough?"

His fingers tightened on the railing. "Maybe, but I wanted to use the money we were finally clearing to make some investments, build up an estate. Law school costs a lot of money, and it would have been for only one of us."

"How do you figure that? A law degree is an investment, too. It wouldn't have taken her long to earn back the initial outlay once she was practicing."

"That's what she said. I suppose it's true, but we'd worked at the store for so long. It was ours, something we'd built together, like our family. If she went off and did something on her own . . ." He shrugged. "The more I pointed out the disadvantages, the more insistent she became. We started to argue all the time. At first it was just about law school, and then she started to nag at me about all sorts of other things. It seemed as though I couldn't do anything right. Finally, when I refused to pay for law school in the fall, she said if the only way she could have some control over her own life was to get out of her marriage to me, that was what she'd do."

"You didn't give her any choice, Brad."

It was not what he wanted to hear. "We made that money together. Any decision about how to spend it had to be a joint one. I didn't want it spent on law school. Hell, she'd started all kinds of projects she'd never finished. I could just see thousands of dollars going down the drain."

Marty didn't think that had been his main concern, but she said nothing. This was his story, his side of the upheavals that had led to his divorce.

"She didn't speak to me for a month after that. When she finally did, she said she'd decided to get a divorce. She cried the whole time she told me, so I thought she'd never go through with it. I agreed to move out for a while, until she'd calmed down. I was sure she'd come to her senses, especially when she thought about our daughter. Andrea hated to see us arguing. She'd . . . well, she just couldn't stand it."

The echo of exuberant music filtered through the closed French doors, a grotesque counterpoint to the painful times of which he was speaking. A shudder ran through her, and she slipped her arms through the sleeves of his jacket, knowing perfectly well that it wasn't the cool night that chilled her. He seemed impervious to the cold, even in his shirt-sleeves, but he'd stopped talking.

Marty gently prompted him. "But she didn't change her mind?"

"No. She got a lawyer, a woman she'd met, and went straight ahead with it. Nothing I said had the least influence on her. I even said she could have the money for law school, but she said it was too late and that we should use some of that money to have Andrea see a therapist for a while until she'd adjusted to the change." Brad pressed his fingers against his temples, trying to clear his head or ease the pain. Marty wasn't sure which. It was a few minutes before he continued.

"She got someone really good for Andrea. We both went occasionally, but not together except once. It didn't work out with both of us there. Andrea came out of it really well, though. She grew up a little too fast, but she seems to have her head together." He shook his head. "But that wasn't what I meant to tell you. I had to get a lawyer and someone recommended Carl Nash. They said he worked hard to get amicable settlements, not this wretched adversary stuff. I guess what convinced me to use him was the fact that he'd apparently gotten some couples back together during their divorces, and I still had hopes."

Marty suddenly knew why Carl had looked familiar. "He's done some mediation for the Family Court, hasn't he?"

"Yeah, I think so. He has a different approach than most of them do. At the time it was just what I wanted. We all sat down together to work things out, the two lawyers and Karen and me. That's how they met."

"Oh, dear. Surely they didn't start seeing each other at a time like that."

"I don't know," he said bitterly. "Karen says they didn't, but she also says they met here once, by accident, and talked for a while. She felt sorry for him."

Marty thought she'd somehow missed part of the story. "Sorry for him? I don't understand."

He stood perfectly still for a moment, his face frozen and his hands clenched on the railing. "His wife and child were killed in a car accident a few years ago."

"Oh, my God."

His fist pounded the railing. "I know it's sad. I feel sorry for the poor bastard, too, but don't you see that's why she got interested in him, because he told her that? He shouldn't have told her that."

"Oh, Brad. Do you think he goes around telling everyone something like that? The reason he told her was because he liked her, not because he hoped she'd like him." Marty felt disappointed at his self-absorbed viewpoint, and a touch of impatience crept into her voice. "You're fooling yourself if you believe Carl stole your wife from you. Sure, she was ready to respond to a sympathetic man after the way you'd treated her. You tried to keep her a prisoner, hoping you could hold on to her because of her natural guilt about your daughter. You're not going to be able to get on with your life until you accept responsibility for your own mistake."

Brad blinked at her in astonishment. "What the hell are you talking about?"

"That's the trouble with you, Brad. You don't even know." Marty sadly stripped off his jacket and tossed it on the railing, where it slid off onto the deck. She didn't bother to pick it up. "I don't know where so many men get the idea women were put on earth to be their personal possessions."

She walked back to the French doors, pulled them open and joined the crowded party, leaving him staring after her. So much for her earlier feelings of tenderness, she thought. Why was it that men expected women to feel sorry for them when they got what they deserved for acting so colossally self-important? She could sympathize with Brad's pain, but she couldn't pat him on the head and tell him he had not brought this all on himself, because he had. He just didn't seem to see it.

What was worse, perhaps, from Marty's point of view, was that he was obviously still absorbed in Karen and her supposed mistreatment of him. It would be perfectly senseless to get involved with a man in that position. Yes, she was attracted to him, and probably he was attracted to her. However, he was not, strictly speaking, available. Though it made her feel unbearably sad, she had to recognize that he wasn't the kind of man she *should* get involved with.

Marty looked around her for someone to whom she could speak. Jessica caught her eye and waved her toward a group standing near the living room doorway. Marty immediately joined them. There were two people she knew vaguely, and she fell right into their conversation. She kept her back to the French doors but sensed that Brad had not yet followed her into the house. After a while, she was asked to dance by the man standing beside her, and she accepted.

The only light in the dining room was from a forest of candles on the table, where various snacks were laid out. Because it was only slightly lighter inside than out, Marty could see through the French doors to where Brad still stood leaning against the railing. She couldn't tell if he had picked up his jacket; she could tell he wasn't wearing it. He wasn't looking into the room, but out toward the yard. With difficulty Marty stilled a strong urge to go out and comfort him.

Five other couples were dancing with lighthearted enjoyment of the music and the movement of their bodies. That sense of pleasure caught hold of Marty as she faced her partner. Dancing was Marty's favorite exercise, one in which the gracefulness of her small body came into its own. As a child she'd dreamed of being a dancer, but more practical considerations had intruded when she became a woman. Considerations like making a living and recognizing that her talents were not great enough to dance professionally.

Still, she enjoyed dancing, and she was good at it, slow, fast, almost anything that came along. There was a liquidity to her movements that seemed to fascinate her partner. He nodded his encouragement and graduated from a rather tame effort to something more ambitious. Marty tried to lose herself in the dancing, pushing Brad as far back in her mind as she could. Like playing a game of tennis, the exertion called forth a deep reserve of energy that made her feel renewed.

When the music stopped briefly, she found that another partner was ready to claim her, and she joined him without hesitation. She couldn't help glancing out toward the deck to see if Brad was still there. He was inside the door now, staring at her, a slight frown drawing the wild eyebrows together. She smiled tentatively—no hard feelings. His expression did not change, though he moved a few steps closer to where she was dancing.

Marty returned her attention to her partner, a man she'd never seen before. Unlike her first partner, he was not a particularly good dancer. He was slightly off from the beat of the music, and he kept leering at her, as though her dancing were somehow suggestive. Few things stirred Marty's anger the way this kind of assumption did, but she kept her face impassive. The music would only last a few minutes.

"I think we should get to know each other better," he said, the contortion of his features almost a smirk.

Marty stared at him. "No, I don't think so."

"Hey, look. You're not here with anyone, are you? We could duck out now and have a good time."

She stopped dancing. "I'm not interested. Excuse me, please."

As she slipped past him, she saw that Brad had positioned himself belligerently behind the man. That was all she needed—Brad making another scene by coming to her rescue. She moved directly in front of Brad and drew her short frame up to its greatest extent. "I don't need any help on this, Brad," she said softly but firmly. "It's not the first time, and it won't be the last, that someone has made me uncomfortable. I'm perfectly capable of taking care of it myself."

For a moment longer his dark scowl remained, and then he suddenly grinned. "It's a good thing. He's a lot bigger than I am."

His abrupt change of face startled, and delighted, Marty. She instinctively reached out and touched his arm, and he swiftly covered her hand with his, squeezing lightly. "Want to dance?" he asked.

"Sure."

Her erstwhile partner had strolled sullenly across the room to the kitchen, without looking back.

Every song so far that evening had been fast. There was no reason to think that the next one would be any different, and yet it was. Jessica had obviously put the music on tape ahead of time, and had tossed in the slow one as either a shock or a surprise. Marty felt disoriented for a moment when the music started and Brad, with a roguish smile, caught her up in his arms.

It had been a long time since Marty had slow danced with anyone. She'd forgotten how two bodies could move perfectly in rhythm with each other. Brad held her close, but not too close. He had a perfect sense of the beat, and Marty could feel a bonding between them as they drifted over the hardwood floor. Neither of them spoke; it would have broken the perfect affinity they had achieved. Marty knew it was dangerous to allow even a few minutes of this kind of accord, but she couldn't help enjoying it. Physical contact with Brad had a powerful effect on her—the feel of his body against hers, the smell of his skin—everything heightened the sense of intoxication. Marty felt slightly unsteady by the time the dance ended.

"Don't go away," he pleaded when she drew back from him. "We should have a fast dance, too. Though, it won't be as much fun."

Marty knew what he meant but she tossed her head and said, "It's much better exercise."

All his pent-up energy came out in response to the faster music. His movement was lithe and graceful, but full of expressiveness. Marty was astonished at how much contact they appeared to have, even now when they weren't touching. Their eyes locked and held, their bodies followed intricate patterns which first one and then the other initiated. The music seemed to come from within them, rather than from the speakers on the wall. Only toward the end of the dance did Marty notice that other people were watching them. She had thought no one else would notice the stunning rapport, the elaborate complexity, the subtle intimacy that they exhibited as a dance couple.

There was a burst of applause for them as the music ended.

Marty flushed slightly and Brad put his arm around her waist, whispering in her ear, "We're not bad together, you know?"

"Just at dancing," she insisted.

"That's what you'd like to think." He was grinning, but the expression froze when he found himself standing right beside Carl Nash. Marty pressed her elbow in toward her waist, trapping his hand there. Brad glanced at her briefly, and then said easily to Carl, "She's really good, isn't she?"

"You both are. It's rare to see that combination of spontaneity and precision." He gestured toward the couples who had continued dancing. "Most of us just manage to keep time—if that."

"It's the first time we've danced together," Brad admitted. Then, looking at Marty but speaking to Carl, he added, "She didn't really come with me tonight. I'm sorry if I made things awkward in there."

Carl smiled his sad smile. "It's all right, Brad. We all have a lot of regrets about our situation."

Marty felt a lump rise in her throat as the two men simultaneously extended their hands to shake. It had always seemed a rather empty ritual to her before, fraught with glad-handed insincerity, except for the notorious handshake after a fight. She'd never seen that before, and almost doubted it existed. It took courage to declare that kind of truce, that promise of no further hard feelings. She swallowed hard as their hands clasped firmly and released. Brad turned to her. "Could we talk out on the deck again?"

Marty couldn't speak, but she nodded.

Chapter Ten

It was even colder on the deck now, and Brad removed his sports jacket again and hung it over Marty's shoulders. "You're going to catch pneumonia this way," she protested. "Why don't I get my own coat, or we could talk inside."

"I'm all right. It's too noisy to talk in there." He paced to the railing and back to her. She could see that he was still keyed up, radiating a kind of energy that needed release. The pacing seemed to help, but mostly he wanted to talk and couldn't figure out where to start again. His hands were jammed in his pockets, his face set with concentration. It was dark on the deck, but his black hair gleamed in the moonlight. Marty went to stand against the railing, needing its solidity to keep her from putting herself in his path and throwing her arms around him. The emotional swings of the evening were taking their toll on her.

"I don't think she did see him during the divorce," he finally said. "I think they were scrupulous about that. They wanted to see each other, though, and that could have influenced how he handled things."

"He was probably just as scrupulous about that, Brad. Why would you think he wasn't?"

"Because she ended up still owning part of the store." He stopped in front of her, scowling. "At his suggestion."

"What was the alternative?"

"I'd have had to take a loan out to pay for her share. The business was worth a lot more than the house, which she got."

"Did you *want* to take out a loan?" she asked.

"No. We'd just paid off our debts the year before but I could have done it. This way she's still involved, and if the business grows, she'll make money from it, without ever doing a thing."

"That's what happens when you own a share of Xerox, too."

His sigh was one of exasperation. "I know that but why did he suggest it? I went along with him because I didn't know anything about the two of them, and afterwards, when I learned, I felt like they'd pulled something over on me. You know what I mean?" He'd stopped in front of her, searching her face with those piercing blue eyes.

"Yes, I know what you mean but I think the reason he did it was because it was simplest for you, not because he and Karen would somehow profit from it. Maybe, too, he wanted there to be some necessary contact between you, in addition to your daughter. If it's been bothering you, though, why don't you just *take* out a loan and buy her out?"

Marty didn't think he'd ever considered the possibility before. It was strange how one's mind could get so caught up with an imagined injustice that one didn't see the simplest solution. He stared at her for a moment, and then said, "Actually, I don't think it's going to bother me anymore, after tonight. He's not the wicked villain I've been making him out to be all this time." He looked away. "Karen had some legitimate complaints, too, I guess."

Marty knew how hard it was for him to say that. As hard as shaking hands with Carl. "It's never entirely one-sided," she said. "Do you still love her, Brad?"

He gave her a perplexed look. "How can I know? When I thought I still loved her, I spent all my time trying to convince myself I didn't and thinking about all the things she'd done wrong. I'm fond of her. How could I change that after all those years? Although, it's a different kind of fondness now. I think . . . we could become friends."

The way he said it, with a kind of amazement, made a shiver run through her. He was trying to be completely honest, sifting through the last year's pain and anger and disappointment to get to the heart of the matter. He had worked hard building defenses, only to find them crumbling, and possibly no longer necessary. His eyes were locked on hers, and he reached for her hand. It felt small in his, enveloped by the strength and warmth of his solid clasp. They turned simultaneously to face the yard, standing close to the railing, their hands tucked between them.

"It's been a hell of a year," he went on. "More than a year, really. The divorce has been final for almost a year, and Karen married Carl a few months after that. It was those months after she first asked for the divorce that were the hardest. Everything seemed to be in complete chaos. Andrea was almost hysterical about our splitting up, and I just confused matters by telling her I was sure Karen and I would get back together. I was sure then that we would."

He looked at Marty, to see if she were going to become angry with him again, she supposed. Marty squeezed his hand, and he continued.

"Andrea's therapy was . . . upsetting for all of us. The therapist said my daughter wasn't likely to accept the reality of the situation if I didn't. Andrea knew Karen wasn't going to change her mind. So all of a sudden it was me who was ruining Andrea's life, not Karen. As if that wasn't bad enough, there was a problem at the store."

"You said it was finally profitable then," she reminded him.

"Oh, it wasn't the overall picture. A young cousin of mine from Illinois had come out to San Francisco. He was my mother's sister's kid, and my aunt especially asked me to hire him. She said he needed some responsibility. I didn't pay much attention to him, but Karen was always warning me that he wasn't working out." Brad flung his hand up in despair. "I mean, how much trouble can you have with a stock boy?"

"Quite a bit, I gather."

He sighed. "Well, he was a complainer, but I didn't think much of it. Every twenty-one-year-old thinks he should be president of the company. I told him we owned the place, and we'd move him up as he proved himself. He didn't have any skills or education to merit it, though. Just about the time I found out about Karen and Carl, I discovered Sam had been stealing from the store. It was a rotten time for me, and I blew up and fired him. Of course, there was hell to pay with the family. They all thought I was overreacting because of the strain of the divorce."

"Were you?"

"Maybe I didn't handle it very well," he admitted, "but under any circumstances he deserved to be fired. My aunt hasn't spoken to me since, so I imagine Sam told her rather a different story than the truth. It all turned out to be just another burden on top of the rest. There were a few months there when every day seemed to bring a new crisis."

Marty shifted so her side was pressing against his. "It must have been a wretched time."

He released her hand and put his arm around her waist, hugging her. "It was, but it got better. Andrea started to feel okay again, and I had hours here and there when I didn't think about the whole mess. I got involved in some new ideas for the store." He paused and looked directly at her, his expression wistful. "But I wasn't sure I was ever going to feel completely alive again until I met you."

His eyes developed a wicked sparkle, and Marty knew he wasn't declaring his undying love. Maybe he was saying that she had more than sparked his dormant libido, but not a great deal more. The problem, for her, was that he had tapped her own desires just as strongly. Right now she wanted to feel his lips on hers, to touch his skin, to hold his body tightly to her, to . . .

"Let's go down in the yard," he suggested, grasping her hand and tugging her toward the stairs.

Marty allowed herself to be drawn along in a kind of trance. There were only three steps down into the yard, which meant it was not significantly far from the party. Yet it was far enough. Unless someone came out on the deck, there was no chance of anyone seeing the two of them as they stood near the house, obscured by the shadows. Brad opened his arms, and

Marty walked into them, her heart pounding almost painfully. She leaned against the hardness of his body, feeling soft and vulnerable by comparison. He did no more than hold her firmly against him for several minutes.

During that time Marty could feel her body responding to his. The chaos and tension inside her grew; her skin felt suddenly warm and sensitive. She was caught up in a euphoria that blocked out all thoughts except his nearness. She could feel the whisper of his breathing against her hair and smell the masculine scent of his body. An aching desire wound through her as she tightened her arms around him.

His lips brushed across her hair, and then grazed her temples. Slowly, they made a path down her forehead, across her nose, coming to rest on her mouth. Warm, firm, pliant, they teased at her lips, soothing, tempting, insistent. Marty's response was instant and equally intense. The pressure, the taste of him, set her nerves on edge, a shaky, delirious balance she could scarcely maintain. She greatly needed the support of his arm around her waist.

He slid his hand slowly up her side, stroking the flesh beneath her dress until his hand cupped her breast. Marty drew back, not because she didn't want him to touch her, but because the sensation was so strong her legs felt incapable of supporting her. Brad cocked his head questioningly.

"Don't you like that?" he asked.

She drew a deep breath. "Yes, I like it. Just . . . not here, not now. I can't seem to keep my balance."

"Come home with me," he urged. "We always seem to end up outside, where there's no way to be comfortable."

"It's not a matter of comfort. It's a matter of . . ."

She tossed her head in annoyance, unable to find the right words. "I'm not ready to sleep with you, Brad. I don't mean to be so blunt, but I can't think of any other way to put it."

"You don't have to sleep with me. I just want to hold you and touch you, Marty." He rubbed a finger against her cheek. "I want you to trust me."

Trust him! It was just like Brad to think it was such a simple matter. He stood there looking supremely confident that she would make that giant leap of faith. This man who told a completely different story from that of her client, this man who had only now, after all these months, made peace with his former-wife's husband, this man who had been so shaken by his divorce that he was just beginning to realize that he no longer loved his ex-wife, how could he ask her to trust him?

On the other hand, he was the man who had just confessed his deepest pain to her, and who had made an honest attempt at clearing up a difficult problem. More than that, he was the man whose touch made her echo with longing.

"I don't know what to say," she whispered. "It's too soon. I'm too confused. There are too many obstacles."

"There's nothing we can't manage. Look, Marty, I promise I won't press you."

He looked so terribly earnest, and so trustworthy. She backed a few paces away from him, trying to break the spell he cast, studying him. After a moment she moistened her lips and said, "You could come to my place with me, just for a while, not for the night, Brad."

His infectious grin appeared. "You have my word of honor. Just kick me out when you've had enough."

Marty shook her head. "No, I'm not going to be the heavy. If you come with me, I have to be able to trust you to know when to leave."

Even in the dim light she could see that his eyes narrowed. *That* didn't seem so trustworthy. She began to turn away, and he held her arm. "All right," he said. "You drive a hard bargain, Marty."

"I'm not a teenager, Brad."

"I never thought you were."

Marty didn't wait for him to park his car behind hers before she climbed the stairs to her apartment and unlocked the door. Grave doubts about the wisdom of what she was doing had already taken hold of her, but there didn't seem to be any excuse for changing her mind at this point. Either she could trust him, or she couldn't. This was as good a way to find out as any.

As soon as the door swung inward, her lhasa apso started yapping ecstatically, bouncing against her with an excess of energy. Marty could hear Brad's quick step just behind her, and the dog instantly offered what was intended as a threatening growl. Only a child would have been intimidated by the small, shaggy beast, however, and Brad reached down to pet her. Misty snapped at him.

"You have to be introduced," Marty explained. "She doesn't like strange men."

"I'm not a strange man," he insisted as Marty calmed the dog. "I'm a very normal man, who's just agreed to some very nerve-racking terms, and I didn't expect some mutt to try to enforce them."

"You don't have to come in, and she's not a mutt."

They stared at each other in the darkness of the entry hall for a long moment. Then Brad shrugged and knelt down so the dog could sniff at his hands. "I want to come in," he said.

"Fine," Marty agreed, a little stiffly. "Maybe you could get a fire started in the living room while I get us some wine."

She flipped a switch inside the door, and a lamp glowed softly beside the sofa. The light barely illuminated several easy chairs, a coffee table, bookshelves along one wall and an antique cabinet. She went to the cabinet and opened the door, pointing out where she kept her stereo and records. "Pick something out, if you like. There should be enough wood for a fire. The matches are on the mantel."

Brad was standing directly behind her when she turned toward the hall. He drew her lightly against him. "Don't be angry with me. I'm just a little . . . on edge."

"Aren't we all?" she asked, trying for the proper flippant tone. Before he could think of a suitable reply, she disengaged herself and strode from the room.

It took Marty only two minutes to pour wine for them, but she stayed in the kitchen much longer than that. Her physical response to this man made her nervous. She wasn't used to having a sexual attraction overrule her better judgment, and her better judgment told her not to get involved with him, certainly not now. He needed time to sort out his complicated emotions; she needed time to get the paternity case out of the way. So why had she let him come back here with her?

He already meant something to her, and her body ached for his touch.

Marty petted the dog absently and closed Misty in the kitchen. She would trust Brad, this once. Carefully juggling the two full wine glasses, she headed back to the living room.

Soft music was playing, and he was bent over the hearth, adding larger logs to the blaze he had going. He had turned off the lamp, and the firelight danced on his face, throwing a huge shadow of him against the opposite wall. His sports jacket had been tossed over the back of one of the easy chairs. Marty watched him for a moment from the doorway, picturing him on a camping trip crouched over an open fire. He had that sort of look about him—naturally athletic, competent, slightly undomesticated and very masculine.

Brad turned to catch her staring at him. He didn't smile, but patted the spot beside him on the rug. "It'll be a minute before it's going well enough to ignore," he said.

Marty kicked off her heels and padded over to where he sat, handing him his glass before she stooped down to seat herself. They touched glasses and sipped without saying anything, but their eyes were locked for several seconds. Then Brad set his glass aside and reached for the tongs to rearrange the logs in the fireplace. "Why don't you lie down?" he suggested, not looking at her. "You'll be more comfortable."

Though it was true, she hesitated. There was something more vulnerable about lying down, somehow. She was vulnerable in any case, she decided as she lowered herself onto her stomach and stared ahead of her into the fire. Brad replaced the tongs in the rack and lowered himself beside her, one arm coming to rest across her waist and the other holding his wine glass. His fingers started to rub slowly against her side.

"I hardly ever have a fire in my fireplace," he said. "Maybe it's because I've never remembered to get in enough kindling and logs. You keep a good supply."

"If we're not having really hot weather, I make a fire about once a week." Marty met his gaze, knowing that her eyes already glowed with the fires that were catching in her. He bent forward to kiss her, his lips tasting of wine. Their mouths joined in breathless need, their tongues twining eagerly. Marty could feel stirrings through her body, urged on by the touch of his fingers on her skin.

He had discarded his wine glass and was tracing the path of her necklace from her back to the wildly beating pulse in her throat. For a moment his fingers lingered there, then stroked down toward the open weave of her dress. Her breasts tingled from the nearness of his fingers before he ever touched them. Because she was lying on her stomach, it wasn't possible for him to do more than caress the smooth skin he could just reach under the neckline of her dress, and yet Marty felt her breathing become more rapid.

Her fingers loosened dangerously on her wine glass, and she managed to set it down, pushing it as far from her as she could. With her hands free, she used one to support herself and wound the other through his wavy hair. Brad rolled her onto her side, so he could run his hand over the mound of her breast, sliding the palm repeatedly over the tip. Marty murmured her pleasure and allowed her own fingers to play sensuously over his ears and neck.

This time it was Brad who drew back, letting his eyes run over the loose weave of her dress from her breasts to her knees. "Would you do something for me?" he asked.

"Probably," she said, smiling.

"That dress would be even more beautiful if you were wearing it without anything on underneath."

Her breath caught in her throat, but she nodded. When she'd tried it on in the store she'd done so without underwear, just to see, knowing she couldn't wear it that way. Her breasts had peeked through the loose weave; the triangle of hair below had been visible. It had made her feel incredibly sexy, like wearing a transparent negligee, and perhaps, even with a slip, that was what the dress suggested.

"Would you wear it that way for me?"

His fingers were resting on one breast, unmoving. Marty *wanted* him to see her in the dress the way she'd seen herself in the mirror that day. Without a word she rose and left the room, returning a few minutes later to stand in the doorway in just the soft, flowing, wheat-colored dress.

"You'll have to come closer," he urged. "There's not enough light over there."

She walked slowly toward him, enjoying the feel of the fabric against her flushed skin. Even in the dim light she knew he'd be able to see her small, firm breasts with their budding nipples, the curve of her hips and the sturdy energy of her thighs. He had risen to meet her, his eyes wide with pleasure.

"You're beautiful," he whispered. "That's the way that dress should be worn."

"I can't very well go out in it this way," she protested.

"No, but in private you should never have anything on under it." He ran a hand over her hips across her stomach and up to her breasts.

Marty's breathing quickened when he reached her nipple. Instead of rubbing it with his finger, he lowered his mouth to run his tongue over the fabric until he managed to get it through the soft weave. His lips closed gently over the nipple, sucking it firmly into his mouth. Marty's knees weakened with desire, and his hand moved tightly against her buttock, supporting her.

She wanted to touch him, to share the pleasure he was giving her, but it was difficult, standing there feeling almost nerveless with consuming longing. Would he read it as a sign that she had changed her mind, was willing to have him consummate this reckless desire? Did she want him to? Even as she tried to sort out her fevered thoughts, he was leading her to the sofa, pulling her down onto his lap, holding her so tightly against him that she could feel his heart hammering.

"It's all right," he murmured against her hair. "I'm not going to forget. You can trust me, Marty. I just want to keep you close to me a little while longer."

Relieved, even though she was so thoroughly aroused, Marty gently stroked her fingers through his hair, marveling at how alive it felt to her fingers. Brad merely held her, his hands no longer seeking to stimulate. They sat quietly cuddled together for a long time, letting their bodies calm, enjoying the simple contact. When the stereo stopped, Brad shifted slightly.

"It's time I went home," he announced gruffly.

Marty slipped off his lap and stood looking down at him. "Yes."

He stared at the vision she made in the woven dress, his eyes at long last rising to meet hers. "Will you wear that dress another time for me?"

"Maybe," she said lightly. Next time, she knew, things wouldn't end this way.

"You're awfully careful with your promises, aren't you?" he asked as he rose.

"Yes. That way people know I'll keep them when I make them."

"I'll remember that." He shrugged into his sports jacket, but his eyes never left her. "If you turned the light on, I could see you better."

Marty laughed and drew him toward the front door. "If you left, I could go to bed."

He pulled her to him for one last kiss. "You're impossible," he groaned as she reached around him and opened the door.

"Only when I have to be," she retorted.

He shrugged and loped down the stairs. Before he was in his car she closed the door and leaned against it, taking a deep, shaky breath. Maybe, just maybe, she could trust him the next time. Tonight she wasn't willing to trust herself any further.

Chapter Eleven

*M*arty fell asleep in a haze of erotic dreams, feeling wonderful, but she awoke filled with doubts. Dazzling sunlight seemed to clear away the soft edges of desire from her brain, leaving a list of facts that profoundly disturbed her. She sat up on the mattress with her knees bent and her chin resting against them, hugging her legs as she stared unseeing at the gleaming brass foot of her bed.

First, she was jeopardizing her own position in the Paternity Unit by seeing an alleged father. At the very least, it was a conflict of interests. Was she strong enough to separate the two facts of her life without doing damage to one or the other—or both?

Second, she hadn't stuck to her resolve not to see Brad until the blood tests were completed. Shouldn't she have walked out of that party the minute she knew he was there? If he had complicated matters, played on her sympathy, that shouldn't have interfered with doing the right thing.

Third, even when she'd lost patience with him, she hadn't actually left. Hoping, probably, that he would convince her again of his good intentions, which he had.

Fourth, she had let him completely mesmerize her with his reconciliation with Carl, and with his sad story of the divorce.

Which, fifth, should have told her other things than it did. When a man was going through the throes of that traumatic a divorce, he did some crazy things, things that later he might not want to think about, things he'd rather forget, even deny.

And . . . what number was she up to? Well, it didn't matter. What mattered was that she hadn't said good-bye to him at the party, but had let him come home with her, let him caress her and turn her into jelly. *Why* did he have that effect on her? She'd met so many other, more logical men to become infatuated with. Why this one?

Marty sighed and hugged her knees closer to her. There was never any accounting for where a woman lost her heart. The same thing went for a man, of course. Besides, it wasn't a matter of losing her heart—yet. It was a matter of sexual attraction. Something much more easily ignored, surely. All she had to do was avoid him, at least until after the test results. Then, well, then she'd have to give more thought to the situation.

Meaning that she'd have to decide whether Brad's chauvinistic tendencies were skin- or soul-deep. She'd have to find out whether she was strong enough to resist his attempts to make her into his image of a woman. She'd have to discover whether he really had gotten over his former wife, or whether he was merely attracted to Marty on the rebound. She groaned and climbed out of bed. The whole process sounded exhausting . . . and it all hinged on the tests excluding him. If he'd lied to her about that, there was no hope for them at all.

And precious little even if he hadn't, she thought grumpily as she padded to the bathroom.

Brad was exhilarated. He'd kept his promise the night before, despite the physical strain to himself, but it was worth it to have won some trust from Marty. He felt sure she would admire his self-restraint, not that he hadn't enjoyed just holding her. There was a special kind of intimacy in it that had touched him on a wholly emotional level. However, that was a little alarming for him to think about, and he preferred to marvel at his own admirable control.

Because it was still a little early to call her, he poured himself a bowl of cereal and ate it while he read the Sunday paper. By 9:30 he decided, she would certainly be up, and he dialed her number as he refolded the paper. The line was busy. Impatient, he wandered around the kitchen for a few minutes and tried her number again. It was still busy.

Well, he'd surprise her then. He'd just show up on her doorstep and tell her they were going to take a drive—up to Mount Tamalpais or down along the ocean, whichever she preferred. They could pick up picnic supplies on the way, or stop at a restaurant. Anything, as long as they could spend the day together.

Brad had completely forgotten that Marty hadn't wanted to see him again until she had the results of the blood tests. She hadn't said anything further about it the previous evening, so he subconsciously assumed it no longer mattered to her. In fact, for the time being, he had entirely forgotten the paternity investigation altogether. It was Marty as a woman in whom he was interested, and her job no more occurred to him that sunny Sunday morning than did his own.

There seemed no reason to change from the blue jeans and plaid shirt he'd put on when he got up, so he simply locked the house on Liberty Street and climbed into his Volvo. It was only a five minute drive to Marty's place, where he parked the car behind a shiny Porsche and tossed several product binders from the passenger seat into the back before he got out.

He took the steps two at a time, jabbed at the bell and stood poised to scoop Marty into his arms the moment she opened her door. Only in the very back of his mind did he consider it possible that she would invite him in for a resumption of their lovemaking of the night before. He certainly wouldn't press her, and he'd look surprised if she *did* seem amenable to a further physical involvement right away, surprised but delighted, of course. Nothing would please him more, but he didn't expect it.

What he did expect was for her to answer her door. He pushed the bell again, longer this time, and clearly heard it ring inside the apartment. He supposed it was possible she was still in bed, even though her phone had been busy earlier. She could have taken a call and then fallen back asleep. Brad pounded a playful but urgent beat on the brass doorknocker, too preoccupied with his concerns to notice that the door beside Marty's had opened.

"Can I help you?" a voice asked coldly.

Startled, Brad spun around so fast the rubber of his tennis shoes squeaked on the terrazzo. The man who stood there was a good six inches taller than Brad, and he looked seriously annoyed. He was dressed in one of those white-collared, striped shirts that Brad thought affected, especially when they were worn with what looked like cuff links. The tie was obviously silk, and the fellow wore gray-wool slacks that fit him perfectly. Brad didn't like the looks of him one bit.

"I wasn't ringing your bell," he said, turning away.

"I'm aware of that. You persist in ringing the bell and knocking, even though it's quite evident there's no one home. I own this building, and I'm asking you to stop."

Brad swung his head around and stared at the man's hard—though handsome—face. Marty had told him she owned her place. Therefore, the man was lying. "No, you don't," he insisted. "Miss Woods owns it."

"Ms. Woods and I both own it." The fellow's eyes narrowed. "Who are you?"

There was no reason on earth why Brad should tell this mannequin who he was. It was something of a shock to learn that Marty owned the building with someone—if indeed she did. She certainly hadn't mentioned it. He cast his mind back to exactly what she *had* said, during their dinner at the Italian restaurant down the street. When he'd asked her if she rented, she'd said no, she owned her place. The discussion hadn't gone any further.

"My name is Brad Macintosh, and I'm a friend of Marty's," he said finally. "I thought she'd be home. When I called, the line was busy."

There was a flicker of name recognition in the man's eyes, Brad thought, but it wasn't a friendly recognition. The fellow pursed his lips and frowned. "One of her paternity cases," he muttered. "I don't think Ms. Woods would like to see you on her doorstep, Mr. Macintosh. If you have business with her, contact her at her office."

Anger pulsed through Brad. How dare this idiot tell him what to do? What right had Marty to discuss him with some stranger? He glared across the short distance that separated the two of them. "I'll do that," he snapped. Without another glance at the man, he went down the stairs and got into his car. Before he pulled away from the curb, though, he noticed that the fellow continued to watch him. Even at the intersection, Brad could see him in his rearview mirror, still standing in the doorway like some kind of bodyguard, for God's sake.

What the hell was going on? Had Marty done this purposely to him? Was she upstairs in the man's apartment, waiting for him to get rid of Brad, or had she gone out, telling him to handle the situation for her? Either was possible. Whether or not either was likely, Brad hadn't the slightest idea. Marty hadn't known he was coming, but she might have guessed he'd show up.

Even if none of these things was true, what right did she have to tell anyone that he was one of her "paternity cases"? Brad felt betrayed, and the feeling was compounded by everything he'd been through in the last few years. He wasn't sure of a great deal these days, but one thing he knew for certain: he wasn't going to get involved with a woman who couldn't be trusted. The hell with her. There were a million women who were just as pretty, just as clever, and just as interesting as she. If he hadn't met them yet, it didn't mean he wouldn't. He would be a fool to let her ruin his life, and Brad was not going to be a fool again.

Bursting with indignation, he nearly ran a red light at the top of Seventeenth Street. His intention at the moment was to show them all—Marty, Karen, Carl— that he was a very exciting man, that any woman in her right mind would be thrilled to have him as her lover. He contemplated going down to one of the nicer Sunday brunch places and finding someone who would appreciate him.

He was in his jeans, though, and it would take too long to get home and get changed. All the interesting women would already be finished with brunch by the time he could get somewhere, or they would have settled for someone less exciting, because he hadn't gotten there sooner.

The smartest thing he could do now, he decided, was go home and read some articles on paternity testing that Marty had given him and which he'd tossed in a drawer. He certainly couldn't rely on her any longer to see him through this mess. Tired, and more miserable than he was willing to admit even to himself, he drove slowly to Liberty Street.

Marty returned in the middle of the afternoon after helping a friend repair a broken window. She had a smudge of putty on her cheek, and her old green slacks and turtleneck sweater were in need of a cleaning. She felt she'd accomplished something. Maybe it was how other women felt when they'd prepared a gourmet meal, she thought as she eased herself out of her car. Misty leaped the gear shift to scurry after her. At least a window usually stayed fixed for a while; a meal was gone in a matter of minutes.

Jim's Porsche was just pulling up behind her car, and she waited on the sidewalk to say hello to him. If she had noticed he had a woman with him, she probably wouldn't have done it, but she was keeping an eye on Misty, who appeared ready to jump up on the Porsche in her excitement. Jim eased his considerable length out of the low car and caught sight of her. "Oh, good, I wanted to speak with you," he said. "Just a minute."

Marty kept Misty from bouncing on his elegantly clad legs while he came around the car and opened the passenger door. He gallantly handed out a woman dressed in a navy suit jacket and skirt. Not one of the beauties, Marty noted, though she was attractive in a subtler way. Everything about her was a little severe, from the French twist to the minimal heels she wore. She blinked uncertainly, as though there hadn't been much light in the car and the sun bothered her. Marty, bent down at an uncomfortable angle, kept a firm hand on Misty's collar.

"Marty, this is Janet Evans. Janet, Marty Woods, who owns the building with me."

The woman offered her hand, and a slight smile which barely lifted the corners of her mouth. It wasn't an unpleasant expression, merely a shy attempt at a warmer greeting. Her handshake was firm, and she told Marty it wasn't necessary to hold onto the dog. "I've already ruined my nylons getting into this ridiculous car. She can't do any worse damage to them."

Misty certainly tried. Marty had rarely seen the dog so instantly taken with anyone, and Janet stooped down to pet her, showing more warmth than she had managed in her greeting to Marty. It wasn't an offensive display, but rather a surprising one; the woman had switched from shyness to real enthusiasm. Marty tried to meet Jim's eyes but he was watching the pair with a curious intensity.

Eventually Janet stood up again, saying, "I used to have a poodle, but I've been thinking of getting a lhasa this time. They're not as nervous."

"No," Marty agreed, "but they're not as intelligent, either."

"That wouldn't matter, unless they could talk."

It was a strange remark, and it took Marty a moment to realize the woman was joking. Marty smiled a bit uncertainly to show she appreciated the remark—and noticed that Jim was beaming at Janet as though she were a particularly bright pupil. Instantly she knew this was the law librarian and that the joke had something to do with a private matter between the two of them. She decided it was time to disappear from the scene and started to excuse herself.

"No, wait, Marty," Jim said. "I wanted to tell you that your paternity case showed up on your doorstep this morning."

"My paternity case?"

"The fellow you mentioned yesterday, the macho one named Brad. I told him he should get in touch with you at the office if he had business, that you wouldn't want him to come here."

Marty felt a sinking sensation in her stomach. "I see. What did he say to that?"

Jim shrugged. "He said he would, and took off. He was a bit feisty for a minute, though. I thought he might take a punch at me."

That certainly sounded like Brad. Marty could just picture him squaring off against anyone who told him what to do, even if his opponent was much bigger than he. "Well, thanks," she murmured.

"Listen, you should be more careful about letting them find out your address." Jim looked truly concerned, though it might have been an act for his woman friend. "You wouldn't want to mess around with some of those guys."

Marty fought successfully against a blush. That wasn't what he meant, in any case. He meant that some of the paternity cases might be violent men. She nodded and scooped Misty into her arms. "Yes, I know. Nice to meet you, Janet," she called as she ran up the stairs and hurriedly let herself into her apartment.

It wasn't difficult to picture the scene. Jim would have been at his most haughty and Brad at his most defensive. Why had Brad come without calling her? Why had Jim bothered to say anything to him at all? Why didn't all of them just leave her alone? Marty dropped down on the sofa where she and Brad had held each other the night before. She ran her hand gently along the pillows. Maybe if she called him she could straighten it out. Maybe he would call her.

It would be best if neither of them made a move now. She still didn't have the test results. Any contact between them would only lead them deeper into a hazardous relationship. Her judgment was getting skewed because of how she felt about him, and that would play havoc with her job. Let it rest until the situation is taken care of, she counseled herself. A few more days and everything will be cleared up.

If he's excluded.

Of course he'll be excluded, she assured herself, patting the pillow nervously. Of course he's been telling me the truth. I wouldn't feel this way about him if he weren't honest.

Yes, I would, she thought unhappily. It could be a

purely physical response I'm having to him, one that has nothing whatsoever to do with his integrity. I will not call him, and if he calls me, I'll tell him to wait for the test results.

Marty was surprised, and not altogether happy, that he didn't call.

It was a long week at work. Marty called the testing lab several times to see whether the results were back. If blood type alone had excluded him, she was sure she'd have known by now. Apparently they were having to go through at least one of the other tests— the red blood cell, HLA or enzyme tests. There was nothing unusual about that, of course. Only a limited number of men were excluded on blood type alone, which was why it was so important that the other tests had been perfected.

The office had been busy all week. Marty had been to court twice, half expecting to find Brad there. She searched her IN box carefully each time she returned from an excursion off the floor. Virginia insisted that she didn't look well, that she might be running a fever.

Brad didn't call, even at the office. She would have thought he'd be more interested in finding out the results. He didn't strike her as a particularly patient man. Still, he knew she'd call when she found out something. She called all the men with the results and sent them copies, but most of them called her several times before that happened.

By Friday she was beginning to feel like a nervous wreck. If she had to live through the weekend without knowing the answers, she didn't think she could bear it. The morning dragged by, and only after urgent persuasion did she agree to go out to lunch with

Virginia. As they returned, a messenger came out of the building, and she *knew* he'd brought the information from the lab. Her feet tapped with frustration as the elevator slowly ascended to her floor. Virginia shook her head in wonder as Marty darted out the door and across to her desk.

The envelope was lying there in the middle of her blotter. Though she tried to calm herself by sitting down, her impatience grew when she had difficulty getting the envelope open. Instead of taking the time to find her letter opener, she ripped off the end, slightly tearing the sheets inside. The important thing she could see at a glance. There were calculations at the bottom of the page. Calculations weren't needed if paternity was excluded.

Chapter Twelve

Marty's eyes skimmed quickly to the name of the putative father. Yes, there was Brad's name: Bradford J. Macintosh. The correct names of mother and child were listed under his. One sheet showed the haplotype testing and another the red-blood-cell antigens. The mother and child shared a great number of common factors, and where they didn't, the alleged father had the proper ones. However, the likelihood of paternity fell into the undecided range, well below the more convincing labels of likely, very likely, extremely likely and practically proved.

That was something.

It was not a typical report. Usually the alleged father was either excluded or fell well within the higher ranges. Marty picked up a note from the technician that accompanied the sheets. "Sorry these aren't more helpful. Unfortunately, both the putative father and the mother have some of the most common blood factors, which keeps the ratio down. There are a few more tests that could be done, but they aren't included in the city's package and wouldn't necessarily be useful. Let me know what you'd like. Joyce"

Marty thumped a fist against her desk. "Damn!"

She found Virginia leaning over her shoulder, studying the results with interest. "Well, it's too bad he wasn't excluded, but those results aren't necessarily going to convince a judge to sock him with support payments at the hearing."

"That's not the point," Marty replied. "I wanted him excluded."

"Maybe Harry won't think the results are good enough to take it any further. Innocent until proved guilty, etc., etc. You said there was no physical evidence in the case."

Marty's fingers tapped impatiently against the result sheets. "I'm not talking about the case. I'm talking about me. I wanted to know for sure that he wasn't the father. This doesn't tell me anything. We might as well not have had them done."

"Ah, I see," Virginia murmured. "It's a personal matter. You've fallen for the guy."

"No, I haven't! Well, maybe I have. I don't know. Why does everything have to be so complicated?"

"That's life, my dear. Are you going to call him?"

Marty groaned. "I'll have to. But not with you hanging over my shoulder. This may be a little tricky."

"I'll bet." Virginia gave a flip of her hand, grinned, and returned to her desk.

It took Marty a moment to steel herself to dial his number, and then Brad's secretary told her he was out of the building. "Will he be back today?" she asked.

"Oh, sure. Probably within an hour or so. Do you want me to have him call you?"

"Please. At the office. He has my number."

And then the long wait began. He didn't call back in an hour. Marty found it difficult to concentrate on her other work, and her mind kept sliding back to the fact that he hadn't called her since Jim had driven him off on Sunday. Was there a special reason for that? It wasn't like him to be so easily deterred. Maybe she should have called him after all, but it was too late to worry about that now.

When he hadn't called by late afternoon, Marty photocopied the test results and put them in an envelope addressed to Brad's office, marking them "personal" so his secretary wouldn't open them. If he didn't call, and she got them in the corner box before 5:30, he'd get them in Saturday's mail. It would be better to talk with him, but she scribbled a note explaining the results and got ready to leave. She was not going to stay at the office late just in case he called after working hours.

The phone rang as she was reaching for her suit jacket. "Paternity Unit. Marty Woods speaking."

"This is Brad Macintosh. I have a message here that you called."

From the chill in his voice, Marty knew there was definitely a problem about last Sunday. Well, it might be best to leave it that way, considering what she had to tell him. Her whole body tensed at the thought of making no effort to straighten things out, but a part of her mind was evaluating the situation on a practical level. The detachment didn't help as much as she'd hoped, but it gave her the strength to say in a calm voice, "We've gotten the blood-test results. You were not excluded. On the other hand, statistically you didn't fall into one of the likely categories. I can't say now whether the assisitant D.A. will want to pursue the case because I wasn't able to get hold of him."

There was a long pause on the other end of the line. "They must have done the tests wrong. I should have been excluded because I'm not the father."

"I'm sure they conducted the analyses just the way they should have. You and the mother both have some very common factors in your blood. The Hummell index for your rating was 'undecided.'" Marty drew a deep breath. "I'm sorry, Brad."

"Not as sorry as I am," he growled. "I want copies of the results."

"I have them ready to put in the mail. You'll have them by tomorrow."

"I want them now."

Marty glanced at the clock on the wall and bit her lip. There would be no one here for her to leave them with if he came by. He had no right to be so imperious in his demand, but she couldn't ignore his frustration. "I'll drop them off at the store on my way home."

"Fine. Just leave them with my secretary."

"Of course." Marty let the phone slide gently onto the receiver. If that was the way he wanted it, she should only be glad. There was no sense in seeing him. Later she would try to sort out why he was being so cold; right now she just wanted to get the task over with.

She slipped into her suit jacket, murmured a goodbye to Virginia and walked out of the building clutching the envelope under her arm. During the walk she refused to think about Brad, or the test results. The sidewalks were crowded, and she concentrated on skirting people, catching lights and dodging cars. Her heel caught once in a hole and slightly wrenched her ankle, but she ignored the discomfort. If she'd known she was going to be taking a hike, she'd have worn her sneakers.

The store was full of people, probably buying supplies for their weekend remodeling projects. Marty went along the side to the office entry and rang the bell. Kerri appeared almost immediately, and Marty handed her the envelope.

"Aren't you coming in?" the young woman asked, surprised.

"No. Not this time."

"Well, I'll give it to Brad right away."

"Thanks."

Marty turned away quickly, feeling the sting of tears at her eyes. Ridiculous! If he wanted to act like a spoiled brat, she should be happy to be rid of him. A good meal would cure her silly sentimentality. She set her mind to deciding what was the most interesting restaurant for dinner. It was too painful to think about Brad.

Brad waited in the reception area for Kerri to return, half expecting her to have Marty with her. Instead she had only a manila envelope, which she turned over to him without a word. He nodded a curt thanks and walked into his office, closing the door firmly behind him. There was no need to see Marty Woods, he told himself. She'd done enough harm to him already. He was perfectly capable of reviewing the test results in light of the reading he'd done on paternity testing.

The forms didn't look quite as he'd expected, and it took him a few minutes to sort out what they meant. The pluses and zeros were clear enough, but the HLA results and the statistical probabilities were more confusing. He ran his eyes over the long list of blood factors, searching for a discrepancy that he knew wouldn't be there. With all those different elements, it seemed impossible that he wouldn't have been excluded, that the child wouldn't have had some factor that neither he nor the mother could have given her. There was none.

Still, he took some solace in the fact that his ranking was only "undecided." Surely that wasn't good enough to try to prove he was the father, especially when they couldn't possibly have any physical evidence to go along with it. Brad sat back in his old wooden chair and drummed his fingers against his desk. Marty had been very convinced of his responsibility when she first met him, which meant the mother told a good story. At a cut-and-dried hearing he wasn't going to have a chance to sway a judge's opinion with his personal charm and honesty. The judge would have heard a thousand of these cases and wasn't going to be impressed by Brad's declaration of innocence.

Without Marty's assistance, Brad suddenly felt enormously discouraged. The child wasn't his, of course, but if a hearing went against him, he would be ordered to pay child support until there was a full-blown trial, which would undoubtedly cost him a fortune. For that sort of thing he'd have to get a lawyer, and a good one. Maybe he should get one for the hearing, as Marty had urged him.

Brad glanced at his watch and found it was almost six. He was due to pick up Andrea for the weekend in a few minutes. Usually the thought of being able to spend time with his daughter cheered him. Tonight he merely wondered how he'd manage to push aside his problems so she wouldn't notice them. Brad believed that it was an adult's responsibility to keep worrisome concerns away from children, but Andrea was a bit too perceptive to make him feel certain he could do so at a time like this.

He stuffed the test results back in the manila envelope, which he folded and thrust into his jacket pocket. Kerri had left for the day when he emerged from his office, so he turned out all the lights and stood for a long moment in the darkened reception area. What he really wanted to do was talk to Marty. His hand moved toward the phone on his secretary's desk, then fell back to his side. She wouldn't be home yet. Worse, he had forgotten for a split second that she was not to be trusted. With a shrug of irritation at himself, he left the building.

By the time Brad arrived at the house, he'd decided he had to talk with someone, even if it was Karen. Maybe she'd know a little more about the legalities of a paternity case after her first year in law school than he did from his discussions with Marty. Funny, he wouldn't have thought of discussing it with her just a few weeks ago. In fact, it would have made him furious if she'd somehow found out about it.

Andrea answered the door, looking like a normal thirteen-year-old in blue jeans and a perfectly acceptable blouse, not one of those strange concoctions she was prone to dream up. Of course, they couldn't go anywhere fancy to eat, but they usually didn't, anyhow. She greeted him affectionately and turned to pick up the suitcase with her weekend's worth of clothes.

"Is your mother home?" he asked.

Andrea regarded him suspiciously. "Yes. She's in

the kitchen. You're not going to argue with her, are
you, Dad? She's had a hard day."

Brad stared at her. "Argue with her? Of course
not."

"Well," Andrea said, hunching her shoulders defensively, "you usually only want to talk with her
when you're upset at her."

Could that possibly be true? Brad tried to think
back over the last year and a half, tried to recall the
few meetings with Karen. There had been the "discussion" about where Andrea would spend Christmas,
and the "discussion" about who was spoiling her, and
the "discussion" about who should share in the payment for her orthodontic work. None of them had
really been discussions at all. He had always worked
himself up to a meeting with Karen by thinking of all
her wrongs against him, and by the time he sat down
with her he wasn't particularly calm.

He ruffled his daughter's black curls, smiling rather
ruefully. "It's nothing like that, Andy. Your mother
and I are going to get on a lot better now. We're not
always going to agree about you, but we're going to be
able to talk more rationally. Tonight I don't want to
talk about you at all. It's something else."

She didn't look as though she completely believed
him, but she nodded solemnly and disappeared toward the back of the house. When she returned,
Karen was following her, wiping her hands on a
dishtowel. Karen, too, looked slightly apprehensive.

"Hi, Brad. Andrea says you'd like to talk to me."

How did you explain to your former wife that you
had no intention of browbeating her? Brad dug his
hands into his pockets, flashed what was meant to be a
reassuring smile, and said, "Just a question I wanted

to ask you, actually. Alone," he added meaningfully with a glance at Andrea.

"Will you keep an eye on the chicken?" Karen asked her daughter.

Andrea hesitated before shuffling slowly off to the kitchen.

Karen led him into the living room, where she seated herself in one of the two armchairs opposite the sofa, her hands folded tightly in her lap. Brad took the other armchair, the one that had been his. He crossed his legs and then uncrossed them, leaning toward her. "I have a problem, Karen."

"Yes?"

"A legal problem."

"I've only had one year of law school so far. I doubt if I'd be able to help you, and Carl isn't home yet."

"I just want your advice, you know, about whether I should get a lawyer or not."

Karen lifted her shoulders in a helpless shrug. "Any lawyer is going to tell you to get an attorney if you have a legal problem, Brad. I could give you names of several good people."

The conversation was not progressing as Brad had hoped. Determined to get to the heart of the matter, he blurted, "I'm being sued for paternity."

For just the briefest moment she stared at him. Then her lips twitched, and though she tried not to, she burst out laughing. She held a hand up by way of apology, but she couldn't speak for a minute.

"This is serious," he protested.

"I'm sorry. I know it is." Her amusement faded, and a worried frown took its place. "Is it your child, Brad?"

"I haven't become some kind of libertine," he said.

"I don't even *know* this woman who says I fathered her daughter."

There was a gasp from the doorway, and Andrea ran into the room, her eyes enormous. "I have a sister? And you never told me? What's her name? What does she look like? How old is she?"

"You two aren't listening to me!" Brad roared. "I don't know this woman! I've never met her!"

"Then a blood test will exclude you," Karen remarked.

Brad waved the manila envelope at them. "The blood test didn't exclude me! It should have. Everyone told me it would exclude me if I wasn't the father. I'm not the father and I didn't get excluded. The probability falls in an undecided range. All I want to know is whether I should get a lawyer to represent me at the hearing if there can't be any physical evidence and the tests are inconclusive."

"I don't have a sister?" Andrea sounded disappointed.

"No, you don't have a sister," he growled. "For God's sake, Andrea, aren't things complicated enough?"

Karen slipped the manila envelope from his hand and pulled the test sheets out onto her lap. She frowned at the maze of letters, numbers, zeros and pluses. "How do you tell if you're excluded?"

"The child has to get each factor from one or the other of its parents. If neither the mother nor I had some particular element that the child had, then I'd be ruled out, because the real father would have to have it."

"It must be kind of rare to get results like this," Karen mused. "Look how often you and the mother have the same factors. Are you sure you're not related to her?"

"Of course I'm sure! I'd never even *heard* of her until this thing came up. The first thing I knew was when some guy served me with a Summons of Complaint. I thought they'd got my name on it by mistake."

Andrea was leaning over her mother's shoulder. "Cheryl. That's the baby's name. How pretty. And the mother's name is Lydia. Didn't we know someone named Lydia?"

"Not this Lydia!" Brad muttered.

"That was Lydia Stoneham," Karen explained. Her gaze lifted to Brad's. "Why would this Lydia Brown accuse you of being the father? How would she know who you are?"

Brad hammered a fist against the chair arm. "I don't know. That's what's driving me crazy, that and the fact that no one believes me. You know I don't lie, Karen. You have to believe me."

"Of course." She turned to Andrea and said, "The chicken's going to burn, love. Please go keep an eye on it."

Andrea's gaze flashed back and forth between them. "You just don't want me to be here because you're going to talk about something 'mature,'" she objected.

Her mother laughed and gave her a purposeful shove in the direction of the kitchen. "That's right. Run along."

Scowling, Andrea stomped from the room.

"What's she talking about?" Brad asked.

"She knows we're going to talk about your sex life and that she's excluded from the discussion."

"Who says we're going to talk about my sex life?" Brad demanded hotly. "I'm not going to talk about my sex life!"

Karen settled back against the plush chair and folded her arms across her chest, imitating his favorite position when they were having a "discussion." She didn't seem at all disturbed by his heated objection. "Brad, do you remember how upset you were when I filed for a divorce?"

"That has nothing to do with why I'm here."

"No, but it might have had a lot to do with how you behaved during that period. I'm not saying I don't believe you. I'm saying you may have drunk too much and taken some young woman home from a bar and slept with her . . . and not remembered it afterwards."

"I never did that! Never! If I wanted to drink, I drank at my house. I only went out with a few women during all that time, and they were ones people fixed me up with. None of them interested me. I never got drunk and took home some woman whose name I didn't even know." Brad raked long fingers through his wavy hair. "Besides, that's not how this Lydia woman says it happened, either. Marty says she can describe my office right down to the swimming trophy. I'm supposed to have gone with her over a period of time."

"Marty?" Karen cocked her head at him. "The Marty I met at the party the other night?"

Brad hadn't meant to mention Marty's name. Reluctantly, he admitted, "Yes, she's an investigator with the Paternity Unit for the district attorney's office."

"Wow! You sure do love to complicate your life."

"I didn't mean to start seeing her." A scowl settled over his features. "And I won't be seeing her anymore."

"That's probably wise, Brad. She could get in a lot of trouble seeing you while she's handling the case."

Her concern for Marty seemed like the last straw to Brad. "Why isn't anyone sympathetic about *my* problem? Some woman I don't even know is suing me for paternity, and all anyone cares about is whether Marty might lose her job. She could get another job! She's competent and clever and attractive and intelligent and she could do a lot better than investigating paternity cases, anyhow! It would probably be the best thing that ever happened to her, whereas everyone seems to think it's just fine that for the rest of my life I may have to support some kid with whom I have no connection!"

He stomped from the room, but not before Karen called, "You should definitely get a lawyer." From the hall he bellowed to Andrea, picked up her suitcase and marched out the door, leaving it open for her to follow him.

Chapter Thirteen

Harry Mills regarded Marty curiously as he sipped his wine. "I thought this case was open and shut."

"Well, it would have been, if the test results were better," she said. Her lunch was still mostly untouched—a hamburger so large it was hard to get her mouth around it. The assistant district attorney was a busy man; he couldn't afford the time to go further than the cafe down the block. "There's always been the problem of not having any physical evidence. Lydia doesn't have any pictures of him, or any letters from him, though she described his office perfectly. She never told him she was pregnant, because he dropped her before she found out." She had to be very careful to phrase this case as she would have any of the other ones she and Harry had gone over for years now.

"How bad could the test results be, if he wasn't excluded?"

"They're rather unusual, actually. He falls in the 'undecided' range. Both he and the mother have factors statistically more common than most people would." Marty forced herself to take a bite of the hamburger and chewed it carefully. "All you have to go on is the mother's word, when you get right down to it."

"Then it will be a challenge," he declared, raising his chin pugnaciously. "I love taking on these smart-ass lawyers the fathers get. They don't seem to understand that at a hearing the judge has heard it all before."

Marty didn't know whether it would help or hinder Brad's case to mention that, so far as she knew, he hadn't gotten a lawyer. "The mother sounds very sincere, but she's alone here and has no one to back up her story. She's young and rather naive; her testimony might be shaken by an aggressive attorney."

Harry considered this for a moment. "What does the father have to say about the relationship?"

It almost embarrassed Marty to tell him, but she kept her voice as neutral as humanly possible. "He says he's never heard of her."

Harry snorted. "Sure thing. That clinches it, as far as I'm concerned. What do we have to lose, anyhow? A few hours of our time, which I grant you is highly expensive time, but it's what we're paid to do. We'd have to justify not pursuing it if we didn't, and you say she's sincere."

"I said she *sounds* sincere."

"What's the difference? Do you have any reason to doubt her?"

When Marty hesitated, Harry's brows rose. "Well, do you?" he asked.

"He's very credible, too. It's difficult to prove something negative. If he actually didn't know her, how could he prove it?"

"He could have proved it by being excluded," Harry said dismissively. "So maybe we lose this one. It can't hurt to give it a try. Is the guy loaded or something?"

Marty winced. "He's reasonably well off, I think. Just coming out of a divorce, though."

Harry nodded his head knowledgeably. "Just the kind of situation where a guy gets involved with someone he'd like to forget later on. We'll go for it, Marty. And we'll win it," he added, confident. "You'll see. I'll get a hearing date for us."

Though her stomach churned, Marty took a bite of her hamburger. It was easier than trying to show any enthusiasm.

Back in her office she drew a deep breath and dialed Brad's work number. There was no reason to believe he'd be any less bristly about this news than he'd been a few days previously about the test results. While the phone rang at the other end, Marty decided to leave a cleverly worded message that would tell him what was happening without conveying anything to his secretary—something like: the case will continue, or the matter will proceed. However, when Kerri answered the phone and heard who was calling, she didn't wait for Marty to say anything further, but put the call straight through.

"Macintosh."

She could feel her spine straighten. He was *not* going to intimidate her. "It's Marty Woods. I wanted to let you know that the assistant district attorney has decided to go ahead with the complaint."

"What does that mean?"

"He'll get a date for a hearing at which the judge will determine whether you're to pay temporary child support. If you want a trial after that, it will be put on the docket. You'll be advised of the hearing date."

There was a long silence at the other end of the line. Marty was just considering hanging up when he said, "You got me into this mess; now I want you to get me out."

"I didn't get you into it, Brad. When I talked with Harry Mills, I pointed out the weaknesses in the case, but he decided to go ahead with it. I can't do anything more than that."

"You could tell him you know I'm not the father."

"He'd just ask me how I know, and what would I tell him? I don't have anything on which to base my belief."

"*Do* you believe me?" he demanded.

She could feel the tension in his voice. It sent tremors along her nerve endings, making her hand shake slightly as she held the phone. "I want to believe you."

"That's not good enough! Why in hell doesn't anyone just believe me? It can't possibly be that difficult. When have I ever lied to anyone? I don't even lie to the IRS, for God's sake! I don't even write off lunches with friends as business lunches! I tell the truth. Ask anyone. Why can't you just believe me?"

"It's my job not to believe you."

"Bull! Your job is to sue the child's father for child support. I'm not the child's father. If I was the child's father, I'd pay child support."

"Brad, I have to go by the rules."

"Rules are for idiots. Rules are for people who can't figure out how to do things right. You're not supposed to follow the rules when they bring about injustice. You're supposed to look for the truth, especially when it's hiding."

Her other hand had begun to shake. "Where do you suggest I look for the truth, Brad?"

"Make that woman tell you the truth. She's lying to you."

"I've talked with her several times. She's very young; I can't harass her."

"Then take me with you to see her."

"What would you do, Brad? Yell at her the way you're yelling at me? You'll have a chance to question her at the hearing, and not before."

He sighed. "I'm sorry. This is driving me crazy, Marty. Why me? What did I do to deserve this?"

Marty frowned at a pencil lying half buried by her desk blotter. What indeed had he done? "You know, Brad," she said slowly, "that might be exactly how you're going to get to the answer . . . figuring out what you did."

"But I didn't do anything! I don't know her, Marty. She never worked at the store. I've even asked some of the people here, and no one has ever heard of her."

"Ask all of them. Ask your friends. Look what you have to go on, Brad. She's been in your office. There's simply no doubt about it. Someone could have told her what's there, of course, but it's unlikely. The only jobs she's had in San Francisco are waitressing ones, so she couldn't have been there as a supplier's rep. And remember, you're concerned with the period of December and January of over a year ago. That's when she has to have gotten pregnant."

"You do believe me, don't you?" he demanded suddenly.

Her voice shook slightly. "I suppose I do, but it's

not going to make any difference in how I conduct the case, Brad. I have a job to do, and I'm going to do it right."

"Your job is to find the child's father."

"And the child's mother insists that you're the one. The blood tests don't exclude you. The assistant district attorney is satisfied. This is a stalemate, Brad."

"No, it isn't. I'm going to pick you up at five o'clock, in front of your office, and you're going to put in some overtime getting the right answer to this one."

Marty drew a shaky breath. "I thought you were mad at me."

"We'll discuss that when I see you," he said and hung up.

"Where are we going?" she asked as she settled nervously into the Volvo.

"To my place."

She had meant which restaurant. It hadn't even occurred to her that he would take her home—now. It was not a good idea, now or later, but she asked only, "Are you going to cook?"

Brad gestured toward a bag of groceries resting on the back seat. "Sure. Andrea's been teaching me how."

Marty's question had been rhetorical, to a certain extent. It had been meant to remind him that she wasn't a cook, and therefore their best bet was to have a meal at a restaurant. She felt dubious about any skill he could have acquired, especially when he hadn't shown the least interest in cooking such a short time ago. "What are you going to make?"

"Nothing too difficult." He turned to study her skeptical expression. "Steak with sautéed mushrooms, and baked potatoes and salad. Something even you could do."

"Maybe. You're going to ask me to sauté the mushrooms, aren't you, Brad?"

"Why not?"

"Because that's the sort of thing I always ruin. Something that sounds really easy and unruinable. I can't be trusted with cooking."

"Which reminds me." His face became suddenly grim. "I'm not at all sure you can be trusted, period. What right did you have telling that male mannequin that I was one of your paternity fathers?"

It took Marty a moment to realize he was speaking of Jim and their encounter on Sunday. "Jim was the assistant D.A. who prosecuted paternity cases before Harry Mills. If I mentioned your name to him, it wasn't some divulging of confidence. Jim knows all about my work, and I know a great deal about his."

"You didn't tell me you owned the building with him."

Marty shrugged. "Why should I? It was the only way I could buy into San Francisco real estate, doing it with someone else. We don't all have the money to buy a house whenever we want a new one." This last was said pointedly, as they pulled into the driveway of Brad's house.

Brad sat unmoving, his mournful gaze on the small, brown, shingled house. "I didn't buy it because I wanted it. I bought it because I had to have a place to live."

"Some people have to rent an apartment when they need a place to live."

"All right, so I could afford to buy a place. What does that have to do with your owning a building with some jerk?"

"He's not a jerk. He has idiosyncrasies, but then everyone I know does . . . including you. For instance, you've sat around mad all week because I only own half of a building when you thought I owned all of it."

"That's not why I was mad."

"Then tell me why you were."

"Because you'd talked to that guy about me; he identified me right off as one of your paternity cases. That's a private matter between you and me, not for general circulation."

"I'm sorry I mentioned your name to him, but wouldn't it have been better for you to call and tell me what the problem was, rather than sulk all week?"

Brad glared at her. "I wasn't sulking. I wasn't going to ever have anything more to do with you."

"*Much* more serious than a sulk," Marty pronounced gravely. "Haven't you noticed it's better to talk something out than hold a grudge?"

"You could have called me."

"After the case, maybe, not at this point. It was better for me not to be in touch with you."

His hands moved to frame her face. "It wasn't good for me. I wanted to touch you. After that night I wanted to have you naked beside me, to run my hands over your body, to feel and taste every silky inch of you." He ran his hands down along her neck, over her shoulders and, pushing back her suit jacket, enclosed her breasts. Marty felt a wave of instant pleasure rush over her, intensifying as his thumbs rubbed insistently over her nipples. As they hardened, he slid one hand inside her blouse and under her bra to catch the peak between his thumb and forefinger, rolling it back and forth until her body tensed with anticipation.

They were sitting in the car in broad daylight in his driveway, and Marty drew back, saying, "Not here, Brad."

"Hm?" He blinked across at her. "Oh, of course not. Sorry. You haven't even seen the house yet."

Marty would willingly have skipped a tour of the house at that moment, but Brad started taking his role as host seriously. He gathered the bag of groceries from the back seat, slid out of the car and came around to open Marty's door. "It only has two bedrooms and one bath, but there's potential for some expansion out the back. I've been meaning to retile the kitchen but haven't gotten around to it yet. The place isn't as clean as it might be; I had a cleaning service in on Friday, but Andrea was with me over the weekend, so it's messed up again."

He led her up a flagstone path to the front door, which he unlocked while balancing the bag of groceries in his other arm. They entered a small hallway with a staircase opposite. Marty felt sure the bedroom was upstairs, but Brad led her to the right, through the dining room into the kitchen. As he set the shopping bag on the counter, Brad gestured toward the oven with his head. "Set it to 425, okay? I want to put the potatoes in to bake right away."

Fascinated, Marty turned on the oven—one of the few things she felt capable of doing in a kitchen. He was already washing off two plump potatoes, which he dried and greased with butter before putting them in the oven. "The cookbook says you shouldn't wrap them in aluminum foil because they retain too much moisture," he informed her.

"Oh."

"They don't get flaky enough. Baked potatoes are supposed to get flaky."

"Right."

"We can leave everything else right where it is," he said, flipping the steaks out on the counter and leaving the salad makings in the bag. "I'll show you the rest of the house now."

This time he paused when they entered the dining room. "I got the oak table when I first moved in, but I haven't bothered to find any oak chairs." He surveyed the room as though surprised to note the incongruity of an antique oak table with metal folding chairs, and nothing else in the whole room. "It's pretty barren, isn't it? Andrea's been after me to do something with it but I haven't really felt like it." His gaze returned to Marty, a faintly puzzled look in his eyes. "Maybe soon . . ."

The look disturbed Marty, and she wandered away from him, through the hall and into the living room. "You seem to have everything you need here."

It was a surprisingly masculine room, with the sole exception of the sofa. The chairs were brown leather and the table, bookshelves and stereo cabinet were dark wood in hard, straight lines with an almost aggressive functionalism. The sofa was whimsical—large, soft-looking and colorful, a complete contrast to everything else in the room.

"Andrea insisted on it," he said, following Marty's eyes to the sofa. "Everything else came from my study at the old house. She said it looked like I was too serious and that guests would need a comfortable place to sit. Try it."

Marty crossed the room and lowered herself onto a puffy cushion. Her body sank slowly into the sofa as though she were being enveloped by an enormous pillow. Startled, she giggled nervously. Brad grinned down at her. "Neat, isn't it?" he asked.

"Yes, once you get used to it. Isn't it impossible to get out of it?"

"No, but don't try yet. I'll join you."

He sat down directly beside her, so close that the shift in the sofa made her list toward him. His arms went around her, drawing her against his chest. "To hell with the house tour," he muttered. "You can see it later."

His lips on hers were eager, their warmth and pressure calling forth a similar response from her. His physical presence was so strong, her reaction so predictable. She was in his house, in his arms. If she wasn't going to go through with this aspect of their relationship, she should say so now. His hand moved surely over her breast, stroking, rubbing, tempting. With a shaky sigh she began to unbutton her blouse. There was no sense in fighting this attraction any longer.

He smiled as he watched her, but not, she thought, because her fingers shook slightly. When the blouse was totally unfastened, he helped her remove it along with her jacket. Then he reached behind to unfasten her bra and tossed it aside. Her breasts seemed small to her, but his eyes devoured them for long moments as she lay back against the sofa, waiting for him to touch them, to make her body sing with desire as he always did. He lowered his head to take one rosy nipple into his mouth, toying it with his tongue, then sucking hard against the stiffening bud.

An urgency coursed through her, a need that grew more powerful with each movement of his mouth. His hands were not still either; one of them massaged her other breast and then slowly descended to the button on her skirt. It hesitated only long enough to effect release. He continued to draw at her nipple as he pushed her skirt, panty hose and underpants down over her thighs. His hand returned to the triangle of hair between her legs, a finger gliding to the most sensitive of spots. Marty felt her body twist with an agony of pleasure.

She kissed the crown of his head, hugging him against her as the fever rose in her body. Though she tried to reach him, to run her hands over his thighs, he whispered against her flesh, "Not yet, sweetheart. I want to concentrate on you for a few minutes. I want to taste more of you." Gently he settled her in a lying position on the sofa, then crouched beside her on the floor. Starting with her lips, he licked and tasted his way down the length of her body, taking his time, and causing her an ecstasy of sensation.

Marty moaned, writhing uncontrollably as his lips and tongue built a rhythm within her body. "Oh, no. Please, I can't . . . Oh, God." The rhythm had taken on a life of its own, rising, rising, rising, until it crashed over her.

"It's okay, Marty," Brad assured her. His hands played soothingly over her shuddering flesh, calming now where they had aroused a moment before. He kissed the glistening skin on her forehead. "It's beautiful to watch you."

Marty's smile was bemused. She closed her arms tightly around him. "Oh, Brad. Come in me now." Her brows drew slightly together. "But use something. We can't take any chances."

His hands stopped in their progress down her body. "But I don't *have* anything, Marty. I thought you'd be protected."

The mists of pleasure were rapidly clearing away

from Marty's head. "Why would I be protected?" she demanded. "Do you think I carry something around in my purse all the time just in case I decide to hop into bed with some man I meet?"

"Of course not, but I thought maybe you'd be on the pill or something."

Marty sat up against the sofa and glared at him. "I don't believe this. You expected *me* to be protected, even though I had no way of knowing that we might make love today, even though we came to *your* house. You expected *me* to be on the pill. Why? Do you think I'm promiscuous, Brad?"

"It's not a question of promiscuous, Marty. Women these days are supposed to . . . you know . . . be prepared for sex whenever they decide to have it."

Marty threw her hands up in despair. "You can't be that gullible. Are all women the same, Brad? Do they all do the same things? Do you think every available woman you meet out on the street is on the pill or has some birth control protection in her purse?" Her eyes narrowed in concentration. "Is that how you got Lydia pregnant? Did you assume she was protected?"

For a moment he frowned uncomprehendingly. Then he exploded. "You said you believed me! Why do you keep changing your mind?"

Marty was vaguely conscious of her nakedness, but she was far more interested in getting to the heart of this matter. She bent toward him, pointing a finger at his chest. "You think all women are basically the same, don't you, Brad? If you're attracted to them sexually, and they're willing, what's to stop you? You're certainly not going to be stopped by a little matter of birth control."

"That's not what I think!" he insisted. "I don't think all women are the same! I thought you'd be on the pill because you were probably sleeping with that guy who owns the building with you."

"That does it!" she shouted, jumping up and grabbing for her bra and blouse. "So now I'm sleeping with Jim, am I? Do you know what sort of woman that makes me, Brad? I suppose it would be okay with you if I slept with both of you. You'd just think that was a wonderful thing. You don't give a flying damn about me!"

In her rage she was having a difficult time hooking her bra. Her fingers kept getting tangled with the flap, and she gave a little stomp of annoyance. Brad stepped behind her and hooked it as though he'd been doing it for years. Marty glared at him as she shrugged into her blouse. "Maybe you think you're just too damned attractive to resist!" she snapped. "I've known more handsome men. I've known *taller* men!"

Instead of being devastated by her low blow, he grinned at her. "Now, now. It's been a long time since I accused you of not being feminine enough for me, and I apologized for it." He watched her pull her bikini underpants hurriedly up her sleek legs. "I'm not going to get any taller than I am now, Marty."

She glanced up at him, and grimaced. "All right. I'm sorry but you're infuriating, Brad. You're being irresponsible, and trying to blame it on me. Everything you've said makes me sound like some kind of floozy." Putting on panty hose when you were upset was very difficult, Marty discovered. She decided it wasn't actually necessary to put them back on, and stuffed them in her purse before slipping on her skirt. When she was dressed more or less to her satisfaction, she faced him directly. "You can take me home now, or call me a cab."

Brad shook his head. "I'm not going to have you

leave in a huff, Marty. You told me earlier I should have talked things out with you, instead of holding a grudge. Now I'm going to insist that you do the same."

They had a short, fierce glaring duel. Marty was the first to look away, and sigh. "All right, Brad, but you aren't necessarily going to like what I have to say."

"Then we'd better eat first," he suggested. "Come on, I want you to help with the salad."

Chapter Fourteen

Marty was surprised at how well they worked together in the kitchen. Because he was new to cooking himself, Brad assumed she knew as little about it as he did and was very specific in his instructions. A satisfactory arrangement, considering her limited skill. While he broiled the steaks and sautéed the mushrooms, Marty managed to turn out two avocado salads that looked just like the picture in the book he showed her.

"Well done!" He gave her a quick kiss on the tip of her nose. "Andrea says it doesn't have to be complicated to look elegant and taste good. I told her I was more interested in easy than elegant."

"It's obviously both, or I couldn't have done it."

"You underestimate yourself."

"No," she said, frowning, "but I may overextend myself when I try to cook. Making one thing is a whole lot simpler than trying to throw together a gourmet dinner with five dishes, especially when you don't know what you're doing."

Brad pulled the steaks from the oven. "Apparently the hard part is getting everything to come out at the same time. Andrea says you just can't start making this and that; you have to set a time when you're going to eat, and work toward it."

"Andrea sounds like one smart kid." Then, because she couldn't help teasing him, she said, "When does she recommend you set the table?"

Startled, he glanced through the door to the dining room, where the table was still bare. "You can't get everything right the first few times," he grumbled.

"Or even the first few dozen," Marty agreed as she pulled drawers open in search of flatware. "I know from experience."

"We're going to get it right together," he insisted. "If I can learn to cook, you can."

"What if I don't want to? What if cooking doesn't interest me?" She stood at the counter, hands full of flatware, glaring at him.

"Well, it didn't interest me a few weeks ago."

"If it hasn't interested me for twenty years, it's not going to start now, Brad."

He shrugged. "Suit yourself." The grease was still spitting in the broiler pan, and he transferred the steaks to individual plates as she moved into the dining room to set the table. He pulled the baked potatoes from the oven and slit them open. Marty searched for the butter, salt and pepper. "There's sour cream in the fridge, too," he said.

"I can't force myself to be something I'm not, just to please you," she said.

"Nobody's asking you to."

"Humpf," she muttered.

"*I'm* changing, aren't I?"

Marty seated herself in the chair he held for her, and sniffed. "That remains to be seen. Making a meal is something girls are expected to learn before they're twenty. Do you expect me to get excited about someone doing it at thirty-five?"

"You're a hard woman, Marty."

"Maybe I am. Sometimes I have to be, for my job. Sometimes I need to be, when I think I may be getting in over my head, like now, with you."

He sat down opposite her, a frown shifting his wild eyebrows. "What do you mean—'getting in over your head'?"

Marty wouldn't meet his eyes. Instead she cut a bite of steak and chewed it thoroughly before she answered. "The steak is terrific, Brad, and you're a good man. We just don't seem to be right for each other, you know? You keep expecting me to be a different kind of woman, and I need you to be a different kind of man."

"What kind of man do you need me to be?" he demanded. "I thought you'd be pleased that I'm learning to cook. The only reason I decided to do it seriously was because you didn't. I could have survived the way I was, but I thought if we were going to, you know, spend a lot of time together, one of us had better know how to cook."

Tears suddenly stung at Marty's eyes. He was trying so hard, and he really was remarkably dear to her. How did she explain that to him, and at the same time show him that their real differences made it impossible for them to mesh? She dropped a spoonful of sour cream on her baked potato and worked it in with her fork, hoping the distraction would help rid her eyes of the unwanted gleam of tears. She suspected it could only be dangerous to show Brad any vulnerability.

Without looking up, she said, "I appreciate your learning to cook. Honestly I do, but I don't *want* you to have to change. I don't want to have to change so we fit together. It doesn't work that way, not in the long run."

"I don't know what the hell you're talking about! And who said anything about the long run, anyhow?"

Marty's gaze swung up to catch the defensive glare in his eyes. "Exactly," she said softly. "I have enough purely ethical reasons not to get involved with you. Knowing there's no future in it just adds to my resolution, Brad."

"I didn't say there wasn't any future! You're putting words in my mouth."

"I don't mean to. Let's say *I* believe there's no future in it and let it go at that, okay?"

There was a slight pause before he muttered, "Your dinner's getting cold. We'll discuss this after you eat."

Marty accepted this decision, but stored it, with the other instances of his high-handedness, in her memory. These instances she intended to produce immediately after she completed her meal and was once again harassed by his questioning. It wouldn't be so difficult to illustrate for him how often he expected her to simply fall in line with his commands. She would make it very clear that she could not imagine a relationship where the man and woman weren't partners. She couldn't tolerate a situation where his opinions or his wishes were supposed to have more weight than hers.

She finished her meal but a stubbornness was growing in her. Yes, it was time she set him straight on several matters. When she set down her fork, she faced him with a militant gleam in her eye.

"Do you love me?" he asked.

The unexpectedness of the question stunned her. For a long moment she sat blinking at him, unable to utter a sound. "That's not at all a fair question," she insisted when she finally managed to speak. "It doesn't have anything to do with what's wrong between us, like your annoying attitude that you're the more important one between us. You assume that my morals are loose, and you expect me to change in the ways you want. And . . ."

Brad waved a hand interrupting her list of objections. "None of those things matter if you don't love me. Do you?"

Marty was *not* going to answer his question. "What do you mean they don't matter? Of course they matter—to me, at any rate."

"Yes, but look, Marty. If you didn't intend to see me ever again, would it make any difference to you if I did socially unacceptable things like eating with my hands? If you didn't care about me, you'd just shrug your shoulders and walk away, right?"

"That's what I'm trying to tell you I'm going to do—walk away."

"No, you're not." He said it with supreme confidence, leaning back against his chair until it tilted off the floor. "Maybe you'd like to, because I tick you off sometimes, but you're too attached to me to walk away permanently." At her narrow-eyed glare he added hastily, "And I wouldn't want you to. I'm attached to you, too."

"Wonderful!" Marty threw her hands up in a gesture of frustration. "You think that solves everything, do you? Is that supposed to make me forget that you boss me around or that you have chauvinist tendencies? Well, it doesn't!"

Brad allowed his chair to settle back down on the floor. His lips were pursed thoughtfully and his brows drawn down into shaggy dashes over his eyes. "You seem to think I didn't learn anything from my marriage. Well, maybe I *did* refuse to figure out what went wrong for a long time, but I think I have it straight now. If I revert to old habits, all you have to do is tell me to shape up. That's not so tough, is it?"

"Of course it's tough! It would make me feel like a nag. No one wants to be a nag."

He reached across the table and clasped her rigid hands. "Don't think of it as being a nag, Marty. Think of it as reeducating me or something. Think of it as the way we're going to manage to be together . . . and that it's important for the two of us to be together."

Marty didn't withdraw her hands from his grip, though she felt shaken by his calm assumption. *Was* it important for the two of them to be together? A kind of anxiety gripped her, making her chest feel tight and her breath come in rapid, shallow gasps. She wasn't ready to admit how important he was to her. She wanted to pretend that this was still a tentative attachment. It was too soon, surely, to have to face what the long-term consequences of her feelings for Brad might be.

Meeting his eyes was especially difficult, but when she did, she found his gaze warm and full of tenderness. "Maybe it is important for the two of us to be together," she admitted, her voice husky. "I don't want to walk away if I don't have to."

"I'm not going to let you, not unless you have a better reason than you've given me so far." He released her hands and stood up. "I forgot to get anything for dessert. If you promise not to disappear, I'll go out and pick something up real quick."

"I won't disappear, but it's not necessary to get dessert."

"I'd like to. It'll only take a few minutes."

Marty watched as he shrugged into a jacket. As soon as he was gone, she carried their dishes into the kitchen and started cleaning up.

Brad returned in a half hour with a frozen chocolate cake and a container of coffee ice cream. "Will that be okay?" he asked.

"Sounds great. I don't really need both cake and ice cream."

"No, but two are better than one." He shoved the package of frozen cake across the counter toward her. "Why don't you open that while I get a couple of plates and a knife?"

Marty uncrimped the aluminum foil and lifted off the cardboard top of the package. Inside, a piece of cake had already been removed, and in its place was a small silver package that could have come only from a drugstore. Marty choked on a laugh as she felt his hands come around her waist.

"That's for a different dessert," he said smugly.

"You lunatic!" she muttered, scooping the tiny package out of the cake container and dropping it on the counter. "This cake has to defrost for a while before we can eat it."

"I can think of the perfect way to spend our time while we're waiting."

"So can I." Marty unfastened his hands from around her waist and held them as she turned to face him. "Thank you, Brad. It's important to me."

"Of course it is," he said, his voice gruff. "It's

important to me, too, and I just wasn't being responsible before. I don't think I ever really thought you were having an affair with that fellow in your building. The main thing I thought was that I hoped to hell you weren't!"

Marty leaned against him, unable to resist for another moment the warmth of his body against hers. "With you, I could be promiscuous," she whispered into his shoulder. She could feel the rumble of his laughter through his chest.

His hands caressed her hair, moving slowly through the curls down to massage her neck. Then he turned her face upward, and his lips traced a path down her forehead, over her nose and ending with her mouth. Marty savored the warm pressure and returned it with sensuous enthusiasm, her arms tightening around his waist. It always surprised her how quickly her body responded to his slightest touch. His hands were still at the back of her neck, with only his lips on hers, but she could feel the desire already working its way through her.

When his tongue slid into her mouth she experienced a tremor of anticipation. The moist tip of it caressed the hardness of her teeth and the velvety softness of the fleshy lining. A slight feeling of suction seemed to draw on the very recesses of her body, tugging at her erotic zones like a moon swelling the tide. She sighed as his tongue darted teasingly in and out of her mouth, too elusive for her to capture. The feeling of chaos increased inside her, the riot of luscious tensions pressing for release.

Brad drew back slightly, running his fingers down her arms. "I think we belong in the bedroom, Marty."

A shiver ran through her, and he cocked his head questioningly. She was too immersed in her need and could not speak; she merely nodded. He clasped her hand, drawing her behind him through the dining room and into the hall. There he slipped a small paper bag out of his jacket pocket before leading Marty up the carpeted stairs. The bedroom into which he took her had a ceiling that sloped downward on two sides, making the room feel like a cave. The feeling was enhanced by the smallness of the front windows, which lent an air of secrecy to the place.

While Marty walked over to the windows, Brad turned on a bedside lamp that cast a golden light over the spartan room. The windows looked out over the street and a partial view of the city beyond. Marty stood there trying to pay attention to the view until Brad moved behind her, pressing his body into the curves of hers and kissing the flesh at her nape. With one hand he drew the curtain cord, closing the beige curtains over the view. Marty turned to meet him.

His face with its wild eyebrows and unnerving blue eyes, had become so important to her that she almost blurted out that yes, she did love him. She wanted nothing more than to be there with him, knowing that their bodies would join, that it would be right for them to share that bed across the room in mutual passion. But it wasn't the moment to tell him that. There would be time to explore these feelings, and he would need time to sort out his own. Right now what seemed most urgent was the desire that sparked between them, that made the breath catch in her throat even when no part of her body touched his, when only his eyes spoke of his delight in her.

Brad carefully began to unbutton her blouse. She stood unmoving as he opened and removed it, hanging it over a straight-backed chair beside them. With her bra still on he cupped her breasts, rubbing his thumbs rhythmically across the silky fabric until her nipples hardened. Again a wave of desire swept through her, causing her to strain forward against his hands. He reached behind her to release the bra, allowing it to slide down her arms and onto the floor. For a long moment he just stared at her breasts, with their firm nipples and swollen fullness. Then he rubbed the backs of his fingers back and forth across the tips, watching her eyes grow sultry and hearing her breath quicken.

Slowly he unfastened her skirt and slid it down, along with her underpants, until she stood naked in front of him. Then, without a word, he stripped himself, revealing his almost painful eagerness for a joining with her. Marty walked into his open arms, feeling his hardness against her lower torso, urgent but not yet insistent. He lifted her against his hips, and she tightened her legs around him so he could carry her to the bed.

They tumbled onto the mattress, flesh on flesh, pulses racing, breath coming almost too quickly. Before their joining each of them seemed to want to touch the other, to feel each inch of sensitive skin, to taste the special flavors of an aroused body. Brad's mouth closed over her nipple, stroking, tugging, kissing, lapping, nursing. His fingers meanwhile trailed over her stomach and down through the patch of curly brown hair to the center of her longing. The ache grew between her thighs.

Her own fingers found him, loving the feel of him and this intimate knowledge of his maleness, his potency. He groaned from the pleasure of her touch, shifting so that she could reach him more easily.

His hands wandered over her, now soothing, now

raising the sensory level so close to its height that she gasped with sharpened awareness. She found that not only her breasts were sensitive to his touch but also the curve of her hip, the hollow of her neck and the bareness of her forearm. His fingers slid into her mouth, and she sucked on them with an urgency that almost frightened her, wanting him in her, on her, a part of her. The fever in her body burned so brightly she felt her skin must be dangerous to touch, but he dared to stroke it, and to leave a moist trail with his tongue, cooling her only momentarily.

Finally, when she thought she couldn't bear the tactile pleasure any longer, when she feared she would collapse from the prolonged dazzle of this arousal, he slid onto her. He did not enter yet, merely lying there as he reached for the paper bag he'd left on the bedside table. She wanted him in her so badly she almost cried out for him not to bother, but watched in silence as his hands moved quickly, surely. She loved him for his care, for his remembering, when he'd so aroused her that she'd long forgotten.

Their hot bodies touched from head to toe, melting against each other with the ache of longing. Brad slid between her legs but not inside of her, moving himself slowly back and forth against the sensitive peak. Her breathing further quickened, her hands clenched against his back, her body arched upward to him.

When he had raised her desire to staggering, unbelievable heights, he seemed to sense the exact moment to enter her. Waves of shattering release crashed on her, taking over her mind as well as her body, engulfing her in a bliss that seemed on an entirely different level from her ordinary life. She clung to him, shaken, whispering his name. He collapsed against her, kissing her face, running his hands lightly through her sweat-dampened hair.

"Oh, Marty," he sighed. "You wonderful, adorable, luscious, exciting woman. How lucky I am to have found you."

Her breathing was only gradually returning to normal. "You're not half bad yourself," she whispered, her voice catching a little.

He wiped moisture from her forehead and kissed the tip of her nose. "Do you still think you could be promiscuous with me?"

She laughed. "What did you have in mind?"

"First off, I think we should do this again soon."

Marty, pretending carelessness, gave a shrug. "I suppose I could go along with that."

"And then I think we should do it frequently after that."

There was a lump in her throat which wouldn't go away when she swallowed. "We'll have to see, Brad. This kind of magic can make you forget some of the other things in your life, even important things."

He traced the line of her jaw with his finger. "It *was* magic, wasn't it? When you find magic, Marty, you don't ignore it."

"I know you don't. I also know magic is illusion; it can fool you. You have to be careful with it."

"You're too cautious, too practical," he scolded. "Sometimes you just have to live for the moment. Like tonight."

"Which I did," she said lightly. "Don't try to bully me, Brad. I'm twenty-nine years old, not twelve. I have to decide for myself what I want out of life . . . and out of our relationship."

With a puzzled frown, he rolled over onto the side

of the bed and propped himself on an elbow. "But I thought you wanted to keep seeing me."

"I do. I just want you to understand that it has to be *my* decision, not just yours."

"I don't see the difference. Either you want to see me or you don't."

"There's a big difference. I wish you could see it." Marty smiled slightly, trying to ease the tension that was growing between them. "Someday I'll manage to get it through your chauvinist head, but I'm not going to waste my time tonight. Right now I want some of that chocolate cake."

Brad leaped out of bed. "Stay right where you are! I'll serve it to you in bed. Then you'll be right where I want you a half hour from now."

Marty shook her head ruefully at his infectious grin, but agreed.

Chapter Fifteen

$\mathscr{M}$ arty saw Brad the next evening, and the evening after that. They seldom discussed the paternity suit. There was nothing new that either of them could say. Marty continued to put the case together as though she'd never gotten involved with Brad. It was the only thing she could do. Until the hearing was behind them, she wouldn't even spend the night at his house, feeling somehow that it would be too compromising. Brad grumbled and coaxed; Marty held firm.

"I have to take care of the dog, too," she said one day on the phone. "She gets lonely if I'm never there."

"You could bring her to my house. As long as she's with you, she won't care where she is."

"That's not really it, Brad. I'm not ready to stay over, on principle. I have my job to think of."

Brad gave a snort of disagreement. "I tell you what,

Marty. Bring the dog tonight, just to see how she likes it." Marty knew he'd try to con her into staying if she had no other excuse than not feeling "right" about it. He might succeed, too. After all, Marty's car was parked in his customer parking area at this very moment. She'd never intended to take advantage of that offer, but he'd urged her. He pointed out how much easier life would be for her and how handy it would be to have the car available not only at the end of the day but at lunch time as well. "It's not going to do anybody any harm," he'd said. He could be so darned persuasive when he wanted to be—too persuasive.

"No, I'm not going to bring the dog over," she said, with finality.

When she went to pick up her car at the end of the day, Brad was on the phone in his office and dangled his house keys at her. Covering the phone with one hand, he said, "I'll be a little late. Would you put the roast in right away? Three hundred and fifty degrees. Then you can go home and bring the dog back with you. I need to get to know her better, so she won't keep biting me. I should be there by the time you get back."

It was no use arguing with him while he was on the phone. Marty shrugged and took the keys, determined not to give in to Brad's pressure. If she crumpled on one thing, he was sure to press his advantage. The next thing she knew, she'd be practically living at his house.

If she had to go to his house first, put on the meat, return home and be back in time to eat, there wasn't going to be time to spend with Misty. That had been her pattern the last few days.

Sometimes Marty thought Brad was particularly Machiavellian.

It was the first time he'd had any reason to give her his keys, and she felt a little strange letting herself into his house alone. Since she would only be there for a moment, she dropped her purse by the door and headed directly for the kitchen.

"Dad?"

Marty stopped dead. It could only be his daughter. "No," she said, and cleared her throat. "It's a friend of his. He'll be along in a few minutes."

A teenager appeared in the living room door and stared at her. "I didn't know. . . . He never told me. . . . Do you live here now?"

"Oh, no," Marty hastened to assure her. She jiggled the keys where the child could see them. "He lent me his keys so I could put on the roast. You must be Andrea. Was he expecting you?"

"No." Reminded of her reason for being there, the girl's eyes grew large with unshed tears. "He's going to be so mad at me. I got a referral."

"What's a referral?"

"Being sent to the principal's office. Actually, it's worse than that. The counselor said one of my parents will have to come in tomorrow. I know Mom has classes, so it's going to have to be Dad."

Marty nodded, as though she comprehended all this, which she didn't. What could a child this age have done to require so alarming a conference? "Well, I'm sure he'll be perfectly willing to go." She turned toward the kitchen. "I should put the roast in, or you could. Brad's told me that you're a good cook." Marty paused and then said, "Maybe it would be a good idea if I just ran along. You can have dinner alone with your father and talk the whole thing over."

The girl wavered. Marty thought Andrea was probably trying to decide whether the embarrassment of describing her predicament to a stranger outweighed the benefits of having that same stranger act as a buffer when her father heard the bad news. After a moment Andrea led the way into the kitchen without saying anything. Marty followed.

The girl removed the roast from the refrigerator, while Marty set the oven. Without looking at her, Andrea said, "Dad thinks it's real important for a girl to be ladylike, you know?"

Marty took the roast from her and popped it into the oven. It was already in a pan and had seasonings on it. Obviously Brad had prepared it that morning. "Yes, I know," she said.

"The reason I got the referral was that I hit this boy at school, not just once, a whole lot of times."

In a neutral tone of voice Marty asked, "Why?"

"Because . . ." The tears that had threatened before now spilled over. "Well, he sits in front of me in class, and when the period started, I had my feet on his chair. He told me to take them off, and I did. Then he pushed his chair back into my desk, and I shoved him away. Then he hit me."

Fury flared in the girl's eyes, instantly drying up the tears. "I didn't hit him right back." The girl looked defiant, her chin coming up. It made her look so much like Brad that under more beneficent circumstances Marty would have laughed. "The teacher in that class has always made fun of me, so I knew he wouldn't help. I just jumped up and ran out of the room. I was going to go to the office. That's what I intended to do, even though I knew all they'd do was pat me on the head and tell me he wouldn't do it again. In the corridor I ran into this girl I knew, and I asked her to go in and tell Pete he was wanted in the office."

Clever, Marty thought, very clever.

"When he came out, I ran down the hall after him and hit him a bunch of times. He's littler than me," she explained.

"Did it feel good?"

Andrea blinked at her, surprised. "Yeah, right then it did. It didn't feel so hot afterwards when the teacher gave me a referral."

"I suppose not, but there's something so satisfying about handling one's own problems." Marty sighed. "I know you'd have been better off not to have done it. Violence is never a solution to anything, but all the same, I think it's terrific you showed you wouldn't stand for that kind of behavior. I'd pick you for my team any day."

Andrea giggled. "What kind of team do you have?"

"I don't actually have one," Marty confessed. "If I did, it would be for women who insisted on taking care of themselves, and you'd qualify."

"My mom would, too. Do you know her?"

"We met recently, at a party, but I didn't get to talk with her."

"Hmm." Andrea heaved herself up onto the counter and stared solemnly at the refrigerator for a while. Then she spoke slowly, carefully. "You're a bit like her, I guess, and that may not be good—you know? She and Dad didn't get along. He's not very . . . ah . . . liberated, I think you'd call it. He's a real dear," she hastened to add. "I love him, but he's not too keen on women who don't depend completely on men, if you know what I mean. He likes feeling responsible for other people."

"I know he does, and I don't feel comfortable letting someone else take responsibility for me."

"You'd be good for him," his daughter said, "but he'd probably drive you crazy, like he did Mom. I just thought maybe I should warn you."

Marty gave her a rueful smile. "I appreciate it, Andrea. It's something I try to keep in mind." Though it's very difficult, she thought. "I'm going to go home now, so you and your dad can have a good talk. Tell him I'll call him later."

"Okay." Andrea hopped off the counter and extended her hand. "It was nice meeting you . . . uh, did you tell me your name?"

"I'm sorry. It's Marty Woods." Marty shook hands, and resisted an impulse to hug the girl. Perhaps Brad would understand why Andrea had behaved the way she had, but Marty couldn't be sure he would. His daughter's actions had not been those of a meek, delicate female. Any psychological pressure Brad put on his daughter would obviously be counteracted by Karen. Andrea would be all right.

It was really none of Marty's business, anyhow. . . .

Marty had taken the dog for a walk, and scraped together a meal of sorts for herself, before she settled in to do the housework. It was the kind of thing she did when she had some serious thinking to do. Thinking distracted her from the mindlessness of wiping down appliances and dusting tabletops that would just become dirty again in a matter of days. The drudgery of the chores seemed worth it if she reached some solution and it was nice to have the apartment clean, of course.

Marty wore cut-off jeans, a paint-speckled shirt and

a bandana tied peasant-style around her hair when she cleaned. She didn't look her best in this outfit, but there was never anyone to see her, so it didn't matter.

As she mopped the kitchen floor, she was trying to determine whether her association with Brad could possibly go anywhere. She was letting herself toy with the idea that she *wanted* it to go somewhere, that she wanted it to become permanent. Mostly, though, she was trying to figure out how she had let herself fall in love with Brad when she'd known all along about his worst qualities. Even his *daughter* knew about his worst qualities.

He was chauvinistic and stubborn and dictatorial.

He was also loving and exciting and adorable.

Marty wiped her forehead with the back of her hand, staring at the floor without seeing it. What she had to decide was whether she could stand up to Brad or whether he'd oppress her with his attitudes. No two people believed exactly the same things. She simply had to figure out whether she would be likely to bow to his pressure.

If she was going to do that, she knew she'd be as miserable as she'd been with Harry, even though there was no comparison between the two men. She couldn't live with that awful feeling of always having to control what she said, of biting down the anger that she couldn't express, of behaving in a way that pleased someone else rather than herself. Misshaping herself for the sake of femininity, or some man's concept of femininity, was something she'd never do again.

She had been telling Brad that all along, in her own way. Sometimes it had taken a great deal of strength for her to insist on being treated fairly. Though he occasionally grumbled, and frequently didn't understand her, Brad seemed to accept her as she was.

Probably he'd learned a lesson from his inflexibility with Karen: if you didn't bend, you broke. Marty could look back over the course of their relationship and see the times that Brad had bent.

A warmth spread through her, making her smile a little tremulously. She didn't think he'd have done that if he didn't care for her a lot. He'd been as generous as she'd been courageous. It was a balance they'd need to maintain, and it wouldn't do them any harm to work at that. Every couple had their sources of friction, though many didn't recognize it. At least Marty and Brad would know, right from the start.

Even before the doorbell rang, Misty had shot down the hall, barking sharply. Marty followed, leaving the kitchen floor half finished. At the door, she asked who it was and was only a little surprised to hear Brad answer. "It's all right, Misty," she said to the frantically barking dog.

When she swung the door open, Brad stood there unmoving, frowning at her. Marty's hand automatically went up to the bandana she'd forgotten to remove. Then she shrugged and said, "I was washing the kitchen floor. Come on in, and I'll finish while we talk."

He followed her down the hall without saying anything. Misty trotted along at his side, casting suspicious glances up at him. Maybe she didn't like the stiffness with which he walked; Marty didn't either. Brad generally had a much easier stride. Marty checked the clock on the stove and was reassured to find that it was only 9:30. For a moment she'd thought perhaps it was much later and he was annoyed because she hadn't called. She gestured to one of the chairs she'd pushed just outside the kitchen door and went in to continue her mopping. He didn't sit down.

"I've just taken Andrea home," he announced.

Marty dipped the mop in a bucket of sudsy water and nodded. The comment didn't seem to require any answer.

"She told me what happened at school today. She also told me what you said about it."

He was glaring at her, and she raised her brows. "So?"

"She's *my* daughter. When something like this comes up, *I* take care of it. You don't even know her, and I'm not going to have you interfering in her life. It's confusing enough for her with the differences between Karen and me. She doesn't need a complete stranger putting in her two cents."

"So what do you expect me to do when she tells me about what happened, Brad, just stand there like a statue and say nothing?"

"You say, 'Your father will discuss that with you when he gets home.'"

"Is that what I say?" Marty asked, sarcasm so heavy in her throat that it almost choked her. "I become a nonperson just because I'm not related to her? Don't be ridiculous. I'm a human being, and I'm going to respond to another human being's needs, whether she's your daughter or not."

"Oh, no, you're not," he insisted. "If you don't promise me you won't interfere, I simply won't have you there when Andrea is around."

Anger coursed through her. She would have liked to shake the dripping mop over this head—or worse. "That won't be necessary," she told him in a voice so cold and hard she barely recognized it as her own. "I won't tolerate that kind of restriction on my behavior, Brad, and I don't want to have anything to do with someone who'd try to limit me that way. I want you to leave now, and I don't want to see you again—unless it's in connection with the paternity case."

She turned her back on him, blindly mopping the section of floor that hadn't been done. Her stomach churned and her eyes blurred with tears. But the anger held her rigidly together. His insistence on her noninvolvement with his daughter was the last straw. She could have lived with everything else, she thought, but this was too much.

"Fine," he growled. "That's fine with me. I don't need someone who's going to make my life more complicated."

Marty didn't turn to watch him stomp down the hall, but she heard Misty barking excitedly and scampering along with him. The front door slammed. The stiffness instantly left her, making her legs feel weak. She dropped to the floor in a sitting position and slumped over so her forehead rested on her knees. Her whole body shook with sobs.

The dog, alarmed by the stormy turn of events, skittered across the wet floor and smashed into the bucket of water, overturning it with a loud crash. Marty heard hurried footsteps on the back stairs and glanced helplessly from the spreading pool of water to Jim's concerned face in the back door window. The dog whimpered, and Jim demanded through the window whether she was all right. Marty was too dazed to do anything but sit there getting soaked.

Jim rattled the doorknob, but it was locked. Misty pranced through the water, fastidiously lifting her feet. Marty sobbed. This state of affairs seemed to continue for a very long time, too long, certainly, for Jim to retain his vaunted patience. "Open the door!" he barked. "Now, Marty! Get off your rear and open this door."

It was easier to obey him than to sit there hearing him yell at her. Besides, something had to be done about all that water. It would be simpler to mop it out the door than to squeeze it back into the bucket. Marty stumbled to her feet. The floor was slippery, and she barely made it to the door without falling. Water seeped out the moment she pushed the door open.

"For God's sake!" Jim protested, stomping his loafers onto dryer ground. "What's going on? Are you all right?"

Marty's eyes were red, and her face was streaked with tears. Her cutoffs were dripping down her legs into her sneakers. She had never felt so miserable in her life. When she said nothing, Jim studied the woebegone woman for a long moment. Then he opened his arms to her, ignoring the devastation her wet condition might wreak on his new suit and his good shoes. She cried against his shoulder while he patted her awkwardly on the back, murmuring, "There, there" in a deep, consoling voice.

It was several minutes before Marty hiccuped into relative calm. With a shaky sigh she backed out of Jim's arms and accepted the handkerchief he offered, not that it did much good. Her face was a swollen wreck by this time, and she shivered in the night air. "Thanks," she said gruffly.

"What's this all about, Marty?"

"Oh, the usual," she replied, trying to make light of it. "Heartbreak, unrequited love, disillusion."

He frowned. "I didn't even know you were seeing someone."

"Well, I'm not—anymore. It was stupid of me to get involved in the first place." She noticed the wet patch on his jacket and said, "I'm sorry. It'll probably dry okay, but if you have to send it to the cleaners, I'll pay for it."

"Forget about the suit. I just want to be sure you're going to be okay. I've never seen you cry before."

"Well, it's not the first time, and it won't be the last. I'm in no condition to talk about it. Right now I need to change my clothes and mop up the kitchen floor." She stood on tiptoe to kiss his cheek. "Thanks, Jim. You're a good friend."

"Do you want me to mop the floor while you change?"

"No. I'll be okay. Really."

Jim considered her for a moment and then nodded. "Yeah, I know you will. Just call if you need anything."

Marty watched him climb the stairs. When he opened his back door, she heard the murmur of a woman's voice. How kind of him to come to her rescue when he had company! She shivered again, which spurred her out of her stupor and into the apartment to change.

Her image in the bathroom mirror was so pathetic she turned away from it. After stripping, she dried herself with a towel and took her robe down from the hook on the back of the door. As she tied the belt around her waist, there was a long hammering on the front door.

Marty knew it was Brad.

If she ignored the hammering, it would only bring Jim roaring downstairs again, and she wasn't up to that kind of confrontation. However, she had no intention of seeing Brad. Before he could knock again, she dashed up the hall in her bare feet, hushing the dog as she went. "What do you want?" she called.

"I want to talk to you."

"I think we've said all the important things. I'm not going to let you in, and if you make a fuss, I'll go up to Jim's. So please leave."

"There are a lot of other things for us to talk about! You were the one who said it was better to talk things out."

"There's nothing to talk out, this time. I have to clean up a spilled bucket of water in the kitchen now. Good night, Brad." She made as much noise as she could going back down the hall. Though she could hear him protesting, she couldn't make out the words. By the time she'd reached the kitchen, she was unable to hear his voice at all. He didn't pound on the door or lean on the doorbell. Marty began to mop the small lake of water toward the back door.

She was startled, and a little frightened, when he appeared there. It was easy enough to get through the weeds in the vacant lot on one side, but he must have climbed over the tall fence as well.

"We have to talk," he said.

"If you're not gone in one minute, I'm going to scream. When I scream, Jim is going to come down here in one hell of a state because he's already seen what a mess I am tonight."

One hand raked helplessly through his unruly hair. "For crying out loud, all I want to do is talk to you."

"What you want doesn't count right now. You're in my house, and I feel threatened because you didn't leave when I told you to leave."

He looked horrified. "You can't think I'd hurt you!"

"Get out, Brad. Now."

"But . . ." He didn't complete his protest. His face

looked suddenly drawn, his eyes dull with pain. "I can't believe you're afraid of me." He sounded stunned. When she said nothing, he turned and left.

Marty had thought there were no tears left but they streamed down her cheeks one after another as though they would never end. She clung to the mop and tried to swallow down the tears, tried to will them into drying up. When this utterly failed, she straightened her shoulders and attacked the water on the floor as though her life depended on completing the job. In time the motion and distraction calmed her somewhat, and she was able to think about the situation.

Had she been afraid of him? No, not that he would do her any physical harm, but she had been afraid of his other powers over her. Because of her love for him, Marty had feared that he would talk her out of her anger, or worse, that he would talk her into bed. She didn't trust him not to take advantage of that kind of power. When two people were equally in love, there was a balance of power. Marty believed she was more in love with Brad than he was with her, and therefore, that he could manipulate her if he wished.

If he had stayed, and talked, and touched her, she would have been mesmerized as usual. They would have made love, but their problems would not have been solved. Knowing Brad, he would have thought he'd "won," that she would continue to see him and obey his unreasonable rules. Marty knew she couldn't, and wouldn't, do that. There was no sense in seeing him—tonight . . . or ever again.

Chapter Sixteen

*B*rad drove back to his house in a strange mood that shifted alarmingly back and forth between anger and sorrow. One minute he was furious with Marty for hinting that he could hurt her. The next he felt stricken that he wouldn't see her again. He couldn't understand either her fear of him or her fury about not being able to interfere in his daughter's life.

Surely there was nothing threatening about him. He'd never so much as accidentally stepped on her toes. How in hell could she be afraid of him? It made Brad feel a little sick to think she could believe him capable of harming her in any way, and angry, too, because he'd never done anything to justify her having such a fear.

As to her insistence on her right to interfere in Andrea's life, that was just plain crazy. Andrea already had a mother and a father and a stepfather in her life; she didn't need another adult expecting obedience. It was hard enough for Brad to hold on to his share of influence over the child without having one more person to compete against.

When Andrea had mentioned talking with Marty, she hadn't indicated any unhappiness with their conversation. It was Brad who saw a great deal wrong with it, who objected to Marty thrusting herself so deeply into his life. For the most part, he'd been able to keep her separate from his previous marriage, even from his business. That made things less complicated for him. Until now, it had not occurred to him that he couldn't keep doing that forever.

Well, now he wouldn't have to worry about it, he told himself defiantly. Marty would never see Andrea again, would never offer any words of comfort or advice. Obviously it was better that way. Wasn't it?

Brad turned into his driveway and shut off the engine, but he remained seated in his car trying to think through the consequences of the night's happenings. Tomorrow he was going to have to go to Andrea's school. He wished he'd told Marty that he hadn't been hard on his daughter about her misbehavior. He was not, after all, blind to the aggravation she'd received. He would have been perfectly happy to throttle the kid who'd hit her.

His mind refused to stay with his daughter's problem, however. It kept skittering off to Marty. Brad found it impossible to believe that he wasn't ever going to hold her again, that she wasn't ever going to walk around his house or help him with dinner again. *How could she possibly have been afraid of him?* He banged his fist against the steering wheel in a fit of frustration. *Didn't she know he loved her?*

Brad froze where he sat, staring blankly at the darkness outside the car. What had made him think that? His feelings for Marty were more than friendly, of course, but surely he wouldn't go so far as to call them love. Would he? Infatuation, certainly, and he had a real affection for her, a protective, caring sort of attachment. Her laugh delighted him, and her body thrilled him. But that was hardly love.

Love was that crazy headiness you felt when you were eighteen, and it was that deep abiding respect you had for a woman with whom you'd shared your life. It was so strong it invaded your very core and had a hold on you that you couldn't possibly ignore. Your thoughts and your emotions were permeated by someone other than yourself. Every facet of your life was affected by the other person's very being.

Not a bad description of how he felt about Marty, given his advancing age and previous experience. There was the headiness of their physical attraction, and his admiration for her strong character. The depth of his feeling for her had increased with each encounter until there was no longer a way to detach this special woman from his heart.

How would he bear not having her in his life? He had come to depend on her, to see her as necessary to his well-being. If he had intended for her to stay in his life, it was only logical that she would have had frequent contact with Andrea. If the situation were reversed, and Marty had the teenager, would he have settled for her telling him to butt out of the child's life?

Never.

Even if they didn't agree on everything, Marty deserved the right to respond to Andrea's presence, and her needs. Andrea wasn't so young that another voice in her life would painfully confuse her. It was Brad who had feared the eroding of his influence over his daughter, a natural fear bred by the last two years, but one which he would have to conquer.

Brad knew it was too late to correct his error. He had frightened Marty, and she wasn't willing to listen to his new understanding of things. She had already let him talk her out of her convictions about dating him half a dozen times. After the way he'd behaved, she wasn't even going to believe him if he told her he loved her. He had manipulated her too many times; it would sound like one more ploy to get his way.

Discouraged, he climbed out of the car and went into the house. As he undressed for bed, he decided he could write her a letter. She would read it, if only to make sure it had nothing to do with the paternity case. That was going to be more difficult, too, the paternity case.

For no particular reason, while he was brushing his teeth he remembered something Marty had said: "You sometimes get blood-test results like that when the woman is related to the man." Brad was sure he wasn't related to Lydia Brown, but as the toothpaste foamed in his mouth a rather startling idea occurred to him.

What other sort of relationship could account for his not being excluded, when he obviously wasn't the father? Having a cousin, perhaps, who was the father?

The thought was so stunning that he stood for some moments staring at himself in the mirror, his toothbrush forgotten. His cousin Sam had lived in San Francisco back in those days. Sam could have met Lydia at the building supply store and conducted an affair with her. There was no reason Brad would have known.

Brad frowned in concentration. When was it he'd had to fire his cousin for stealing from the store?

Surely around the same time he'd found out about Karen and Carl. Was that the right time, if Sam was the child's father?

Hurriedly he rinsed out his mouth and patted his face and hands dry. This was no time to worry about why Lydia would have accused *him* if it was his cousin who was responsible for her pregnancy. All he wanted to find out was exactly when he had fired Sam. There was no way he could find that out without going to the store.

Waiting until morning never occurred to him. When Brad decided to do something, he did it instantly, no matter that it was late. He got back into his clothes and loped out to his car. He tried not to think about Marty as he drove to the deserted store, parked in his usual space and jumped out.

It was so dark in the shadow of the building that he fumbled trying to find the office-door key, and then had trouble inserting it into the lock. So intent was he on his errand that when a loud voice demanded, "What do you think you're doing, buddy?" he jumped, and dropped his keys.

A patrol car was stopped at the curb, and a spotlight shone directly on him as one of the two officers climbed out of the car. Brad walked toward him, protesting his innocence. "It's my business, officer. I'm Brad Macintosh."

"Sure, fella. Let's see a little I.D."

Brad dug into his pants pocket to retrieve his wallet. It wasn't there. He patted the front of his jacket and the rest of the pockets—nothing. "Well, I must have left my wallet at home," he admitted, "but it's still my business. I have a key to the office door."

The officer looked more than skeptical. "Just because you have the key doesn't mean it belongs to you," he said. "Why would you drive down here at this hour of the night without your wallet? You've probably been driving without a license, too, haven't you?"

"You didn't stop me when I was driving, and I have a license—in my name, Brad Macintosh. It just happens I forgot it at home." Brad regarded the policeman with ill-concealed frustration. "Look, officer, I can prove this is my business. Ask me anything about it."

"Why are you down here at this hour?" the policeman asked again.

"Because I want to check the personnel records to find out exactly when I fired my cousin Sam."

There was a bellow of laughter from inside the patrol car. The officer inside shook his head in admiration. "You've got to admit, Joe, it's a unique explanation." To Brad he said, "Why didn't you wait until morning?"

Brad did not wish to discuss his difficulties with these men. On the other hand, now was perhaps not the time to become evasive with them, either. He made an impatient gesture with one hand. "An idea occurred to me just a few minutes ago, something important, and I wasn't willing to wait until morning to check it out."

The officers shared a dissatisfied glance. The one in the car stared at Brad for a long time, then asked, "When did you open the store here?"

Brad rattled off the exact date.

The policeman nodded and gestured his companion back to the car. "I remember," he said, "because it was the day I got transferred to this area of town. My new partner pointed out the store and said it would help the neighborhood. Try to remember to take your license with you when you go out at night, Mr. Macintosh."

"Yeah, I will." Brad watched, relieved, as the patrol car drove slowly away. It was beginning to seem that everything associated with this paternity suit, and Marty, was fraught with alarming consequences.

From his earlier search, Brad remembered that the file he needed was in the storage room, and he snapped on lights as he passed through the halls. Sam's file was in the second drawer of the filing cabinet in the smallest storage room, just where Karen had directed him the first time. Brad flipped it open to the angry note he'd written the day he'd spoken with Sam. *"January 16. Fired for stealing materials from the store. Two weeks' severance pay, though he doesn't deserve it. Sam seems to think I 'owed' him the stuff because I 'didn't pay him well enough.' Idiot!"*

Brad remembered then how angry he'd been. It wasn't just because Sam was related to him, but because he'd been warned by Karen that Sam wasn't to be trusted, and he hadn't seen it. He was angry all the time then, that month when he'd found out Karen and Carl were interested in each other. Sam's irresponsibility and dishonesty had goaded him into a real outburst.

Looking back on it now, Brad could see that he'd poured onto Sam all the anger he'd felt toward Karen, since she was available and she wasn't. Not a particularly admirable thing to do, but he'd been under incredible stress at the time.

According to his mental calculations, the baby must have been conceived that January. After the humiliation of being fired by a raving cousin, had Sam gone out and grabbed the first woman he'd seen? The thought made Brad shiver, but he remembered almost immediately that Lydia's story was that the child's father had an affair of several weeks with her.

One of the elements that had long bothered him about her story, her ability to describe his office, now fell into place. It certainly wouldn't have been beyond Sam's flagrant idiocy to bring her into the office after hours and strut around the place. Had he actually told her he was Brad?

Brad couldn't remember all the elements of her story. Though he and Sam bore a vague family resemblance, no one could possibly mistake one for the other. For one thing, Sam was in his early twenties compared with Brad's thirty-five.

The possibility of mistaken identity had occurred to Marty, he remembered now. She had made Lydia describe him originally, and later she'd shown her the picture taken at the blood-testing place. Lydia had positively identified him from the photograph.

Brad carried his cousin's file to the main office, flicking on the light as he entered. The reception area, and his own room beyond, looked particularly ratty to him in the stark light. It was the first time he'd been forcibly struck by the need for new furniture here, and there were two dead plants. He shoved these thoughts aside, however, since there were more important matters to consider at the moment—like whether Sam was the father of Lydia's baby.

How could he possibly find out? Brad sat down at his desk and drew a pad of paper toward himself, jotting down his thoughts as they came to him. First he'd have to check with each of the employees who'd been working at the building supply store at the time Sam worked there. Some of them might have known he was seeing Lydia. If not, he might have mentioned something else that would be useful.

Brad tapped his pen impatiently against the desk. He could call Sam, of course. Somehow it didn't sound like a good idea, not yet, at any rate. He wanted to have something more substantial than a guess before he tackled his careless young cousin. Right now, a guess was basically all he had.

It had always seemed that there had to be some connection between Brad and Lydia. Otherwise, why would she have chosen to blame him for the paternity? How would she even have known who he was? Perhaps Sam was only a guess, but Brad had a solid gut feeling that it was the right guess. Sam fitted the puzzle in a lot of important ways.

Brad wanted to share his discovery with Marty immediately. Twice his hand went out to the phone, and twice it fell back. It was too late, and she'd hang up when she heard his voice. In the morning he could call her at the office, but he shuddered at the impersonality of it. Better yet, in the morning he'd be sitting on her stoop. In the bright daylight he wouldn't frighten her, and he'd explain right away that he had something to tell her about the paternity case. Maybe she'd let him drive her to work while he talked.

He tucked the file under his arm, switched off all the lights as he walked through the outer office and hallway and carefully locked the door as he left the building. Before starting the Volvo, he sat for a while staring unseeing into the darkness of the night.

The introduction of Sam into the paternity case was simply going to further confuse Marty's job. It wouldn't necessarily have any bearing on her relationship with Brad. Her loyalties would still be torn between believing him and doing her job properly.

Brad felt slightly apprehensive about how she would respond. With a sigh he started the car and drove home.

Marty was awakened by raised voices outside her flat. Though this had never happened before, she might not have thought much of it except that they were Brad's and Jim's voices. She hastily slipped into her old robe and tied it around her waist as she ran down the hall. Misty raced along with her, working herself into a frenzy that forced Marty to scoop her up before she could open the door.

Brad and Jim stood confronting each other, rigid with hostility. Jim was holding his morning newspaper like a potential weapon, and Brad's fists were clenched at his sides. Jim switched his angry gaze to Marty.

"This idiot says he has to see you. He's the one I chased off a while back." And, his eyes said, he's undoubtedly the cause of last night's trouble.

Her breath caught in her throat, but she managed to say, huskily, "I don't want to see you, Brad."

"It's about the paternity case—something new, and very important."

Jim interceded, stepping protectively between Marty and Brad. "You can call her at her office about the paternity case. There's no excuse for your showing up here." He turned to Marty. "You go back inside. I'll take care of this."

Brad looked as if he wanted to slap his opponent.

Marty wrapped her arms firmly around the dog and tried to meet Jim's eyes. "I appreciate your help, Jim, but I have to take care of this matter myself. Mr. Macintosh knows that I don't wish to see him here, but I want to make sure he understands that I'll be perfectly happy to have him call me at the office, if he has something to tell me about the paternity case."

"I was going to drive you to work," Brad said. "I want to show you a file folder I have in the car. What I've discovered could make a big difference to the case."

Jim hadn't moved, but his gaze flickered rapidly back and forth between Marty and Brad. Marty stood there shaking her head mutely the whole time Brad talked. When he was finished, she said only, "You can call me at the office." Then she turned and went into her apartment, closing the door softly behind her.

Leaning against the door she could have heard if either of the men said anything. All she heard was Brad loping down the stairs and Jim shutting the door of his apartment. After a moment an engine started, and a car drove off down the street. Marty went to the front window to make sure Brad had indeed left. She was astonished that he'd had the nerve to show up on her doorstep after what had happened the night before. Even if he'd managed to concoct some story of a discovery in the paternity case, not for a minute did she believe it was anything significant.

When he didn't call her at the office, she was sure she was right. It had simply been a ploy to make amends, and he'd known better than to try to pursue it over the phone, where she could hang up so easily. Though she ached with the loss of him, she felt it was better that they have no contact whatsoever. If he had called about the paternity case, she would have spoken with him, but it would have been difficult. This way was much better.

Because she didn't hear from him even as the hearing date approached, she assumed he was going to get a lawyer. Harry didn't mention being contacted by the defendant's attorney, but it seemed almost a foregone conclusion that he had been. Marty didn't bother to ask. Everything associated with Brad was too painful to delve into just now. Later, she expected to be calmer about it. When the hearing was finished, she would start to put him out of her mind entirely.

Getting through the hearing was becoming a goal of hers. Now that she and Brad had fallen into their natural positions as adversaries, she should have felt more comfortable. All she had to do was think of the state's interest in the case and proceed as though she believed every word Lydia Brown had ever told her, but Brad was in the back of her mind all the time, whispering his innocence.

On the day she went over all the material with Harry, she couldn't seem to settle down. Her hands kept fluttering among the papers, her feet tapping nervously against the linoleum floor of the conference room.

"What's up?" Harry demanded.

"Nothing. It just doesn't seem to be a very strong case, with the inconclusive blood tests and all."

"This is only a hearing, Marty. We don't have to convince a jury, just a judge who's seen it all before. You told me the mother is very positive about everything."

"Oh, she is. I'm having her come early tomorrow so you can talk with her." Marty ran a hand distractedly through her curly hair. "Surely Mr. Macintosh's attorney can poke holes in our case. Who's acting for him?"

Harry grinned. "As far as I know, no one. I'm telling you, Marty, we've got it sewed up."

If it wouldn't have been impolitic, she would have

groaned. What was Brad thinking of? If she'd been helping him, he might barely have squeezed by without getting someone. On his own he was just going to lose the slim chance he had of making a decent case for himself.

She wanted to wring his neck . . . and hug him. She wanted to force him to listen to reason . . . and lie holding him beside her. She wanted to yell at his obstinance . . . and whisper her love in his ear. He drove her crazy with his chauvinist stand on everything . . . and made every sensual tissue in her body swell with desire.

The hearing was the next day. Marty could not do a thing to help him. One way or another, it was too late.

When Brad left Marty's apartment for the last time, he had every intention of calling her as soon as she got to her office and presenting her with his theory about Sam and Lydia. The more he thought about it, though, the more convinced he became that there were good reasons not to do it. For one, if Marty could be as cold and impersonal as she'd just been, then her sympathies could not possibly lie with him anymore. She might take the information and use it against him by preparing Lydia to fend off any surprise suggestion at the hearing.

If she did indeed still feel sympathetic toward him, but was unwilling to act on his behalf because of her job and her determination not to see him, then telling her would only add to her difficulties. He had made her life difficult enough already, and he wasn't going to try to clear up their various misunderstandings until after the hearing—if then. If she seemed agreeable and was even speaking to him, he might try to clear things up.

To the astonishment of all three of them, Brad sat down with Andrea and Karen and Carl to talk about his paternity problem. No one laughed at him. Carl offered to represent him gratis, but Brad accepted only free legal advice. Together they planned his strategy, and Karen suggested a reasonable way to handle Sam and his family. Andrea walked him to the door.

"Is Marty helping you, too?" she asked.

"Her job puts her on the other side of the fence, sweetheart."

"But she could help you if she wanted to."

Brad lifted a careless shoulder. "We're not seeing each other right now."

Andrea nodded solemnly. "I liked her, but I didn't think you two would stay together. She seemed real independent, and you don't like that kind of woman."

"How can you say that?" he demanded. "I liked your mother, and she's independent."

"Yes, but she had to divorce you because you wouldn't let her do what was important for her. The same thing would have happened with Marty," the girl insisted. "I even sort of warned her, you know, because I didn't want to see her get hurt."

"Oh, for God's sake!" Brad glared at her. "Is it too much to ask you to let me handle my own affairs? This is none of your business."

"It would be. If you'd kept on seeing her, she'd have been like Carl was before he and Mom got married, like a friendly uncle or something. We had to work it out from the first time we met. You don't just suddenly have a stepfather or a stepmother, you know. You have to find a place for them in your life."

Andrea stood on tiptoe to kiss his cheek. "I'd have been happy to do that with Marty, but don't worry.

I'm determined to like whoever you end up with, if it kills me."

"How do you know I'm ever going to end up with someone?" he asked, his voice gruff.

"Because you need a woman in your life. You're not a loner, even if you pretend you are sometimes." She smiled sadly. "It would have been nice if it had been Marty."

Brad opened the front door before he spoke. "Yeah, it would have been nice," he muttered as he stepped out into the cool evening air.

Chapter Seventeen

The courtroom was one of the smaller ones in City Hall but it had all the usual wood trim and paneling. Marty had frequently sat in the witness chair beside the judge's high bench and even more frequently waited in the visitor seats. She knew the clerk, the bailiff, the court reporter. She knew how comfortable the chairs were, and how much sunlight made its way into the room on a sunny morning. The courtroom was as familiar to her as her own office.

Yet it felt subtly different this morning because Brad was sitting there, at the table reserved for the defendant. Harry sat at the other table with a bulging briefcase; Brad had only a file folder. Brad didn't look at her, even when Harry motioned her over to ask a question.

Marty felt sure he must be curious about Lydia, but he didn't turn to look at either her or the expert witness from the blood-testing laboratory. He wore the brown tweed suit she'd seen him in at the other paternity trial, and he looked expectant—not nervous or intimidated or angry. He didn't exactly look like an attorney because there was that aura of unruly energy about him, but he looked competent and eager. Marty's heart beat faster just looking at him.

Lydia sat with her hands folded in her lap. Harry always liked the mothers to dress conservatively, and she had complied. She looked a little lost in a navy skirt and bulky, black sweater both of which were too large for her. When questioned by Lydia, Marty had smiled and said, "You look fine. Is your neighbor watching Cheryl for you?"

"Yes." She wound a strand of long, fine hair around her finger. "I'll be finished by noon, won't I?"

"Sure. This is just the hearing. It would take longer for a trial, but this should move along pretty quickly." Marty gestured with her head toward Brad. "You do recognize Mr. Macintosh, don't you? I'd hate to find we had a mix-up at such a late date."

"Oh, yes. He looks a little older, though."

Marty eyed her sharply. "But you're sure this man is the father."

Lydia's chin came up. "Definitely."

Well, she'd do fine on the stand, but Marty could no longer believe her, not when her assertion was in direct contradiction with Brad's. Marty had gotten to know him too well to believe he was lying to her. He might be archaic and stubborn and impulsive, but she knew he had told her the truth. The hearing was likely to be a very painful experience, all things considered.

The bailiff called out for them to rise and Judge Stoller appeared in his black robes. He was an older man, with gray hair and a lined face. Marty had always thought he looked worn out by hearing so many tales of antisocial behavior, but she'd never known him to be less than thorough in the trials and hearings over which he presided. He nodded now to Harry and Marty before regarding Brad with speculative eyes.

"Do you plan to represent yourself, Mr. Macintosh?"

"Yes, sir, I do."

"You realize that it's customary to be represented by counsel in an action such as this, do you?"

"I do, but I decided to handle it myself."

"Very well. We'll be a little lenient in accepting testimony, Mr. Mills, since Mr. Macintosh won't be familiar with all our procedures and since this is only a hearing. I presume that will be acceptable with you."

Harry half rose. "Certainly, your honor."

The judge explained the order of business to Brad, who maintained a respectful attention. When Lydia took the stand, Brad studied her with his head cocked to one side, but his expression remained enigmatic.

Harry questioned the young woman clearly and concisely. He had her identify Brad and acknowledge a birth certificate for her daughter which had Brad's name on it as the father. Marty was watching him when this paper was introduced, and she saw his dark brows draw together in a frown. When he was given an opportunity to question her, the first thing he asked was, "What's my full name, Miss Brown?"

"Brad Macintosh."

"No, Brad is short for something, and I have a middle name. What are they?"

Lydia looked to Harry and then the judge for help. Neither offered any suggestions, and she shrugged. "I don't know. You never told me."

"Are you sure I'm the man you met at Macintosh Building Supply?"

"Very sure."

"You're willing to testify under oath that I am the father of your child?"

"Yes."

Marty's heart ached for Brad. He really had nothing with which to shake Lydia's story, and he seemed confused about exactly how to proceed. When the medical evidence was introduced, there would be even less he could do to exonerate himself. A lawyer would have tried to poke holes in Lydia's story by confusing her with questions about time and place. Brad was too gentlemanly to do that. He turned to the judge and said, "I want to bring someone into the courtroom for her to identify. Is that all right?"

"Certainly. If it's pertinent to the case."

"It is."

Brad moved to the back of the courtroom and pushed open the door. The first person to enter was Kerri, his secretary, and Marty couldn't understand what good she was going to do Brad. A young man followed her into the room, someone Marty had never seen before. He was slightly taller than Brad and had wavy black hair and blue eyes. It did not occur to her that he looked particularly like Brad, though if someone had pointed out the superficial resemblance she would have agreed.

Someone who works for the store, Marty thought, someone who saw Lydia there, perhaps, and can at least identify her. Marty swung her gaze back to Lydia on the witness stand, and her heart nearly stopped. Lydia's face had become so pale Marty thought she would faint. Before she could rise from her seat to offer aid, though, the judge had suggested that Lydia might like to take a break. Lydia merely shook her head.

Brad returned to a position in front of the witness stand. "Do you know the man who just came into the courtroom?"

There was a long silence. Lydia stared at the newcomer, and he stared back at her. Only when his face softened from a distant coolness to an apologetic smile did she speak. "Yes, I know him."

"What's his name?"

"Sam Moore."

"Do you know how he's related to me?"

Harry looked as if he were going to object, but the judge waved him to silence.

"He's your cousin."

"Where did you meet Sam?"

"At the store, the building supply store."

Brad nodded and turned to look, briefly, at Marty. She met his eyes without flinching. In fact, what she felt more than anything was a vast sense of relief. So he really had wanted to tell her something that morning. But he had decided against it, obviously. She vaguely remembered mention of a cousin, but it was nothing that would ever have led her to suspect what was now unfolding.

"Did you see Sam outside the store? Did you date him?"

Lydia's hands were knotted in her lap. Her anxious gaze moved from Brad to the judge to Marty to Sam. She couldn't seem to make up her mind what to answer. Sam spread his hands, but still she sat mute.

The judge bent toward her with a stern expression on his face. "Perjury is a punishable crime, Miss Brown. Do you know what perjury means?"

"I'm not sure."

"It means lying under oath. I want you to tell the truth now. You would be doing a grave injustice to any man to accuse him of fathering a child that wasn't his. This court will overlook previous inaccurate testimony if you'll now provide us with the whole truth."

Lydia's lips trembled, but she nodded her head. "I don't remember the question."

Brad responded immediately. "Did you see Sam outside the store? Did you date him?"

"Yes, we went together for a while."

"When was that?" Brad asked.

"In December and January."

Brad made her be specific about the years, and then he put the important question to her. "Is Sam Moore the father of your baby?"

Tears overflowed her eyes and dribbled down her cheeks. Lydia brushed them away with her fists. She looked directly at Sam when she answered. "Yes. He's my baby's father."

By the time the revelation was made, Marty realized, everyone had come to understand what it would be. There was no indrawn breath, no commotion, no pounding of the gavel. Harry began wearily stuffing materials back into his briefcase. He would want to blame her, but Marty knew he couldn't do it. She had given fair warning.

Brad was not finished with the witness, Marty discovered. It wasn't good enough to have her relieve him of paternity. He wanted to know a great deal more. Marty didn't blame him.

"Why did you tell Ms. Woods, in the Paternity Unit, that I was the father of your child?"

"Because you have to tell them someone was, and

Sam went away before I knew I was pregnant. I didn't know where he lived." Lydia stared at her clenched hands. "You were mean to him. You fired him without a reason, and you never paid him enough money. You wouldn't promote him to a better position. It seemed fair that you should have to pay for the child, to make up for all the bad things you did to Sam."

When Brad turned to glare at him, Sam shifted nervously in his seat. A bubble of laughter floated up through Marty, making her feel almost light-headed. She caught Brad's eye, and winked. His eyebrows twitched, but he gave no other sign of having noticed.

He turned back to Lydia to ask, "Wouldn't it have been easier for you to come to me when you found out you were pregnant? I could have told you where Sam was."

The idea seemed new to her. She frowned, trying to think through the implications. "Well, I suppose I didn't think you'd tell me, or that it wouldn't do any good, anyway. Marty had mentioned they couldn't sue people out of state, and the purpose was to get the child support. If you knew it was Sam, then they couldn't get the child support from you."

"But the blood tests might have excluded me," he pointed out.

"You're cousins. You must have the same kind of blood. It's not as if it were someone not related to you."

Marty groaned. It was difficult to explain the intricacies to someone who had preconceived notions, and, against the odds, Lydia had turned out to be more or less correct this time. Brad hadn't been excluded—so much for the sophistication of their testing techniques.

"I guess that's all," Brad said, starting to walk back

to the defense table. "Except, if it's possible, I'd like the birth certificate changed so it has Sam's name on it instead of mine."

The judge grinned. "I think we can manage that, Mr. Macintosh. The court appreciates your efforts to straighten the matter out and regrets any inconvenience you may have been caused." He proceeded to dismiss the case, with various pertinent remarks, but Marty paid only a minimum of attention to his voice.

She should have been trying to figure out how the state could get Sam Moore to support his child, but she would let Harry worry about that for the moment. Right now she wanted to observe Brad. She might have expected him to be cocky, having won out over all of them in spite of the odds against him, but he just looked tired, suddenly. One of his hands rested on the solitary file folder, the other on his knee. He stared straight ahead, as though he wasn't really listening to the judge, either. It was hardly a triumphant stance.

After the judge had dismissed the case, all eyes went to Lydia, who took a tentative step toward Sam. His expression was a confusion of embarrassment, pride, fear, hope and bravado. Marty had rarely seen such a disparate blend. He rose from his seat but seemed unable to move. Marty would have liked to give him a push in the right direction.

It proved to be unnecessary. Though his legs were apparently paralyzed, he managed to reach out a hand toward Lydia. She grasped it like a life preserver. "Will you come and see her?" she asked, her voice soft as a whisper. "Her name's Cheryl. You told me once you thought that was a pretty name."

"Yeah, I do," he said gruffly. "I want to see her."

Distracted by this reunion, Marty was startled to find Brad at her elbow. She turned toward him and dropped her voice to say, "I'm glad you found out the truth of it. Even though Ṣam is your cousin, you should have been excluded, you know, except that all of you have such common blood factors. I'm sorry for the nuisance everything has been. Did you have to pay to fly him out here?"

"His mother split it with me. He does have a job. If he won't come up with child support, my aunt and uncle will do it for him. They feel obliged. Sam's so flaky it's hard to tell whether he'll feel obliged or not." He stared straight into her eyes, as though he were trying to convey some message.

Marty looked away. "We can't go after him for paternity because he lives out of state. If he or his parents contribute to the child's support, it's entirely a voluntary thing, but it will affect how much A.F.D.C. Lydia gets."

"Maybe I could bring him to your office tomorrow to straighten all that out."

"I don't have anything to do with the A.F.D.C. payments." Marty dug through the pocket in her purse and came up with a card. "Here's a number you could call to make an appointment. They'd be able to answer any of your questions."

He stuffed the card in his pants pocket. "Okay, forget about Sam. I want to talk to *you*."

Marty had tried to prepare herself for this possibility. She had told herself she would be calm and reasonable, but here she was standing in front of him. Her heart raced, her hands trembled, and her throat felt swollen shut. The only thing she could do was shake her head, and she shook it violently.

A look of pain crossed his face. "Marty, I wouldn't hurt you for the world. Where did you get this crazy idea of being afraid of me?" He sounded as bewildered as he looked.

She couldn't let him believe that, so she forced herself to speak. "I'm not afraid of you, Brad, honestly. I simply don't think it would be a good idea for us to see each other again. Our differences are too great."

"You always said we could get things straightened out when the paternity case was behind us."

"That was before you convinced me it would be impossible."

"I could change your mind." He took hold of her arm in his urgency. "I know you were right about Andrea. I just hadn't faced it then."

Marty felt as though she'd been shocked. His touch on her arm and his words both sent a jolt through her. Confused, she said, "I don't know what to say, Brad. Seeing you just seems to tear me apart sooner or later. Maybe it's best just to leave it the way it is."

Brad wasn't given a chance to respond. His cousin appeared beside him, with Lydia in tow, insisting that they be taken to Lydia's apartment building, so he could see his daughter. It would have been senseless for Brad to try to continue his discussion with Marty, and she was relieved. This way she'd have time to think about whether she should see him again.

"I'll call you," he said as he allowed Sam to tug him toward the door of the courtroom. "Soon."

Marty nodded, but she didn't intend to be available for the rest of the day. Instead of returning to the office, she went home, giving Virginia strict instructions not to let Brad know where she was. Marty knew he would find her soon enough. . . .

Chapter Eighteen

$\mathcal{M}$arty hoped that if she turned on the stereo and played some classical music, it would help to make her thinking more rational. She sat down on the sofa and slid off her shoes as the music began to pour from the speakers, but she found that it only made her restless. When she thought of Brad, she was unable to maintain the calm she so desperately needed right now. Just thinking of him evoked a physical excitement in her, which was not necessarily a point in his favor, she tried to tell herself.

That sort of heady effect could overpower more important considerations, like whether they were compatible. It was vital that she *think* rather than simply feel. Oh, if she went with her feelings she'd just hop in her car and drive over to his house to wait for him, and she'd probably take the mesh dress with her!

Marty needed to think about the hard realities, like

his automatic response of cutting Marty out where Andrea was concerned. Could that possibly bode well for a continuing involvement? It seemed to her that every time he was confronted with a new situation, his response was to think he was right and she was wrong.

Yes, but every time he had also been willing to re-evaluate, she reminded herself. He was willing to learn from his mistakes and change his mind. That was a marvelous quality in a man, one far too rare in her experience. Maybe it was she who had become too rigid as she realized the strength of her attraction to him. Her own fears that she would let him ride roughshod over her might be keeping her from seeing that he was more adaptable than she had at first thought.

Perhaps he'd *become* more adaptable since she'd met him. Maybe he'd realized how much it had cost him to be inflexible, since he had fallen in love with a woman who needed to maintain her sense of self. Marty knew he was in love with her, just as she was with him. The only question was whether they made sense together, whether they would be good for each other—in the long run. There was no sense seeing him again unless this could be a permanent relationship. It would be too painful for her.

Misty, who had been curled up at her feet, bounded up and toward the front door, barking sharply. Marty moved to the front window, afraid, and yet hopeful that she would see Brad charging up the front stairs. She had to talk to him, but she wasn't sure she was ready yet.

It was a woman who climbed the stairs, with a key poised in her hand. Marty was sure she'd seen her before but couldn't quite remember when. She heard the woman enter Jim's apartment. It was very odd that a woman should have a key to Jim's apartment. Marty frowned in an effort of recollection.

Then she saw Jim drive up and park his Porsche in the driveway. As he was climbing out of his car, Brad's Volvo appeared in the street. Just what she needed, she thought, another clash between the two of them! Her mouth felt dry as she slid her feet into her shoes and raced to the door, almost stumbling over Misty in her haste. The dog darted out the door before Marty could catch hold of her collar.

Jim had a large grocery bag in his arms. He halted beside Brad's car with a stern look on his face. Brad grinned up at him. "How's it going, counselor?" Brad asked, springing out of the driver's seat.

He sounded so cocky it almost made Marty laugh. There was never any keeping Brad down for long. If Jim had seemed to come out on top at their last encounter, Brad had no intention of letting that happen again. He slammed his car door with an aggressiveness nicely calculated to irritate Jim.

What Brad hadn't counted on was the dog. Misty attacked him, barking ferociously and nipping at his shoes. Somehow it detracted from his confident image.

It was Jim's turn to look smug, which made Marty want to pinch him. He hadn't noticed her yet, and he said to Brad, "I believe we've already determined that Ms. Woods doesn't want you here."

Brad reached down to pick up the yapping dog, and Misty snapped at him. "Stop that," he said in his firmest voice. Misty slunk behind the car.

Now Marty did laugh, and the two of them turned to face her, both speaking at the same time. "This idiot has shown up again," Jim proclaimed, while

Brad said, "Between your neighbor and your dog, it's impossible to get a decent welcome here."

Marty scooped the dog up into her arms. "The paternity case was settled this morning, Jim. Brad is no longer involved."

"Does that give him some right to come around and harass you?" Jim demanded, glaring at Brad.

"He isn't here to harass me," she said.

"How do you know?"

Marty turned to Brad. "Are you?"

"No," he admitted, his eyes sparkling. "Harassment wasn't what I had in mind."

Marty flushed. "You see?" Jim didn't look convinced, so she added, "It's okay, Jim. Brad and I are involved personally, and don't scold me about it. I just saw the law librarian let herself into your place with a key."

Jim drew himself up to his full height. "I wasn't going to scold you about it, but I'll have you know that Janet and I are planning to be married."

"Well, congratulations!" Marty cried. "That's wonderful."

"Marty and I are going to get married, too," Brad interjected.

She stared at him. "Since when?"

"Probably since the day we met, if you want to get technical about it, but more recently it's just sort of seemed the right thing to do."

"Don't I get a chance to discuss it with you?"

"Sure, if you think it's necessary."

Jim shook his head at the two of them, as though they were crazy, and disappeared into the building with his sack of groceries.

When he was gone, Marty suddenly felt nervous

with Brad. Surely he had mentioned getting married just to be one up on Jim. Brad didn't suffer arrogance lightly. He stepped over to her now and kissed her lightly on the lips.

"I'd like you to tell your dog, once and for all, that she's to be nice to me, because I intend to live in close proximity with her from now on." He held his hand out for the dog to sniff, but his eyes were intent on Marty.

She shivered from the tremor that ran through her. "Let's go inside," she suggested.

He followed her up the stairs and through the open door of the apartment. The music had stopped, and Marty walked into the living room to turn it on again. Then she turned to face him. "What did you mean about Andrea?"

Brad clasped her hand, twining their fingers together. He tugged her gently toward the sofa. "I'm going to tell you lots of things, but I want to be comfortable while I do it. After all, it's been a rough few weeks, not being in touch with you."

Being in touch with him now, literally, was having its usual effect on Marty. She knew she'd be better off withdrawing her hand if she wished to think clearly. Still, if she wanted to be realistic about her involvement with Brad, she was going to have to work things through from exactly where they were, clasped hands and all. That was the way it was between them.

"I sat down and talked with Andrea the other day," he said, "about your reaction to my telling you not to involve yourself in her life. I'd already realized that I was afraid of losing my influence over her. She's only thirteen, and I'm her father." He raked strong fingers through his hair. "She told me no one else could ever take my place or her mother's. She was happy you'd talked to her that day and she had hoped you'd be around to do it again."

"Do you feel that way, too?" Marty asked through trembling lips.

"Yeah." He squeezed her hand and brought it up to his lips. "I hadn't thought about it from your point of view when I came on so strong. I'm sorry, Marty. It was like the last link to the old ways, the old days, and I rushed in just like I always had. I won't do it anymore—if you'll remind me." He smiled broadly. "You'd have to be around, all the time, to do that."

Marty could feel the pulse pounding in her throat. She wanted to laugh or cry or both. He overwhelmed her—emotionally, mentally and physically. It was senseless to try to combat those feelings. There was nothing she wanted more than to be with him. So she leaned across and hugged him, holding him tightly against her and whispering in his ear, "I love you, Brad. You're a little bit crazy and a little bit stubborn and a little bit macho, but you're wonderful. I've never met anyone quite like you."

"I should hope not. Does that mean it's settled?" he asked hopefully.

"That what's settled?"

"That we'll get married, of course."

Marty ran a finger across his lips. Was that what she wanted? Yes, there was really no other choice. She felt sure she'd be able to hold her own because he had come to accept her as she was. "Do you love me?" she asked, just to be sure.

"Of *course* I do. Didn't I say so? You see what you do to me? I'm mad about you. I can't imagine living without you. Do you know what I was thinking when I questioned Lydia on the stand this morning?"

Marty shook her head.

"When I asked her if she knew my full name, I was thinking that I didn't know yours. How was I going to apply for a marriage license if I didn't know?"

"Well, chances are I'd be there with you, so it wouldn't be a problem. However, it's Martha Jane Woods."

"Good. I like to get these little matters out of the way." He glanced down to where Misty was untying his shoelaces. "I love you so much I'll even let your dog chew up all my shoes."

Marty laughed. "That won't be necessary. She's really very good when you get to know her."

"I'll look forward to it," he promised. Then he gathered Marty into his arms, kissing her with the intensity of a man in love, a man committed to an exciting new partnership.

As they kissed, the earth moved, the building shook, crystals clinked against glass, vases rocked on the mantelpiece. Brad drew back with his wild eyebrows raised. "If we can do that when we kiss," he said, "just think what we can do when we make love. California will probably fall off into the ocean."

The earthquake diminished, and Marty rose from the sofa, her face flushed. "Let's chance it," she urged, and led him down the hall to her bedroom.

ENTER:

Here's your chance to win a fabulous $50,000 diamond jewelry collection, consisting of diamond necklace, bracelet, earrings and ring.

All you have to do to enter is fill out the coupon below and mail it by September 30, 1985.

Send entries to:

In the U.S.	Silhouette Diamond Sweepstakes P.O. Box 779 Madison Square Station New York, NY 10159
In Canada	Silhouette Diamond Sweepstakes Suite 191 238 Davenport Road Toronto, Ontario M5R 1J6

NAME_____

ADDRESS_____

CITY_____STATE/(PROV.)_____

ZIP/(POSTAL CODE)_____

BCD-A-1

RULES FOR SILHOUETTE DIAMOND SWEEPSTAKES

OFFICIAL RULES—NO PURCHASE NECESSARY

1. Silhouette Diamond Sweepstakes is open to Canadian (except Quebec) and United States residents 18 years or older at the time of entry. Employees and immediate families of the publishers of Silhouette, their affiliates, retailers, distributors, printers, agencies and RONALD SMILEY INC. are excluded.

2. To enter, print your name and address on the official entry form or on a 3″ x 5″ slip of paper. You may enter as often as you choose, but each envelope must contain only one entry. Mail entries first class in Canada to Silhouette Diamond Sweepstakes, Suite 191, 238 Davenport Road, Toronto, Ontario M5R 1J6. In the United States, mail to Silhouette Diamond Sweepstakes, P.O. Box 779, Madison Square Station, New York, NY 10159. Entries must be postmarked between February 1 and September 30, 1985. Silhouette is not responsible for lost, late or misdirected mail.

3. First Prize of diamond jewelry, consisting of a necklace, ring, bracelet and earrings will be awarded. Approximate retail value is $50,000 U.S./$62,500 Canadian. Second Prize of 100 Silhouette Home Reader Service Subscriptions will be awarded. Approximate retail value of each is $162.00 U.S./$180.00 Canadian. No substitution, duplication, cash redemption or transfer of prizes will be permitted. Odds of winning depend upon the number of valid entries received. One prize to a family or household. Income taxes, other taxes and insurance on First Prize are the sole responsibility of the winners.

4. Winners will be selected under the supervision of RONALD SMILEY INC., an independent judging organization whose decisions are final, by random drawings from valid entries postmarked by September 30, 1985, and received no later than October 7, 1985. Entry in this sweepstakes indicates your awareness of the Official Rules. Winners who are residents of Canada must answer correctly a time-related arithmetical skill-testing question to qualify. First Prize winner will be notified by certified mail and must submit an Affidavit of Compliance within 10 days of notification. Returned Affidavits or prizes that are refused or undeliverable will result in alternative names being randomly drawn. Winners may be asked for use of their name and photo at no additional compensation.

5. For a First Prize winner list, send a stamped self-addressed envelope postmarked by September 30, 1985. In Canada, mail to Silhouette Diamond Contest Winner, Suite 309, 238 Davenport Road, Toronto, Ontario M5R 1J6. In the United States, mail to Silhouette Diamond Contest Winner, P.O. Box 182, Bowling Green Station, New York, NY 10274. This offer will appear in Silhouette publications and at participating retailers. Offer void in Quebec and subject to all Federal, Provincial, State and Municipal laws and regulations and wherever prohibited or restricted by law.

SDR-A-1

READERS' COMMENTS ON SILHOUETTE SPECIAL EDITIONS:

"I just finished reading the first six Silhouette Special Edition Books and I had to take the opportunity to write you and tell you how much I enjoyed them. I enjoyed all the authors in this series. Best wishes on your Silhouette Special Editions line and many thanks."

—B.H.*, Jackson, OH

"The Special Editions are really special and I enjoyed them very much! I am looking forward to next month's books."

—R.M.W.*, Melbourne, FL

"I've just finished reading four of your first six Special Editions and I enjoyed them very much. I like the more sensual detail and longer stories. I will look forward each month to your new Special Editions."

—L.S.*, Visalia, CA

"Silhouette Special Editions are — 1.) Superb! 2.) Great! 3.) Delicious! 4.) Fantastic! . . . Did I leave anything out? These are books that an adult woman can read . . . I love them!"

—H.C.*, Monterey Park, CA

*names available on request

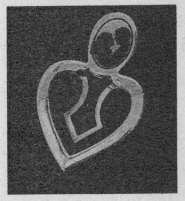